Also by Amy Rose Bennett

THE BYRONIC BOOK CLUB SERIES
Up All Night with a Good Duke
Curled Up with an Earl
Tall, Duke, and Scandalous

Tall, Duke, and Scandalous

AMY ROSE BENNETT

sourcebooks
casablanca

Published by Sourcebooks Casablanca, an imprint of Sourcebooks
P.O. Box 4410, Naperville, Illinois 60567-4410
(630) 961-3900
sourcebooks.com

Printed and bound in Canada.
MBP 10 9 8 7 6 5 4 3 2 1

*To, Richard, my hero, forever. I love you, always.
Also, to my dear mother-in-law, you're one of the
strongest women I know, and I love you dearly.*

Chapter One

London: Belgravia. Saint Valentine's Day, 1859

MISS JANE DELANEY BURST THROUGH THE FRONT DOOR OF Halifax House in a flurry of green silk skirts and ruffled petticoats. Breathless with rushing and bristling with ill humor, she came to an abrupt halt at the bottom of the stone steps, then frowned as she scoured Chester Square. Well, *attempted* to scour. The heavy shroud of fog obscured much of the barely lit expanse of cobblestones and the enclosed park beyond.

Curses. Her family's carriage was nowhere to be seen amongst the other coaches, nor her mother or Jane's stepsister, Kitty Pevensey, for that matter. Had they really left her behind at the Halifaxes' masquerade ball? Her mother *had* been complaining of a megrim and she could be single-minded whenever she felt unwell and was desperate for a dose of her "nerve tonic." But Jane had only been gone ten minutes. Kitty, who tended to be absent-minded, had apparently left her brand-new fan "somewhere" in the ballroom. And because it was a loss that "simply couldn't be borne," Jane had been sent on a mission to retrieve it.

Jane had eventually located the fan in the supper room, but clearly her search had taken too long. Her glove-clad fingers curled into fists at the realization she *had* been abandoned.

Forgotten about just like Kitty's blasted fan.

She gave a disgruntled huff, then swiped at one of her domino mask's drooping feathers as she considered her options.

On the long list of "Calamities That Had Befallen Miss Jane Delaney" of late, this was on the less disastrous end of the scale. But still…Jane's already stretched-tighter-than-a-bowstring patience was about to snap.

The sounds of merrymaking seeped into the square as the door of Halifax House opened to grant exit to another set of departing guests.

Jane sighed heavily as the tittering couple brushed past her, barely sparing her a glance. She certainly didn't relish the prospect of a mile walk through the dark streets to the Pevenseys' town house in Pelham Crescent. The most sensible thing to do would be to hail a hansom cab in one of the busier thoroughfares. Luckily, she always kept a few coins in her reticule.

Mind made up, Jane hugged her velvet cloak more tightly about herself in a vain attempt to ward off the chill night air as she started toward Sloane Street. If either of her dear friends and fellow Byronic Book Club members Lucy or Artemis were home—during the Season proper, they resided in nearby Eaton Square and Belgrave Square respectively—she would have knocked on their doors, seeking refuge. But alas, Lucy was in Scotland with her deliciously gruff husband, William, the Earl of Kyle, and Artemis was still ensconced in Devonshire at Ashburn Abbey, the country estate of her broodingly handsome husband, the Duke of Dartmoor.

While Jane was thrilled her childhood friends were blissfully wed, it appeared she'd been relegated to the ranks of spinsterhood. Although, once upon a time, she'd longed for a husband and children. But courtesy of a capricious turn of fate and a lily-livered man, both of which had left her deeply scarred in more ways than one, that ship had sailed long ago.

It seemed that some things—no matter how much one secretly yearned for them—were never meant to be.

Jane lifted her fingers to her left cheek and brushed over the disfiguring scar that arced from her left ear down to her mouth. Thanks to her mask and its strategically placed feathers, she hadn't needed to endure too many shocked stares or pitying glances at the Halifaxes' masquerade ball. Not that she wasn't used to such reactions from strangers by now. But still, it was nice to feel ordinary and unnoticed for once.

A grand town coach pulled by two pairs of perfectly matched grays lumbered into view and Jane paused to wait for it to pass by. Until recently, she'd been like those blinkered creatures. Head down, plodding forward along a path toward some foggy destination that was always a bit uncertain and out of reach. But now... Now perhaps a rudderless boat tossed about in a storm-swept sea with no safe port in sight would be a more accurate description of her current state of being.

Oh, but Jane longed for a safe port. And fulfillment. She might have given up on her dream of finding a husband and having a baby, but she couldn't help being a *little* envious of her friends' situations. Like Artemis and Lucy, she wanted to make a difference in the world. To champion the rights of women. To help others in some way. Because of her own fraught history, it was a drive within that was hard to deny.

It also seemed like an impossible feat given her present situation. A situation that was becoming more precarious by the day...

Jane glanced toward the indistinct silhouettes of the town houses in Eaton Square. Both Artemis's and Lucy's wealthy, titled husbands were so smitten with their wives that they were hugely generous.

Now, if a mysterious Byronic hero with deep pockets popped onto Jane's horizon and offered to solve all her problems with a flick of a pen over a checkbook, wouldn't that be wonderful?

No, it was money Jane needed, not a man. *Money*. And desperately, before she drowned in a whirlpool of anxiety and scandal and ruined dreams.

A miracle wouldn't hurt either.

Through the shifting darkness, the sounds of unbridled carousing floated toward Jane—music and laughter and chatter interspersed with wild whoops and cheers. It seemed someone else was hosting a Saint Valentine's ball this evening. Perhaps there'd be a hansom cab in the vicinity.

Jane followed the hubbub easily, and before long the lights of the town house pierced through the fog. As soon as it hove into full view, she frowned. She knew this house. Lucy had once pointed it out to her as they'd passed by. It was the residence of the Duke of Roxby.

If society's gossipmongers were to be believed, the present duke, Christopher Marsden—a former army officer and Crimean War hero—was one of the country's most notorious scoundrels. A profligate, licentious cad who'd inherited the dukedom from an ancient uncle early last year. At least according to the *London Tatler*, a newspaper that was little more than a scandal rag. Jane should know because she also penned articles for the publication.

Indeed, to her shame she'd also recently begun to contemplate the idea of secretly feeding gossip to the *London Tatler*'s "social column." She'd certainly been attending enough high-society functions with Kitty—Jane was frequently enlisted as a chaperone—and she often gleaned all manner of juicy tidbits while waiting on the edge of the ballroom.

Of course, it was not within Jane's nature to do something so grubby and low, but she was so frantic with worry that she might have to. *For the money,* she reminded herself. *For your family.* Namely for her grandfather, the proprietor of Delaney's Antiquarian Bookshop. And to save her mother from destroying her reputation and jeopardizing her marriage.

Blast her mother. If it weren't for Leonora Pevensey's addiction to high-stakes card play, Delaney's would not be in danger. The fact that her mother had put her share of the business up as collateral when she'd lost a large sum at the whist table was unconscionable. Jane loved that bookstore almost as much as her paternal grandfather did, and she would *not* let anything happen to it.

As for her desperate need for money to solve her own dire problem… If Jane's blackmailer revealed her own scandalous secret, she'd be devastated.

Crushed.

Ruined…

Somehow Jane pushed the deeply distressing thought aside. She could only deal with one pressing issue at a time.

A hansom cab clattered by, heading toward Roxby House, and Jane hastened her steps in that direction. Only, by the time she reached her destination, it was to discover a masked gentleman leaping into the cab, and within the blink of an eye it had taken off.

Ugh. Jane batted the drooping feather away from her face once more. She'd have to head back toward Belgrave Street again. She turned and looked toward the front door of Roxby House. It stood wide open, the bright light of an enormous gaslight chandelier spilling out onto the stone steps. And there was no one—not a single footman or a butler—guarding the entry hall, monitoring who could come and go.

How odd.

Perhaps the scandalous duke didn't much care who

attended his parties. Rumor had it that his soirees were on the wilder side and not for the fainthearted, or indeed anyone who wished to maintain some semblance of a reputation. It was not the sort of place Kitty Pevensey would be allowed to set foot in. Not that Kitty's debut would matter all that much if it was learned her stepmother had a terrible gambling habit. Or her new stepsister was being blackmailed.

Another frisson of cold fear trickled down Jane's spine. If she couldn't help her mother secure the funds to pay off her gambling vowels in the next week or two, there was a very real chance her grandfather might lose his entire bookstore.

But what if…? Jane studied the open doorway to Roxby House. What if she swallowed her scruples and sneaked inside and observed some of the antics of the elite? The *London Tatler's* chief editor wouldn't pay her an enormous sum in exchange for scandalous gossip, but it would be a start. It would be better than nothing. And really, if the Duke of Roxby was in the habit of leaving his front door open for just anybody to waltz in, what did he expect?

Desperate times call for desperate measures, after all.

Before she could think further on it—before she lost her nerve—Jane lifted her crinoline skirts and rushed up the stairs into Roxby House.

"Oi. You there, miss."

Oh no. Jane froze in the middle of the grand vestibule. Off to one side by a pair of enormous marble columns stood a burly footman wearing a scowl along with fine livery. How foolish of her to think there wouldn't be anyone stationed at the door.

Unfurling Kitty's fan, Jane raised it to hide the line of her scar not obscured by the mask, then pasted on a smile as she turned around. It seemed a bit of playacting would be required to gain admittance.

She fluttered her eyelashes in the manner of a brazen minx who had every right to be attending the Duke of Roxby's ball without an invitation. "You mean me?"

"Yes, you." The strapping footman's brows arrowed into a frown as he looked her up and down. "What's the password? You can't go in until you tell me what it is. His Grace is very particular about who attends his soirees."

Somehow Jane managed to swallow a snort of laughter. *Particular?* By the sounds of it, a Roman orgy was taking place within these walls. As her mind scrambled to come up with a suitable password for a Saint Valentine's event that most likely bordered on the bacchanalian, several coatless "gentlemen" bolted across the space between her and the footman. It appeared they were engaged in some sort of crude game of rugby as one chap tossed an oversized ham to another fellow before they all stumbled through an arched doorway into a gaslit gallery.

"Wine, women, and song?" she asked hopefully.

The footman crossed his arms. "You don't know what it is, do you?"

"How about 'tits'?" she suggested, puffing out her less-than-ample chest. She would not be put off.

"No."

"Cock-a-doodle-do?"

The footman was stony-faced.

"Does it really matter if I don't know it?" she asked.

"It does. I'll give you one last try before you're out." The servant gestured at the still-open front door with his thumb.

Borrowing a curse from her dear friend Artemis, Jane muttered, "Beelzebub's ballocks."

"What was that last bit?" asked the footman.

"Ballocks?" replied Jane.

"In you go," said the footman. "The ballroom is down that hall to your right." Then he grinned. "Have fun."

Well, that almost seemed *too* easy… However, Jane wasn't about to look a gift horse in the mouth. After murmuring "Thank you," she hurried away.

The first thing that struck Jane as she entered a high-ceilinged gallery embellished with the sort of frescoes and gilt moldings that might grace the Doge's Palace of Venice was the level of noise. It could only be described as overwhelming. A deafening, discordant cacophony that was bound to give one a headache. All the doors to every vast room were thrown wide open, revealing one tableau of debauchery after another. In the ballroom, a small string ensemble doggedly played a rousing mazurka, while masked men and scantily clad women with champagne glasses in hand laughed and cheered and pranced about with gay abandon.

In another crowded room hazy with the smoke of hookah pipes, a man in a rumpled, half-open shirt sat hunched over the keyboard of a monstrously carved pianoforte as he played a darkly dramatic nocturne. However, almost everyone's attention was riveted on a naked woman who was reclining on top of the piano, while another male guest was furiously painting the licentious scene.

Jane didn't like to think of herself as a prude, but even she found herself blushing at the idea of so many people blatantly ogling the artist's muse.

But that wasn't the worst of the debauchery. In the adjacent dining room, several couples in various stages of undress were fornicating on a table between the glassware and platters and several upset bottles of wine.

Good Lord above. Jane had never seen so many bare breasts and behinds in all her life. Her face burning, she rushed past and turned down another hall. She doubted she'd be able to report on any of this activity. It was too shocking even for the *London Tatler* to print. She had no idea if the duke himself was anywhere about. He obviously didn't care what went on beneath his roof.

There was also no doubt in her mind that she'd made a mistake coming here. She was clearly wasting her time and really should go before something untoward happened.

She just needed to find her way out. But that was easier said than done. Everywhere she turned was bedlam.

To Jane's relief, she soon found herself in a far quieter, deserted gallery, and halfway along, a gleaming oak-paneled door stood ajar. It was an enormous library that seemed to be devoid of occupants. The room was cloaked in dense shadows. She really should press on and escape this madness, but instead she crossed the threshold. Perhaps it was the vastness of the room with its impressive bookcases or the welcoming pull of the flickering flames in the enormous black marble fireplace that she couldn't resist. The familiar scents of leather and beeswax and the pleasant mustiness of old books drifted toward her, beckoning her inside.

And then she recalled something else she knew about the Duke of Roxby. Well, not the new duke but the old duke. Jane's grandfather had once mentioned that the man had been an eccentric character and had amassed a large collection of very rare books.

Very *expensive* books.

Curiosity sparking, Jane decided to take a quick look. She couldn't resist. Antique book collections were her personal form of opium. Over the years, she'd spent countless hours in her grandfather's shop, helping to catalog the antiquarian titles he sold, dusting and storing them carefully, and even repairing books in the store's workshop. Books were in her blood. Surely the new duke wouldn't mind. It wasn't as though she was going to fornicate between the shelves or construct a makeshift set of wickets from a stack of books for a drunken cricket game.

Ignoring the nervous fluttering in her belly, Jane carefully closed the door behind her. Her reverent gaze wandered over the shelves as she contemplated where to start.

There. Over by the far wall near a wrought-iron staircase that led to an upper gallery she spied tomes stored in a glass-fronted cabinet that might warrant a look. Hopefully the doors weren't locked. But then nothing else that was of value in this house appeared to be kept under lock and key.

She traversed the plush Turkish rug and upon reaching the bookcase reached out and tried the brass handle. *Yes.* It *was* unlocked.

When she perused the titles on the spines, her heart did a little jig of excitement. Oh, wouldn't she love to spend hours and hours in this place, cataloging everything. Reading to her heart's content.

She dared to run a gloved fingertip along the edge of a very old copy of *The Canterbury Tales* by Chaucer. Without even examining it, her instincts told her it was a first edition. Probably late fifteenth century. Possibly printed by William Caxton.

A man like the Duke of Roxby didn't deserve to own such a treasure.

As Jane reached for the book, her mask's troublesome feather drooped over her left eye. With an annoyed huff, she blew it out of the way, but it immediately flopped down again.

Ack. What harm would it do if she took off her mask? No one else was around. It would only be for a minute or two. Decision made, Jane put Kitty's fan and her own reticule on a nearby table, then removed the domino.

Once unmasked, she carefully slid Chaucer's book out from the shelf and opened its delicate pages with suitable reverence. *Aha!* Her instincts had been correct. This volume *had* been published by Caxton. It was priceless.

It would fetch a small fortune at auction...

Jane swallowed. Her breath quickened. Temptation curled its hooks into her. Whispered wicked thoughts in her ear. Made her ignore the sharp prick of guilt inside her chest. Her gaze darted to the library doors, but they were still firmly closed.

If truth be told, Jane had always been sensible. Practical and dependable. Since her nineteenth summer when she'd thrown caution to the wind and put her faith in the wrong man, she'd been the sort of woman who'd never put a foot wrong. She didn't lie or cheat or act rashly. She certainly didn't steal.

But...if she made a hasty retreat from Roxby House with this book in her possession, would anyone notice it was gone? Did the Duke of Roxby even know that he owned something so precious?

He probably doesn't value it at all, Jane told herself, even as her conscience quailed in horror at what she was about to do. *He's too busy hosting orgies where anything and everything goes. His guests almost certainly pilfer the silver and Lord knows what else all the time.*

And what she was thinking about stealing—no, *rescuing* from this madhouse—was one little book that was practically falling apart...

This book... This was the miracle Jane desperately needed. And of course the money she'd make from its sale was going toward a very good cause. She could pay off her mother's gambling debt and save her grandfather's bookstore and...and she might be able to extricate herself from her own precarious predicament too. It wouldn't be long before her blackmailer demanded another payment. A payment she couldn't possibly make.

A soft noise made Jane jump and she nearly dropped *The Canterbury Tales*. Whirling around, her gaze darted about the room, but she didn't see anyone lurking by the fire or between any of the bookcases or by the duke's enormous desk. The soft rustling sound must have been a log crumbling to ash in the grate. Blowing out a sigh of relief, she contemplated the best way to conceal this book on her person. Her ball gown didn't have a pocket. Her reticule was far too small. She could hide the book in the folds of her cloak, but what if the footman at the front door noticed she was clutching something against her body?

Her caged crinoline skirts were so voluminous, she could practically hide a person—or even half a library—beneath them.

Yes. What if she carefully tied the book to one of her legs with a garter and stocking? No one at all would notice one foot was stockingless. She just had to make it out the front door. It was the only way to ensure success.

Jane put the book down on the table, then slipped off a pump. Hiking up her skirts and petticoats, she then placed her foot on a padded chair and rolled up her drawers to her knee. Untied her garter, then swiftly whipped off her silk stocking. Within less than a minute, she'd firmly strapped the book to her upper thigh.

She smiled at her handiwork. *There, that will do.*

And then a distinctly masculine voice, laced with sardonic humor, drifted toward her from the deep shadows to her left. "As much as I'm enjoying the show, I must stop you there."

Oh my God. Jane froze. Her heart almost stuttered to a complete stop before taking off at breakneck speed.

Snatching a breath, she slowly turned her head. How had

she not noticed that there was someone else—an impossibly tall, broad-shouldered man—lingering here in the library with her?

Watching her every move in silence. Observing her in the act of stealing one of the Duke of Roxby's priceless books.

She'd been caught red-handed.

And she wasn't wearing a mask.

Chapter Two

"I–I..." Jane dropped her skirts and slid her bare foot to the floor. Her knees were shaking so much, she doubted she'd be able to bolt from the room. "Well, this is rather awkward," she finished in a voice husky with mortification and a good dose of fear. And smothering guilt.

Drawing a steadying breath, she peered past the man's imposing silhouette and spied a wingback chair secreted in a curtained window embrasure. A cut crystal tumbler sat on an occasional table beside it. The man must have been sitting there the entire time.

Oh God. If the floor had opened up and swallowed her whole, Jane would have been most grateful. Anything would have been better than these excruciatingly painful moments. The entire room seemed to be hushed and listening. Waiting.

"Oh, I don't know about that," the stranger said. While one of his wide shoulders was propped casually against the wall, Jane had the feeling that if she made any sudden move, he would pounce. "The words 'amusing' and 'intriguing' spring to mind. You've certainly aroused my interest in more ways than one."

Jane's cheeks burned. Surely he didn't mean that. Without thinking, her gaze fell to the man's lean hips, but of course he was still cloaked in darkness so she couldn't see if the sight of her removing her stocking had affected him. She couldn't even discern the stranger's face. But his superior, mocking tone along with the idea that he'd been watching her and hadn't said a word rankled. Some wicked imp inside her made her say, "Actually, sir, I meant it must be awkward for you. Do you make a habit of hiding in dark corners and spying on others?"

"Or," he drawled smugly, "perhaps I'm simply lying in wait to catch out pretty book thieves."

The retort forming on the tip of Jane's tongue died as soon as the stranger stepped into the golden pool of light cast by a nearby gas lamp. In fact, all she could do was gasp. Even the word *handsome* wouldn't have done this man justice.

He was starkly beautiful. His face, all lean planes and sharply cut angles, was framed by tousled, light-brown locks that bordered on leonine. Golden stubble shaded his perfectly hewn jaw. Even though his evening attire was the epitome of sartorial elegance, Jane wasn't sure if the man reminded her of a marauding Viking or an avenging angel who'd descended to earth. If he'd drawn a flaming broadsword from a sheath strapped to his back to smite her, she wouldn't have been the least bit surprised.

Even *light brown* was the wrong phrase to describe the stranger's hair. As he raked a hand through that lustrous tawny mane, the lamp's glow picked out strands of deep guinea gold and copper and rich caramel. And then of course it was impossible not to be mesmerized by the man's arresting eyes. Set above carved, high cheekbones, they were the ice-cold blue of an arctic wasteland. Indeed, his gaze as it met and trapped Jane's was sharp and hard and penetrating. There was no warmth there, only acute interest and some other emotion she couldn't quite identify.

It was Jane who looked away first, to break the disconcerting glamour that had ensnared her.

She cleared her throat. "Well…" Beneath her skirts, she surreptitiously reached out with her bare foot in search of her discarded pump. "I...er...should probably be going." There was no point in refuting the man's accusation that she was a book thief, just as there was no point in paying any attention to his false flattery about her looks. Brazening her way out of this situation was the best she could hope for.

Well, she could also pray that the handsome stranger didn't say anything about her thievery to the duke. And then she nearly expired on the spot when the man held out one hand and said, "Before you do go, I'd like my book back."

"*Your* book?" Jane whispered as a wave of foreboding engulfed her.

The man's perfectly chiseled lips twitched with a wry smile. "Yes, *my* book. *The Canterbury Tales* published by William Caxton. While I admire your taste and the fact you know a valuable work when you see one, I really don't wish to part with it. I'm sure you understand."

"You're...you're the duke." It wasn't a question. In that moment, Jane *knew* it.

The man sketched a mocking bow. "I am indeed. Christopher Marsden, the sixth Duke of Roxby. And you are?"

"Horrified."

Genuine rather than sardonic amusement flickered in the man's eyes. "Come, come, I'm not that frightening, am I? I did ask that you return my book with an appropriate degree of politeness, did I not?"

"You did," agreed Jane. "But I would politely ask you to face the other way while I remove it from..." She grimaced and gestured at her skirts. There was no hope for it. She would not be leaving here with her much-needed "miracle" after all.

The duke laughed. It was a deep throaty chuckle that Jane felt all the way to her toes. "And have you abscond while my back is turned, Miss Horrified? I don't think so."

Jane lifted her chin. "Doubtless you'd catch me before I even made it halfway across the room."

"Doubtless," he returned. "But I'm sure you can appreciate that I don't quite trust you. It will be easier this way."

"A gentleman *would* turn away," returned Jane stiffly.

The duke bared his teeth in a wolfish grin and his blue eyes gleamed. "Ah, but everyone knows the Duke of Roxby is no gentleman. Don't mistake an occasional bout of politeness for gallantry."

"Very well," Jane huffed. Her remorse and embarrassment coalesced with bristling indignation as she placed her bare foot on the chair again and raised her skirts. *At least he hasn't threatened to have me arrested and then hauled off to Newgate Prison,* she reminded herself as she plucked at the knots in her ribbon and stocking. *It could be worse.*

Fate must have been listening and in that moment decided to punish Jane for her hubris. Because things *did* get worse. Her trembling fingers couldn't undo the tight knots. She was all thumbs. And if she tried to slide the book from its bindings, she'd be sure to damage it.

"I...um..." Jane glanced over to the duke, who was watching her ineffectual plucks with an expression that might have passed for amusement. Although it could very well have been annoyance. "You wouldn't happen to have a nice sharp letter opener at hand, would you, Your Grace?"

He made a scoffing noise, then marched over to the desk. When he returned with the requested implement, he eyed Jane narrowly. "Again, I hope you'll understand when I say that I don't trust you. I'm afraid that *I'm* going to have to cut those ties."

Jane snorted, even as her blood began to thrum at the idea that the duke's large hands would soon be touching her drawers-clad thigh. "I only tried to pilfer a book. I'm not a murderess. I promise I won't stab you."

"Ah, but it's a very *expensive* book," said the duke. "People will do all kinds of things for money. And I don't know you." He drew close, and Jane caught the scent of his cologne—something spicy and rich like sandalwood with a touch of citrus. "Now, hold still," he said softly as he bent low. "This will be over in a moment."

His long fingers gripped the book, and with a flick of the letter opener's wickedly sharp silver blade, the silk bindings split in two with nary a whisper. Which was a shame because as the duke's fingers brushed her leg, an involuntary shiver of longing spread across Jane's skin and an agonized whimper escaped her throat. The soft sound was loud in the silent library.

Oh dear God. Why must her body betray her in this way? Would this humiliation never end? Jane didn't want to want the duke. He was arrogant and a cad and ungentlemanly and…

He was probably going to let her go.

Many men in his position wouldn't. She should count her blessings.

But then again, maybe she shouldn't count them *too* soon…

Even though the duke had his precious book in hand, he hadn't moved away. Jane pushed down her skirts, and when she looked up, he was unabashedly staring at her face.

At her scar.

She opened her mouth to say something along the lines of "It's rude to stare," but all of a sudden she couldn't make her lips and tongue work. Not one syllable emerged.

She was transfixed. The duke's bold, ice-blue gaze traced its way down the unsightly slashing mark to where it ended at the corner of her mouth. There his attention lingered for the briefest of moments before dipping to her chin. Then he examined her nose, and then her furrowed brow. Her bright-red cheeks.

She had the oddest notion that he was studying each of her features. As though he were trying to commit her face to memory.

Leaning toward her ear, his nostrils flared ever so slightly as though he were also sampling her scent. It was nothing special or exotic. Just Pears Soap and lily-of-the-valley water.

While these moments were strangely intimate, they were also peculiar and unsettling. Jane suddenly felt like a butterfly pinned beneath a sheet of glass—a curiosity—rather than a woman being admired.

At last, the duke's torturous scrutiny ended. "Remarkable," he murmured before he stepped away and crossed to his desk.

Remarkable? Bizarre seemed more fitting, but Jane kept her thoughts to herself. She didn't need her unruly tongue to get her into any more trouble tonight. Dragging in a much-needed breath, she held onto the arm of the chair as she lowered her foot and slid on her shoe, then retrieved the rest of her things, including Kitty's fan.

When she turned around, it was to discover the duke had propped one lean hip on his desk. And he was still holding Chaucer's book.

Jane affected a laugh. "All's well that ends well," she said, trying for a light and breezy tone. Instead, her voice sounded brittle and high-pitched. It was obvious she was nervous.

"Oh, our little tête-à-tête hasn't ended," said the duke quietly.

Jane swallowed. "What do you mean? As pleasant as this has been, it's rather late"—she gestured toward the library's long-case clock that showed it was nearing 1:00 a.m.—"and I don't wish to turn into a pumpkin."

"Tell me why you tried to steal my book and you may go." The duke's frosty gaze was uncompromising. "I'll know if you're lying so I wouldn't bother."

Jane gave a mirthless laugh. "Obviously I need money, Your Grace. It's a very *expensive* book after all."

The duke's attention drifted over her attire, and Jane knew he was assessing its worth. It was unmistakably haute couture. A gift from Artemis last Season, in fact. Even though the ball gown suited Jane well—the emerald-green silk complemented her brown hair and green eyes—it was not the kind of gown she usually wore. Of course, the duke didn't know that. He would surmise that she didn't *look* impoverished. But people needed money for all sorts of reasons.

The duke clearly thought so too. "Money for what purpose?"

Oh, but he was blunt. Jane's gaze fell to the volume in the duke's hand. "It's a complicated matter," she said stiffly. "One that's difficult to discuss with a stranger."

"I understand 'complicated' more than you could know."

The duke's voice was so soft, so imbued with compassion that Jane's gaze shot to his face. In some ways, the change in his demeanor was the most surprising thing that had happened tonight.

Or was it a trick? Some ploy to invite her to share a confidence that he could then use against her? How he would do that she had no idea, but her instincts told her to be wary.

"I…I don't know if I can trust you," she murmured.

He nodded. "Will you at least share your name with me?"

Jane decided she could make this one small concession. "Miss Jane Delaney."

"Ah," he said. "That makes sense."

"What do you mean?"

He raised the book. "You knew the value of this straightaway. I presume you have an association with Delaney's Antiquarian Bookshop in Sackville Street off Piccadilly?"

Jane couldn't hide her astonishment. "You know about Delaney's?"

"I inherited a vast antique book collection from my great-uncle. Of course I do."

"I've never seen you in the sho—" She broke off.

Oh no. She'd inadvertently admitted she was very well acquainted with her grandfather's business. If she'd put her grandfather's reputation in jeopardy because of her own foolish, rash actions, she'd never be able to forgive herself.

"Your Grace," she said, "what happened here tonight... I want to assure you it had nothing to do with the proprietor of Delaney's. It was I and I alone who decided to come here. I'm the one who tried to take your book to serve my own ends. I accept full responsibility—"

The duke held up his hand. "That's quite enough self-flagellation, Miss Delaney. I'm not going to send for the police."

"You're not?"

"No. But that doesn't mean there won't be any consequences for your actions."

Jane's heart began to thump against her breastbone. "Con-consequences?"

The duke placed the book down very carefully upon the desk. "You don't need to look so alarmed, Miss Delaney. I don't bite..." His wide mouth curved into a rakish grin. "Well, I do sometimes, but only when invited to."

Heat suffused Jane's cheeks. She'd never blushed so much in her whole life. "Your Grace, please speak plainly. It does grow rather late, and I don't wish to worry my family unduly. I still need to make my way home."

"Very well. You do have a point. We shall finish this conversation tomorrow." He sighed and rubbed his brow as though he was suddenly weary beyond measure or even had a megrim coming on. "I mean, later on today. I expect to see you back at Roxby House at three o'clock. Sharp."

Jane dipped into a small curtsy. "I'll be here, Your Grace." She had no doubt in her mind that if she didn't turn up at the allotted time, the duke would come and find her.

"Right." The duke pushed to his feet and gestured toward the door. "Let us depart."

"Wait… You're coming with me?" Did he think she would try to steal something else on her way out?

But then he said, "Only to the front door. I know how wild things get here in the wee small hours. It would be curmudgeonly of me not to see you out safely."

Jane inclined her head. "That's very kind of you, Your Grace."

Once she'd redonned her mask, the duke offered his arm, and he escorted her through the halls. Carousing guests called greetings as he passed by, and he acknowledged all with a wave and a tilt of his head. But he didn't stop to talk with anyone, and Jane was grateful.

They gained the grand entry hall and the footman on duty bowed as soon as he saw his master.

The duke addressed him. "Please arrange suitable transport for my guest here." He turned to Jane and raised a brow. "I take it that you don't have a carriage waiting outside?"

"No, I don't. A hansom cab will suffice." Jane lifted her chin. "I have enough for the fare."

The duke smirked at her show of pride. "Tell the cab driver to return here for his payment," he said to the footman.

And then the Duke of Roxby astonished Jane again when he bowed over her hand. "Until we meet again, Miss Delaney," he said in a low voice meant only for her. And then he turned on his well-shod heel and quit the entry hall, leaving Jane with the sense that she might have unwittingly jumped from the frying pan straight into the fire.

Chapter Three

THICK GRAY FOG WREATHED THE ENORMOUS EQUESTRIAN statue sitting atop the Wellington Arch as Christopher rode his black Thoroughbred gelding, Apollo, beneath it and into Hyde Park beyond. His valet, and former batman, Frederick Featherstone—the only person he trusted entirely on this earth—followed dutifully behind on a dappled gray.

Even though a headache was brewing at the back of Christopher's skull and his eyes were gritty from lack of sleep—he'd only managed four hours after last night's Saint Valentine's ball—it felt good to be in the saddle. He might not be an officer in Her Majesty's cavalry anymore, but that didn't mean he didn't still relish an early morning ride. Rain, hail, or shine, there was nothing Christopher found more invigorating.

His mouth twisted in a grim smile as he directed Apollo toward Rotten Row. Once upon a time when he was a military man, he would have said that indulging in a good bout of bed sport with a willing widow or an occasional tumble with a prostitute would have been the most rousing activity he could think of. But not lately. Not since his life had abruptly changed course seven months ago...

Pushing thoughts of that horrendous time aside—in particular, the day when his life had all but gone to hell—Christopher's mind drifted back to the events of last night instead...and the beautiful would-be book thief who'd stolen into his library.

Miss Jane Delaney... Her cheek might be marked with a

distinctive scar, but that didn't lessen the young woman's attractiveness in his eyes. Or how intriguing he found her. He wasn't even irked that she'd tried to steal a priceless book from his collection. Which was odd in and of itself. Of course, he was richer than Croesus. His great-uncle had left him a very healthy dukedom. While the theft wouldn't hurt him in a financial sense, he knew he'd be furious if anyone else had tried to pilfer something so precious. And rightfully so.

But he wasn't furious. Not even a little bit. And perhaps that was the most damnably strange thing of all about last night's encounter with Miss Delaney.

Christopher could well and truly declare, hand on his heart, without a lie, that this particular young woman, out of all the women he'd crossed paths with of late, was truly captivating. Perhaps even unforgettable. And he had no idea why.

If he did nothing else today, he would find out all he could about Miss Delaney.

He had to. She was a puzzle. An enigma.

A rarity. In his world at least.

The mere thought of seeing her again this afternoon at three o'clock stirred Christopher's blood with excitement. If luck was on his side, he might even see Miss Delaney sooner when he stopped by Delaney's Antiquarian Bookshop to do some reconnaissance. He'd subtly quiz its proprietor of the same name—surely he and Jane were related—to find out if he had anything to do with Miss Delaney's attempted theft. While Christopher wouldn't jump to any conclusions yet, he would readily admit he was burning with curiosity to find out what was really going on. His gut told him Miss Delaney had never done anything like this before. But one never knew...

Christopher reined in Apollo at the head of Rotten Row and turned to regard the man who drew alongside him on his gray mount. He was barrel-chested with bushy muttonchops, and when he spoke, his rough Yorkshire accent combined with his familiar yet distinctive gravel-toned voice reminded Christopher of the rumble of distant artillery fire. "I take it ye'd like to race to the end of the Row like we usually do, Yer Grace?" said Featherstone.

Christopher inclined his head. "Yes, as far as Kensington Gardens. Then we'll follow the bridle path back and have a second round."

The Yorkshireman grinned. "Or best of three? I'm game if you are, Yer Grace."

"Done," agreed Christopher.

They both kicked their horses, and their Thoroughbred beasts, used to the routine, took off like a pair of exploding cannonballs, hurtling down Rotten Row at breakneck speed.

Hooves thundered over the muddy ground and the stands of trees, cloaked in their gray shrouds, loomed like spectral watchers on either side of the deserted track. It was early on a chill winter's morning and only the most dedicated equestrians would be out and about.

Apollo beat Featherstone's gray by a nose, and as Christopher wheeled his mount around to face his valet, an earsplitting crack—a shot—rent the air and Christopher's hat went flying.

What the blazing hell? Christopher's training as a cavalry officer took over as Apollo shied. Ducking down, he quickly brought the horse under control.

"Take cover in the trees, Yer Grace," rumbled Featherstone. "I'll—"

He got no further because all at once a rider—a dark-haired man in a greatcoat—burst from the copse of ash and oak from whence the shot had come. His bay horse bolted across the park, heading toward the Queen's Gate entrance like the hounds of hell were at its heels. And perhaps they were because both Christopher and Featherstone took off, racing on their mounts through the thick-as-pea-soup miasma in hot pursuit.

But the fog was both a blessing and a curse. While it had possibly saved Christopher's life—the shooter's line of sight had undoubtedly been affected—it hindered the chase. The roiling veil not only obscured vision but also muffled sound, and it wasn't long before Christopher realized the perpetrator had managed to get away. And he'd lost Featherstone too.

Damn it all to hell. Frustration rushing through his veins, Christopher reined in Apollo at the edge of Prince Albert Road and Kensington Gore. Early morning traffic—carts, carriages, hansom cabs, and a packed omnibus—clogged the thoroughfares. As he scanned the shrouded streets, his gaze darting this way and that, he couldn't see hide nor hair of a rider on a bay horse. The bastard had disappeared.

When another rider emerged from the blanketing fog, drawing close, Christopher immediately stiffened, and he reached for the pistol he always kept tucked in his greatcoat... But then he recognized the dapple-gray horse, and when the barrel-chested man spoke, his harsh-as-gravel voice and Northern brogue were both familiar to Christopher's ear. "It's only me, Featherstone, Yer Grace."

Christopher inclined his head. "I can't believe someone took a bloody shot at me in Hyde Park," he grated out between clenched teeth. Now that the initial shock and the thrill of the chase were wearing off, cold hard anger seeped into Christopher's chest. The headache at the back of his skull throbbed in earnest. He'd need to take another dose of laudanum when he got home.

"Neither can I," replied Featherstone. His bushy brows

arrowed into a frown. "Do you think we should go to Scotland Yard?"

Christopher shook his head. "There's no point. There's nothing to go on. Nothing concrete to report. The cur's long gone." Just like the first attempted shooting last July, only five months after he'd inherited the dukedom. And the second time when someone had attempted to knife him in a dark London alley in early December. And now this…

Featherstone nodded. "He's been watching you. He knows yer habits."

"Yes," agreed Christopher grimly. He raised a hand and pressed his gloved fingertips against the scar above his left ear. He could almost feel the hot sting of the bullet that had grazed him seven months ago on his country estate. A supposed accident.

As for *this* incident… Christopher's gut told him that shot *had* definitely been meant for him. It *couldn't* be an accident. Hyde Park wasn't a damn hunting ground.

No, that bullet had had Christopher's name on it, and the problem was he had no idea who wanted him dead or why. One thing was certain: He had to take action. He had to find out who was responsible for these attempts on his life. He couldn't go on like this… For months and months he'd been waiting and wondering. If nothing else, now he had a semblance of clarity. Now he was sure.

"Just to be safe, I suggest we return to Roxby House via a circuitous route and then regroup," he said. Featherstone agreed with a nod and a grunt.

As he and his valet cantered back through Hyde Park toward the Serpentine, Christopher's thoughts strayed to Miss Jane Delaney and the moment he'd realized she was different from everyone else.

His life was complicated enough. Becoming more complicated by the day. But maybe he needed this particular woman to help him. He'd find out later on this afternoon if his instincts about her were correct.

Chapter Four

"JANE, I KNEW YOU'D FIND MY FAN. YOU'RE A GEM," proclaimed Kitty Pevensey with a bright smile as she drifted into the morning room of 21 Pelham Crescent like a spring blossom on a breeze.

"It was no bother," said Jane, only just stifling a yawn. She pushed her cup of tea away and contemplated the idea of sending for coffee. When she'd finally crawled into her bed, she'd barely slept a wink. Which wasn't surprising, given everything that had transpired last night at Roxby House. Or truth to tell, the tangled mess that was her current life. "How is Mama? Her megrim must have been fierce considering you both quit Halifax House before I returned to the carriage."

Her stepsister at least had the decency to look sheepish as she took a seat opposite Jane. "Mama is still abed," Kitty said as she took great pains to lay a linen napkin over her skirts. She was clearly avoiding Jane's gaze. "And as for leaving you behind, well, *I* wanted to wait for you. But you were taking too long, and Mama insisted that you would be able to make your way home easily enough. Which you clearly did…" Kitty helped herself to a cup of tea before pinching a piece of toast from the rack. "All in all, I did have a splendid time at the Halifaxes'. There's nothing quite as fun as a masked ball."

Jane, if she'd spoken her mind, would have remarked she didn't find any balls "fun." But she shouldn't let her own cynicism about courting rituals spoil Kitty's good humor.

While she was a little flighty and self-absorbed at times, Kitty Pevensey was, on the whole, a pleasant young woman with a decent dowry and Jane was certain it wouldn't be long before a raft of suitors would be calling at the Pevensey residence once the Season proper began.

Unless, of course, scandal crashed down on Leonora Pevensey. And on Jane too...

Jane eyed her own piece of toast and the congealing boiled egg in its china eggcup and grimaced. She had no appetite this morning. Not when her stomach churned with nerves every time she thought of her coming interview with the daunting Duke of Roxby.

She had no idea what the duke's idea of "consequences" would be. As she'd tossed and turned in her bed, her mind had struggled to fathom what he truly meant. Hours later, she was still completely baffled.

He might have mentioned that she was "pretty" and then declared that her face was "remarkable," but surely he didn't mean that. Jane supposed that he *might* ask her for sexual favors in return for her continued freedom from prosecution—a despicable act to be sure. But a man as rich and handsome as the duke would surely have his pick of beautiful women to invite to his bed. Jane had certainly spied many such women partaking in all sorts of amorous shenanigans during his soiree. But if that *was* the duke's agenda—to tup her—why hadn't he propositioned her last night? They'd been alone in his library while orgiastic mayhem reigned just outside the door.

Jane sighed and replenished her tea. She was under no delusion that her facial scar did not diminish her attractiveness. Not that it bothered *her* particularly. She was used to it now and the way others reacted to it. It was part of her, and she couldn't do anything to change it. There was no point crying over spilled milk or dogcart accidents or fair-weather fiancés. Her mother, on the other hand, had never reconciled with the reality that her only daughter's face was disfigured. Or that Jane had let her family down by ruining her prospects of making a good marriage to someone else.

Someone with deep pockets.

Jane sometimes wondered if Leonora Pevensey silently blamed her daughter for her addiction to gambling too.

She should really go and seek her mother out. Make it plain that she, Jane, couldn't save her mother's reputation and Delaney's Bookshop all on her own. Mind made up, she excused herself from the table and made her way upstairs to her mother's bedchamber.

While Leonora Pevensey was still abed, she was wide awake and sipping hot chocolate as she went through her correspondence. Upon seeing Jane, she flapped at the window with a handful of letters. "Jane dear, please close the curtains a bit. Even though it's a dull day, it's still far too bright in here. Hannah was overzealous when she drew them earlier, and now I fear my megrim will return." She pressed her fingertips to her temple. "I can already feel it pulsing here. I'll need another dose of my nerve tonic soon if it doesn't fade."

"Of course, Mama," said Jane. Her mother frequently had headaches and Jane suspected half of them were manufactured. It was her mother's way of avoiding anything unpleasant.

But Jane wasn't going to back down. There was too much at stake.

Once the bedroom was suitably dim, she perched upon the edge of her mother's overstuffed mattress. "Mama…" she began, but Leonora Pevensey held up a hand.

"Now, Jane. I know you are going to berate me about last night. I can see that militant look in your eyes and I won't have it."

"That's not what I want to talk about," said Jane as patiently as she could. "We need to discuss the issue of your debt."

Jane's gaze darted to the bedchamber door, but it was firmly closed. Good.

Henry Pevensey was out of town on business, but Jane wasn't sure if Hannah, her mother's new lady's maid, could be trusted. To be on the safe side, she lowered her voice as she continued. "How are we to cover it? You know Father would never have wanted you to gamble away your share of the bookstore. He bequeathed it to you—"

"Well, your father died, Jane, and the money he *did* leave me barely covered our living expenses," her mother huffed. "I know you've had some work and contributed to the household too, but *I* had to take up cards to make ends meet. A fifty percent share in a quaint bookstore is almost useless when there are substantial bills that need to be paid. For a solicitor, your father was not very canny with his investments."

Jane sighed. What her mother said was true to some extent. After George Delaney had died seven years ago, Colin, Jane's older brother, had inherited the family home at Heathwick Green but had subsequently sold it. As a result, her mother had needed to watch her pennies to keep their rented London town house over her head and Jane's.

Lately, Jane had begun to wonder if her mother had actually been losing money for some time but hadn't let on. It was rumored that the Whisteria Club—an exclusive female-only card club that her mother had been invited to join two years ago—was notorious for high-stakes play. While Leonora's new husband, Henry, was comfortably off, Jane was certain he'd be horrified to discover his wife had a gambling addiction and had accrued a debt she had no hope of acquitting.

Jane sighed, striving for patience. "Be that as it may, Mama, now that you've wed again, you don't have to rely on your winnings at the card table anymore. And it isn't at all fair that you've put Grandfather's business in jeopardy. You know how much he loves that shop."

"Oh, I'm so sick of hearing about Joseph's precious store," her mother snapped. "You're always there, slaving away for next to nothing. Joseph should have sold that shop long ago. It's about time he retired."

"Mama, I cannot believe you're saying all this," returned Jane heatedly. "Please, you need to reconsider. There must be something else you own—a piece of jewelry, perhaps—that we could pawn that would at least cover some of the debt."

Her mother's peal of laughter was shrill. "I've already sold it all, Jane. Everything I own, apart from my new wedding ring and the amethyst and pearl parure Henry gave me as a wedding gift, is all paste. Every last stone. It's all worthless. And I won't sell the parure." She hiked up her chin. "It's beautiful and I couldn't do that to Henry. Selling the bookstore is the only way. I'll get at least fifteen hundred pounds for the sale. That will be more than enough to cover my debt and replace some of my jewels."

Jane shook her head. "No. No, I can't let you do this. Grandfather will be heartbroken if you force him to give up his shop."

I will be heartbroken.

Ever since the devastating dogcart accident that had changed the course of her life, Jane had found hours and hours of solace in Delaney's. It was her refuge from the world. A safe place. Her grandfather understood this. Her best friends, Artemis and Lucy, understood this. In fact, many of their Byronic Book Club meetings had taken place at Delaney's. Its shelves were brimming with the Gothic novels they all adored.

The books containing the Byronic heroes they loved so much. The men who didn't fail their heroines when they needed them most.

Her mother should know the importance of the store to Jane. Shouldn't she? Unless she knew and didn't care...

"It's simply the way it is," said her mother stiffly. "We all have our crosses to bear. I have an unmarriageable daughter and a bequest that's not worth the paper it's written on. Well, not unless I sell it. It's time."

Hot tears burned at the back of Jane's eyes. "I can't believe you would be so heartless."

Her mother sniffed and wrapped her bed jacket more tightly around herself. "Come, Jane. It's not as though you don't know that you're not marriage material anymore."

"That's not what I mean," snapped Jane. "My looks and marriageability do not signify." She drew a breath and strove to rein in her runaway temper. "Please, at least give me until tomorrow to try to come up with another solution."

Her mother paled and gripped Jane's arm. "Don't you dare ask your well-heeled friends for that money. I'd die of mortification if they found out about my habit. And I don't wish to be beholden to anyone."

"I understand, and I'm not going to," said Jane. "Aside from the fact Artemis and Lucy are both away, I would never burden them with *your* problem." She shoved away the thought that she had a pressing problem too.

Leonora Pevensey's eyes narrowed. "Then what are you going to do? Steal the Crown Jewels?"

Jane sighed heavily. "I...I don't know. But I'll think of something."

Or someone, she thought as she returned to her own bedroom. A wicked duke with an unexpected knowledge of rare and valuable books, perhaps? Could she persuade him to invest in her grandfather's store?

But why would he, Jane? What can you offer him?

Sexual favors?

She nearly laughed as she stared at her reflection in the looking glass above her dressing table. She'd had sexual intercourse but once in her life. With her erstwhile fiancé, Miles Dempster, and she could hardly characterize that experience as wonderful. All in all, it had been disastrous and not worth the pain—both physical and emotional—it had caused her.

In fact, the memory of that time still caused her pain. It was the reason she wanted to make a difference in other women's lives. By publishing a series of educative pamphlets about sexual congress and ways to prevent conception, she hoped that other women wouldn't make the same mistakes she had all those years ago. Then they wouldn't have to experience the terrible loss and anguish she'd endured.

But now she was being punished for her past history and her controversial plan by a person unknown. Her blackmailer.

But maybe, just maybe, you could ask the Duke of Roxby for help, Jane… He has the money you need to solve all your problems.

But would he be moved to help her? After what she'd done last night?

She had no idea. He was a stranger after all. And by all accounts a scoundrel. A seducer of women…

Even though Jane would be on her guard when she met with the duke in a handful of hours, her pulse began to race. The man was far too handsome, and simply thinking about him and his wicked reputation made her feel vexed and fretful. While she had practical knowledge about the mechanics involved when it came to sexual intercourse, she knew next to nothing about *giving* pleasure.

She suspected the Duke of Roxby knew all about pleasure though. Both the giving and receiving. And then she chided herself for being so foolish. Anyone would think she was a naive and starry-eyed debutante, not a no-nonsense, world-weary spinster.

A desperate spinster with a secret that could destroy her.

Jane eyed her somber reflection again. She couldn't blame her mother for *this* particular problem.

The fact that Miss Jane Delaney had a blackmailer was entirely her own fault.

Somehow, some way, she would extricate herself from this mess. And if that meant asking a handsome stranger for help, she would. Maybe it was pride, maybe it was her own need to be independent, but Jane wouldn't go to Lucy or Artemis.

She would *not* be the burden—a cross to bear—that her mother believed her to be, not to anyone else.

Chapter Five

THE DOORBELL OF DELANEY'S ANTIQUARIAN BOOKSHOP tinkled as Christopher pushed inside. He'd never visited the store before. He usually sent Featherstone to make the occasional purchase here or at the nearby Hatchards.

Despite the clumsy attempt to take his life in Hyde Park earlier today, Christopher refused to go to ground. In fact, he was more determined than ever to find out all he could about Miss Jane Delaney and why she had been tempted to steal a priceless book from his library. Part of him still rather hoped that he'd bump into the intriguing young woman before their meeting at three o'clock.

But as his gaze scanned the downstairs floor of the shop with its myriad well-stocked bookcases, he couldn't discern a slender, dark-haired young woman with a prominent facial scar in amongst the few customers perusing the titles on display.

Neither was there anyone in here who looked like they meant to do him harm. At least at first glance. All Christopher saw was a quaint, small business that seemed successful enough and ordinary people going about their day. He didn't sense anything untoward—anyone casting him furtive looks or looking uncharacteristically tense as though poised to strike. He didn't feel a prickle of preternatural warning that would make him reach for the pistol concealed in his coat or the knife strapped to his ankle.

Besides, no one would be expecting him to visit this particular store this morning. It was out of character for the

"Debauched Duke of Roxby" or whatever moniker the gossip columns had decided to dub him with today.

Behind the counter was a tall, pewter-haired gentleman sporting neatly trimmed muttonchops and wire-rimmed spectacles that were precariously balanced upon the end of his long nose. Christopher also made a mental note of the gent's dark-gray sack coat and pristine white shirt. His neatly tied neckcloth and black wool waistcoat. A silver watch chain and the edge of a red silk kerchief poking from a pocket.

Christopher assumed he was the proprietor of the shop and addressed him as such when he approached.

"Mr. Delaney?" he inquired.

The gentleman smiled warmly. "I am. Joseph Delaney to be exact," he said in a pleasantly deep voice. His consonants were crisp, his accent cultured. "What can I assist you with, sir?"

"I've heard that you restore and also value rare books."

"I do. And so does my granddaughter."

Aha. So, Joseph Delaney had a granddaughter. "Is she here this morning?" Christopher asked in a tone he hoped was innocuous.

Not innocuous enough, though, because Joseph Delaney frowned. Behind his spectacles, his eyes narrowed with suspicion as he gave Christopher a swift glance up and down. "No... no, she isn't. But I'm sure I can be of assistance, good sir. I've been in the book business for nearly forty years and my reputation is first-rate, even if I do say so myself."

Ah. So Joseph Delaney was both proud of his professionalism and protective of those in his immediate sphere. Christopher instantly liked the man.

"I have a rare, very old book I'd like you to value," said Christopher. "If you have the time. A rough estimate of its worth would be fine."

Delaney's gaze immediately sharpened with interest. "Of course, Mister…"

"Marsden. Major Christopher Marsden. The Duke of Roxby."

"The Duke of…" Joseph Delaney's face paled to the color of parchment paper. "Of course, Your Grace," he continued with a small bow. "Please forgive my error. It's not often that such an elevated customer crosses the threshold of my store. I am most honored."

"That's quite all right, Mr. Delaney. You weren't to know. Now, about this book." Christopher withdrew the silk-wrapped package from his leather satchel and then placed it on the wooden counter. "It's a first-edition copy of *The Canterbury Tales* printed by William Caxton. Late fifteenth century. I've heard that there aren't many copies still in existence. While I'm not looking to sell it, I hoped to gain an idea of what it would be worth at auction."

"Well…" Delaney cleared his throat. "Let's take a look at it." He withdrew a pair of pristine white cotton gloves from a drawer and put them on before he carefully unwrapped the silk cover from the book. His touch was deft yet careful as he examined the volume both inside and out. "The blind-tooled calfskin cover is in very good condition, considering the book's age. And so are the pages and woodcut illustrations. There's nary a tear or staining." Delaney placed the book reverently back upon the piece of silk. "It's difficult to say what some might be willing to pay for this, but at a rough guess, I imagine it would fetch a price in the vicinity of eight to ten thousand pounds. At least."

Christopher nodded. His great-uncle had already had the book valued by an auctioneer several years ago, and Joseph Delaney's estimate was not dissimilar. But it hadn't been the man's opinion he was interested in. It was his reaction upon encountering such a valuable work. While Delaney's eyes had gleamed with professional interest, Christopher hadn't detected any overt covetousness in the man's manner. Nor had he picked up any signs of alarm. Miss Delaney must have spoken the truth last night when she'd claimed that the owner of Delaney's had had nothing to do with her decision to steal Christopher's book.

"Thank you." Christopher rewrapped the volume and slid it carefully back into the satchel. "I should probably have this kept under lock and key. I know book theft isn't common, but one never knows."

"I would recommend that too, Your Grace," said Joseph Delaney, his face a picture of earnest innocence. "That book is undeniably valuable. It's such a shame my granddaughter, Jane, isn't here to see it. She would appreciate its full worth too."

Delaney was either a superb actor or completely clueless about his granddaughter's attempted crime. Christopher smiled. "Perhaps another time."

Later today, in fact.

As soon as Miss Jane Delaney walked through his library door again, Christopher would know if she was the woman he needed.

Chapter Six

"THIS WAY, MISS DELANEY."

Jane followed the footman into the depths of Roxby House. It wasn't the same fellow she'd encountered last night, but while his manner was pleasant enough, he was no less physically intimidating.

Jane was beginning to wonder if the duke's criteria for hiring these men was based on their height and shoulder width alone.

As she progressed through the town house, she was also struck by how immaculate everything was—how shiny and bright and in perfect order. Fresh hothouse flowers elegantly spilled from vases, and pale winter sunlight streamed through clear-as-crystal windowpanes. It was also eerily quiet. The rabble had gone, and now the pristine halls echoed with nothing but the click of heels—the footman's highly polished shoes and Jane's own half boots—on the gleaming marble floors.

In fact, it was so silent that Jane imagined the footman would be able to hear the erratic thud of her heart when they paused before the paneled-oak doors of the library.

As the fellow knocked, Jane heard a clock within the library chime the hour: three o'clock.

"Enter," called a deep voice from within, and Jane shivered with a combination of nervous anticipation and burning curiosity. She fancied she was going to her doom. Or about to meet the devil incarnate. Which was utter nonsense.

The Duke of Roxby is only a man, she reminded herself

sternly. *And if he meant you harm, you'd already be in prison. So chin up and do not betray the fact that you're intimidated by him. Or worse, attracted to him.*

The Duke of Roxby was sitting behind a vast mahogany desk, attending to some kind of correspondence or paperwork, but he pushed it aside as soon as Jane stepped into the room.

Her memories from last night hadn't done the man justice. Once again, she was taken aback by how breathtakingly handsome he was. Indeed, it was hard to maintain eye contact with him without becoming flustered. Nevertheless, Jane steeled herself to appear unruffled in all other respects, even if telltale color might flood her face at some point during this encounter. She dropped into a sedate curtsy as he rose to his feet.

"Miss Delaney. I'm impressed by your punctuality," he said in that beautiful rich baritone voice of his. Just like last night, the duke's gaze lingered on her face, unashamedly wandering over all her features, including her scar.

Irritation sparked. Ignoring the duke's compliment, Jane asked, "Is there something amiss with my appearance, Your Grace?"

The duke was infuriatingly indifferent to her verbal dig. "Not at all, Miss Delaney," he said smoothly. Gesturing toward an arrangement of leather wingback chairs by the fireplace he asked, "Would you care to take a seat? I can send for tea or coffee. My cook makes excellent petit fours."

But Jane held her ground. "The sword of Damocles has been hanging over my head all day, Your Grace. So if you don't mind, I'd like to get straight to the point of this meeting rather than dillydally over tea and cake. I don't have an appetite for unnecessary pleasantries."

The duke inclined his head. "Of course, Miss Delaney." He sat down behind his desk again and indicated that Jane should take one of the heavy Jacobean-style chairs on the opposite side. "Business it is."

"Thank you." Jane settled herself onto the velvet-upholstered seat, resting her reticule on her lap like a prim schoolmistress. She'd dressed smartly but plainly for the occasion in a plum woolen gown with a starched white collar, and her brown hair was scraped back into a tightly pinned, no-nonsense bun. "Shall we begin?"

"We shall." The duke's ice-blue gaze met Jane's as he rested his forearms on the desk. "Let me preface this meeting with the reassurance that the consequences I have in mind for you are not punitive at all. I do not seek to manipulate you or take advantage of you. I am a fair man. A considerate man, despite what you may have read about me in the newspapers."

Jane raised a brow. "Oh? So you *are* a gentleman, not a reprobate of the lowest order?"

The duke smirked. "I wouldn't go *that* far, Miss Delaney. Let's just say that I'm..." He stroked his clean-shaven chin. "Misunderstood."

"Hmmm." Jane frowned. "What you say may be quite true, but I still don't understand what you want. Because you *do* want something from me, don't you, Your Grace?"

"I do." The duke drummed his fingers upon the leather blotter and his expression grew thoughtful, as though he were weighing up his next words. However, Jane suspected it was all for show. She imagined that the duke was the sort of man who would always have a strategy up his sleeve. He knew exactly what he was going to say, and after a pregnant pause, he did. "In actual fact," he continued, "I simply want you to listen to what I'm about to share with you. And then I'm going to make you an offer."

"An offer? What sort of offer?" Jane's mind spun with possibilities, none of them good.

The duke narrowed his gaze. "I wouldn't jump to conclusions just yet. Hear me out, that's all I ask."

Jane sat up straighter. "Very well," she said, and she made a concerted effort to stop her thoughts careening toward anything nefarious or scandalous.

"Thank you," said the duke, and for once he sounded sincere. And also strangely somber. "I'm going to take you into my confidence, Miss Delaney. You see"—another pause—"I have an affliction."

An affliction? Jane's mouth dropped open. Surely the man was lying. Apart from her friends' husbands, the Duke of Dartmoor and the Earl of Kyle, Jane had never met a man who appeared to be more in his prime. "Is this when you tell me that your beauty is a curse and that's why you shut yourself away from all the revelry at your soirees or whatever you want to call them? Because you can't bear all the fawning and adoration? All those women—or perhaps men as well—throwing themselves at you."

The duke's mouth quirked with a wry smile. "No. Not quite," he said. "Although I'm flattered that you think me beautiful. I've never heard anyone describe me in that way before."

Heat scalded Jane's cheeks. "Yes. Well. 'Handsome' is what I really meant to say. In any case, being physically attractive can hardly be classed as an affliction."

"Agreed," said the duke. "But your assumption about the nature of my condition is incorrect. Some scars are hidden, wouldn't you agree? And you did say that you would listen."

Oh dear. Jane's chest tightened with guilt. How awful she must seem. How callous. "I did," she said. Even though she had no idea what the duke's malady might be, she added, "And I apologize unreservedly for my thoughtless words, Your Grace. My own affliction, so to speak"—she gestured at her left cheek—"has perhaps influenced my thinking. I shouldn't have mocked you. That was unaccountably rude."

"I understand," replied the duke gravely. "And your apology is accepted."

Jane bent her head in acknowledgment. "Please...do go on, Your Grace. If you feel that you can."

As her gaze met the duke's, Jane sensed that something had shifted. The impenetrable veneer of perfection surrounding the man had somehow crumbled a little. The light in his eyes was softer. His manner less cynical. He suddenly seemed less other-worldly and more human. A trifle uncertain, perhaps.

Vulnerable.

Jane knew exactly what that felt like, and for that reason she was inclined to give him the benefit of the doubt, whatever he said next. She *would* listen.

The duke leaned back in his chair as though settling in for a protracted conversation. "To help you understand the nature of my ailment, Miss Delaney, I must go back in time. You may or may not have heard that I inherited the dukedom from my elderly great-uncle about a year ago. That prior to that time, I'd been serving in Her Majesty's army as a cavalry officer. For almost a decade to be exact."

"Yes, I have heard something along those lines," said Jane. "It was in the newspapers."

The duke's mouth twitched with the ghost of a smile. "Amongst other things, I'm sure. What you might not have read in the London papers was that seven months ago I suffered a significant fall while riding on my Hertfordshire estate. In fact, I've been told that I lost consciousness for several hours. The local physician had even suggested employing a procedure called trepanation to alleviate the pressure inside my head. He feared I might die otherwise."

"Trepanation?"

"Yes. I'm told the doctor drills a hole in one's skull to drain the excess blood away from one's brain."

Jane gasped. "Good Lord, that sounds utterly barbaric."

"Quite," said the duke dryly. "In the end, trepanation wasn't necessary because I came to. But..." He paused. "I do wonder if the doctor had conducted the procedure whether I would have been better off. I suppose I'll never know."

The duke sighed. "But I digress. In the days following the accident, Featherstone—my erstwhile batman who now serves as my valet—reported that I seemed dazed and a bit confused. It isn't unheard of after such a heavy fall and subsequent head injury. I had no memory of the incident or the entire preceding day. I was forgetful and kept losing track of time. Most of my symptoms abated over the next fortnight. All but one." He met Jane's gaze directly. "I didn't recognize anyone anymore. No one at all. Even those as familiar to me as the back of my own hand."

Jane's brow furrowed. "You had amnesia?"

"In a sense. But a peculiar form of amnesia. I could remember everything else about myself and my life. After the initial period of general confusion passed, I knew where I was, who I was, the day and the year. All of my memories from early childhood, my school days, my university days, and my time in military service were completely intact. The fact that I was an only child and that my parents were deceased. My first few months as the Duke of Roxby. What I *couldn't* recall was anyone's face. Every single person—Featherstone, my doctor, my household staff, my colleagues—had become strangers to me. And even after all this time, they still are. It's like the blow to my head resulted in a strange form of blindness for faces and faces alone. I can *see* faces. I can note individual features as I regard them. But I cannot remember them as a whole. As soon as I look away, the image in my mind blurs, then disintegrates to nothing."

Jane's frown deepened as she endeavored to understand. "I–I can't even imagine it," she murmured. "How terrible. To not know with whom you are speaking. It must be horribly disconcerting. Nightmarish even."

"It is. Although I have developed certain strategies that help me manage to some extent," said the duke. "I'm practiced at recalling other features about a person to help keep them in my memory, even if it's only for a short while. I note things like height and build, hair color, attire, the timbre of the person's voice. The context of our conversation and where we are. But of course that only works for a brief period of time. The very next day, or even minutes later, in a different setting, if that same person has trimmed his beard or changed the color of his suit and the handkerchief in his waistcoat pocket, I might not have a clue who he is. Which can be awkward, to say the very least. Actually, it has the potential to be disastrous. In fact, it might end me."

Jane shook her head. "Surely not."

"Oh, I assure you that I'm entirely serious, Miss Delaney. I'm sure you can appreciate that as a duke I have many responsibilities. I cannot be seen to be weak or incompetent. By anyone. Especially by those in the peerage." A shadow crossed his countenance. "I fear that one day I might be accused of being mad or deemed an imbecile who cannot manage his affairs. I'll be declared non compos mentis and then locked up in an asylum for the rest of my days."

"But you don't seem either of those things to me," said Jane. "Mad or imbecilic."

"Ah, but I've learned to mask my affliction," said the duke. "To hide it. But sometimes I slip up. And being on my guard at all times is wearying beyond measure. In fact, the only souls who know I have this singular form of blindness are my physician, who is sworn to maintain patient confidentiality, and my batman, whom I trust implicitly. And now you, Miss Delaney. I feel that I can trust you."

"Me?" Jane couldn't hide the note of shock in her voice.

The duke's gaze was direct. Unflinching. "Yes. You."

"But…but why? You hardly know me. We've only just met. And I certainly wasn't at my best last night."

"Because, Miss Delaney, your face, out of an entire sea of unrecognizable faces, is the only one that I can remember. I cannot account for it, but it's locked in here." The duke pointed at his temple. "Indeed, from the moment I saw you in this library, your features seemed to be tattooed onto my brain. So yes, even though we've only just met, you alone are not a stranger to me. And that is why I believe that I can trust you. When you haven't been able to recognize anyone at all, a familiar face is not only an extraordinary thing…it's welcome. I cannot explain it any other way."

For the second time since she entered the library, Jane's mouth fell open. "I… Why…?" She drew a breath. "I'm flabbergasted, Your Grace. Your disclosure is a lot to take in."

All sorts of questions darted through Jane's head: *Why me? Why my face? Is it my scar?*

Of course, it must be your scar. The duke has stared at it often enough, Jane.

But is he telling the truth?

That's what Jane really wanted to know. But then if the Duke of Roxby wasn't being honest, what purpose would deceit serve? Why manufacture an elaborate lie about an affliction she'd never heard of?

Jane didn't want to be suspicious, but after her ill treatment at the hands of Miles Dempster, it was not in her nature to trust others easily. And then of course there was that whole issue of being blackmailed. Being on guard was as natural to Jane as breathing.

"It's not just that, though, is it, Your Grace?" she managed at length. "Perhaps the *only* reason for sharing your secret with me is because you know something about me too. Something shameful that I tried to do. A secret that you could easily use against me if I betray you."

"Ah, so cynical, Miss Delaney," said the duke. "But you see, who would believe the word of a supposed madman?"

Jane inclined her head. What he said made sense if she followed his thread of logic through to the end. But still she felt the need to provide a counterargument. "Who would believe the word of a spinster who needs money so desperately that she tried to steal a duke's priceless book? You'd only have to convince the bobby who showed up on your doorstep that I was guilty. A Crown prosecutor would take care of the rest."

"Perhaps…" The duke's brows arrowed into a forbidding frown. "Look, we could go back and forth about the whys and wherefores for the rest of the afternoon, but the honest-to-God truth is I need you, Miss Delaney. I'm not just concerned that my affliction will be exposed to the world." He leaned forward. A muscle twitched in his lean cheek. "I'm also worried that someone is trying to kill me."

"What?" Shock whipped the breath from Jane's lungs. "You can't be serious, Your Grace."

"Oh, but I am. Deadly serious," returned the duke gravely. "What I didn't disclose to you earlier was that the reason I fell from my horse—and if you recall, I mentioned I've been a cavalry officer for many years, so I'm an excellent rider—was that someone took a shot at me. The bullet grazed me here." The duke lifted up a sweep of his light-brown hair to reveal a livid scar along the left side of his temple.

"Oh my God," breathed Jane. "You're lucky you weren't killed."

"Indeed," said the duke as he let his tousled locks fall back into place. "The local constabulary was called in to investigate, but in the end it was deemed to be an accident. Nothing more than a local landowner or poacher who was out hunting rabbits or pheasants on the edge of my estate and missed his mark. It didn't help that I couldn't remember a thing about the incident. There was talk in the local village of course, and a brief mention in the local gazette, but the story went nowhere." He shrugged. "Men fall off their horses every day."

"But you don't think it was an accident," said Jane.

"No. Not now. Well, I did at first. I had no real reason to think it was anything else but bad luck. But the more I thought about the incident and how odd it was, the more suspicious I became. Especially when there was a second attempt a few months ago. And then a third. This very morning in fact."

A cold sliver of apprehension slid down Jane's spine. "You're not joking, are you?" she whispered.

"No, I am not, Miss Delaney," said the duke with such solemnity that Jane knew he spoke the truth. "The worst part is," he continued, "I cannot remember what the perpetrator or perpetrators look like. I don't even know if I've caught a glimpse of their faces. Only that on each occasion it was a male of indeterminate age. The second attempt happened when I was walking home late one night in Town in early December. A man darted out from an alley and lunged at me with a knife. I was able to disarm him easily enough, but then he got away. Then during my ride in Hyde Park earlier today, someone took another shot at me."

Jane couldn't suppress a gasp of horror and the duke's mouth twisted with a wry smile. "I wouldn't worry too much, Miss Delaney. Clearly, he missed." Then the duke snorted. "Well, he put a neat hole through my hat before he beat a hasty retreat. My valet and I gave chase, but it was a foggy morning, and he was also on horseback, so it wasn't too hard for him to disappear."

The duke sighed heavily. "Truth to tell, I feel like I'm being hunted by a ghost, Miss Delaney. I have begun compiling a list of potential suspects—people who might bear me a grudge of some sort or other—but the list is very short. I clearly have an enemy. A dangerous enemy. The frustrating thing is I can't even go to Scotland Yard. Who'd believe a man who can't remember who he's talking to? Who hasn't a shred of any real evidence? Who doesn't even know why he has a target on his back? I'm hardly a credible witness."

Jane drew a shaky breath as she tried to order her chaotic thoughts. For someone who'd almost been murdered earlier today, the duke possessed an unusual degree of sangfroid. Of course, he *had* been to war. But being shot at on the battlefield was surely different from being shot at in Hyde Park... There was much more to the man than met the eye.

"To say I'm shocked by all of this would be an understatement," she said gravely. "You said earlier that you need me, Your Grace. However, I fail to see how I can help. I understand that you *want* to trust me, and I assure you I am trustworthy, despite my actions last night. But—"

The duke held up a hand. "You promised that you would hear me out, Miss Delaney. And that included listening to my offer. I have a proposition for you. One that will benefit you as well as me."

Jane resisted the urge to squirm or fidget. Or blush. The

duke was regarding her with unnerving intent again. With a penetrating, sharper-than-crystal incisiveness that cut through her own defenses. "You're going to offer me money," she murmured huskily as trepidation made her pulse flutter madly. "The question is what do you want from me in return?"

"Yes, you are quite correct," said the duke. His light-blue gaze was cold and calculating as it drifted over her face. "The debt you owe, the one you are reluctant to talk about, whatever it is I will cover it. But in return…"

Jane lifted her chin. Firmed her voice. "I won't become your mistress, Your Grace." Because really, what else could a duke want with a spinster like her?

But the duke shook his head. "That's not my intention, Miss Delaney. You misunderstand the nature of my offer." He inhaled a breath. Caught her gaze. "I'm going to ask you to be my wife."

Chapter Seven

I'M GOING TO ASK YOU TO BE MY WIFE.

Jane couldn't believe what she was hearing. "You can't be serious," she gasped. "I–I don't know you. We…we don't know each other. At all."

The duke cocked an eyebrow. "But it would solve your financial woes, no?"

"Yes…yes, it would. Of course it would. I mean, it's undeniably generous that you would offer to cover a debt that you know nothing about. But…" Jane shook her head as she grappled with the full import of what the duke had suggested. "I think I need a drink. Not tea or coffee. Something stronger."

The duke pushed to his feet and strode over to an oak cabinet, upon which sat a silver tray and several crystal decanters. "Brandy? Sherry? Whisky?" he called over his shoulder.

"Brandy will suffice. Thank you."

When the duke returned, Jane placed her reticule on the desk and took the proffered crystal tumbler with a murmured thanks. Her thoughts were careening out of control like a herd of panicked horses, and she couldn't seem to slow them down or make sense of them. She took a sip of the brandy. Then another.

The duke had reclaimed his seat and was sipping his own drink. His expression was thoughtful as he regarded her over the rim of his glass.

"You still haven't told me how much the debt is, or how it was incurred," he said at last, interrupting her riotous thoughts.

"No. I haven't." Jane made herself meet the gaze of the man who'd just made the most outrageous proposal in all of Christendom. At least she could answer *this* question. "One thousand pounds," she said. "It's the amount needed to save my grandfather's bookstore."

"Delaney's."

"Yes. My grandfather doesn't even know he might lose the store. You see, my mother inherited a share of the business— fifty percent to be exact—when my father passed away. And she"—Jane's cheeks grew warm with embarrassment—"she recently lost her share in a high-stakes card game. She put the shop up as collateral to buy herself some time to raise the money she owed, but she hasn't been able to. The payment to clear the vowel is due in a week. So I decided to try and raise the funds myself. And when temptation presented itself last night..." She shrugged. "You know the rest."

The duke put down his glass, reached across his desk's blotter, and pulled a small book toward him. He picked up a silver pen, the nib hovering over a crystal inkwell as though he were about to dip it in. "I can write out a personal check payable to you for that amount right now, Miss Delaney," he said. "If you say yes..."

If I say yes...

Jane swallowed. Despite the fact she'd had another mouthful of brandy, her mouth was as bone-dry as the Sahara in midsummer. Her stomach was aswarm with a thousand butterflies and her mind was tumbling with a thousand thoughts.

What would life be like married to the Duke of Roxby? What sort of man was he really? She'd assumed that he was simply a jaded rake who didn't care about anything other than the pursuit of pleasure. While that still might be true to some extent, she'd also seen another side of him. A more vulnerable side.

If someone wished him dead, he was clearly in deep, deep trouble.

"How...how would this work? This marriage?" she asked in a voice husky with nerves.

The duke put down his pen and his mouth twitched. "Well, first of all, I would get a special license from Doctors' Commons—"

"No. That's not what I mean." Jane frowned. "Someone wants you dead, Your Grace, and you seem to believe that I will be able to assist you because you feel that you can rely upon me. I'm a known quantity, so to speak. I trust you have some sort of plan to draw the murderer out?"

"Yes. I do," he said. "But I need you to be my eyes. To help me recall the people that I encounter on a daily basis while I try to work out who is trying to end my life. I won't lie or try to sugarcoat it. This will be no ordinary marriage of convenience. It will be quite a dangerous undertaking."

"I see." Jane pressed her lips together. "Might I play devil's advocate though, Your Grace? Perhaps you don't actually need a wife. For instance, if I were to become your personal secretary, would that suffice? If you don't already have one, that is. I'd be with you during the day, and I could reliably observe anyone you meet with and verify his or her identity. Aside from that, I'm hardworking and quite experienced with cataloging and letter writing and taking dictation—"

But the duke shook his head. "No. That wouldn't work. If you were simply my secretary, it would invite far too much comment if I took you out and about Town with me at all hours of the day and night. There'd be too much speculation about the nature of my relationship with my pretty new employee and your reputation might suffer."

Jane almost laughed at that. "Well, while I'm flattered that you've complimented my looks, Your Grace, I must question your logic. Being married to the most scandalous duke in London will surely affect my reputation as well, don't you think?"

"The most scandalous duke in London... Hmmm..." The duke sighed. "While I do understand why you would think that, I would remind you that appearances can be deceiving, Miss Delaney. And no, as my wife—a duchess no less—you'd be well respected. I will assert again that we'd need to live together. In close quarters. As husband and wife."

Jane's grip tightened around her glass. "How close?" she asked.

The duke shrugged. "You'd have your own suite of rooms. Of course, we'd need to consummate the marriage so it's legally binding. And one day, I'd expect an heir. In fact, considering someone is trying to end me, I'd like to father a child sooner rather than later. Once I have a son and I am no longer in danger, we could go our separate ways. Lead separate lives. I have many properties and I could set up a household for you anywhere you like. Would you be amenable to that?"

Jane blew out a shaky sigh. The duke wanted a baby.

Of course he did.

Before she could draw another breath, Jane's heart cramped with sorrow and pain as long-buried emotion rose like a specter from the grave of her past. For years, she'd suppressed the desire to have a child. Since she'd been injured and Miles had forsaken her when she'd needed him most—since she'd been consigned to spinsterhood—Jane had not permitted herself to think of babies or motherhood as a real possibility. Not ever. She'd never once allowed herself to dwell on all the what-ifs and might-have-beens of that long-ago day when Miles had proposed and had made love to her when she'd said "yes." She'd tried very hard to obliterate all her memories of the accident on that very same day, as well as during the weeks of pain and loss and grief that had followed. And for the most part, she'd succeeded.

But now... Now the Duke of Roxby was proposing marriage to her.

And he wanted an heir to cement his family line.

A baby...

A fierce yearning surged as if from nowhere, momentarily stealing Jane's breath.

She couldn't deny it. She wanted a baby too. She'd *always* wanted a baby.

She'd never *stopped* wanting a baby. Jane knew Artemis and her Dominic had been trying for a child since they wed, but she'd steadfastly crushed the envious pang in her chest. She hadn't let her own longing escape from the locked box in her heart.

But this offer of marriage was her chance to make her own secret dream come true. The unexpected revelation after all these years shook Jane to her core.

Trying for a baby meant she would also be spending an inordinate amount of time in the duke's bed.

A stranger's bed.

Jane's gaze slid to the duke. He was watching her. Waiting for her to respond.

If she did this, if she said yes, she could save her grandfather's store. And she could have the baby she'd secretly longed for since she was nineteen.

She might even be able to pay off her blackmailer. But she would hold her tongue about that particular problem for the moment. What she wouldn't stay silent about was a concern she had about the duke.

"I have my own stipulation. My own condition," she said firmly, even though her insides were trembling.

"Oh, yes?" The duke's tone was slightly amused.

"For me to agree to your proposal, you must also agree that you will no longer host these outrageous parties you're so famous for. Not only that, but I must also insist that you stay faithful to me while you try to beget a child. I do not want to end up with the pox or the clap or some other hideous disease."

The duke arched a brow. "I commend you on your forthrightness, Miss Delaney. And just in case you're concerned that I'm not in perfect health—well, aside from this cursed facial blindness—I am. I'm as strong and vigorous as a cavalry horse."

Jane gave a small humph. "I'll have to take your word for that, Your Grace."

He flashed a roguish grin. "I'd be happy for you to put me through my paces at any time."

Jane couldn't help but laugh. His charm was infectious, and she realized if they wed, she'd have to be careful and guard her heart. "Let's not put the cart before the horse, Your Grace. You haven't yet agreed to my first stipulation—that you will cease holding these wild soirees you seem to be so fond of."

"Ah, but what I haven't told *you* yet, Miss Delaney, is that these debauched events are all a ruse."

"A ruse? Really?" Jane snorted in disbelief. "The couples fornicating in your dining room looked real enough to me. As did the naked woman on your pianoforte."

"True. However, I'm sure you can appreciate that for someone in *my* particular situation, it's better to be viewed as a devil-may-care libertine. There are fewer expectations for one to perform one's duty with any degree of precision. If I don't show up to a parliamentary session"—he shrugged—"hardly anyone bats an eyelid. If I'm not seen at White's or Brooks's or Boodle's, everyone assumes those particular clubs are too sedate for my tastes. If most people believe you're a drunkard, and the people you surround yourself with are inebriated, it's easier to explain away verbal faux pas. In fact, one can simply talk in generalities, and no one really notices if you only refer to them as 'old chap' or 'my dear.'"

Jane studied the duke closely, looking for any sign of guile. But she hardly knew him well enough to tell if he was lying. "If what you say is true, Your Grace," she said after a moment, "your ruse, while elaborate, is clever, I'll give you that."

The duke inclined his head. "Thank you." His shoulders rose and fell on a sigh. "Even though I've come to think of it as a necessary evil, I will confess that I too grow weary of the hubbub and constant mess in my house. The completely shallow interactions. And yes, the petty theft by people I barely know. My footmen can only do so much to police how many trinkets and how much silverware gets stuffed into pockets and down corsets and beneath skirts. So yes, I will happily agree to your stipulation, Miss Delaney. The Duke of Roxby will dispense with his wild-rake persona and become the epitome of the devoted husband once he's wed. He shall 'settle down.'"

Jane fiddled with her glass. She wanted to believe the duke.

The problem was she didn't know if he *was* telling the truth. She suddenly wished Artemis and Lucy were in Town. Lucy's husband, Will, in particular. He'd also served in the Queen's army. He might even know the Duke of Roxby. Well, Major Christopher Marsden and his reputation as an officer, at least.

Jane sighed and put down her unfinished brandy. "Your Grace, your offer to marry me and bail my family out of their financial mess is more than generous, but I feel that I need some time to consider it. Committing myself to a man I barely know is quite a momentous undertaking. May I have a day to think on it?"

"Of course, Miss Delaney. I understand perfectly," said the duke. He got to his feet. This meeting was clearly over.

Jane rose too and retrieved her reticule. But as she reached the door, the duke said, "I have one final request too, Miss Delaney."

Jane stopped. Turned around. "Yes...?" She couldn't fail to notice that there was an intent look in the duke's eyes as he crossed the Turkish rug, reaching her in a handful of long-legged strides.

"Before you go," he said, his voice low, "I'd like to suggest that we kiss. It seems to me that it's difficult to agree to spend a lifetime with someone if you haven't even sampled the merchandise." His mouth quirked with a wry smile. "So to speak. I can't deny that I haven't been thinking about it. From the moment we met, in fact." His gaze dropped to her lips. "Have you? Thought about it too, Miss Delaney?" he murmured. "What it would be like? To be in my arms? To feel my mouth pressed to yours? How I would taste?"

"I..." A searing blush heated Jane's cheeks. She wasn't shy about kissing. Far from it. She'd blushed because the duke had read her as easily as a book. He'd detected her desire for him. "I will admit that the thought has crossed my mind," she whispered. "Once or twice." There was no point in denying it.

His smile was slow. Heart-stoppingly appealing. "Did you think about it when you were alone in your bed last night? I know I did."

Jane's pulse fluttered like a trapped hummingbird. Her breath quickened and her corset felt far too tight. "Yes..." She couldn't lie. It had been so long—a whole decade—since she'd been kissed or even felt the pull of desire.

Well, that wasn't quite true... When she lost herself in books featuring brooding Byronic heroes—the sort of racy Gothic romance novels her friend Artemis wrote—she certainly became aroused. And when she was alone in her bed, fantasizing about these fictional men, she sometimes sought satisfaction by her own hand. She wasn't ashamed of what she did. She wasn't a saint and neither was she made of stone. She was human after all.

And surely she wouldn't lose her head, or her heart, over something as mundane as a kiss. Miles had kissed her numerous times while they'd been courting. Besides, if she said yes to the duke's proposal, it wouldn't be long before she'd be sharing more than kisses with this man. Just because she was determined to protect her heart, that didn't mean she'd deny herself the chance to experience physical "love" again. In fact, right at this moment, she would own to feeling a great degree of eagerness to share a bed with the duke. And not only because she wanted a baby. She wanted to experience true passion.

She wanted this man to show her pleasure.

"I meant it when I said that you are pretty." The duke raised his hand and gently caressed Jane's scarred cheek. He was standing so close, she could feel the heat of his body. Smell his deliciously heady cologne. "But I could see it in your eyes that you didn't believe me. On both occasions. You probably won't believe me when I say it now."

Jane inhaled a quick breath. Even though the truth might hurt, she had to know. "It's my scar, isn't it? That's why my face is so appealing to you. That's what makes it stand out."

The duke frowned. "Perhaps… I don't really know." His gaze locked with hers. "Does it matter?"

Jane swallowed. "Yes. I mean, no… To be perfectly honest, I'm not sure." And that was the truth. It had been so long since any man had paid Jane the least bit of attention that she wasn't sure how she felt. She reminded herself that the duke was a practiced rake and was likely to say what she wanted to hear to get what he wanted from her. But a wholly feminine part of her yearned to be desired by a man like him, even if it was for the wrong reason.

The duke slid a hand about her waist. Drew her closer. "It's not just that. That's not all that I remember about you. There are so many other things of note." His voice grew husky as he murmured, "I know you have deep-green eyes and rich brown hair as lustrous as polished mahogany. Hair that should not be pinned back so severely, but falling unbound about bare shoulders." His fingers brushed along a taut tendon of her neck, making her shiver. "I know you have alabaster skin that's so delicate, it readily reveals even the slightest flush of heat. And how could I forget your scent—delicate floral soap and something that is simply Miss Jane Delaney. And your voice." He bent low and whispered in her ear, "How lovely and smoky and sensual it is. I'd recognize it instantly, even in a crowded room. The sound of it makes me burn for a taste of you…"

Jane closed her eyes. Oh, but he was a master at this. She knew in that moment that this man's kisses would be anything *but* mundane. "It does?" she whispered.

"Yes…" His breath drifted across her cheek.

"You're trying to seduce me, Your Grace. Woo me into submission."

"Woo you. Court you. Seduce you… Why, yes, I am. You can't deny the attraction sparking between us, can you, Miss Delaney? Or may I call you Jane?"

Jane opened her eyes. "You may." He was offering his hand in marriage, and if she said yes, they'd soon be sharing a bed. She'd allow him the intimacy.

The duke smiled. The light in his eyes wasn't cool but a smoldering blue as he murmured, "And you may call me Christopher."

"Christopher," Jane repeated. Her fingers curled into his

lapels. Rightly or wrongly, she couldn't say no to this. She *wanted* this. His kiss. She wanted *him*. "You do have a point, so yes, I'll agree to your suggestion. I would like to sample the merchandise too."

"Thank God," he groaned.

Within the space of a heartbeat, the duke's mouth was upon hers. It was a forceful kiss. Searching. Passionate. Deep. Not the sort of kiss one bestowed upon an inexperienced miss in the first flush of womanhood.

The duke—Christopher—had correctly surmised that she wouldn't quail in the face of such naked want. That she wanted him to fan the embers of their mutual lust into something hot and bright and all-consuming.

Jane could tell by the way he pushed her against the door, trapping her there with his long hard body. It was in the way his mouth commanded hers. His lips were firm yet as plush as warm velvet, the strokes of his tongue bold yet gentle. The way one of his hands cradled her face while the other gripped her nape. He was setting her aflame, making her want and burn and forget who she was.

He made her feel alive. Real. A woman of flesh and bone. Of panted breaths and tingling nerves and a racing heart. She was somehow more than the drifting shadow she'd been for so long.

Oh, how she'd missed this heady feeling of being desired. The knowledge that a man like this could want her was potent indeed. If she couldn't have love, she could at least have this.

When the duke pulled away, he was breathless too. And he was smiling, his blue eyes gleaming. He might even be a little smug. "Well, Jane, suffice it to say I think that the sampling process was most gratifying. What say you?"

"I would agree, Your Grace… I m-mean Christopher." Had the duke noticed she was trembling with need as she clung to him? How overwhelmed she was by his kiss? No wonder he seemed self-satisfied. She might be easy to seduce, but one thing she wouldn't do was fall in love. Never again.

"The only problem is…" Christopher's thumb brushed across her kiss-swollen lower lip. "Now that I've tasted you, Jane, I want more." His gaze, bright and piercing, met hers. "Don't keep me waiting. I'm not a patient man. I want your answer tomorrow."

She inhaled a shaky breath. "You shall have it."

The duke stepped back and opened the door. "I'll be here. Three o'clock, shall we say?"

Jane nodded. "Yes."

"Good."

As the library door closed behind her, Jane wondered if this was how it would feel to make a deal with the devil himself.

The way her body thrummed, it appeared that for the most part she would quite happily burn.

———

As the door shut behind the delectable Miss Jane Delaney, Christopher groaned. Let his head drop against the cool panels of the door.

Good God. What the hell was he doing?

Maybe he *was* going mad.

Since he'd first come up with the idea that he would propose to this woman earlier today—offer her a marriage of convenience—he'd thought of it as purely transactional. Purely business.

A military campaign, as it were—an exercise—in tracking down his killer.

He did truly need Jane Delaney to be his eyes.

He hadn't realized that he would also want her in his bed with a hunger that bordered on insatiable.

It was a novel sensation. For a man who'd felt dead inside for months on end, he couldn't account for this sudden surge of ravening need...

Of course, he'd admired Miss Delaney's long legs and slender figure as soon as she'd set foot in his library the night before. He was aware that she was an attractive woman, despite the fact that her face had been marked with a prominent scar. Her intelligence, her fearless manner, and her devotion to her family were admirable qualities too. He sensed she had a good heart.

What Christopher hadn't counted on was his all-but-primitive reaction to her nearness. When she'd entered his library this afternoon, when she'd perched herself so primly on the chair in front of his desk, all he could think about was the lust inside him sparking to life once more and searing through his veins.

Of acting on that lust and taking Jane Delaney in exactly the way he wanted to. Her enthusiastic response to his kiss had been everything he'd hoped for and more. He hadn't been able to mask his own sense of deep satisfaction as he'd taken in her desire-glazed gaze at the end of their kiss. It was gratifying to learn his lust wasn't one-sided.

She's been thinking about me when she's alone in her bed...

Her frank admission only added fuel to Christopher's barely banked desire. Ignited his mind with all sorts of libidinous fantasies.

He wanted to free Jane's glorious hair from that hideous bun. Unbutton her plain purple gown with that awful prim collar. Remove all her skirts and her corset and drawers to reveal the treasures beneath. Pleasure her until she was sprawled boneless and sated on top of his desk.

He'd known then and there that he would have to have her in his arms every night until he'd had his fill. And the only excuse he could come up with that would guarantee that eventuality was insisting that he wanted to get a child on her.

Of course, one day he *would* need an heir, and perhaps a spare.

But right now? Now, when his life was being threatened and his head was such an addled mess?

Christ. Starting a family would undoubtedly add another layer of difficulty to an already complex situation. Yet another matter for him to deal with. Another distraction.

Like Jane.

Oh, but what a delectable distraction she was.

Despite his attraction, despite his simmering lust, Christopher was determined not to develop any sort of deep emotional attachment to her. He'd been disabused of the notion that true love matches existed—at least for him— some time ago. He might have lost his ability to discern faces, but he certainly wouldn't be easily duped into losing his mind over a woman.

Yes, his life was complicated enough. He didn't have time to waste being besotted with anyone, even if she did have spectacular legs and bewitching green eyes.

Christopher strode over to the drinks tray again and poured himself another brandy. Gulped it down in a few swallows then poured another. He could feel a headache coming on. Brandy was not the answer, but perhaps it would douse the fire of unquenched desire surging through his body, thickening his cock. Calm the chaos in his brain.

He both wanted and needed Jane Delaney in his life. At least she desired him too.

Without a doubt, she needed his money.

Christopher trusted that when she walked back into Roxby House tomorrow, her answer would be yes.

It had to be.

Chapter Eight

Jane stifled a yawn as she poured cups of steaming tea for her grandfather and herself. He was still upstairs in his small apartment above the bookstore, getting ready for the day ahead. A glance at a nearby clock confirmed that it was almost time to unlock the front door of Delaney's and let in the first customers. Although, given the fact that it was raining cats and dogs outside, Jane doubted that many people would be out and about on such a dismal morning.

It was the sort of day made for staying indoors and pondering weighty problems. Even though the gas lamps were all lit, the bookstore's atmosphere was decidedly gloomy. It was almost as though it was a sentient being and knew its future was at stake.

Jane made a small scoffing sound as she stirred a small lump of sugar into her grandfather's tea. She was becoming more fanciful by the day.

If she said yes to the duke's proposal, the bookstore would be safe.

Her mother's reputation would be safe.

As for her own reputation…Jane wouldn't rest easy until she'd put an end to this blackmailing business. But as she'd been telling herself, she could only tackle one problem at a time. As much as she'd like to enlist Christopher Marsden's help—or even that of Artemis and Lucy—Jane just couldn't.

Aside from the fact she was too embarrassed, ultimately she

was determined to sort out this particular mess on her own. If she did marry Christopher, she was certain she'd be able to deal with the matter quietly and efficiently. He needn't find out. Besides, he had enough to worry about. Jane couldn't even imagine what it would be like to be looking over one's shoulder all the time, wondering if someone was going to end you. It would be nightmarish. Especially in Christopher's case because everyone except her was a stranger to him. He certainly didn't need to take care of yet another problem.

Jane sighed and sipped her tea. The scalding heat on her tongue was welcome. It helped to clear her head.

The main reason she felt that she couldn't share her own oh-so-awkward predicament with Christopher was that she didn't know him well enough. She had no idea how he'd react if he learned she was being blackmailed for something that she'd done. Or to be more exact, for something that she *wanted* to do. In fact, he might even stop her from carrying out her plan. And she couldn't have that. This project of hers—a project of her heart—was very much a secret and needed to remain so for it to work.

For her own safety.

Oh, what a pickle she was in!

The hateful words of her blackmailer's latest letter invaded Jane's mind. It had been pushed through the letterbox in Delaney's front door early one morning a week ago. Jane didn't need to dig it out from the locked drawer in her grandfather's workroom at the back of the shop to recall exactly what it said…

> *You don't deserve a happy life, Miss Delaney.*
> *You must be held to account for your sinful ways.*
> *To ensure my continued silence, you must pay a deposit*
> *of fifty pounds on the 21st of this month. Like last time,*
> *deliver it to Mudie's Lending Library at 10:00 a.m.*

precisely. Place it in Mr. Dickens's book The Pickwick
Papers. *Then walk away. Out the door.*

Do not look back.

*I'll be watching, and if you don't do exactly as I say, your
shameful dirty secret—those filthy words you wrote—
will be exposed to everyone.*

*Your wicked character picked to pieces in the papers.
You'll be the laughingstock of London.*

Shunned.

*Do not make the mistake of thinking that I won't do it.
You'll be informed when you can collect your depraved book.*

In hindsight, Jane probably should have kept her journal with
the first draft of her series of pamphlets—*A Practical Woman's
Guide to Self-Determination and Lasting Fulfillment*—locked
away in her bedroom at her mother's house in Kensington. But
how was she to know that someone would break into Delaney's
and rob the store, just after Twelfth Night? The local constabulary had been called, a report had been made, but because
nothing particularly valuable had been stolen—Joseph Delaney
kept most of the store's takings in a locked safe in his rooms
above the shop—not much effort had been expended on the
investigation.

A few bits and pieces from the workshop—a brass-handled
magnifying glass, a pewter knife, and some scissors, along
with some loose change in a drawer—had been taken. And, of
course, a leather-bound journal.

Jane's journal.

Jane could hardly tell the police—or her family and friends,
for that matter—that her notebook contained what amounted to
a manual detailing everything a woman should know about sexual
intercourse and practical methods to safeguard against pregnancy.

It was the sort of information *all* women needed. So they would have choices in life. In Jane's mind, it was an updated, much clearer version of Richard Carlile's much maligned work, *Every Woman's Book, Or, What is Love?* which was published over thirty years ago. If she could spare even one woman from making the same terrible journey she'd made when she was nineteen, she would.

But despite her desire to help others in a meaningful way, Jane feared she might fail. It rankled her no end that perhaps the theft of her notes would have amounted to nothing if she hadn't thoughtlessly written her name on the very first page of the book. But she had, and there was no point in lamenting the fact now.

Just as there was no point in lamenting the fact she had no idea who the culprit was. Not a single clue. It might be a complete stranger, but then again it might not. She'd gone over and over who she knew and who would be despicable enough to blackmail her, but no one came to mind. She had journalist associates at the *London Tatler*, but no one bore her a grudge or considered her a rival, let alone "wicked" or "sinful." As far as she knew. As for the other shop attendants who worked at Delaney's, Jane had known them for years, and they were all on good terms with both her and her grandfather. Besides, why would anyone break into the store in the dead of night when he or she could easily steal the notebook in a quiet moment? She couldn't make sense of any of it.

The sound of her grandfather's footsteps on the stairs heralded his arrival in the shop.

"Jane, my dear. You're here early this morning," he said as he joined her behind the shop counter.

She smiled. "The rain woke me, and I couldn't sleep. I thought it might be better to make the trek from Kensington to Piccadilly before the morning traffic got too bad." She would often walk the two miles from Pelham Crescent to Delaney's, but because of the downpour, she'd caught an omnibus instead.

Her grandfather gratefully accepted his cup of tea. "Are you all right, Jane?" he asked after he'd taken a sip. "You don't seem your usual self."

She forced another smile. While she'd love to confide in her grandfather, she didn't want to worry him. "I'm fine," she lied. "Really. The horrid weather isn't helping though. And of course I miss Artemis and Lucy."

Her grandfather nodded. "It seems like ages since you and your friends held a Byronic Book Club meeting here. But it shouldn't be long until Artemis and Lucy return to Town, no?"

"I expect they'll both be back in a few weeks," said Jane. It felt like Artemis and Lucy had been her friends forever. In actual fact, they'd all grown up in Heathwick Green, just outside of London. Their Byronic Book Club had formed during their adolescent years because of their mutual love of novels, especially Gothic novels, and the brooding heroes that frequented their pages. They might have gone their separate ways over time, but they'd never disbanded their "book club." In fact, in many ways it had sustained them, especially after both Jane and Artemis had ended up nursing broken hearts one long-ago summer when they were both nineteen. The fictional men they encountered in their favorite books like *Jane Eyre* and *North and South* and *Pride and Prejudice* fell in love, and despite their flaws, they gave their heroines what they needed. They made them happy. Whereas real men—spineless cads like Miles Dempster—often broke women's hearts and then walked away.

"You could always jump on a train," suggested her grandfather. "I'm sure both of your friends would love a visit from you."

"Oh, I couldn't leave you—"

"To fend for myself?" Her grandfather smiled. "I might be

old, but I'm not infirm, my dear. I'm sure your mother and Kitty and even your brother and his wife can do without you. You do too much for them all."

"I know," said Jane. And it was quite true. She was the chaperone for Kitty and various Delaney cousins when the occasion called for it. She was the sometimes nanny for Colin's children. She earned extra income when she could, writing articles and literature reviews for various newspapers. And of course she worked at Delaney's.

And then a terrible wave of guilt and loss flooded Jane's chest as she realized that accepting the Duke of Roxby's offer would mean that she would never be able to work here again. It was acceptable for Artemis, the Duchess of Dartmoor, to be the patroness of her own ladies' academic college. Lucy, as a countess, could quite happily travel the world with her husband, conducting her botanical research. As the Duchess of Roxby, Jane would not be permitted to work in a bookstore.

Of course, her grandfather would hire someone else to cover her shifts. All the same, Jane would miss being here at Delaney's. Most of all, she'd miss her grandfather's company.

When she looked up, it was to discover her grandfather was watching her. "I have something to tell you that might cheer you up," he said.

Jane smiled. "Oh, yes?"

"You'll never guess who was in here yesterday morning." Behind his spectacles, his eyes gleamed with excitement. "The notorious Duke of Roxby himself. He asked me to estimate the value of a priceless book."

Jane fought to keep her expression neutral. She wasn't sure if she was annoyed that the duke hadn't said anything to her yesterday about his visit to Delaney's. It almost felt like he was spying on her behind her back. But part of her was also intrigued. "Oh," she said after an awkward pause. "How much is it—? I mean, which book?"

Obviously she knew, but she had to ask.

Her grandfather beamed. "It was a first edition copy of *The Canterbury Tales* published by William Caxton."

"My goodness," said Jane. A memory of the duke cutting the precious book away from her leg made her pulse flutter.

Fortunately, her grandfather didn't seem to notice she was a little unsettled as he continued, "Yes, indeed. The estimate I gave was rough, but because the copy was in such good condition, I suggested that it would fetch eight to ten thousand pounds at auction."

Jane nodded. That had been her thought too when she'd first laid eyes on the book. Before she could stop herself, she asked, "And is that all the duke wanted?"

"It would seem so," said her grandfather.

At that moment the store's clock chimed the hour, nine o'clock, and he put down his tea. "Right, time to open up, my girl. If you wouldn't mind checking through that new box of books that came in late yesterday and sorting out which customer has ordered what, I'd be most grateful. I'll man the counter."

"Of course," said Jane. Doing something menial would perhaps take her mind off her myriad worries. And while she would love to do what her grandfather suggested—take a train to Ashburn Abbey in Dartmoor to see Artemis or even to Scotland to see Lucy—she couldn't. The duke wanted his answer this afternoon, and Jane knew that whatever advice her friends gave her, she would most likely ignore it. She certainly wouldn't ask for or accept their money.

Jane's troubles were her own and she wouldn't burden anyone else with them. It was not within her nature to do so. And besides, she couldn't deny the unleashed yearning deep inside her to have a baby. Now that she'd acknowledged it, it was an insistent beat in her blood. A constant tick, tick, ticking in her mind.

She was nearing thirty and she might never have this opportunity again.

It seemed that she'd made up her mind already. Before long—for better or for worse—Jane was throwing her lot in with a man she barely knew. A man with a complicated life. A life that could very well be in danger. And he wanted her to help him catch a would-be murderer. She had no idea what his plan was in that regard, but she would do what she could to help. In many respects, he was not the man everyone thought him to be, and she couldn't deny that part of her was intrigued by him. He had hidden depths she was only just beginning to learn about.

She was certainly looking forward to becoming physically intimate with him...

Some might say that what Jane was about to do was foolhardy.

It was undeniably dangerous.

But she was going to take a leap of faith and do it anyway, come what may.

———

After Jane climbed the rain-slick steps of Roxby House, she made herself pause before she rapped on the shiny black door. She took a moment to snatch a few deep breaths even though it was cold and drizzling and miserable.

She was still wearing her rather ordinary plaid taffeta gown that she'd donned first thing that morning. While it suited her well enough, now she was rather wishing she looked a tad more stylish. She was about to become the Duke of Roxby's fiancée, and it would have been nice to at least look the part.

The towering footman who answered the front door and relieved her of her umbrella and bonnet was different again. An icy shiver slid down Jane's spine. She supposed if there was a potential murderer out there, it would make sense for the duke to station physically intimidating staff at the entrance to his house.

Another male servant appeared—an older gentleman who introduced himself as Shelby, the duke's butler. As he escorted Jane through the house, she heard the melodious ebb and flow of a pianoforte. A nocturne by Chopin perhaps.

"Is that your master playing?" she asked Shelby.

The man smiled. "It is, Miss Delaney. He's quite accomplished. At least I like to think so."

"You're not wrong at all," she said. It seemed the scandalous duke with the glacial blue eyes had hidden talents she was hitherto unaware of. But then she'd never expected the Duke of Roxby to have an appreciation of rare and expensive books either. She couldn't help but wonder what else she might soon discover about her prospective husband-to-be.

She already knew he was an excellent kisser.

When the butler ushered Jane into Roxby House's drawing room but a moment later, her pulse was cavorting about with nervous expectation.

As soon as the duke caught sight of her, he ceased playing the lyrical nocturne and rose from his seat. "Miss Delaney," he said with a perfectly executed bow. "I see you're punctual as usual."

"I... Ah, yes," she said. "I'm not one to drag my heels. There's no time like the present and all that."

Jane suddenly wondered if being on time made her come across as too eager. Too money-hungry. But then she chided herself for being ridiculous. If she really was that avaricious, she would have said yes to the duke's marriage proposal yesterday. She'd made the man wait a whole day for her answer.

The butler had already quit the room, and she and the duke were alone. Jane's gaze drifted to the pianoforte, now free of naked muses. In fact, the whole room looked quite different by the light of day. It was tastefully furnished in deep shades of blue and gray with touches of gilt here and there.

The duke smiled as his gaze wandered over her in a leisurely fashion before returning to her face. "You look well, Jane," he said. And then his forehead creased with a slight frown. "It's still all right that I call you Jane, isn't it?"

Jane smiled back. She liked that he appeared concerned about her opinion on the matter. "Yes, it is, Christopher... It's still all right to address you by your first name too?"

He laughed. "To be perfectly honest, I'm not used to being called 'Your Grace' yet. I'm not sure if I ever will be."

He gestured toward a cluster of chairs by the ornately carved gray marble fireplace. "Would you care to take a seat? I'm anticipating there's much you'd like to discuss."

"Yes..." Jane selected an elegant shepherdess chair and Christopher folded his large frame into the opposite seat. "Before I give you my answer," she said, "I feel that I should clarify a few details about our arrangement."

"Go ahead. I'm listening." His disconcerting gaze touched hers.

Jane cleared her throat. "At the risk of sounding mercenary, and even though I don't have a dowry, I would like to ask if you would afford me some sort of allowance or pin money should I become your duchess. I'm familiar enough with noble marriages to know that it's quite customary. My good friend Artemis, the Duchess of Dartmoor, has one. As does my other friend, Lucinda, the Countess of Kyle." She paused. "Her husband was a major with the Scots Greys and served in the Crimean conflict as well. You may have known him back then as William Lockhart. His grandfather is the Duke of Ayr."

Christopher's eyebrows shot up. "You have well-connected friends indeed, Jane. And yes, I do know Major Lockhart, or should I say Lord Kyle. Not well, mind you, but I have crossed paths with him. As for the Duke of Dartmoor...I may have encountered him, albeit briefly, at White's before I lost my memory for faces. I think I also heard him speak in the House of Lords on one occasion. I was pleased to hear that he's wed again."

"He's very happily married," said Jane. "Artemis, Lucy, and I are actually childhood friends. We grew up together in Heathwick Green near Hampstead Heath."

"Ah, I know of it," said Christopher. "A lovely spot."

"It is."

The duke frowned. "Forgive me, Jane, but considering you do have such wealthy friends, I must ask... You didn't think to ask for their help, but instead chose to steal one of my books?"

Jane clasped her gloved hands together in her lap. "For one thing, I honestly didn't think you'd notice anything was missing from your library. When I entered Roxby House, I did it on a whim. I originally intended to glean some gossip to sell to the newspapers." And then Jane explained her connection to the *London Tatler*. "I–I know it sounds grubby and awful, and you might think ill of me, but I do think you should know that was my original intention when I stole inside. Before I saw your bookcase of rare titles, that is."

Christopher frowned but didn't say anything.

Jane licked her lips, her mouth suddenly dry. "I...er... My friends have their own lives, and I did not wish to burden them with my family's financial woes. Aside from that, hardly anyone knows about my mother's addiction to high-stakes card play...and I'd rather it stay that way. And so would she." She resisted the urge to look away from Christopher's steady gaze. "She remarried recently, to a well-to-do banker, and my mother cannot afford for any scandal to be attached to her name."

"I see." Christopher steepled his long fingers beneath his chin. "I can well imagine that your mother does not want that sort of secret to get out. However, it seems to me that you take on the problems of others far too much, Jane."

"I know," she said, then closed her eyes for a moment, gathering her courage. "The thing is, Your Grace—I mean Christopher—when you mentioned yesterday that you would need an heir sooner rather than later, part of me realized that I do indeed want to have a baby. That being said"—Jane sat up straighter and drew a bracing breath—"I should let you know that I am almost thirty. I'm getting older and perhaps I'm not as...as fertile as a younger woman."

Christopher raised a brow. "Jane, I can assure you that wedding some fresh-out-of-the-schoolroom debutante who knows nothing of the world is, and always has been, the farthest thing from my mind. But while we are exchanging confidences, I should let you know something about me and my stipulation about wanting an heir..." He adjusted his position as though he were a little uneasy. "It is true that someone in my position does need a son to continue the family line. And it does trouble me that I may not achieve that end if something else untoward happens to me. But..." He blew out a sigh. "Look, there is no easy way to say this."

All of a sudden, Christopher's eyes smoldered with a burning blue intensity that made Jane shiver from the inside out. "When I saw you for the very first time, I knew that I had to have you. That I wanted you in my bed. I can't explain it. It's...it's not the sort of lust that one generally admits to in the company of a lady. So when I proposed this marriage of convenience, I decided that I would tell you that my need for an heir was pressing. It was—it essentially still is—an excuse to seduce you.

"While I can't promise you love—I'm afraid I'm rather cynical when it comes to that emotion—I also don't want a cold, passionless marriage. And even though you'll have your own suite of rooms, I want you in my bed as much as possible." He leaned back, watching her. "I want you, and I mean to have you in any and every way that I can. How do you feel about that particular disclosure, Jane?"

The Duke of Roxby wanted her. In his bed… Rather a lot, by the sound of it.

Jane's heart began to beat hard and fast against her breast.

Goodness, the man didn't believe in beating about the bush, did he? But then what was the point in avoiding the topic of sexual relations? They were striking a deal after all. As to his declaration that he couldn't promise her love, well, she was fine with that too. She liked the fact he was being honest. And it would be far easier to protect her heart if they kept things "businesslike." If both of them understood the terms of their arrangement. In fact, she relished the opportunity to at last undo the buttons and tight laces that had kept her passionate side in check for so long.

And the more time she spent in the duke's bed, the better her chances were of conceiving.

Jane could hardly wait.

Chapter Nine

JANE DELANEY DIPPED HER HEAD AND APPEARED TO CONtemplate everything Christopher had said. Whether she was embarrassed or chagrined or felt something else entirely, he couldn't be sure. But as the silence extended he wondered, with growing dismay, if he *had* gone too far. If he'd shocked Jane with his candid admission about his desire and the fact their union might very well be loveless.

But then, thank God, she lifted her gaze and met Christopher's directly. "I don't have a problem with any of that," she said in that low, smoky, distinctive voice of hers that secretly drove Christopher wild. "And I appreciate your frankness. In the interest of reciprocating that honesty, I think you should also know that I'm"—she raised her chin a notch—"I'm not a virgin."

"Neither am I," said Christopher with a wry smile.

"I mean, I wouldn't like to suggest that I'm terribly experienced in that regard," she added after a pause. "I..." She frowned and then puffed out a breath as though she'd reached a decision. "Ten years ago, I fell head over heels in love with a man. He proposed to me, and after I accepted we consummated our union. But shortly afterward, this happened." Jane gestured at her cheek. "We were both in a dogcart accident. He was driving, and then..." She shrugged. "Well, suffice it to say he didn't wish to get married after that. He pretended as if he'd never even asked me the question in the first place."

Fury gripped Christopher's chest. "The blackguard. He jilted you? After hurting you like that?"

Jane's lovely mouth tilted into a sad smile. "It would seem so. But I suppose in a way the incident revealed that he was not the sort of man one could rely upon. That his feelings for me were superficial." She knotted her hands together in her lap. "What I'm trying to say, Christopher, is that I welcome the opportunity to share your bed in the begetting of a child. I...I do not wish this to be a cold, passionless union either. While it seems that neither of us is looking for love—I certainly don't expect that and no longer possess the starry-eyed delusions I once had—I would hope that we will at least be able to form an amicable relationship based on mutual respect."

"I concur with your thoughts, Jane. It seems that we are 'on the same page' in a manner of speaking."

"Yes..." She smiled softly and her green eyes glowed warmly like a forest pool lit by sunlight on a summer's day. And Christopher was transfixed. What was it about this woman that had him in such a lather? He was not the sort of man to wax lyrical about anyone's eyes, or be stirred by a voice or even the scent of a woman's soap.

Now a pair of long slender legs definitely stirred him. He looked forward to exploring Jane Delaney's in great detail in the not-too-distant future.

This afternoon, if she would let him...

But then Jane's expression changed. Grew serious. "Christopher, while we are negotiating the terms of our marriage, I do feel that this is also the time for me ask you about another matter." She shifted in her seat as though she were a little uncomfortable. "You've mentioned that I shall have my own suite of rooms here at Roxby House, and that one day, when we agree to lead separate lives, you will provide me with my own residence. Which is all very appreciated, of course. But might I also be permitted to employ a lady's maid? I'm afraid I do not have one of my own."

Christopher held up a hand. "That goes without saying. And when you have your allowance, I'd urge you not to be too frugal with your purchases. I am a generous man and I do understand that you will need a new wardrobe. I will not have my duchess attired in anything but the finest gowns and jewels. You shall even have your own carriage and horses. My only request is that when you finally choose a maid, you have her background thoroughly investigated. Since the third attempt on my life, I've taken to verifying the staff in my employ. It might seem unnecessarily careful to you, but I'd rather not have a would-be murderer living under my roof."

"Oh, of course," said Jane. "I understand completely. In fact, I shall ask my friends Artemis and Lucy to help me find someone suitable with impeccable references."

"Excellent," said Christopher. "I take it that your answer to my proposal is yes?"

Jane drew a breath as her clear, unwavering gaze met his. "Yes, it is. I'll agree to be your wife."

Christopher found himself smiling. "You don't know how happy and relieved it makes me to hear you say that." It wasn't a lie. Again, he couldn't account for the feelings this woman so effortlessly evoked in him. There was fierce arousal, yes, but lurking beneath that there was a sense that this arrangement might just work out for both of them. The more cynical part of him would argue that he felt that way simply because she was the one person in the world that he could truly recognize. But…but…he also *liked* her. The bits of her personality that he'd seen so far, anyway.

He stretched out a hand. "Come here, Jane. Your fiancé wishes to kiss you," he said, and he was thrilled when she immediately complied. As soon as she put her hand in his, he pulled her across his lap and claimed her mouth, reveling in that warm, honeyed recess and the way she welcomed the incursion of his tongue. How he adored the way her own sinuous tongue, softer than velvet, twined around his, and tasted and caressed him just as thoroughly. When her slender body relaxed against him, she unashamedly pressed her breasts against his chest, and he couldn't suppress a moan of appreciation.

He couldn't wait to have Jane beneath him, naked. Or on top of him, or however she goddamn pleased. His blood heated and his cock twitched.

Yes...

It had been months and months since he'd lain with a woman. He hadn't lied to Jane when he'd told her that his parties were all an elaborate ruse.

Truth to tell, he hadn't even felt aroused for months, and he'd begun to suspect something was very wrong with him other than his peculiar form of blindness. Perhaps it had something to do with the injury he'd sustained and the strain he'd been under, wondering if someone might discover his secret and use it against him to undermine his standing and even question his sanity. And of course if someone was trying to kill him and when that person might strike again. Lately, he'd begun to worry if he would ever feel true desire again at all.

But with Jane here in his arms, with her hands buried in his hair and her sweet, hot mouth ravishing his with equal ferocity, he knew the part of him that had been dormant for so long was at last coming back to life. In fact, he was afire.

He needed more than Jane's kisses. He wanted all of her.

He boldly cupped one of her breasts and groaned when he felt the jut of her nipple even through the layers of her bodice and corset. He slid a button at her throat undone, followed by a second and a third. And then he pressed his mouth to the fragrant, satiny flesh he'd exposed. Relished in the feverish flutter of Jane's pulse beneath his questing lips and the way she shivered and moaned when he dragged his tongue along her neck and nipped at her shoulder.

He was in the process of undoing a fourth button when there was a knock on the door.

Fucking hell.

Christopher only just stifled the crude curse as Jane gasped and stiffened in his arms. He raised his head and prayed for patience and words that weren't other obscenities.

"Yes?" he called. His eyes sought Jane's, but she was frantically setting her bodice to rights.

"I'm sorry, Your Grace." Shelby's muffled voice filtered through the door. "But you have a visitor. She says it's urgent."

She?

Christopher ran a hand through his hair. "Shelby, I don't care if it's the bloody Queen herself. Now is not a good time."

"It's all right," said Jane. She slid off his lap and smoothed her skirts. "I–I don't want to interrupt your day. I'm sure you have a thousand other things to do."

"No, it's not all right," grumbled Christopher. "And you're not interrupting me at all." At least his erection had started to subside. He pushed to his feet, and after adjusting the fit of his coat to make sure he appeared respectable, he strode over to the door and flung it open.

Shelby—at least he thought it was the butler—had the decency to look shamefaced. "It's a Mrs. Daphne Marsden, Your Grace. She didn't leave a card because she insists that she's part of your extended family and that you are well-acquainted. She says the matter has something to do with her son."

"Ballocks," muttered Christopher. Then he sighed. "Very well, Shelby. Send her in, along with a suitably inviting afternoon tea tray." He knew that if he didn't deal with whatever matter had put his cousin-in-law in a flap, it would only get worse as time went on. Best to nip the issue in the bud now.

Once Shelby had gone, Christopher turned back to Jane. "Daphne is the widow of my cousin, Thomas Marsden, who died on the battlefield in Crimea," he explained. "Their son, Oliver, is my second cousin, and he's next in the line of succession. Well, at least until I produce my own son. Because my great-uncle, the former Duke of Roxby, was one of Oliver's guardians, it seems I have inherited that privilege too."

"I see," said Jane. She tucked a loosened lock of glossy brown hair behind her ear. "Do I look all right? I can leave if you'd prefer..."

"I want you to stay," Christopher said firmly. "And you look perfect. Hopefully, this won't take too long. Actually..." Struck with inspiration, he crossed to an oak sideboard and snatched up a picture in a silver frame. "If you wouldn't mind taking a look at this," he said, passing it to Jane. "It's a photograph of Daphne Marsden with my cousin. I don't like to be suspicious of everyone that I encounter, but I'm hoping that you'll be able to confirm that the woman who walks through my drawing room door is the same woman in the picture. My butler has only been in my employ for the last three months, so he hasn't met Daphne before."

"I would be happy to," said Jane. There was a small line between her fine dark brows when she raised her gaze from the photograph. "It must be so awful not knowing who anybody is. Doubting who you see in front of you."

"It's certainly disconcerting," said Christopher with a wry smile. "Especially when one looks in the mirror and sees a stranger staring back."

Jane paled. "You don't know your own face?"

"No. I can catalog all of my features individually. I know I have blue eyes, a straight nose, and a wide mouth. That I have a scar near my hairline. And I can tell if I need a shave. But I don't recognize my reflection as my own. The only part of me from the neck up that I can reliably identify is my hair. It might be unfashionably long at the moment, but it helps to remind me that the man in the mirror *is* actually me."

"I'm so sorry, Christopher." Jane put down the silver frame, then reached out and touched his arm. "That must be so unsettling. I'll do what I can..."

Her voice trailed away as there was another knock on the door and Shelby announced the arrival of Daphne Marsden.

A petite woman dressed in black entered the room with sure, swift steps. From what Christopher could recall about his cousin-in-law, this woman matched the one in the photo, at least on a superficial level. Her face with its regular features—blue eyes, small nose, unremarkable brown hair—could have belonged to anyone at all. She *might* have been Queen Victoria for all he knew.

He glanced at Jane, and she tilted her head ever so slightly as if to indicate that yes, this *was* Daphne Marsden. "Cousin," he said with a gentlemanly bow, "it's been a while since you paid a visit to Roxby House."

"Four whole months to be precise, Your Grace," replied Daphne in clipped tones. Her gaze flitted to Jane. "I apologize if I'm interrupting anything." Her expression was frosty with disapproval. It was clear that she suspected the scandalous Duke of Roxby was "up to no good" with an unchaperoned woman.

Which he had been, but Jane was also his fiancée. Christopher smiled. "Mrs. Marsden, allow me to introduce you to Miss Jane Delaney. We've just become engaged. This very afternoon in fact. You are the first to hear the felicitous news."

If Christopher had pulled a wet fish out from his coat and slapped his cousin-in-law across the face with it, she would have looked less shocked.

At his pronouncement, Daphne immediately blanched and her mouth dropped open. "Engaged?" she repeated. Her gaze shot to Jane. "To her?"

"Yes," said Christopher. "To Miss Delaney."

"How do you do, Mrs. Marsden?" said Jane in her smoky, smooth-as-satin voice. Her green eyes twinkled with amusement. She was clearly enjoying the fact his stuffy cousin-in-law was flummoxed.

"I...er... How do you do, Miss Delaney?" returned Daphne. She drew back her shoulders and turned to Christopher. "As I'm sure you're quite busy, Your Grace, perhaps it would be best if we got straight down to business."

"Of course," said Christopher. "Won't you take a seat?"

As they all settled by the fire, afternoon tea arrived. Jane played the part of mistress of the house and dispensed everyone's tea with aplomb. No one touched the array of petit fours and sandwiches.

"Now," said Daphne after she'd taken a birdlike sip of tea, then set her cup aside, "I suspect you know already why I'm here, Your Grace."

Christopher knew, but resisted the urge to say "Money." Instead he said, "I take it the urgent matter my butler alluded to has something to do with Oliver."

"Yes," said Daphne. "You may or may not recall that Oliver is due to start his first term at Eton in the not-too-distant future, and while his fees are covered by his trust fund, I'm afraid insufficient monies have been allocated for other necessary expenses, such as clothing. He's a growing boy of thirteen, Your Grace, and my widow's jointure is not sufficient to cover the cost of a whole new wardrobe for him every few months."

"I see," said Christopher. "Boys of his age do shoot up like saplings."

"Two hundred pounds should cover it, Your Grace. Good leather shoes are especially expensive and—"

Christopher held up his hand. "I shall go to the library straightaway and write you a check for three hundred pounds. Will that do?"

"Yes. It will. Thank you," said Daphne with an incline of her head.

When Christopher returned a few minutes later, he noted the atmosphere in the drawing room was decidedly chilly.

In hindsight, he probably shouldn't have left Jane alone with the woman. Daphne was a bit of a pernickety prig. But then Jane didn't strike him as a shrinking violet who'd wither beneath Daphne's disdainful stare. Even though he was still getting to know Jane, he trusted that she would be able to hold her own in almost any situation.

"Is there anything else?" Christopher asked his cousin-in-law after he'd furnished her with the signed check. Now would be the perfect opportunity for Daphne to offer her congratulations to him and Jane, but the woman shook her head.

"No, I believe that's all, Your Grace. I'd best be on my way," she said, sliding the check into her reticule before rising to her feet. She cast Jane a strained smile that clearly said "I'd rather choke on cut glass than say anything remotely civil to you." And then she dipped into a barely there curtsy and quit the room.

"Well, I never," said Jane as soon as the door clicked shut.

"She doesn't approve of me and the way I've been conducting myself," said Christopher. "I can't say that I blame her. What I do blame her for, though, is her insufferably rude treatment of you."

Jane shrugged and got to her feet. "She doesn't know me. And I *am* unchaperoned. She's bound to assume that we... That you and I..." She wrinkled her nose. "It wasn't until the tea service arrived that I realized I hadn't done my buttons up correctly."

Christopher snorted. "You're a twenty-nine-year-old woman. You don't need a bloody chaperone. And we're now engaged. In my books, that means you and I can do whatever we damn well please."

Jane smiled. "Yes. I agree."

"Good." Christopher reached out a hand to draw Jane into his arms, but she neatly sidestepped him, heading toward the door too.

"I'm afraid I must go as well," she said over her shoulder as he followed. "My family is expecting me... Although..." She turned to face him. "I know your cousin-in-law just asked you for money, but I did wonder if it would be possible to ask for the check that will cover the cost of my mother's gambling debt. It might take a few days to clear at the bank, and I would hate it if my grandfather discovered what's been going on."

"Ah, I have it here already." Christopher reached into his coat pocket and withdrew a second banknote in the amount of one thousand pounds. As he passed it to Jane, he said, "I will call on your grandfather tomorrow to inform him of our engagement. No doubt he might like to have a say in what goes into the marriage contract."

"Goodness. A contract," whispered Jane.

"It's customary. I could discuss the terms with your mother and her new husband instead. I'm sure Mr. Pevensey—he's a banker, yes?—would drive a hard bargain, but because he's not a blood relative..."

"I would prefer it if you saw my grandfather. Of course, there's my older brother too. Colin is a solicitor at a firm with offices near Fleet Street. But he's training to be a barrister and is usually caught up with a thousand pressing cases."

"Very well. Joseph Delaney is the man I shall see. However, before you leave..." Christopher leaned a shoulder against the doorjamb. "I want to thank you for confirming Daphne's identity."

"It was nothing at all. I'm glad I could be of assistance." Jane's brows furrowed with concern as she added, "I'm happy to do more. In fact, I've been meaning to ask you about your plan to catch your would-be killer."

"I don't want you to worry unduly," said Christopher quietly. He slid a crooked finger beneath Jane's chin and tipped up so her gaze met his. "Not on our engagement day. We can discuss all of that unsavory business another time, if that's all right with you."

"Of course," she murmured.

The worried light in her green eyes faded as Christopher lightly brushed his fingers across her cheek. A petal-pink blush bloomed in the wake of his touch, and he wondered if other parts of her body would flush in the same way.

He cleared his throat which was suddenly tight with uncharacteristic nervous tension. "There's one more thing I need to do before you go." The last time Christopher had become engaged—three years ago—it had ended in disaster. *But,* he reminded himself, *this union will be different. It won't be based on lies. It isn't based on false promises of undying devotion.* Reaching into his coat pocket again, he withdrew a square-cut emerald and diamond ring. "This is for you," he said gruffly as he reached for Jane's left hand and slid it onto her ring finger. It fit perfectly. "So everyone knows that we are indeed betrothed."

"I..." Jane bit her lip as she studied the ring and its glittering jewels. "It's beautiful. It must be worth a small fortune. Thank you, Christopher. I'll keep it safe."

"I'm not sure of its worth or its history, but I found it in amongst the Roxby family's jewel collection. I chose it because it reminds me of your eyes. Their remarkable color was one of the first things I noticed about you." Good God, had he really just said something so romantic, perhaps even mawkish? What the hell was wrong with him? Christopher flashed a wicked grin to lighten the moment as he added, "Well, apart from your spectacular legs. They're unforgettable too."

Jane's answering smile hovered between hesitant and endearingly hopeful. Perhaps she didn't believe he was sincere. He could hardly blame her, given his reputation.

Nevertheless, she said after a moment, "I love the ring *and* your compliments. Actually, I'm quite overwhelmed by your generosity."

"After I've spoken with your grandfather, I'll obtain a special license. We can wed anytime after that. I'd suggest a date sooner rather than later."

"I concur," said Jane. "Three days from today perhaps? On Saturday? Would that suit?"

"Done." And then Christopher braced his arm against the doorframe and kissed Jane once more. "Now go," he murmured when he at last pulled back, "before I decide to sling you over my shoulder and cart you off to my bedroom for an evening of wicked pleasure."

To Christopher's delight, his fiancée reached out and quite boldly slid her hand beneath his coat and waistcoat and placed her hand on his chest. Through the fine linen of his shirt, her touch burned, making his blood heat and his already half-aroused cock stir even more.

"It's been ten years, Christopher," she returned huskily. "Don't tempt me."

As Jane slipped out the door, Christopher was left with the sense that this marriage might actually result in mutual satisfaction in more ways than one.

Chapter Ten

IN THE GLOOMY INTERIOR OF THE HACKNEY, THE ENGAGE-ment ring on Jane's finger glimmered like a silent rebuke. The answer to her own pressing problem was right here in front of her. She could go straight to a pawn shop she knew of near Delaney's Bookshop and sell it. She'd get hundreds if not a thousand pounds for it, and then she could claim that she'd lost it or was robbed in the street by a footpad.

She could pay off her blackmailer and maybe even buy her very own printing press so she could produce and distribute her pamphlets to women all over London.

But how could she do that to Christopher? It would be unconscionable. This might be a marriage of convenience, but she wouldn't stoop so low. She'd secure the fifty pounds she needed to appease her blackmailer another way.

An image of the searing desire in her fiancé's blue eyes entered Jane's mind and she shivered.

She couldn't lie to herself. She wanted to be in this man's bed. She wanted to spend countless hours enjoying all the wicked pleasures she was certain he could show her. And she wanted to have a baby.

More than anything, she wanted that. What she couldn't afford to do was destroy the fragile trust that seemed to be developing between her and Christopher. If she disposed of this engagement ring to serve her own ends—and if he found out why—she might very well ruin everything.

Yes, she would have to think of something else. Her black-mailer was expecting payment in less than a week, but hope-fully she'd have pin money very soon. Although she wouldn't have access to that until *after* she and Christopher wed...

Even though that was cutting it fine, it was best if she bided her time. She wouldn't panic. She'd managed to save her grand-father's shop and her mother from the brink of scandal. All was not lost. Yet.

The hackney pulled up outside 21 Pelham Crescent, and Jane dashed through the sheeting rain and into the house. One thing she hadn't thought enough about was how she would break the news to her mother that she was now engaged.

There would be questions. Many, many awkward and alto-gether difficult questions. Jane was not looking forward to this coming interview, but she supposed it was best to rip off the plaster now, and quickly. There was no point in putting off the inevitable, no matter how unpleasant.

She found her mother with Kitty in one of the upstairs par-lors, taking tea by the fire. As soon as Jane entered, her mother frowned at her over her teacup. "Jane, goodness gracious, girl. At least you could have changed your gown before coming in here. Your hem is mucky."

Jane ignored her dig. If it wasn't her attire her mother was displeased with, it was usually something else. Her hair was too messy or dressed too plainly, or she had unsightly ink stains on her fingers, or she was looking far too maudlin or careworn. "I have some news. Rather momentous news, actually," she said.

Kitty's eyes shone. "Oooh, that sounds exciting. Do tell."

Jane smiled, then met her mother's curious gaze. "I'm engaged," she said, but before she could utter another word, her mother's mouth fell open.

"Engaged?" Leonora Pevensey gasped. "You can't be serious."

"Indeed, I am," replied Jane.

Kitty clapped her hands. "Oh, how wonderful. I'm so happy for you, Jane. But to whom? Do we know him?"

"I shouldn't think so," said Jane. "I'm sure you've heard *of* him though."

"Oh, do stop playing games and tell us his name," sniped her mother.

"It's..." Jane drew a fortifying breath. "It's the Duke of Roxby."

"What?" Her mother put down her teacup in such a hurry it clattered on the saucer and tea sloshed over the edge onto the table. "You must be joking."

Jane raised a brow. "I assure you I'm not."

"But...what? How? It's not possible," declared her mother. "You're...you're hardly a catch, Jane."

"Because I'm akin to the spoiled apple at the bottom of the barrel that no one wants to buy?" returned Jane. She couldn't hide the bitterness in her voice.

"Well, that's rather blunt when you put it like that, but yes."

"Because my face is scarred."

"It's not only that, Jane. You know it's not," said her mother.

Jane narrowed her gaze. With effort, she reined in her rancor as she replied, "Not everyone is so quick to judge and condemn another for her past actions. Some might even forgive another for the unforgivable crime of being in love and then acting on those feelings."

"Ahem," Kitty interjected. "Forgive me. But I'm a little confused."

Jane faced her stepsister. "Our mama believes I'm soiled goods because I'm no longer a virgin and—"

"Jane!" Her mother sprang to her feet. "That's enough. I'm beginning to think you are quite touched in the head. This nonsense you are spouting is beyond the pale."

"Well, I don't think the duke's betrothal ring is a load of nonsense," returned Jane, and then she held out her left hand so that her mother and Kitty could see the evidence for themselves.

Leonora Pevensey's eyes widened to the size of saucers and Kitty squealed.

"Where did you get that?" whispered her mother. "Don't tell me you stole it."

"Of course I didn't," said Jane, even though she had attempted to steal an even more expensive book only two days ago. "The duke gave it to me this afternoon. He chose it because he thought the emerald was a good match for my eyes. Despite what you think, Mother, the duke—or should I say Christopher?—actually thinks I'm quite pretty."

Her mother's eyes narrowed. "What did you do, Jane? I know you did something you shouldn't have."

Ignoring her mother's accusation, Jane lifted her chin. "The duke has also given me a sizable check to cover the cost of your—"

"Jane! I said enough," snapped her mother. Her gaze shot to her stepdaughter. "Kitty dear, if you wouldn't mind repairing to another room for a short while, I would very much appreciate it. Jane and I have a few—"

"Awkward matters to discuss," finished Jane. Her mother wasn't the only one who'd had enough. She was tired of her mother's put-downs and ongoing refusal to acknowledge she had a problem with gambling.

"Oh, very well," said Kitty. "I'll go to my bedroom. I have some correspondence I need to attend to anyway."

As soon as the door shut, Leonora Pevensey rounded on Jane. "How...how dare you mention anything to do with my little problem in front of Kitty?" she hissed. "If she goes to her father—"

"*Little* problem?" Jane repeated with a snort. "Losing one thousand pounds in a card game and then sacrificing your father-in-law's livelihood in order to hide what you've done is not little, Mama. And while I'm not expecting any sort of praise from you, at least you could thank me for bailing you out of the mess you landed yourself in. If it weren't for this marriage that I've agreed to—"

"To a scandalous duke who must be mad," said her mother with a derisive snort. "You still haven't explained how all this has come about." Her face paled. "You're…you're not pregnant, are you?" she whispered. "After what happened last time with Miles Dempster…"

"As hard as that is for you to believe, no, I'm not," said Jane stiffly. "But you just said it yourself. Clearly the duke must be mad, because why else would he wed someone like me?"

When her mother didn't say anything to contradict her summation, Jane rolled her eyes. "Well, thank you very much, Mother," she said. "In any event, in a few days' time I *will* be the Duchess of Roxby and then your shameless, burdensome daughter will be off your hands altogether. I thought you'd be happy about *that* if nothing else." She headed for the parlor door. "And by the way, when the check clears, you will tell me how I can settle the vowels on your behalf."

Her mother sniffed. "Well, thank you very much for not trusting me, Jane. And for going to a complete stranger for money when I told you I didn't want anyone else to know. Because I'm sure your duke wanted to know what the check was for."

"You gave me no choice," returned Jane. "And I would ask that this never happens again out of respect for your family. You must end your association with the Whisteria Club. Your gambling has to stop. Because if there is a next time, I might have to go to your husband." And with that, she quit the room.

She had a grandfather to inform, a check to deposit, vowels to pay, a blackmailer to foil, and a wedding to plan.

If Jane's blackmailer were to be believed, it seemed there was no rest for the "wicked."

Chapter Eleven

THE VERY NEXT MORNING, JANE SENT TELEGRAMS TO Artemis and Lucy from the telegraph office in Regent Street, just off Piccadilly. She'd have to face her friends sooner rather than later. They'd no doubt want to know why Jane had made such a life-changing decision seemingly out of nowhere. As her grandfather had pointed out, both of Jane's friends were only a train journey away.

Both telegrams ran along similar lines:

> *I have news to share. Momentous news. I'm getting married in two days' time! On Saturday! To the Duke of Roxby. I know it's an unexpected turn of events, but I hope you'll be happy for me.*
>
> *Much love,*
>
> *J*
>
> *P.S. I know you might not be able to get back to Town in time, but I would love it if you could.*

As Jane quit the telegraph office and headed back toward Sackville Street and Delaney's, she braced herself for the day ahead. No doubt Christopher would be meeting with her grandfather.

She'd already broken the news to him about her engagement late yesterday. After she'd deposited Christopher's check at her bank, Coutts & Co on the Strand, she'd dropped by the bookstore before returning to Kensington. As she'd responded to her wily grandfather's quizzing, she'd realized that she and the duke probably should have discussed the whys and wherefores of their engagement in greater detail so their stories would match.

Even though her grandfather had been astounded at first, somehow Jane had managed to convince him that marriage to the Duke of Roxby was what she truly wanted. That the rumors about the duke's scandalous behavior were greatly exaggerated and that he was keen to settle down. That even though they'd only known each other a short time—she was vague about the exact circumstances of their meeting—they'd bonded over their love of rare books. At least when she'd admitted to her grandfather that she wanted to start a family, that part hadn't been a lie.

Of course, Jane hadn't disclosed anything else about the Duke of Roxby's current situation, or the pragmatic nature of their marriage bargain. Or the fact someone might be trying to kill him…

This union might not be a love match, but Jane would still do what she could to help the duke track down whoever was trying to hurt him. She would be riddled with unease until she knew Christopher was safe. He would be the father of her child, after all.

He was already another child's guardian…

As Jane paused to cross the madly busy thoroughfare that was Piccadilly, she cast her mind back to her encounter with Daphne Marsden. Even though the woman couldn't have been more than a few years older than Jane herself, her son, Oliver, was about to start Eton.

When Christopher had left them alone together in the drawing room, Daphne had said not one word to Jane at first. The woman had simply sipped her tea and looked everywhere *but* at Jane as though Jane didn't exist. When Jane had tried to make an innocuous comment about the weather, Daphne had blatantly ignored her remark, but then had asked in a frost-laden tone about her family connections and where she hailed from. Upon Jane mentioning that her grandfather was the pro-prietor of Delaney's Antiquarian Bookshop, Mrs. Marsden had given an imperious sniff and had not made any further remarks. She wouldn't even be drawn into conversation about her son.

It was obvious Daphne Marsden thought that Jane was beneath her, even though she would soon be the next Duchess of Roxby. Jane wondered if the woman would attend the wed-ding, or shun both her and Christopher. She supposed she would find out soon enough.

It was a little after ten o'clock when Jane entered Delaney's. Hoskins, one of her grandfather's shop assistants, informed her that her grandfather was upstairs with another gentleman. Cupping his hand beside his mouth, Hoskins then whispered in a melodramatic fashion, "It's the Duke of Roxby."

"My goodness," said Jane, even though she wasn't the least bit surprised. But she would own to being a trifle nervous. As much as she wanted to go upstairs and listen in on the discus-sion taking place, it wasn't the done thing. Instead, she picked up a duster, a cloth, and some beeswax polish and began to tidy the books and shelves downstairs. There was some bookbind-ing that needed seeing to in the workshop, but it was intricate work and Jane didn't have the concentration for it.

An excruciating half hour crawled by, but then at last Joseph Delaney appeared in the shop, closely followed by Christopher.

"Jane," her grandfather intoned as he crossed the floor and

enveloped her in a warm hug. "My Jane. How simply marvel-ous, my dear girl." When he drew back, there were tears in his eyes. "I know I was perhaps a bit circumspect last night when we spoke, so let me say this now. Congratulations. I'm so happy for you."

"I'm so glad you approve." Jane really was relieved. Of course, it wasn't as though anyone could prevent her from mar-rying, but her grandfather's blessing meant the world to her.

Christopher had begun talking about solicitors and the con-tract that would be ready to sign that afternoon. "And the wed-ding shall take place at Roxby House. If that's all right with you, my dearest fiancée." Christopher patted his coat pocket. "I have the special license right here."

"Yes, of course," said Jane. "I'm looking forward to it."

"As am I," returned Christopher, his voice low. His blue gaze flickered with heat before he turned a thoroughly engaging smile on her grandfather. "If you're not too busy, Mr. Delaney, what say we all repair to Fortnum & Mason's for a celebratory cup of tea? I hear their cakes are particularly good."

"They are indeed," agreed Jane's grandfather. "I'm sure Hoskins here can hold the fort. Can't you, Hoskins?"

The young man nodded, his gaze darting from his employer to Christopher, where his attention remained. It was obvious he was in awe of the duke. But then, Jane could understand that. She was more than a little in awe of her fiancé too.

Jane donned her gloves and bonnet, and Christopher offered his arm to escort her outside. Joseph Delaney strolled alongside them as they made their way down Piccadilly. Fortnum & Mason's was but a short distance away, on the other side of the street.

As they paused on the edge of the curb, waiting for a gap in the traffic, Christopher bent his head and murmured in her ear,

"Being engaged suits you, Jane. To be perfectly frank, if your grandfather wasn't with us, I'd be whisking you off to Roxby House for something a tad more thrilling than tea and cake."

"Whatever do you mean?" returned Jane. "There's nothing more delightful than sinking one's teeth into a treacle tart or a lovely sticky finger bun. At least I think so."

"I'm more of a muffin man, myself," said Christopher, his eyes twinkling.

Jane's breath quickened. She had the distinct feeling they were not talking about cake at all. Although she suspected that whatever her fiancé was referring to would be equally if not more delicious.

She was in the process of formulating a suitably ribald rejoinder when all of a sudden someone—a man—crashed his shoulder into Christopher's back and Jane lost her grip on his arm. Knocked off-balance, Christopher stumbled forward toward a hansom cab hurtling their way. The horse shied and whinnied, rearing up on its hind legs, and Christopher's top hat went flying just as Jane managed to haul the duke out of the way and back onto the pavement.

The horse's hooves had missed Christopher's head by the merest of whiskers and Jane's heart had almost stopped.

"Jane. Oh my God." Christopher clutched at her upper arms. His blazing blue eyes bore into hers. "Are you all right?"

Jane's mouth dropped open. "Am *I* all right?"

"Yes, you were almost struck by that horse's flailing hooves."

"So were you, Your Grace." Joseph Delaney was as white as a sheet. "I would admonish Jane for putting herself in harm's way too, except for the fact that she saved you."

"I..." Jane swallowed as a delayed surge of fear sucked the air from her lungs. "You could have been killed," she whispered. Her whole body was trembling like an autumn leaf, and she was grateful Christopher was gripping her so tightly, keeping her upright. "That man..." Her gaze darted among the faces in the crowd that had gathered about them, but she didn't recognize anyone at all. "The man who pushed you..."

"Did you see who it was?" asked Christopher. His mouth was a grim line.

"No. It all happened too quickly," said Jane. "All I saw was a glimpse of a man in a black coat and dark hat. Did...did you see anything, Grandfather?"

But her grandfather shook his head. "No, I was looking at my pocket watch. I have no idea what was happening until I heard the horse's whinny and the cab driver's shout. Did someone push you, Your Grace?"

But Christopher shrugged, all studied nonchalance. "I'm not certain. Someone did knock into me from behind, but perhaps it was an accident."

He caught Jane's gaze and there was something about his expression that made Jane agree. "Yes... I'm sure you're right." Her fiancé clearly didn't wish to discuss the fact that someone may very well have tried to kill him. It would surely alarm her grandfather. Aside from that, the stranger might still be lurking nearby, waiting for another opportunity to strike.

By this time, the small crowd of onlookers that had gathered had begun to disperse now that the kerfuffle had ended. Even the cab driver had driven off.

"I don't know about you, but I'm not sure if I feel up to going to Fortnum & Mason right now," said Jane. Her knees were shaky, and she felt as though she'd been running and couldn't quite catch her breath.

A chill mizzling rain had begun to fall, and she started to shiver. Christopher frowned down at her, concern etched in every feature. "No," he said. "I don't think I'm up to it either."

He caught her grandfather's eye. "Mr. Delaney, my carriage is only a little farther along the street, up near Burlington House. I think it would be a good idea if I took your granddaughter to her mother's house."

Her grandfather nodded. "I think so too, Your Grace." He touched Jane's arm. "You're looking decidedly pale, my dear girl. Go home and rest. We have all the time in the world to celebrate."

Jane tried to smile, but couldn't manage more than a twitch of her lips. "Are you sure?"

"I am. Now go before you catch your death of cold. I'm certain your fiancé will take good care of you."

Christopher steered Jane toward his carriage. It was easy to spot because his coat of arms was emblazoned on the side. As they approached, a footman leapt down to open the door and let down the steps.

Although Jane didn't recognize the fellow, he was attired in the appropriate livery. She realized that the servant's attire was probably the only visual clue that Christopher could rely upon to reassure himself that this staff member was truly someone who was loyal to him and not an imposter with dark deeds on his mind. She decided then and there that she would make it her business to get to know all of the staff at Roxby House so she could verify their identities too. If someone was devious enough, they could easily produce a counterfeit copy of the Roxby livery and infiltrate the duke's household. The idea made Jane feel even more unsettled, and her heart cramped with sympathy for Christopher. She had no idea how the man slept at night.

As soon as the carriage door closed, Jane wilted onto the velvet-upholstered seats with a shuddering sigh. "Good Lord, Christopher," she murmured. "I can't believe that someone actually attempted to kill you in broad daylight in a busy street in the middle of Town."

As the carriage moved off, Christopher pulled down the blinds at the window, shielding them from anyone looking in from the street. "Neither can I," he said as he settled on the seat beside her. His expression was grim. "These attacks are becoming more brazen. And more frequent."

Turning to her, he studied her face. "And you, Jane. I don't know whether to berate you or—" He broke off, a muscle working in his jaw. "You could have been hurt. Or worse." All of a sudden, he gathered her into his arms. Crushed her against his wide chest. "I can't thank you enough for putting yourself in harm's way to save me," he murmured against her hair, his voice low and rough. "We're not even wed and already you've been thrust into danger. I would understand if you wanted to change your mind about marrying me."

Fear spiked in Jane's chest, and she pulled back from Christopher's embrace. "Heavens no. I do wish to marry you. I sincerely do." It wasn't only about the money she'd have access to, and it wasn't just about the baby that he might be able to give her. It was suddenly about Christopher and what *he* needed. "I know we barely know each other but..." She drew a deep breath. "I'm drawn to you, and I want to help you. I can't explain it. So rest assured I'm not going to end this—whatever this is between us—before we've even begun. Despite the risks."

Christopher searched her eyes. "Very well. If you're sure."

"I am," she said. After a pause she added, "Do you think we should go to the police? To Scotland Yard? My friends Artemis and Lucy have both had dealings with a very good detective there. His name is John Lawrence. I'm sure he'd listen to your concerns."

"Not yet." Christopher sighed and raked a hand through his

hair. "I need evidence that's a little more concrete than a few near misses and my gut feeling."

"You mentioned you have a list of suspects."

"Yes..." The carriage rocked as they turned a sharp corner, and Christopher lifted the edge of the blind to look outside. "We'll be at Roxby House shortly," he said. "We can talk about them at length once we're inside."

"You're not taking me to my mother's house in Kensington?"

"No." Christopher's unflinching gaze returned to her face. "I'd prefer to talk to you in private. We have much to discuss, including the timing of our wedding."

Alarm flickered inside Jane. Good heavens, if the duke wanted to delay their nuptials for more than a week, how on earth was she to secure the money to keep her blackmailer quiet? If Christopher found out about any of that, he might change his mind about marrying *her*. "You...you don't wish to get married in two days' time?"

"No," he said. "After what just happened, I think we should get married without delay. This evening, in fact. If you don't have any objections."

Jane's pulse rate kicked up a notch. "Won't we need witnesses for the ceremony? A minister? And even though I'm not the sort of person who likes large parties, I was hoping that we might host some sort of wedding breakfast for close family and friends. I'm sure my friends Artemis and Lucy would love to attend. I've sent both of them telegrams about our upcoming nuptials on Saturday."

"My butler and valet could stand in as witnesses," said Christopher. "And I'm certain I can find an Anglican minister to officiate at short notice. As for a party, we could always host a small gathering—a dinner or soiree of some kind or even a celebratory ball—anytime at all. You can invite whomever you'd like." He smiled. "My staff are used to that sort of thing."

Jane bit her lip. He'd thought of almost everything. "And then there's the marriage contract," she added. "Not that I want to bring up the subject of money again. My grandfather seemed happy with the terms you discussed?"

"Yes, he was satisfied," Christopher said. "However, because you are of age, you can sign the contract yourself after you've read through it. It's your decision, after all. I'm expecting a courier to deliver a copy to Roxby House by noon. But of course if you'd like your brother to look it over too, that can certainly be arranged." A groove appeared between Christopher's brows. "I know I'm rushing you. You can say no. Part of my reason for making haste is that the sooner we are wed, the sooner you will be provided for in the event of my death." His mouth twitched. "Not that I'm planning on dying early, but I will own to being rather ill-starred at present."

"I . . ." Jane tried to gather her runaway thoughts. "But . . . you hardly know me. Why would my future matter to you? You have enough to worry about."

Christopher reached out and stroked her jawline with a featherlight touch. "I know enough about you to recognize that you are worthy of the title 'duchess' and that you deserve everything that goes along with that. It appears to me that you would risk almost anything for those you care about. A rare and most admirable quality. Aside from that"—he picked up one of her hands and rubbed his thumb along the sensitive inch of bare flesh on the inside of her wrist, just between her glove and the end of her sleeve—"you shouldn't spend your days hiding in the shadows of bookcases, dusting shelves, all the while worrying about how you are to cover the debts of others."

A sliver of guilt penetrated Jane's heart, overriding the warm glow Christopher's kind words evoked and the pleasurable sensations his touch aroused.

This man thought she was worthy despite her humble background. But he didn't know *everything* about her. He wasn't aware that she was being blackmailed or why. And she would continue to deceive Christopher in order to hide her scandalous secret for some time to come. Could she live with that? This was supposed to be a marriage of convenience, not a marriage based on deceit and false expectations.

As Jane looked up into her fiancé's far-too-handsome face, she contemplated confessing all. But how would he react to the news that she wanted to publish and distribute a pamphlet that would broach controversial topics such as how to prevent conception and venereal disease, as well as the joys of sexual intercourse, whether one was married or not? A duchess would *never* do something like that. If it ever came to light that she was the author and publisher of such a pamphlet, society would ridicule her and brand her a wicked woman. She'd be ostracized. She might even be arrested and prosecuted for disseminating lewd material and corrupting the minds of the Queen's subjects.

No, Jane couldn't risk sharing her secret. Not until she knew Christopher better. He might have hosted wild soirees, but that didn't mean he'd be comfortable with his wife spearheading a project of such a controversial nature. For the time being, she would have to tamp down her guilt and hold her tongue.

"Jane," Christopher prompted gently, "tell me what you're thinking. You've gone awfully quiet."

Jane met her fiancé's eyes and prayed her smile seemed genuine. "I think your idea has some merit. So yes, I agree, Christopher. There's no sense in delaying. We'll marry this evening."

Christopher raised her hand to his lips. Even that light brushing kiss across the kid leather of her glove made Jane's flesh tingle with delicious anticipation. "I can hardly wait," he murmured, his blue eyes glowing.

If he'd asked Jane how she felt in that moment, she would have readily attested to a degree of impatience too. Despite all of her other reservations and doubts about the future, she was absolutely certain that she wouldn't regret spending the night in the arms of the Duke of Roxby.

Chapter Twelve

WHEN CHRISTOPHER'S CARRIAGE PULLED UP OUTSIDE ROXBY House, he was bemused by Jane asking if she could meet all his household staff straightaway. "If I am to be duchess in a few short hours, I think it would be a good idea if I become familiar with everyone's faces."

Christopher exited the carriage, then assisted Jane to alight. "An excellent idea," he said. "Featherstone keeps an eye on who's who and what's what, but he can't be everywhere at all times. It might take a few minutes, but I'll arrange a receiving line." He tucked Jane's hand into the crook of his arm. "It's about time you were introduced as my duchess-to-be."

Within the space of five minutes, the entirety of Roxby House's twenty staff members were assembled in the entry hall. Christopher introduced Jane as his fiancée and explained that they would be wed that very evening. After the congratulations faded away, Christopher led Jane down the line. Aside from Shelby, she really didn't know anyone else, but Christopher was impressed that she took the time to learn something about each one of them. Not only their names but where they hailed from and how long they'd been at Roxby House. Everyone curtsied and smiled with due deference.

Christopher couldn't help but smile to himself. He was certain his entire staff would be relieved that there were changes afoot at Roxby House. An end to the nights of wholesale debauchery and the countless hours of cleaning that went along with it would no doubt be welcomed by all.

Christopher was quietly relieved about not having to continue the ruse too.

Once the introductions were complete, Jane turned a charming smile on everyone. "I'm going to be perfectly frank with you. I'm actually terrible with names, so please do forgive me if I don't remember them all at first." A faint line appeared between her brows as she turned to Christopher. "Actually, I have an idea, Your Grace. Do you think we could arrange a small badge for everyone? Something in pewter with each person's name engraved upon it? Or names could be embroidered onto uniforms at a pinch."

How brilliant his fiancée was. And perceptive. Christopher was touched she'd thought of something so simple that would make a world of difference to him. He inclined his head. "Of course we can, my dear. Shelby. Mrs. Harrigan..." Christopher addressed the man he believed was his butler, and the housekeeper whom he rarely saw most days. The enormous bunch of keys dangling from her waist was about the only thing that set her apart from all the other female staff attired in black gowns with pristine white caps and aprons. "Between the two of you, do you think you could arrange something? I'll allocate the additional funds required to the household budget."

Shelby and Mrs. Harrigan bowed and curtsied respectively. After Christopher dismissed everyone, he beckoned over the man he thought was Featherstone. "I'd like a word with you. Meet me and Miss Delaney in the library in ten minutes."

His valet inclined his head. "Of course, Yer Grace." His mouth curved into a grin. "And might I be so forward as to say I can already see that you and yer bride are well suited."

Christopher snorted. "If it was anyone but you, Featherstone,

I would tell you to keep your opinion to yourself. But thank you. I think I've chosen well."

"I can hear you two, you know," said Jane, stepping forward. She caught Featherstone's gaze. "I'm pleased to hear you approve. I might also venture to say that I'm impressed to hear about your loyalty to His Grace."

Featherstone puffed out his chest. "Indeed, I am, Miss Delaney. He's the best of men. I've followed him into battle, and I would lay down my life for him any time, any place."

"Not many men would inspire such loyalty. Now I'm doubly impressed," said Jane.

Christopher raised a brow. "I can hear you two, you know."

Jane laughed. "More's the pity. I hope we're not fanning the flames of your ducal arrogance. I suspect your sense of self-importance is rather inflated already."

"Me? Arrogant?" scoffed Christopher.

"You *were* an officer in Her Majesty's cavalry, and now you're one of the highest-ranking peers in the realm," returned Jane. "You must own to some degree of arrogance, Your Grace. You're certainly not the shy and retiring type by any means."

"No, His Grace is not either of those things," agreed Featherstone with a grin. "Loud and proud, more like. Especially when he's addressing troops or making a parliamentary speech or even a drunken toast. Whatever the case may be."

Christopher donned a scowl. "Don't I pay your wages, Featherstone? Where's your loyalty now? Don't tell me that my charming fiancée has you turned around her little finger already."

"I'm simply being honest, Yer Grace," said Featherstone. "And yes, perhaps Miss Delaney has."

Jane's cheeks took on a delicate glow and Christopher's thoughts immediately rushed to how she would look later tonight when she was naked and flushed and boneless with pleasure in his bed.

An overwhelming urge to have his fiancée before they exchanged vows suddenly shot through him. If Christopher were honest with himself, it wasn't lust alone that compelled him to seduce Jane. Both of them could have been killed less than an hour ago, and he needed to feel alive. To connect with this woman on the most basic, visceral level and lose himself in her for a few hours.

Aside from that, it had been so very long since Christopher had bedded anyone. Or even felt the desire to do so. And without a doubt he wanted Jane. His blood was already beginning to heat; his cock was stirring. But devil take him, he had things to attend to first.

He dismissed Featherstone and then escorted Jane to the library.

As soon as the door closed, he had her up against one of the bookcases, bracketing her with his arms.

"Arrogant, am I?" he growled playfully.

Jane's green eyes sparkled with challenge and amusement. "Well, if the shoe fits, Your Grace..." She shrugged a shoulder. "Might I also add high-handed, impatient, and demanding to that list? You did ride roughshod over my plans to return to my mother's house. Am I to wear this dull blue workaday gown to our wedding?"

"I don't give a toss what you wear to our wedding. You can turn up in a potato sack for all I care. And you haven't seen demanding yet, you gorgeous, damnable wench," he muttered, pressing his hips against hers, crushing her skirts. "Or perhaps I should say 'witch,' because you do indeed have me transfixed and I'm utterly aching with the need to have you." And then he was kissing Jane like there was no tomorrow and this might be his last chance to taste her. To drink her in. To breathe her essence and take it into his lungs. To feel her warmth and absorb it into his world-weary soul.

It was deeply gratifying to discover that Jane seemed to want him just as much. She kissed him back with a frantic fervor that matched his own. Her mouth was hot and slick, and she readily opened for him when he dragged on her lower lip with his thumbs. Oh, how sweet were her moans and the way her tongue danced and dueled with his. How delicious the taste of the silken flesh beneath her jaw and fragrant hollow by her ear. He was starving. Hungry for more.

Desperate. But he should curb his craving and wait for tonight when his time with his bride wouldn't be rushed.

Curse this infernal situation he was in. Christopher buried his face in Jane's neck and simply inhaled her scent. He had a killer dogging his heels and he would not let whoever it was succeed. Not when he could have *this.*

With a sigh, he forced himself to pull back, releasing Jane from the cage of his arms. "As much as I would like to make you mine right now," he said, "I'm afraid I have other pressing matters to attend to. Featherstone will be here any minute, but before he arrives, I want to apprise you of certain things."

"Things to do with what happened on Piccadilly?"

"Exactly."

Jane ran her hands down her rumpled skirts. "It was definitely a man who pushed you. But as to what he looked like..." Her brow dipped into a frown. "It all happened so quickly that I didn't catch a glimpse of his face."

Christopher sighed heavily. "Yes... That's been the problem each and every time. And even if I *had* seen the culprit, there's no doubt that I wouldn't be able to remember him."

He crossed to the sideboard and poured himself a brandy.

"Even though it's not yet noon, I feel the need for a fortifying drink. I can send for tea, or would you like a brandy too?"

"I won't refuse a brandy," she said. "Actually, I'm surprised you didn't have a flask on hand in your carriage."

"That was rather remiss of me," agreed Christopher, handing her a tumbler. "An officer should be prepared at all times. I must be going soft in my dotage."

"Oh, I don't know about that," murmured Jane. "It didn't feel like that a few moments ago."

Christopher laughed. He gestured to the chairs by the fire. "Shall we?"

Once they were settled, Jane asked, "So, who *is* on your list of suspects? I'm dying to know." Then she winced. "My apologies. That was not the best choice of words."

Christopher smiled. "No harm done. At least not yet." He took a pull of his drink as he settled back in his seat. "I have three candidates—all men—with reasonable motives to consider. A fellow I trounced at cards over a year ago. A subaltern officer who was court martialed for 'conduct unbecoming an officer' based on my testimony. And the third…" He paused, wondering how Jane would respond to his next disclosure. "Well, to be perfectly honest, this last one's rather awkward. It's the husband of my former fiancée."

"Goodness," said Jane, her eyes widening in surprise. She sipped her brandy before she met his gaze again. Was that a hint of hesitancy, perhaps even concern in her expression? "I had no idea you'd been engaged before. And I'm sorry it didn't work out the way you'd probably planned." Her mouth curved in a small sad smile. "I know how that feels. To have loved and lost. Unless you didn't love her, of course… Which is perfectly all right. I mean, we're engaged, and we aren't in love." She ground to a halt, then grimaced.

"I'm making all sorts of assumptions and blathering on. I should let you finish."

Christopher inclined his head. "It's quite all right. And you're not wrong. I did care for my fiancée, so it seems we are both battle-scarred by love..." He blew out a sigh and put down his brandy. "Six years ago, when I was merely Major Christopher Marsden, I was smitten by a young woman from a respectable family. Marguerite or 'Daisy' Byrd was her name back then, and we met through mutual acquaintances in London. A month before I left England for the Crimea, we became engaged. But she..." He flexed his fingers on the arms of his chair. "Daisy had difficulty waiting for me. Which I do understand. It's not easy being the fiancée or wife of a military man."

"Yes, I imagine it wouldn't be," said Jane softly. "All that worry. But if you love someone...wouldn't you wait for that person? Be there for them through thick and thin?"

Christopher cast her a wry smile. "Well, I'd like to think so, but evidently Daisy didn't. She jilted me via a letter and then married another man. A fellow by the name of Simon Cosgrove."

"And he's another one of your suspects?" Jane's brow furrowed. "I'm confused though. You're the wronged party, not this Simon. Why would he bear *you* a grudge?"

"Because of what Daisy did after I'd returned to England and had inherited the dukedom."

"This was last year? Before you were shot?"

"Yes... She propositioned me at a society function in April. She told me that she should never have jilted me and that she was still in love with me. Even though I was not interested in starting an affair with a married woman, she persisted and eventually she turned up at here at Roxby House. In June. I'd thrown an end-of-Season ball." Christopher hesitated, choosing his words. It was best not to go into *too* many details.

"In any event, her husband found out about her pursuit of me. Nothing of import ever happened between Daisy and me, but Cosgrove was adamant that the new Duke of Roxby had every intention of leading his wife astray. I suspect he wanted to call me out—we exchanged words at the horse auctions at Tattersall's a week after the ball—but of course he knew of my military past and no doubt I would have bested him in a duel..." Christopher shrugged. "I can't discount the idea that jealousy could drive a man to take matters into his own hands. If Cosgrove loves his wife and still sees me as a threat to his marriage, who knows what he might do."

Jane nodded in apparent agreement. Although her expression had grown a little pensive. "I see," she said. "Jealousy is a strong emotion, and your reasoning is sound. But what about your other suspects? What can you tell me about them?"

Christopher ran a hand down his face. The fact that Jane was still here, listening to such personal admissions without judgment, filled him with relief and gave him the push to continue on no matter how unsavory the subject. "I will try to summarize," he said, reaching for his brandy again. "When I joined Brooks's Gentlemen's Club shortly after I inherited the dukedom, I ended up in a card game with the second son of a baronet—a fellow named Harry Wexford—who could ill afford to wager the small fortune that he did. I had no idea, but apparently Sir Gideon Wexford was so incensed by his son's actions that he disowned him. If I'd had any idea of Harry Wexford's situation, I certainly wouldn't have played that game. I've since heard rumors that Wexford hasn't been doing very well, so clearly he's someone who might bear me a grudge."

"Yes, he might," agreed Jane. "I imagine Sir Gideon must have been at his wits' end to take such drastic action. Given my own mother's penchant for gambling beyond her means, I can understand how immensely frustrating it can be. It's a difficult problem to deal with."

"Yes, I agree," Christopher said grimly. "Part of me feels terrible about what happened, but I honestly had no idea until it was all too late. It does play on my mind that Harry Wexford is now estranged from his father."

"I'm sure it's not your fault," Jane said softly. "And the other suspect? He was a subaltern?"

Christopher grimaced. "That business happened soon after I'd returned from the Crimea. I caught a junior officer by the name of Phelps—a lieutenant in my cavalry regiment—in flagrante with my commanding officer's wife. He was drunk and physically threatened me, leaving me little choice but to report him. He was discharged with disgrace. I'm not sure where he is now or how he's faring, but I'm sure he blames me for ending his military career."

"Well…" Jane arched a brow. "That *is* another strong motive. The question is how do you find out if any of these men bear you so much ill will that one of them *is* actually trying to kill you?"

"While I'm reluctant to approach Scotland Yard at this juncture, that doesn't mean I'm going to sit on my hands," said Christopher. "This is where Featherstone comes in. I've mentioned before that I trust him implicitly. His cousin, Jack O'Connor, is a former bobby who's recently begun to offer his services as a private detective. After I've met with this O'Connor and I also deem him to be trustworthy, I'm going to task him with finding out whatever he can about my suspects in the way of background information. I've lost track of Phelps since he was discharged. And Wexford, as far as I know, has gone to ground. Cosgrove resides here in London, so he should be easy enough to investigate. O'Connor will be able to observe their movements and discreetly nose around for any gossip or rumors that seem related to my case. Someone within their immediate spheres might have heard one of them expressing their intense dislike for me."

"I see," said Jane. "I think that's a very sound idea. Once you have some more information to go on, perhaps you can also arrange 'accidental encounters' with each of your suspects."

"I intend to do just that. And…" He caught Jane's gaze.

"I trust you would like me to be involved with that? So I can verify the identity of whoever you speak with?"

"Yes. I would appreciate it. Very much." Christopher put down his brandy on a nearby table. "I know that what I'm asking you to undertake is dangerous, but I do really need your help."

Jane nodded. "Considering we will soon be wed, I think it's also within my best interests to find out who is behind these attacks." Her cheeks turned a delightful shade of pink. "To begin a family, you need to be here. And I'd hate to think our child would grow up without knowing his father."

Christopher couldn't help but be charmed by her blush. "You make very valid points, my dear Jane," he said in a low voice calculated to stir her even more. She was an intriguing mixture of uncertainty and eagerness. A buttoned-up spinster on the outside, yet he'd warrant a siren lurked beneath. As soon as they were wed, he was definitely going to coax the siren to come out and play. "Considering the near miss we both had this morning," he continued, "I vote that we start on that family almost straightaway."

Jane gave a little laugh. "Good heavens. Has there ever been a more eager bridegroom? I haven't even signed this marriage contract you keep talking about."

"Very true." Christopher glanced at the longcase clock. It was almost midday. "It should be delivered shortly. After I've spoken with Featherstone about employing his cousin, I'll need to go out to locate a minister. That should give you an uninterrupted hour or two to read it."

Jane nodded. "And after I've signed it, I'd like to return to my mother's house to pick up a few things." She cast him an arch smile. "Despite what you declared earlier, I will not be wearing a workaday gown or a potato sack to my wedding."

"At the risk of sounding far too arrogant, I'll allow it. But only if you go in one of my unmarked carriages and several of my burliest footmen accompany you. I'll not risk your safety either."

Jane inclined her head. "Very well. It's not every day one is almost run down in the street."

Christopher couldn't disagree with that.

———

The marriage contract was generous. So generous Jane was thoroughly flabbergasted.

She put down the papers on Christopher's desk and leaned back in his chair. She was alone in Roxby House's library. Her fiancé was so confident she'd agree to the terms that he'd gone out to secure a minister to conduct the service.

He was undeniably arrogant and high-handed. A man accustomed to giving orders and having them obeyed. Strangely, Jane didn't seem to mind.

She picked up the contract again and flipped through the pages to the last one where she had to sign. Not only would she have access to an allowance that was worth a small fortune, but Christopher was as good as his word and would also gift her one of his country estates—an unentailed manor house in nearby Bedfordshire—as well as another town house here in London when they eventually decided to live separate lives.

And she didn't even have a dowry. Her mother had lost it all long ago.

The truth of the matter was clear: Jane would never go without. Nor would any of the children she and Christopher had. Although…Jane couldn't account for the entirely unreasonable pang she felt at the prospect of living alone in the country without her husband. And then she sternly reminded herself that her situation was completely different from Artemis's and Lucy's. Both of her friends had found love matches, whereas she had not.

Even though Christopher *appeared* to be kind and generous and thoughtful, she shouldn't be lulled into a false sense of security. Miles had been charming and appeared to care for her…right up until the point that he'd abandoned her. Only time would tell what sort of man the Duke of Roxby really was.

But then Jane cast her mind back to those moments in the carriage straight after the "almost accident" on Piccadilly. Christopher *had* seemed genuinely perturbed by the idea that she might have been hurt too. And touched that she would intervene to protect him.

Even now, she couldn't explain why she'd done what she'd done. It had all happened so quickly. For the most part, she'd reacted instinctively.

But… Jane picked up the cup of tea at her elbow and took a fortifying sip. The stab of acute terror she'd felt as she'd seen Christopher stumbling toward that oncoming hansom cab had been genuine. Heart-stoppingly real. If she closed her eyes and pictured those petrifying moments all over again, her stomach pitched and her chest felt far too tight.

If Christopher meant nothing at all to her, surely she wouldn't feel this way.

It was a sobering thought.

But then she wasn't an automaton that felt nothing at all. And Christopher was helping her in significant, material ways. She was grateful for the money he'd given her to save her grandfather's store. She was excited that at long last she could realize her dream of having a baby. God willing, of course. She could pay off her blackmailer, and before long that horrid business would be over with once and for all.

Yes, Jane was thankful. And of course caught in a fever of lust. That was all. These hot fluttering emotions gathering in her breast and low in her belly had nothing to do with love. She desired Christopher and wanted him to make love to her, and that was an entirely different kettle of fish altogether.

She and Christopher would make love tonight. She simply had to sign the contract...

Jane put down her teacup, picked up her husband-to-be's pen, dipped the nib in the crystal inkwell, and then signed the document with a flourish before she could change her mind.

Jane Helena Delaney

Done.

Now all she had to do was return to 21 Pelham Crescent, change into a suitable gown to get married in, and pack a few other personal items in a carpetbag. Hopefully, neither her mother nor Kitty would notice what she was doing. All going well, in a few hours' time she'd be the Duchess of Roxby.

For better or worse, a whole new chapter in her life was about to begin.

Chapter Thirteen

"I PRONOUNCE THAT THEY BE MAN AND WIFE TOGETHER, IN the name of the Father, and of the Son, and of the Holy Ghost," declared the ancient vicar who Christopher had managed to procure from nearby St. Peter's Church. "Those whom God has joined together, let no man put asunder."

"Amen," murmured Christopher. And then despite the fact Jane's immediate family was gathered in Roxby House's drawing room as witnesses, he kissed his bride with a vigor that would no doubt be described as indecorous. The muted gasps and clearing of throats said it all. But Christopher didn't care. Interlopers be damned. If people were going to invade his town house, they would have to accept him as he was. He would do whatever he pleased in his own home.

He was the debauched Duke of Roxby after all.

And now he was married.

He released Jane from his kiss, and by the way she was smiling and the fact that her eyes were glowing, she didn't seem to mind that they'd both shocked the stockings off her family.

Jane's mother, Leonora Pevensey, stepped forward and embraced Jane. Or perhaps it was Jane's sister-in-law Rachel, or even her stepsister Kitty, because the woman was wearing a circlet of flowers in her hair and that seemed like something a debutante would do, not a married woman. Christopher had tried to take note of what everyone was wearing and any other distinguishing features that would help him to discriminate one person from another when Jane's family had first arrived en masse. But as usual it was challenging.

Aside from Joseph Delaney with his distinctive pewter hair and the fact he wore glasses, Christopher really couldn't tell Jane's brother, Colin, apart from Henry Pevensey, her stepfather. Both men sported somber suits and similarly styled muttonchops. Christopher would have to keep Jane close at hand lest he trip up and her family question his rightness of mind if he started mistaking one person for another.

In fact, as the guests mingled and sipped champagne and helped themselves to lobster patties and mushroom vol-au-vents—Mrs. Harrigan and Roxby House's cook had somehow managed to whip up a makeshift wedding breakfast at the drop of a hatpin—Christopher realized that aside from Joseph Delaney, almost everyone was keen to toady up to Jane's new husband, despite his notoriety.

Thank God for Jane. She deftly inserted each person's name into the start of every new conversation so he knew who he was talking to. He wanted to kiss her every time she declared, "Oh, Mama, I've been meaning to tell you…" or "Now, Colin, you and Rachel must tell my husband about…" or "Dear Kitty, I can't quite believe…" et cetera, et cetera. Christopher wondered how he could have survived this long without this woman in his life.

It seemed she could skillfully and effortlessly help him to navigate group social situations with an adroitness that was impressive. He didn't have to concentrate quite so much or worry he would make a fool of himself. Or act the part of the "arrogant duke" who was dismissive of those who spoke to him (when in truth he was simply feigning disinterest so he could discontinue a conversation that had him floundering).

At one point when there was a lull in the chitchat,

Christopher drew Jane aside. "I want to thank you for cleverly identifying who's who for me," he murmured. "Your perceptiveness is quite astounding."

Jane's eyes held a compassionate light as she held his gaze. "I've been thinking about what it's like when you bump into someone and you can't quite place them. How disconcerting it is that he or she knows you, but you can't recall that person at all. And this happens to you every single day. I can't even begin to imagine how you've managed all this time."

Christopher cast her a wry smile. "Neither can I. Pretending you know who you are talking to requires considerable vigilance. But with you by my side, Jane, I can relax a little more."

"Yet you still held all those parties," said Jane.

"I think I mentioned before that it's easier when most of the people around you are inebriated."

A slight frown knitted Jane's brow. "I must apologize for foisting my family on you this evening. When I went home to collect a few things, I was waylaid by my mother. As soon as she saw that I was packing a carpetbag, she knew something was afoot. And I would never wear something as fine as this"—she gestured at her blue silk gown—"unless I was accompanying her and Kitty to a function."

"Do not be concerned. It was foolhardy of me to think that I could get away with marrying you in secret when your family lives close by. And I can see how close you are to your grandfather, Jane. It would be a shame for him to miss this moment in your life."

"Yes, marrying a duke is not something that happens every day. I never..." Jane drew a deep breath. "I never dreamed I would marry anyone at all. Not after—" She broke off and shrugged a shoulder. "Well, not after my dogcart accident. But you already know all about that. Over the years, I told myself time and again that I didn't want a family of my own. That supporting my mother and grandfather and brother's family was enough. But…" She blushed a little. "It seems I was wrong about that."

Christopher gave her a rakish smile meant only for her. "I look forward to making a family with you. You can have as many children as you like. You know that I want you. That since we met I've barely thought about anything other than all of the different ways I can bring you pleasure. Actually, if your family doesn't depart soon"—he grasped her arm and leaned closer—"I might have to throw them all out."

She laughed. "Believe me, I'm of the same mind."

They fell into companionable silence and sipped their champagne as Christopher cast his gaze about the room. Every time he was confronted with a stranger-filled crowd, Jane would be his anchor. His safe and familiar place.

Although at this moment she was both a comfort and a torment. A torment simply because he couldn't claim her in a physical sense. He hadn't lied when he'd professed that his every waking minute was filled with thoughts of what they'd do together when they were alone. Jane might be the Duchess of Roxby, but she wasn't completely his yet. He wouldn't be satisfied until she was, and patience was not his strong suit.

A pulse began to beat in Christopher's skull and the champagne he was drinking suddenly tasted sour. The gas lamps made him squint, and the chatter around him seemed to swell and pound and swamp his senses.

Damn it all to hell. Why was he beset by one of his infernal megrims *now?* When a headache like this began, there was no stopping its progression. Christopher had been ignoring the tightness in his neck all afternoon, hoping it would go away, but now the throbbing pain in his temple had started up in earnest.

There was no hope for it. He would have to retire to his rooms and take a dose of laudanum and sleep it off. As much as he wanted to make love to Jane, it seemed their conjugal union *would* have to wait.

It made him want to gnash his teeth and growl like a beast.

He put down his champagne flute and turned to his lovely wife. "Forgive me, Jane. I must excuse myself..." He swallowed as a wave of nausea hit.

Jane paled and gripped his arm. "Christopher. What's wrong?"

He forced a smile that he suspected was more of a grimace. "Just a headache," he gritted out. "No one's poisoned me. I'll be in my rooms if you need me." And then he strode from the drawing room before he cast up his accounts in the middle of his wedding celebrations.

———

"How is he?" murmured Jane. She was in the hallway outside the Duke of Roxby's suite, and she perversely felt like she shouldn't be here, even though she was now Christopher's wife. At least in name.

Featherstone offered her a small smile, perhaps to reassure her that she wasn't intruding. "Resting comfortably enough, Yer Grace. His Grace has taken a dose of laudanum. That and sleep are the only things that seem to help when he gets one of his headaches."

Jane nodded. It was the same way with her mother. Well, when she really did have a headache and wasn't feigning one to avoid something unpleasant. "I wish there was something else I could do," she said. "Do you...do you think I could go in and sit with him?"

"Of course, Yer Grace. Of course," said the valet, opening

the door to admit her. He pointed across the opulent sitting room to another doorway that stood ajar. A sliver of lamplight spilled out onto the plush Aubusson rug. "Just go through there. I'll leave you in peace. But do ring if there's anything you need."

Jane nodded. "Thank you."

Christopher's chamber was as richly furnished as the sitting room. But Jane was barely aware of the gleaming oak furniture as she quietly crossed the room to the enormous four-poster bed swathed in heavy drapes of blue and antique gold. Her gaze was riveted to the man lying beneath the satin counterpane and crisp white sheets.

Her husband.

Jane's heart clenched with compassion as she hovered by the bed. Even though Christopher was cloaked in shadows, it was evident he was fast asleep. He lay on his back, one bare arm flung above his head, his leonine locks tumbling across his furrowed brow. His dark-brown lashes caressed his cheeks, and his sharply cut lips were slightly parted. Even in repose, he didn't appear relaxed. It was as though he had the weight of the world resting upon his very broad, beautifully carved shoulders... Shoulders that were also bare...

Goodness. Her husband was shirtless beneath the covers. Jane inhaled a shaky breath as she sank into a nearby armchair. She really shouldn't stare. It wasn't right to ogle an unconscious man or even imagine what else might lie beneath the sheets.

She dragged her gaze back to Christopher's face. He made a small noise in his throat, then murmured something incoherent beneath his breath, and Jane wondered if he was dreaming. She prayed he wasn't having a nightmare.

She glanced at the mantel clock. It was only nine. Her family had departed a half hour ago, and after unpacking the few items she'd brought with her to Roxby House, she'd found herself at loose ends.

She hadn't changed out of her wedding finery, such as it was. But she supposed she should, even though she'd probably be cold. She'd packed a highly impractical light lawn nightgown fringed with delicate lace to wear to bed. The tiny bit of feminine vanity that still lurked deep inside her heart made Jane want to look fetching on her wedding night. Her plain old flannel nightgown would not do. Of course, she'd also anticipated that Christopher would keep her warm...

That certainly wouldn't be happening tonight. Given how unwell Christopher had seemed earlier and how heavily he slept now, it didn't feel right to slip beneath the bedcovers to lie next to him uninvited.

Jane sighed wearily. She should really go back to her own suite of rooms and read a book or write a letter and put aside her disappointment that her wedding night wouldn't be everything she'd imagined it would be. After all, they had all the time in the world to get to know each other.

As long as this wicked person who was trying to harm Christopher didn't succeed...

A shiver passed through Jane that had nothing to do with the cold, drizzly night. No wonder her husband suffered headaches.

She rose and silently approached the bed. Would Christopher mind if she brushed his hair away from his troubled brow and dropped a good-night kiss there? Surely that would be permitted.

Her heart hammering, she dared to sweep his tumbling locks to one side...and then Christopher stirred and his eyelids fluttered open. His hand reached for hers, and even though his gaze appeared unfocused and drowsy, he clearly recognized her.

"Jane," he whispered. His syllables were slightly slurred, his voice little more than a low rasp. "Lie with me, love."

Love... He'd called her "love." Of course, he didn't mean it, but a tiny throb of acute yearning pulsed through Jane's chest. Made her defenses crumble just a little. She should turn and leave the room. Walk away before she began to believe this could be more than a marriage of convenience. But she couldn't. The desire to feel wanted, to lie beside a man—this man—was almost impossible to resist. It *was* her wedding night...

"Of course," she murmured. She brought Christopher's hand to her lips and then slipped off her shoes. She couldn't very well hop in bed in her present attire. Would Christopher watch her as she got undressed? He'd certainly seemed to enjoy watching her expose her legs in the library a few nights ago.

Her gaze went to her husband's face, and she thought she detected the gleam of his eyes beneath heavy, half-mast lids.

But as she lifted her skirts and untied the ribbons and tapes securing her crinoline cage and petticoats about her waist, his eyes drifted closed again.

Never mind, she told herself as she loosened her bodice and shed her gown, then unhooked her corset. *You can undress in front of him another night.*

By the time she'd stripped down to her chemise and had unpinned her hair, Christopher was obviously fast asleep again. Nevertheless, the invitation to join him in bed had been issued and she wasn't going to ignore a ducal edict.

Hadn't she promised to love, honor, and obey her husband only a few short hours ago?

Well, while she wasn't in love with Christopher, she could definitely own to caring about his well-being. And she could certainly honor and obey him.

She turned the bedside lamp down as low as it would go and

then carefully climbed into the bed, slipping beneath the covers to lie down beside her husband.

The night was chilly, and he was warm, and it took everything in her to remain still on her side of the mattress. To resist the urge to curl herself around Christopher's long-limbed body and rest her cheek on his bare chest. She dared not even move too close to him lest she discover he was entirely naked.

Jane's pulse quickened at the notion, and all at once she didn't feel cold anymore. Oh, but she was a lustful creature. How she'd remained celibate and devoid of desire for a man for so long—unless it was some mysterious imaginary hero who she'd encountered in a book—she had no idea.

She only had to wait a little longer to experience lovemaking with her husband. This beautiful stranger who could pass for an archangel.

She'd already waited a decade. Surely she could manage to wait a handful of hours. With any luck, she'd fall asleep and be wakened by Christopher's kiss…just like Sleeping Beauty. In the near darkness, her mouth quirked with a wry smile.

She was neither a princess nor beautiful. And while Christopher had the looks of a handsome prince, this relationship was based on lust and procreation and what each of them could do for the other.

That would have to be enough.

Chapter Fourteen

CHRISTOPHER PRIED HIS EYELIDS OPEN AND GROANED AS HE squinted at the shadowy velvet canopy above his bed.

While he was groggy with the laudanum and sleep, and his vision was a tad blurry, he knew that his headache had faded.

Thank God.

And then a burr of irritation penetrated his brain when he recalled that he and Jane had exchanged vows, but then he'd gone and deserted her. He hadn't given her the wedding night she deserved.

Damn it.

He yawned and scrubbed a hand down his face. Somehow he'd make it up to her. He imagined she was fast asleep in her bed in the neighboring suite. Would she be pleased if he entered her bedchamber and woke her up for a conjugal visit, or would she send him away with a flea in his ear?

He turned his head toward his bedside table where a lamp still burned, and he reached for his pocket watch; Featherstone always left it there for him to check the time. It was early—not quite six o'clock. The fire had died in the grate and the room was cold. Rain pattered against the windowpanes, although under the covers he was warm as toast.

Christopher yawned again…and then he froze when he felt the covers beside him move and a small, decidedly feminine murmur penetrated the silence of the room. Whipping his head to the other side, he spied a tumble of rich brown hair draped across the pillow next to him. A glimpse of pale shoulder and a slender upper arm clad in diaphanous fabric and lace.

Jane. His duchess.

My wife.

Desire sparked in Christopher's veins, heating his blood. When had Jane joined him for the night? He frowned as a vague, dreamlike memory stirred. She'd stood by the bed, bending low as though to kiss him. He'd reached for her and then she'd begun to shed her clothes… And then…nothing. He couldn't recall anything else. He must have fallen asleep. Curse the bloody laudanum. It relieved his pain but also made him drowsy as hell.

It was clear that something else *had* happened though. Jane had hopped into bed with him. And it was evident she wasn't wearing much at all. A flimsy chemise or wisp of a nightgown.

Christopher smiled. He'd take it as an encouraging sign.

He turned on his side and moved toward Jane's warm, beautiful body. Close but not quite touching. She was facing away from him, her breathing gentle and even.

Closing his eyes, Christopher inhaled, taking in the intoxicating scent of delicate flowers and warm sleepy female.

His cock, already standing to attention, began to throb in earnest.

Christ, how he wanted this woman.

Christopher drew a deep breath, then ever so gently brushed Jane's silken tresses to one side. Leaning forward, he placed a soft kiss on her bare shoulder, and she stirred a little. Made another one of those soft, delicious sounds in her throat that aroused him even more.

"Jane," he murmured before he bestowed another kiss on smooth-as-satin flesh. Beneath the sheets, he dared to place a possessive hand on her hip. "Are you awake?"

"Mmm…" Jane arched her back and then she stilled. "Christopher?" she whispered and then she rolled over to face him. Her smile was sleepy but welcoming as she softly added, "Good morning, Husband."

"Good morning, Wife," he whispered back.

"Are you feeling better?"

"Much…" He reached out and brushed a strand of tangled hair away from her deep-green eyes. "I'm sorry about last night. Ever since my so-called riding accident, these headaches… They come out of nowhere and there's little I can do except take laudanum and rest."

Concern shadowed Jane's gaze. "I'm so sorry. And you don't need to apologize. It's not your fault."

"I know, but…" Christopher slid a finger beneath the flimsy sleeve of her chemise. "I need to make amends."

"I can think of a few things you could do to achieve that…" Jane bit her lip. The way her teeth pushed into the soft pillow of her bottom lip had Christopher groaning.

"I know you don't believe me," he murmured, "but you're beautiful."

Her gaze grew clouded as it searched his. "My scar doesn't bother you?"

"No. Of course not. I'm a former soldier. You'll soon see I have scars all over my body too. You've seen the bullet graze along my temple, but I also bear other marks. Scars from stray bullets and even a few bayonet slices. Do you think they will affect how you see me? Does the fact my brain is damaged, and my perception has been altered, make me less attractive to you?"

"No, not all. Not one little bit."

He smiled. "So why should this"—he touched her cheek with gentle fingers—"make any difference to me either?"

Jane frowned. "It *has* made a difference though. It's why you can remember my face. And perhaps it's the last shreds of my feminine vanity speaking, but I do sometimes worry that the disfigurement is all you see. It's rather hard to ignore."

Christopher's chest tightened. He had to reassure this woman that he didn't only value her for a facial feature—a disfigurement, as she'd called it—that had somehow magically changed his perception. A feature that he knew had caused her great heartache. It horrified him to think that society, even her own family, regarded her as less worthy because of it.

That she saw herself as a woman who was unwanted.

"No, of course it isn't all I see," he said softly. "I *do* see all of you. Or rather, I *want* to see all of you." He feathered a kiss along the line of her jaw. Caressed her arm lightly. "Let me make love to you, Jane. Let me show you how much I desire you. Let me learn all the ways to please you."

Her mouth curved in a small teasing smile. "If you're sure you're up to it."

Ah, that was better. "Oh, I'm sure," he murmured, pushing his hips forward so his rock-hard cock grazed her belly. She wouldn't be in any doubt now that he was ready.

Even in the dim light, he could see that her cheeks had flushed to a deeper color.

"You certainly are, Your Grace," she whispered huskily. Her hand found him, and she gave his pulsing length a tentative squeeze that made him see stars.

Christ.

"Jane," he groaned and buried his face in her neck. He was hopelessly in lust with this woman, and he couldn't wait to make her his.

Jane's breath caught as Christopher groaned her name against her neck. His mouth was hot on her skin and his long, lean body was pressed hard against hers. Her fingers, still wrapped about his bare cock, squeezed him again, and he muttered a curse and nipped at her ear.

She smiled. Desire was burning her from the inside out, searing through her veins. Gathering between her thighs, making her slick and yearning and mindless with need. And Christopher hadn't even begun to "make amends."

Before she could formulate another thought, his hand was at the back of her head, grasping her nape, and his mouth was on hers. It was a crushing, plundering kiss. A desperate sliding of lips and a frenzied tangle of tongues. A mingling of breaths and moans while hands grasped and kneaded and limbs entwined.

It spoke of mutual need and want, but also a desire to claim. To know.

Not only "to have and to hold," but to belong...

Even if this joining, this coming together, this sense of being "at one" with Christopher was make-believe—a romantic fantasy like the ones in the Gothic novels Jane read—she wanted it so, so much.

And, it seemed, so did her new husband. Jane's blood and whole body sang with the intoxicating notion that this passion, this wild compulsion to explore and possess wasn't one-sided. For ten long years, she'd convinced herself that no one would want her like *this.* That a man like Christopher could be this mad for her. Could be this hungry and overcome by lust.

How wrong she'd been.

Christopher's mouth burned a path down her neck, nipping and sipping and grazing until he reached the neckline of her chemise. And then he flipped the covers away and unerringly claimed one of her achingly hard, sensitive nipples, suckling it through the thin fabric. Tugging on it with his teeth and then laving it until the lawn was wet and the tip was a taut, ruddy peak.

Drawing back, he admired his handiwork. "Wine," he said. "I think your nipples might be the same hue as claret held up to the firelight. A deep rosy-red and even more delicious, I'd warrant." He grinned wolfishly. "Let me check." And then he hauled down the garment, exposing her breast so it was bared to his gaze.

Jane's bosom was on the smaller side, but Christopher didn't appear to mind. "I was right," he murmured huskily, gently pinching and then circling her pebbled flesh with a fingertip. "Perfectly round breasts tipped with wine-red nipples. Just made to fit my hand."

His palm covered her, squeezing gently, and then he was drugging her with a long, slow, mind-dizzying kiss. His tongue stroked and tasted until Jane was breathless and frantic for more. She wanted to press her naked body to his. Feel his touch, his mouth, everywhere.

And it seemed Christopher's thoughts were aligned with hers. Raising his head, he tugged at her chemise and muttered, "Take this off or I'll be forced to rip it off."

She laughed. "You'll have to let me go first."

Christopher released her from his arms just long enough for her to sit up and shimmy out of the garment. As soon as she tossed it away, Christopher dragged her down and covered her body with his. The curve of his long, hard length jutted fiercely into her belly, and her wet, aching sex clenched in anticipation of what was to come.

He grasped one of her wrists and effortlessly pinned her arm above her head with one hand. "I'll not let you go again, Wife," he growled, capturing her other wrist so that she was effectively pinioned. The idea that she was at his mercy, that he could do whatever he wanted with her, thrilled rather than terrified Jane.

She trusted Christopher would offer her nothing but pleasure. His earlier words ran again through her head as he began to feast upon her neck while simultaneously teasing her nipples with his free hand. *Let me learn all the ways to please you.*

It had never been like this with Miles. Their hasty coupling had been but a poor, pale shadow compared to this experience with Christopher. Miles had proposed while they'd picnicked on Hampstead Heath. After she'd said yes, he'd fumbled beneath her skirts, feeling for the slit in her drawers, and deeming she was ready enough with a few tentative, fiddling pokes of his fingers, he'd then pushed himself inside her. It had hurt, and Jane had cried out, but that hadn't deterred him from thrusting a few more times and spending. Jane had told herself that the encounter was romantic and wonderful, when really it was rushed and clumsy and awful.

There'd been no all-consuming kisses. No sweeping caresses or flesh-tingling, teasing strokes. No thought to giving her pleasure at all.

But Jane didn't want to think about her former cad of a fiancé. Not when Christopher was arousing such exquisite sensations with his lips and teeth and tongue and wickedly clever fingers.

It was only when she began to writhe and beg for mercy that he released her wrists. But it seemed her delicious torment was only beginning.

Christopher worked his way down her body, worshipping her rib cage, the plane of her belly, the ridges of her hips with his mouth and hands. And just when she thought he might touch her where she needed him most—her sex was slippery and throbbing with fierce arousal—he moved right down to the end of the bed and flipped her onto her stomach before he proceeded to rain a trail of teasing kisses and wicked licks from her ankles, up her calves, and then to the backs of her knees. His warm breath and his lips on the inside of her thighs made her squirm and twist her fingers into the sheets. Made her tremble and twitch and whimper.

By the time he reached the curve of her behind, Jane was a quivering, goosefleshed, thoroughly addled mess of thwarted desire. "Please…" she moaned into the pillow, arching and circling her hips. "Please, Christopher…"

He placed a hot, open-mouthed kiss on one of her buttock cheeks. "Tell me what you want, Jane." His voice was low and commanding. "And don't you dare tell me that you don't know what it is that you want me to do to you. Nothing is too wicked for the scandalous Duke of Roxby." He kissed her other cheek; then his tongue flickered along the valley between them. "I'll do anything you ask. Anything at all. I'm yours to command."

Jane shivered. Could she say it? Could she ask Christopher to do something that she'd always longed to experience? An act that was entirely carnal yet breathtakingly wonderful? At least according to her married friends.

A decadent act that Jane had often fantasized about in the middle of the night when she'd been alone in her bed, touching herself as she dreamed of dark Byronic heroes. Wicked rakes like Christopher who would do all manner of erotic things to her body…

It appeared she would have to voice her request, because Christopher remained steadfastly silent as he hovered behind her. Curse him.

Or perhaps…perhaps he would find it stimulating too if she brazenly stated what she wanted. It seemed words could arouse just as much as hands and mouths.

Lifting her head, she turned to catch Christopher's gaze over her shoulder. "I want you to kiss my quim," she whispered, her whole face burning as the breathless words tumbled out. "Lick it and taste it and—"

She got no further as Christopher flipped her onto her back and then thrust his shoulders between her thighs, spreading her wide. "Like this?" he asked, his voice rough and ragged with lust before he slid his tongue between her folds and dragged it through the welling moisture. The licking caress was long and slow, and when he reached her clitoris he suckled it, making Jane gasp and arch her hips. Her hands speared into his hair, her fingers twisting. She might have called out "Yes" in response to his question. Or perhaps it was an inarticulate moan of joy. In any event, it was enough for Christopher as he proceeded to do everything she'd asked of him and more.

Good God. Her friends had been right. This was heaven. It was too wonderful for words. It was the most exquisite, maddening torture too. How on earth had she lived this long without...

Ooooh...

Jane's thoughts shattered as everything in her tensed and bowed and all her nerve endings caught alight. Waves of glorious, overwhelming sensation pulsed and rushed through her body, and she was swept away. Tossed into the waiting arms of bliss.

When the pleasure at last abated, Jane sagged back against the pillows, boneless and exhausted yet replete. She wanted to thank Christopher in kind. She knew she could also use her mouth on him. And of course she wanted to explore his beautifully sculpted body. To stroke her hands across all of his sleekly muscled planes and to find all of the sensitive, secret places and hollows that she could torment with her fingertips and lips and tongue. She wanted him to beg for mercy too.

But that wasn't to be. Her husband had other plans. Within

moments, he'd crawled up her body until he was hovering over her. "Forgive me, Jane," he rasped against her ear as one of his knees gently coaxed her legs apart. "I'm desperate to have you. It's been so long since... I want to claim you. Come inside you..."

"There's nothing to forgive," she whispered, her hands sliding over his smooth, hard back. "Take me. Spend your seed inside me. My body aches for your possession too."

"Thank God," Christopher groaned. He dragged the broad head of his rock-hard member along her slick folds, parting them, and then he fitted himself at her entrance. "Wrap those spectacular legs around me, love," he murmured. "I'm about to make you mine."

———

Christopher was so aroused, he was almost certain he'd lose control before he was even inside Jane. She'd told him she wasn't a virgin but that didn't mean he could go charging in holus-bolus like the bloody cavalry. It had been years since she'd had sexual congress, and he was well endowed. He'd take care entering her, go slowly even if it killed him. Gritting his teeth, he pressed forward in a series of gentle nudges, and when Jane did nothing but sigh and wrap her legs more securely around him, he took it as a sign that he wasn't causing her any undue discomfort.

Praise be to God. Christopher thrust his throbbing cock into her tight, slick sheath all the way to the hilt, and then he pressed his forehead to Jane's. "Christ, you feel good. So damn good," he groaned. "Like hot, wet velvet."

A breathy laugh escaped her. "How poetic, Your Grace. I, on the other hand...I feel like I've been invaded and conquered and plundered."

"I'm not hurting you too much, am I?" Christopher studied

her face, but her eyes were as clear as a forest pool, her brow unfurrowed.

"No..." She brushed her lips against his. "Not at all. I never dreamed that being stuffed so full with something so big and hard and hot could feel so wonderful."

"You're certainly doing wonders for my masculine pride." Christopher grinned then dipped his head to steal a deeper kiss. "But the conquering and plundering isn't over yet, darling. The ride has only just begun." And then, because he could no longer bear to stay immobile, Christopher rocked his hips back and forth, sliding his straining cock in and out of Jane in slow, smooth, measured strokes. Her hands curled around his shoulders and she moved with him. When he glanced at her face, he could see that her eyes were closed and her lips were parted. He prayed she was enjoying this as much as he was.

Her sex felt so right, clasping him so tightly. So perfectly. It was like she'd been made for him.

But taking Jane slowly soon wasn't enough. Christopher's body urged him to increase the pace. Plunge harder and faster. And he did.

As his cock hammered in and out of Jane, he claimed her mouth, absorbing her soft, ragged moans and pants. He had to taste her. Have every little bit of her. Even the sweetly erotic sounds she made.

Raw, hungry need spurred him on. His orgasm was starting to gather force like an oncoming firestorm, and when Jane's sex began rippling around his pounding length, Christopher almost cried out in relief. It meant he could let go. Succumb to the overwhelming urge to lose control.

He fumbled between their sweat-slickened bodies and he roughly, clumsily thumbed Jane's clitoris...and then all at once a pleasure-drenched cry tumbled from her lips. The sound of her finding ecstasy was enough to trigger Christopher's own climax. His whole body spasmed and shuddered as he lost himself to the moment, his seed erupting inside Jane in a series of hot, urgent bursts.

Yes...

When he was spent, he collapsed on top of Jane and then rolled to the side, taking her with him. He sought her mouth and kissed her with lingering, gentle thoroughness. When her fingers curled into his hair, tenderness sparked in his chest.

Tenderness? Christopher frowned as he tucked Jane's head beneath his chin. He was not a tenderhearted man by nature. For years, he'd been a cold and clinical cavalry officer dispensing brutality on the battlefield. Making hard decisions, setting aside his emotions. Keeping them in check was as natural to him as breathing or swinging a sword or firing a pistol. Even when his fiancé, Daisy, had rejected him, he'd taken it in his stride after the initial heartbreak had faded.

He didn't believe in happily-ever-afters, and he'd only just met Jane. He was mistaken about what he was feeling. The warm glow suffusing his limbs and his chest were merely remnants, dying embers of the passionate bed sport they'd enjoyed. Lusty lovemaking had nothing to do with love. He was simply sated and also pleased that he and Jane appeared to be entirely compatible in bed. If he had her as much as he wanted to, it probably wouldn't be long before she was with child, and then they could go their separate ways as most couples in a marriage of convenience did.

Only, that wasn't quite true.

Christopher would be dependent on Jane for the foreseeable future. At least until he worked out who was trying to kill him.

He sighed. As much as he would like to lie abed with Jane

all day, he had things to do. Aside from the usual matters of business he needed to deal with, he wanted to speak with Featherstone's cousin and provide him with the information necessary to begin an investigation. Christopher had been sitting on his hands for far too long about all of this. Some sort of action was long overdue.

It seemed there was no rest for dukes with targets on their backs.

Chapter Fifteen

THE ONE-THOUSAND-POUND CHECK THAT CHRISTOPHER had written for Jane cleared the day after their wedding, so Jane decided to get rid of her mother's deuced gambling debt. There was no point in letting it hang over her head, or rather her grandfather's bookshop, like a dark and menacing thundercloud, not when she could disperse it.

She had enough problems of her own to contend with.

Her mother had disclosed to her that the Whisteria Club was on Pall Mall, not far from St. James's Square. The club's existence was supposed to be a well-kept secret amongst society's elite and admittance was by invitation only or upon the recommendation of "a current member in good standing."

Besides a plain carpetbag which contained all of the cash— Jane didn't possess any sort of checkbook, let alone one that bore her new name, the Duchess of Roxby—she also carried a letter of recommendation from her mother. Christopher had offered to come with her, but the club was strictly "women only" so there wouldn't have been much point. Aside from that, she was going to see Artemis straight afterward at Fortnum & Mason's tea rooms for a Byronic Book Club meeting even though Lucy was still away. Tellingly, her friend had sent a note round to Roxby House that very morning stating she was back in Town—she'd apparently arrived late last night after receiving Jane's telegram—and of course she couldn't wait to catch up on all of Jane's "momentous news" that she'd read about in the papers.

Which meant Jane was about to be interrogated about her new husband and why she'd married in such haste rather than waited two more days as originally planned.

Jane didn't want to keep things from her friend, but really, part of the story wasn't hers to tell. It was Christopher's and she wouldn't betray his trust.

Jane touched her gloved fingers to her lips as Christopher's carriage drew up outside the grand town house where the Whisteria Club was located. Christopher had kissed her soundly before she'd quit Roxby House, and she fancied she could still feel the impression of his mouth upon hers. In quiet moments, her thoughts invariably strayed to their wedding night—or should she say morning?—and how wonderfully fulfilling it had been. How passionate and considerate a lover her new husband was. In fact, he was considerate all around. He'd insisted that she take his coach, along with several burly footmen for protection. Aside from the fact she was transporting a great deal of money, Christopher wanted to ensure that she was physically safe too.

Jane was touched that her husband seemed genuinely concerned about her well-being. It was a novel sensation—being cared for by a man. Although Jane had to keep reminding herself that Christopher was looking out for her simply because she would be the mother of his children. She shouldn't mistake the passion they shared in the marriage bed for something else.

A footman named Beattie, the same one who'd interrogated her on Saint Valentine's Day, handed Jane down from the coach and then escorted her to the club's entrance. Jane had dressed in a well-cut gown of dark-green velvet and hoped she looked like a duchess even if she didn't yet feel like one.

The footman on the door of the Whisteria Club looked over her mother's letter of recommendation and then, with a sniff, admitted her. As she removed her bonnet and gloves, Jane took a moment to observe the beautifully appointed entry hall, which was a study in white marble and gilt-trimmed furnishings. Purple, mauve, and white wisteria spilled from enormous vases and also adorned the archway leading into the main club room. The proprietor of the club, the Dowager Viscountess Aylesbury, clearly wished her wealthy guests to feel at home.

Even though it was midafternoon, the hubbub of women chattering indicated that gambling was popular at any hour as the footman showed Jane to Lady Aylesbury's office, a small private parlor that was also stylishly decorated. The dowager viscountess was seated behind an elegant rosewood desk, looking through a ledger, but she looked up as the footman announced Jane.

Out of habit, Jane dipped into a curtsy, and then she chided herself because she was now a duchess and Lady Aylesbury was only a viscountess, so according to etiquette their roles should be reversed.

"The Duchess of Roxby, you say? I wasn't aware that the duke had wed." Lady Aylesbury raised an imperious brow as her gaze wandered over Jane. Her eyes narrowed when she took in Jane's scar and her slightly worse-for-wear carpetbag. She was clearly skeptical of Jane's claim that she was a duchess.

"Yes," replied Jane just as imperiously. She would not be rattled by this woman's superior manner. Lady Aylesbury was a gaming-hell owner, for heaven's sake. "We're newly wedded. As of yesterday, in fact. It was announced in the *Times* this morning if you wish to check."

"No, that won't be necessary. I'll accept your word." The viscountess waved Jane over to a chair before the desk with a beringed hand. "So, what can I do for you, Your Grace?" she asked, her manner cool and businesslike. "I take it you wish to become a member here and you possess a letter of recommendation?"

Heavens, the woman was not easily daunted. But Jane would

not be put off. "Not quite," she said. She didn't bother to pass over her mother's letter or sit because she wouldn't be staying long. "I'm Leonora Pevensey's daughter and I'm here to settle her debt."

Lady Aylesbury sniffed. "I see. I wasn't aware Leonora had a daughter, let alone one so elevated." Her gaze dropped to the carpetbag. "I take it you've brought the money with you, then?"

"Yes." Jane placed the bag on the desk, then undid the buckled clasps. "I have the one thousand pounds in here. In cash."

The viscountess pulled the bag toward her, then looked inside. "I'll have this counted, mind you, but all looks in order. The member who won it will be most pleased this has been settled in a timely manner. There was concern in some quarters that your mother might not be able to afford the debt. Putting up a bookstore as collateral is not usually the done thing, but I allowed it, given your mother has been a club member for some time."

"The concerns you mentioned are definitely warranted," said Jane. "Let me be frank... Aside from me, no one else in my family knows my mother is a member of the Whisteria Club, and after this particular incident I worry that she's developed a habit of playing fast and loose with money she does not have. Although my circumstances have recently changed"—Jane paused to smooth a strand of hair away from her face so that the viscountess would catch a glimpse of her wedding band and impressive engagement ring—"I am not the sort of person who will stand by and allow my mother to fritter away money on something as inconsequential as a game of whist. To that end, I would ask that you rescind her membership."

The dowager viscountess's eyes glittered. "It's not up to you, Your Grace. Whether a member is in good standing or not is decided by me and me alone."

"Well, be that as it may"—Jane met the woman's gaze directly—"let me make one thing very clear. I shan't pay any other debt my mother accrues. Not one penny. This will be the *only* vowels that I shall cover. This is not an opportunity for you to help yourself to a large slice of the Duke of Roxby's fortune."

Lady Aylesbury shrugged. "Well, let me make *this* one thing clear. If her vowels are *not* paid, it won't be my fault if some juicy piece of gossip about the Duke of Roxby's mother-in-law ends up in the papers."

Jane inwardly bristled. Oh, but this woman was cold-blooded. She suddenly wondered if the dowager viscountess could afford such a lavishly appointed house because she was in the habit of issuing threats to her members in order to get them to pay up straightaway.

Well, two could play a cutthroat game. Jane affected an air of nonchalance even though she was stewing with anger just below the surface. "I would reconsider, Lady Aylesbury. If only for the comfort in knowing that if you do as I ask, I will not tell the *London Tatler* the names of those women who frequent your club. My mother has provided me with a very long list. I suspect that you, Lady Aylesbury, have more to lose than I do in the gossip stakes." She leaned forward. "And don't think I don't have the backbone to follow through with my threat. I haven't come so far with a face like this without being ruthless. Not many women can say they tamed a man with a reputation as notorious as the Duke of Roxby's. You do *not* want to cross me."

There, take that, thought Jane as she straightened. Most of what she said had been bluff and bluster, but the dowager viscountess wasn't to know that.

Indeed, the woman looked decidedly pale as she regarded Jane across the scuffed carpetbag full of money. "Very well, Your Grace," the viscountess said stiffly. "Your mother's membership is canceled, effective immediately. She will never cross the threshold again. And neither shall you."

"A most satisfactory outcome," said Jane. She couldn't

suppress a small self-satisfied smile as she added, "I shan't take up any more of your time. I have an appointment with my very good friend, the Duchess of Dartmoor, and I don't wish to keep her waiting. You may keep the carpetbag."

With that, Jane swept from the room, sashaying through the club with her head held high. In moments like these, even she would admit that being a duchess had much to recommend it.

When she gained the entry hall, she paused to redon her bonnet and gloves. As she wrestled with pulling her glove's finger over her engagement ring, the footman on duty opened the door to admit another club patron. The woman didn't pause to remove her hat or gloves and hurried past quickly.

Jane glanced up, and then she frowned. There was something vaguely familiar about the retreating figure. Jane hadn't even caught a glimpse of the woman's profile, but she had the peculiar notion it was Daphne Marsden.

The snooty footman refused to confirm or deny her suspicions when she asked him for the woman's name, and Jane left with a sigh. She was probably mistaken, and really it was neither here nor there if her husband's cousin-in-law enjoyed a game of whist every now and again. Not everyone was addicted to gambling away everything they had like her own mother.

But no more. Delaney's bookshop was safe, and Leonora Pevensey was no longer a member of the Whisteria Club. Her mother would be miffed with her for being so high-handed, but Jane knew it was the right thing to do, for all their sakes.

═══════════

"Jane!" Artemis Winters, the Duchess of Dartmoor, enveloped Jane in a huge hug, right in the middle of Fortnum & Mason's tearooms. "Or should I address you as 'Your Grace'?" Other patrons who were taking tea turned in their seats to observe the commotion, but Artemis didn't seem to care.

A bluestocking with a bold-as-you-please personality, the Duchess of Dartmoor was impervious to the stares and whispers of others. And she often drew admiring stares. Today, Artemis was beautifully attired in a haute couture gown of rich amber silk that showcased her enviable figure and brought out the color of her auburn hair and brown eyes to perfection.

Jane smiled. "So I'm forgiven for getting married sooner than expected?"

"Of course." Artemis gestured at a nearby table. "I've already ordered tea and cakes and sandwiches. Don't think I'll let you leave here without spilling all of the gossip. You must tell me everything."

Jane took a seat. "I will. It's a shame Lucy can't be here too. I did send her a telegram, but she has so much farther to travel." Kyleburn Castle, the Earl of Kyle's seat, was in Ayrshire, Scotland, and it took a good day to reach London, even by train.

"I'm sure she'll arrive this evening," said Artemis as she laid a napkin across her lap. "But now that we are together, you cannot keep me in suspense a moment longer. I shall expire if you do."

Jane laughed. "To be perfectly honest, I'm rather relieved that you're not hauling me over the coals about all this."

"*Pfft.*" Artemis deftly dispensed Jane's tea exactly the way she liked it. "As if I would ever do that. We've been friends forever and you are the most considered person that I know. If you've decided to wed the Duke of Roxby, you must have a very good reason. I respect any woman's choice to live her life the way she chooses. And that includes you, my friend." But then Artemis frowned as she handed Jane her cup of tea. "Of course, I'm assuming this marriage *is* your choice. That you haven't been coerced into doing anything that you don't want to. Because that's another kettle of fish entirely. And you know I will eviscerate anyone who has the gall to hurt you."

"It *is* my choice," said Jane, although she knew she would have to choose her words carefully from here on. "But by the same token, I will readily admit that it's not a path I was expecting to go down..."

Artemis stirred her tea. "I certainly wasn't expecting to marry Dominic either. And Lucy never planned on marrying Will."

"You both married for love though."

"True," said Artemis. A thoughtful look crossed her face. "But considering the speed with which you've wed your duke, I suspect that's not the case for you, Jane. I know I've been away for weeks on end, but I rather suspect that if you'd met a man and fallen head over heels in love, you would have shared that fact sooner with me and Lucy."

"You're not wrong at all," said Jane. "The duke and I... I mean Christopher and I, we aren't in love."

Artemis's mouth quirked with a smile. "In lust then? You know I won't pass judgment. Dominic and I were certainly in lust before we fell in love. I'm sure Lucy would say the same about her and Will."

"Yes...we are most definitely 'in lust,'" Jane admitted as memories of this morning and what she'd done with Christopher drifted through her mind. She lowered her voice lest anyone was eavesdropping. "And I'm pleased to say Christopher is a stupendous lover. He's..." Jane bit her lip, considering her next words. "Perhaps I should say the term 'conjugal bliss' would be a fitting descriptor to sum up our situation."

"Excellent," said Artemis with an approving nod that set her auburn curls bouncing. "You're halfway there then."

Jane's laugh was wry. "I don't know about that. We agreed upon a marriage of convenience. A happily-ever-after is not something that I'm expecting to eventuate. I'm not keen to risk my heart with a man I barely know. Especially after Miles."

"I understand completely." Artemis's brown eyes softened with compassion. "As you know, Dominic and I had an engagement of convenience. But with time, he convinced me that it was safe to love again. So perhaps it will be the same for you and your Christopher."

Jane sighed. "I have no idea." And she really didn't. She attempted a smile. "Perhaps… It's very early days yet."

"It is." Artemis caught Jane's gaze. "While we're being candid, it would be remiss of me not to broach the topic of your husband's reputation. Libidinous rakehells might have a particular appeal when depicted in a book—I mean, my own Gothic novels feature irresistible rogues all the time—but I think it's quite a different matter when it comes to real life. Alas, some men simply cannot be tamed."

"I agree," said Jane. She paused to add a lump of sugar to her tea, even though she normally drank it unsweetened. She'd have to tell Artemis an approximation of the truth about this particular matter. "However, I'm pleased to report that Christopher has pledged to me that he will no longer host wild parties at Roxby House. He claims he wants to settle down and start a family."

Artemis raised a brow. "He wants an heir? Straightaway?"

"Yes…" Jane drew a breath. "And…and I want that too."

Artemis reached for Jane's hand. "You know, all these years I did wonder if you wanted a baby. But all three of us—Lucy, you, and I—were so determined to put on brave faces and denounce all men and the institution of marriage, especially after Guy de Burgh broke my heart. And of course after Miles let you down so very badly."

Jane smiled back at her. "You mean all men save for the Byronic heroes we encountered in the Gothic romance novels that we adore. That they were the only men worthy of our devotion."

"Yes," said Artemis. "But time has taught me that not all men are cads, and marriage can be quite liberating…if it's to the right person. Who'd have thought that outspoken, spinster-ish Artemis Jones would be so happily wed and with—" She broke off and her cheeks bloomed with a bright-pink blush so out of character for Artemis that Jane studied her friend with new eyes. Was Artemis's face a little fuller? Did her bust seem a little more generous? Was she in fact glowing?

"Artemis…" Jane dropped her voice and squeezed her friend's hand. "Are you with child?"

Artemis nodded and her brown eyes shone. "Yes, I am," she whispered back. "It's early days, of course. But I've missed my courses twice, so I'm so very hopeful that yes, I am pregnant. I estimate the due date is sometime in October. I mean to tell Lucy as well. As soon as she arrives in Town."

"Oh, Artemis. I'm so happy for you and Dominic." And Jane meant it. She truly did. "I'm sure Lucy will be thrilled for you too."

The maternal pang in Jane's chest turned into a spark of hope for herself. She and Artemis were of a similar age, and part of Jane worried she'd left it too long to have a baby. But apparently not. Artemis's thoughts must have been traveling along similar lines as she said, "I'm sure it won't be long before you're in the family way too."

"I hope so," said Jane. And then she laughed. "That does not sound like me at all, does it? It's funny how you think you have your life all mapped out, and then all of a sudden you're blown off course and heading in a completely different direction."

"I know the feeling well," said Artemis. She selected a few more sandwiches. "But truth to tell, I would be most intrigued to hear how you and the Duke of Roxby met. Dominic has told me all he knows—that the duke inherited the title about a year ago but that he's not politically active. Not that that's a bad thing… Aside from Roxby's rakehell reputation, Dominic isn't aware of anything else untoward. And yes, I know I'm being nosy, but you are one of my best friends, Jane. You cannot blame me for being curious."

"I don't, and I would expect nothing less from you, Artemis. And I actually appreciate it," said Jane. "As for how Christopher and I met…" She paused and sipped her tea. Lying didn't sit well with Jane, but half-truths would have to do again. "We actually bonded over books, of all things. The former Duke of Roxby, Christopher's great-uncle, had amassed a rare-book collection and Christopher brought one of the titles into Delaney's for appraisal. A fifteenth-century first-edition copy of *The Canterbury Tales*, to be precise. We seemed compatible in many ways, and he feels that he's reached a time in his life when he should father an heir. And because I'm not getting any younger, and deep in my heart I do want a baby…" She shrugged a shoulder. "When he proposed, I couldn't think of a reason at all to refuse him."

"I see," said Artemis. "And the reason for you marrying yesterday rather than tomorrow as you'd originally planned?"

Ugh. Her friend wasn't going to let her off easily after all. Stalling for time, Jane selected a cucumber sandwich. "Despite Christopher's reputation, he really is quite noble," she said after a slight pause. "It's also true that he's quite passionate and, well…" Her face heated. "Let's just say he was impatient for our wedding night. As was I. It's been some years since I last…" She glanced up at Artemis. "I never told you that Miles and I made love after he proposed to me. We'd been drinking champagne out on the Heath and it was all so romantic and, well…I succumbed to temptation. I know women aren't supposed to crave physical love—we're certainly not supposed to engage in sexual congress outside of marriage—but after a decade, I did want to experience intimacy again. I see how happy you and Lucy are, and I wanted that for myself too. Even though love isn't part of the equation for Christopher and me, I can't deny that I'm going to enjoy the lovemaking, and hopefully one day the consequences of that."

Artemis's smile was full of understanding. "It's not wrong to want physical love. I wish society as a whole wasn't so judgmental. It's unfair that unwed women are supposed to be chaste their whole lives but men can do as they darn well please. But enough about that, because if I talk too much longer about it, I'll get in a snit about society's hypocrisy and put you off your tea and cake."

Jane toyed with her cup. Perhaps she *could* confide in Artemis about her pamphlet scheme and her odious blackmailer. They both possessed similar views about the education of women when it came to sexual congress. But Artemis had begun to talk about her ladies' academic college and the fact that her adolescent stepdaughter, Lady Celeste, would be attending science classes this term, a situation both Artemis and the duke's daughter were thrilled about. It had apparently been Lady Celeste's dream to study astronomy for some time, but the Duke of Dartmoor had been resistant to the idea because dukes' daughters usually didn't attend any sort of school or college. But Dominic Winters was besotted with his wife, and Artemis did have quite the knack for getting her way.

Hopefully, Jane would soon have access to her own pin money. It might be naive and wishful thinking on her part, but once she'd paid her bothersome blackmailer the fifty pounds that had been demanded, she prayed that would be the end of the matter. For good.

Chapter Sixteen

"Ah, Jane, I'm glad you're back," said Christopher. And he meant it. He was seated behind his desk in the library, going through various dull-as-ditchwater reports put together by his estate stewards in Hertfordshire, Buckinghamshire, and Yorkshire, and he was happy for the distraction. His wife—he was still getting used to that phrase—had been out visiting her friend Lucy, the Countess of Kyle, who also resided in Eaton Square.

Apparently Lucy had returned to Town the day before, and she'd invited Jane and their other mutual friend, the Duchess of Dartmoor, over for a Byronic Book Club meeting. What that precisely entailed Christopher wasn't sure, but he understood that it was some sort of tradition Jane had been maintaining with her friends for years.

"Featherstone's cousin Jack O'Connor will be here in about ten minutes to discuss the suspects on my list," he added as Jane closed the library door. "And if you have the time, I'd like you to sit in on the meeting too."

"Of course." As Jane approached his desk, dusky blue skirts swaying, Christopher really wished he could catch a glimpse of what was below all of that dashed fabric. Now that his desire to have sexual intercourse had roared back to life, he couldn't seem to stop thinking about much else other than pleasuring his wife. It didn't matter that he'd made love to Jane for hours last night. He couldn't seem to appease the fire in his veins. In fact, if O'Connor wasn't due to arrive any minute, he'd have had

Jane's skirts flipped up and his head between her legs faster than a Covent Garden pickpocket could strike.

"I have some pictures here. One is a photograph of my former fiancée, Daisy," he said as Jane reached his side. "I know because her name is written on the back. And this sketch is of Neville Phelps, the lieutenant who was court-martialed. It's a cutting from the *Illustrated London News*. I believe they're both good likenesses. At least according to Featherstone. They're complete strangers to me now."

Jane leaned across him to pick up the photograph of the blond woman. "She's very pretty," she said, her brows drawing together in a slight frown.

Christopher shrugged. "To be perfectly honest, I used to think so. But her actions have revealed her to be a duplicitous, contrary creature. And now, of course, I wouldn't know her from a bar of soap. It's a shame I don't have a picture of her husband, Simon Cosgrove, Esquire… That would be useful. I have no idea how to describe him other than he's male and about my age. That goes for Harry Wexford as well."

"Perhaps this Jack O'Connor will be able to help out in that regard. It would be handy for me to know what all these men look like too." Jane put down Daisy's photograph and then said softly, "I hope the pewter name badges the staff are now wearing are helping you at home, at least."

When she stroked a lock of hair away from his brow, Christopher caught her hand and kissed it. "They certainly are, my clever wife. I'm thankful Mrs. Harrigan and Shelby were able to arrange them so quickly."

"I'm glad we can all be of help." She leaned back against the desk. "While we're on the subject of staff, Artemis and Lucy have helped me to choose a lady's maid. She's from the Kyles' own household up north, so I'm certain she can be trusted. She's a young Scotswoman by the name of Elsie. She can start straightaway."

"That's very generous of Lady Kyle."

Jane smiled. "It is. But I've known Artemis and Lucy forever, and there's nothing they wouldn't do for me." After a slight hesitation, she added, "I hope it's not too sensitive a subject, but I've lately wondered why you haven't more close friends you could confide in. Considering your years in the military."

Christopher gave her a wry smile and leaned back in his chair. "Well, I do have some friends that would fit that bill, but unfortunately they still serve and have been deployed overseas. But this business with Lieutenant Phelps..." Christopher picked up the man's photograph. "Some members of my regiment took against me when I testified at the man's hearing. They disagreed with what I did, and we're friends no more."

"You told me that you reported Phelps because you caught him with your commanding officer's wife."

"Yes..." Christopher sighed. "It was at a regimental dinner, and the pair were *not* discreet. In actual fact, anyone could have walked in on them, but it happened to be me. And I liked and respected Colonel Bellamy. I couldn't let the matter go. The man deserved to know he was being cuckolded by a junior officer."

"I think you did the right thing," said Jane. "You shouldn't feel guilty."

Christopher looked up at her. "Here, don't you go thinking that I'm a good man or any sort of hero, Jane. There are things that I've done in my past that are not honorable."

His wife's brows gathered into a frown. "Things that you've done in battle?"

Christopher flexed his fingers on the blotter of his desk. His knuckles were scarred and mishappen, and there was a faint red mark from the slice of a bayonet blade across the back of his left hand. They were not the hands of a gentleman. "One does what one must to survive. But it's not only that," he said at length. "There are other things..." His words trailed away as he thought about Daisy and the last time he'd seen her. Of how much of a hypocrite he'd been.

"It's all right. I understand." Jane covered his left hand with hers. "You don't have to tell me everything about yourself, Christopher. Nobody's perfect and most people have secrets."

Christopher's gaze shot to his wife's face. There was something about the way she made that last pronouncement that sharpened his curiosity. "Does that include you, Jane?"

She gave him an enigmatic smile, but there was something else, a shadow behind her green eyes that aroused his suspicion even more. "A woman always has secrets of one kind or another, Your Grace. An element of mystery adds to our allure, don't you think?"

"Undoubtedly," said Christopher, then because he couldn't help himself, he pulled her down onto his lap. He wouldn't question her further. She'd share her secrets when she was good and ready. He kissed her neck, right behind her ear. The spot that he'd learned made her shiver and her nipples peak. He raised a hand to her bodice to check.

She laughed softly. "Christopher," she admonished, pushing his hand away from her breast, "you said the private detective would be here soon. And I have something else to ask."

"I did." Christopher sighed. "Ask away, Wife. But don't expect me to be perfectly behaved while you speak. You'll remain on my lap. Even if you won't let me touch and tease you, I can at least breathe in your delectable scent."

"Very well," she said with a sigh that sounded resigned and long-suffering, but Christopher could tell she was playacting because her cheeks were flushed and her eyes were glowing, and she was as malleable as a soft pat of butter.

She drew a breath and traced a vein on the back of his hand

with a fingertip. "I wondered when I might have access to my pin money. I only have one ball gown, and aside from a day gown in velvet and one in silk, I find my wardrobe is sadly lacking. I'm afraid I won't look the part of a duchess in worsted wool and plain black stuff—"

"Fret no more, love. Tell me what you need, and you shall have it. My man of business is setting up a bank account for you, but he's obviously taking too long to get things organized. It's also Saturday, so I expect we won't hear anything until Monday." Christopher pulled open a drawer in his desk and removed a small bundle of rolled-up pound notes. "Here's one hundred pounds. Will that do in the interim?"

Jane bit her lip as she took the money and tucked it into her sleeve. "Yes. Yes, that will do nicely," she murmured. "Thank you." Then she smiled. "If you'd said no, I would have had to pilfer some of the silver or one of your jeweled tie pins like a common sneak thief."

"Well, we can't have that," said Christopher. "But can I make one request?"

Jane arched a brow. "Which is?"

"Make sure you acquire some flimsy night attire as well." He brushed a kiss across her cheek, then murmured in her ear, "I want to see you in gossamer-thin silk and lace and clinging satin. The more transparent the better."

"Very well, Your Grace." To his disappointment though, Jane slid off his lap. "I shall make an appointment with the modiste on Monday afternoon and see what I can arrange."

"Feel free to set up an account there too. I should have suggested that from the outset."

"Oh, would you like the one hundred pounds back then?"

There was a slightly worried edge to Jane's voice, a brittleness in her tone, that made Christopher study her face. "No, it's yours to do with as you wish. Don't ever be afraid to ask me for money. I might be many things, but ungenerous is not one of them."

"Thank you." She smiled, then swooped down to kiss him on the mouth. Christopher snaked a hand into her thick, silky hair and was about to pull her onto his lap again when there was a knock on the door. *Damn it.*

No doubt Jack O'Connor was here. Christopher sighed and released his wife from his embrace. "Come in," he called when Jane had retreated to the other side of the desk.

The private detective was a tall, well-built Irishman who Christopher estimated to be in his early thirties. He bowed with due deference as he was introduced, but Christopher noticed there was more than a roguish twinkle in the detective's bright-blue eyes as he greeted Jane.

Cheeky sod. Christopher swore that Featherstone had mentioned the man was courting a young woman.

Nevertheless, the Irishman was all business as Christopher explained what he required—locating and gathering information on his three main suspects, surveillance of their movements, and digging up any rumors about grudges any or all of them might harbor against the Duke of Roxby. O'Connor asked insightful questions, and at the end of the meeting, Christopher was confident he had engaged the right man for the job. Hopefully it wouldn't be too long before the private detective had something concrete to report.

It certainly would be a damn sight better than floundering around in the dark, which was how he currently felt about his situation. Or like a sitting wood duck just waiting to be shot.

Thank God for Jane, who'd already made his life that little bit easier.

He'd met her less than a week ago, and already he trusted her more than he could say.

Chapter Seventeen

MUDIE'S SELECT LIBRARY STOOD IN NEW OXFORD STREET, not far from the British Museum. Although Jane could have taken one of Christopher's many carriages—in fact, one was presently being outfitted with brand-new velvet upholstery just for her—she decided it was best if she made her own way to this appointment to pay off her blackmailer.

All going well, within a few hours Jane would be free of this blasted mess she'd ended up in. At least she hoped so. It all depended on how greedy her blackmailer was.

Hopefully not *too* greedy. With any luck, this last payment of fifty pounds would be enough. And if it wasn't, Jane would have to rethink her strategy of giving in to the blackmailer's every demand. She might have to put on her considering cap and come up with a way to stop them for good. Because enough was enough and she really wanted to devote herself to helping Christopher deal with his own not-insignificant problem. Being hunted by a nameless, faceless killer was certainly a much worse prospect than being blackmailed.

Jane had dressed smartly yet sedately for the occasion in one of her plainest gowns, an affair in navy wool trimmed with black military-style frogging. There was no sense in drawing attention to herself, and really she'd been honest with Christopher when she'd told him her wardrobe was sadly lacking. She had an appointment scheduled with Artemis's preferred modiste, Madame Blanchard, at eleven o'clock. Which meant she had plenty of time to get this skullduggery over and done with at Mudie's.

Even though it was still quite early, Mudie's book emporium was a hive of activity when Jane entered. Maids and footmen and other customers were crowded around the main counter and all the bookcases on the ground floor and the level above. Employees armed with books bustled about with an air of efficiency that couldn't be faulted.

Jane was impressed. It made Delaney's Antiquarian Bookshop seem quite a modest affair in comparison. Yet her grandfather catered to a different clientele. Artemis's Gothic romance novels—or to be more precise, Lydia Lovelace's novels (Artemis used a pseudonym)—probably wouldn't be found on Mudie's "select list" of books. It was well known that the proprietor of the library, Charles Mudie, would not stock any title of "questionable character or inferior quality." Novels containing brooding Gothic heroes with seduction on their minds would not be tolerated.

Jane traversed the floor of the library, looking for the section where Charles Dickens's books were kept. Her blackmailer had to be lurking nearby somewhere, hidden in plain sight, watching and waiting for her, poised to grab the book Jane was to leave the money in. If he or she wasn't, there was a very good chance someone else might pick up the book. It was a huge risk to take.

This will be over soon, Jane reminded herself firmly as she scanned the shelves searching for a copy of *The Pickwick Papers*. Strange how last time—when the stranger had demanded only twenty-five pounds—she'd also placed the money in another of Dickens's novels, *Bleak House*.

There, at the end of a shelf at her eye level, was Dickens's book. Her blackmailer mustn't be overly tall considering Jane could reach the volume easily. Every sense on high alert, her skin prickling beneath her wool gown, Jane imagined she *was* being watched as she slid the book from the shelf and placed an envelope containing the fifty pounds inside the front cover. Then she very carefully pushed the book back in place and stepped away. To her left was an enormous marble column and then a passageway leading to another room, but no one appeared to be lingering in the shadows. To her right were several women, all in bonnets and coats, heads down, perusing books, and a little farther along was a tall gentleman with a monocle and a shiny top hat pulled low on his brow. Perhaps he sensed she was staring, as he cocked his head in her direction and raised a quizzical brow. Jane offered him a weak smile, then turned away to her left.

If she ducked behind the column for a moment or two and then peeked around it...

"Jane!"

She swung around and there, standing right behind her, was her friend Lucy, the Countess of Kyle, as pretty as a picture in blue silk, her face framed by flaxen curls.

"What...what are you doing here?" Jane stammered. And then she covered her mouth with her hand. "Oh, I'm so sorry, how inexcusably rude that sounded. I was startled because I wasn't expecting to see you." Before Lucy could say a word, Jane grasped her by the elbow and began to usher her over to the next set of bookshelves on the other side of the marble column. "Let's move somewhere quieter so we can chat." If Jane didn't retreat in time, her blackmailer wouldn't collect the money and then...and then her scandalous secret would be exposed to the world. She couldn't risk such a disastrous outcome.

When they were safely concealed, Jane angled herself in such a way that if she peered around Lucy's shoulder she might be able to catch a glimpse—

"I was visiting the Banksian Herbarium at the British Museum across the street," began Lucy. "I needed to check on something for the paper on Scottish medicinal herbs that I'm writing, and when I exited the building I saw you come in here. Are you borrowing anything interesting? I'm afraid I let my subscription to Mudie's lapse long ago and..." Lucy frowned, her lavender-blue eyes shadowed with concern. "Are you all right, Jane? You look a trifle...unsettled."

Jane attempted to affect a carefree laugh. "Oh, I'm fine. Really. I'm just..." And then she frowned. Someone who looked vaguely familiar had walked behind Lucy. A woman she couldn't quite place. And then a chill snaked its way down her spine as it dawned on her who it might be. "Lucy, do you remember the governess who used to work for Dominic before he wed Artemis? That horrid, spiteful creature who threatened to expose Artemis's authorial identity? Is that her over at the main counter? In a black cloak and bonnet?"

Lucy turned her head ever so slightly and cast the woman a discreet look over her shoulder. "Perhaps..." she said, turning back to face Jane. "I'm not sure, to be honest. I only caught a brief glimpse of her that one time we had a Byronic Book Club meeting at Dartmoor House. When the duke was in such a terrible state. If Artemis were here, she would be able to confirm it."

"Hmmm," said Jane. "I could have sworn Artemis told us that Dominic's sister, Lady Northam, had found the governess another position with a family way up north. In Liverpool or somewhere like that."

"Yes, I think you might be right," said Lucy. She shrugged. "Perhaps she found another position back in London? It's been over nine months since all that horrid business happened."

"Yes, perhaps... In any event, I think we should inform Artemis. I recall the governess had to sign some sort of contract when she was dismissed to ensure that she wouldn't make trouble for Artemis in the future. But I rather think Artemis should know she's back in Town."

"Yes, I agree," said Lucy. "With her academic ladies' college doing so well, Artemis can ill afford any sort of scandal getting out. Aside from that"—Lucy lowered her voice—"it wouldn't be good for the baby if anything untoward happened and caused her an undue amount of stress."

Jane glanced back toward the counter, but the woman in question had disappeared into the crowd. "Sharp," she said. "I think her name was Miss Sharp."

"You're right," said Lucy. "It was. I mean it is. Rosalind Sharp."

As they exited Mudie's arm in arm, Jane did wonder if Miss Rosalind Sharp *might* be her blackmailer. It wasn't as though the woman hadn't tried something similar when she'd coerced Artemis into deserting the duke, her fiancé. But Jane couldn't imagine the governess breaking into Delaney's Bookshop in the middle of the night. A window had been smashed, and according to the police officer who'd investigated the crime, the lock on the front door had been bashed and broken with something heavy like a hammer. So had the lock on the workroom drawer where Jane's journal had been hidden. Jane couldn't see Miss Sharp, a short, slight woman, doing something so brazen and violent.

When Lucy heard where Jane was headed next, she offered to accompany her to Madame Blanchard's. "We can take my carriage. It's over there on the corner of Hart Street. Perhaps we could also send word to Artemis so she can join us too," she said. "I'm sure she would love to help you try on dresses."

Jane laughed. "I'm sure she wouldn't. You know she hates visiting the modiste even more than I do. But I would value her opinion as well as yours. Otherwise I'll order a surfeit of green and brown gowns and not much else."

"Well, we certainly can't have that," said Lucy. "Although green is your color." She caught Jane's bare hand and raised it so that the weak winter sunlight made her emerald engagement ring glitter. "It seems your duke recognizes that fact too. He has good taste." Her smile was sly as she added, "I cannot wait to meet him. Talk about Town is your husband is quite handsome."

"He is," said Jane. "I'll be sure to organize a dinner in lieu of a wedding breakfast very soon." She'd yet to broach the topic with Christopher. No doubt a large gathering would be difficult for him to navigate. To keep track of everyone when one couldn't recall their faces would be altogether taxing. But perhaps an intimate dinner with only Artemis, Lucy, and their respective husbands would be manageable. Will, Lucy's husband, with his Scots accent would be easy to identify in conversation. And Lucy had blond hair and Artemis had red. Christopher might even find it useful to form an acquaintance with Will, who had strong connections with Scotland Yard. If Mr. O'Connor the detective couldn't come up with any useful information, perhaps Will's former colleagues could. But Jane was getting ahead of herself. "I'll talk to Christopher and let you know."

"I look forward to it," said Lucy as one of her footmen handed Jane into the Earl of Kyle's carriage. "Otherwise I'll be forced to creep up and down Eaton Square hoping to catch a glimpse of him through the window."

"Oh goodness, Lucy," Jane said with a laugh as her friend took the seat opposite her. "We cannot have that. And do not be a stranger. Feel free to call on Roxby House anytime. Christopher is very charming."

Perhaps even too *charming*, thought Jane as the carriage moved off. So charming she might be in very real danger of losing her heart to him. And she didn't want that. Not if he'd never feel the same way. She'd believed him when he'd told her that he couldn't promise her love.

In some ways, it would be better if she fell pregnant almost straightaway, because then she wouldn't be in Christopher's arms every night. His lovemaking was far too addictive. No doubt it would be hard to give that up even when she was with child. But they'd both agreed that they would go their separate ways and live apart from each other once she was increasing.

But Christopher might still need you to be his eyes, Jane reminded herself. Until the person who wanted him dead was caught, she would stay with him, no matter the danger.

No matter the cost. It was the right thing to do.

Chapter Eighteen

THE NEXT DAY, JANE'S COURSES ARRIVED ALONG WITH another letter from her blackmailer, this time demanding one hundred pounds.

Not knowing its significance, her grandfather had sent the innocuous-looking envelope along to Roxby House. As Jane sat in her own bed, feeling sad and sorry for herself because of cramps and the fact she wasn't with child—despite all of the times she and Christopher had made love—her mood only descended further into the doldrums upon seeing the horrid words and even more excessive demand in the cursed letter.

> *You didn't do exactly as instructed, Miss Delaney.*
> *Or should I now say the Duchess of Roxby?*
> *You waited and watched for me, and for that mistake you must pay a price.*
> *It's obvious you have even more to lose given your recent elevation, and therefore much more to give.*
> *The only way to safeguard your reputation is to pay me an additional one hundred pounds. I'll expect it a fortnight from now, on the 7th of March. At 10:00 a.m. precisely.*
> *Place it in Mr. Dickens's book Oliver Twist. If you dare look for me again, I will not hesitate to twist the thumbscrews on you and expose every vile thing I know.*
> *Whether I do relinquish your filthy book or not is entirely dependent on you.*

This time, do what I've explicitly instructed, or your doom will be upon you.
There will be no second chances.

To Jane, it appeared her blackmailer would never be appeased. Considering whoever it was knew that she was now a duchess, it seemed that he or she would keep milking Jane's money for the foreseeable future. She'd been so very foolish to think her last payment would be enough.

To Jane's relief, Christopher was solicitous of her condition and her melancholic mood over the next week. Of course, he didn't know the whole reason why she was feeling so dejected. As much as she wanted to confide in him, something inside her held her back.

Establishing intimacy in the bedroom was all well and good—and Jane certainly had no complaints in that regard. But if she told him the truth about her blackmailer, would Christopher decide to wash his hands of her sooner rather than later, even before she was with child? Would he banish her to the country to thwart her pamphlet-publishing scheme? She had no idea if he would be an ally or not.

Yes, it worried her that she was abusing Christopher's trust by not being honest with him from the outset. By the same token, Jane couldn't even be honest with her best friends.

As always, she wanted to fix her own mistakes. But perhaps this time she might need to accept that she couldn't.

As the week dragged on, Jane's courses eased but her anxiety about how to rid herself of her blackmailer didn't. To keep her mind busy—she couldn't work at Delaney's anymore and Christopher had so many staff on hand at Roxby House she barely had to lift a finger—she began to catalog all the books in Roxby House's library.

Aside from a visit midweek from her irate mother when she'd discovered she'd been ousted from the Whisteria Club by Lady Aylesbury, Jane saw no one but Roxby House's servants and Christopher. Well, when he wasn't up to his elbows in paperwork she saw her husband, usually at the dinner table. Lucy was busy arranging her research trip to warmer climes such as Mauritius with Will—they were due to depart in late spring—and Artemis was heavily involved with overseeing the management of her academic college.

As the seventh of March drew inexorably closer, Jane knew she would have to act to catch the perpetrator. Money was no longer an issue. She could easily obtain the one hundred pounds that had been demanded. But if she handed it over, who was to say there wouldn't be another demand? And then another?

She couldn't go on like this. She'd have to swallow her pride and ask for help. But whom could she ask? Whom could she trust? Who was skilled enough and would be discreet enough to help her?

The answer came to her when Christopher asked her to sit in on another meeting with Jack O'Connor. As the Irish private detective delivered a succinct summary of his investigation so far, Jane's mind began to buzz with the idea that perhaps she could enlist the man's help herself. In a quiet moment when Christopher wasn't around...

"Jane?"

She jumped in her seat and almost dropped her tea. "Pardon me, Your Grace," she said. "I was woolgathering." She gave an apologetic smile. "I'm afraid I've lost track of what was being discussed."

Christopher was studying her with a slightly inquisitive gaze. "Mr. O'Connor was just saying that Harry Wexford, the chap I trounced at cards, has unfortunately met with an untimely end in a tavern in Islington named the Blue Anchor."

"Aye. To be sure," said Mr. O'Connor. "He'd been attendin' a rat pit match—"

"Rat pit match?" repeated Jane.

Christopher shot Jack O'Connor a narrow-eyed look before turning his attention back to her. "It's a cruel blood sport involving dogs, often terriers, catching rats. Bets are placed on which dog can kill the most rats released into a pit in a certain amount of time."

A shiver of horror prickled across Jane's skin. "How utterly barbaric."

"Agreed," said Christopher. "It's a sport that should be banned, if you ask me. Mr. O'Connor was saying that Wexford got into a dispute over the result of one of these so-called matches and was fatally injured in the ensuing brawl. The police haven't been able to identify a particular perpetrator because so many men joined in the affray."

"It was right before Christmas," continued O'Connor. "Hardly anyone knows about it because Sir Gideon has done a good job of havin' it all hushed up to save the family from further scandal. Word about Town in some quarters is that the baronet is quite a proud man and he'd had enough of his son's wild ways and habit of livin' beyond his means."

"How awful," murmured Jane. "And tragic."

"Terribly so," said Christopher. A shadow passed across his countenance. "And I cannot help but feel responsible in some way. I was the one who bled Harry Wexford dry at the gaming table."

"You can't know the background and history of everyone you come across," said Jane. "Surely the establishment Brooks, wasn't it?—bears some responsibility too for permitting such high-stakes play. And the other members who perhaps knew that Harry Wexford couldn't afford to lay such a large bet. He must have had friends at the club."

"Perhaps," said Christopher. "In light of Mr. O'Connor's findings, though, it would seem that Harry Wexford wasn't involved in the last two attempts to do away with me. Which leaves Neville Phelps or—"

"Your former fiancée's husband, Simon Cosgrove," finished Jane. She didn't want to be a jealous sort of wife, but she did wonder what sort of woman would seek out the man she'd jilted after he'd inherited a title and a great fortune. A married woman no less. Daisy seemed rather mercenary.

But then, you married Christopher for his money too, Jane reminded herself. *At least at first. You haven't married for love.*

Mr. O'Connor was speaking again. "I've also managed to track down Simon Cosgrove and his wife. They currently reside in Cavendish Square. He works in mercantile insurance and is on the board of the North British Insurance Company. They have offices in Waterloo Place. Cosgrove"—the Irishman flipped over a page in his journal—"has a mistress who resides in rooms in Chelsea, and it appears he visits her once a week. So I suppose it's not the happiest of marriages." O'Connor looked up at Jane and then winced. "My apologies if I've been, er"—he cleared his throat—"too blunt mentionin' Cosgrove's mistress, Your Grace."

"No, it's quite all right," Jane said. "I'd rather know the details than be kept in the dark." She caught Christopher's eye. "I wonder if that's why Daisy propositioned you. If her husband has engaged a mistress, perhaps she's noticed his waning interest. But surely that would mean Cosgrove is *less* likely to be put out if his wife also has a wandering eye and therefore less likely to be concerned about you being a rival for his wife's affections."

Christopher shrugged. "It's not uncommon for men to be hypocritical in that regard. He might feel that he can tomcat about, but also believes that his wife should remain faithful."

Jane regarded her husband across the expanse of his desk.

Did Christopher feel that way? He'd promised not to host any more wild parties and to remain faithful...at least until she was with child. But what if he'd lied? Did he possess double standards? And what would happen after she was pregnant? After she'd produced his heir and they went their separate ways? Would he engage a mistress?

Jane really didn't want to think about him taking another woman to bed. Of giving someone else the pleasure he gave her. Because if she examined her feelings too closely, she might have to face the fact that she'd begun to care about her husband a little too much. Despite her resolve to protect her heart...

But, she reminded herself sternly, what was most important at present was catching whoever it was who was trying to kill Christopher. They'd barely begun as a married couple, and unless they made any headway Jane might be a widow before too long.

The very idea of that made Jane's stomach tumble. She needed to put her petty fears and jealousies aside—yes, she was jealous of the idea of pretty blond Daisy Cosgrove pursuing her husband—and instead help Christopher just as she'd promised.

She turned her attention back to Mr. O'Connor, who was telling Christopher about the Cosgroves' plans over the next few days. "Simon Cosgrove plans to take his wife to the Royal Italian Opera House for a performance of *Il trovatore* tomorrow night. It's the last performance of the season before Lent." The detective grinned. "One of the Cosgroves' footmen is most accommodating with supplying information for a few extra coins."

"Excellent work," said Christopher. He caught Jane's gaze. "I think we shall also go to the opera tomorrow night. I have a box at the Royal Italian Opera House. And if we happen to bump into Simon Cosgrove and Daisy"—he shrugged—"so be it."

"You're not worried about coming face-to-face with Simon Cosgrove?"

"I'd rather provoke a reaction in a public place than a dark alley," said Christopher. "If I poke the bear the right way, he might slip up and say something to incriminate himself."

Jane drew a breath. "I have a suggestion too. I think it would be a good idea for me to find out what Simon Cosgrove looks like. So I can keep an eye out for him tomorrow at the theater, or on any other occasion. His Grace doesn't have a photograph of him, but do you, Mr. O'Connor?"

When the answer was no, Jane caught her husband's eye. "Perhaps I should go to Waterloo Place with Mr. O'Connor this afternoon. Then he could point out Mr. Cosgrove to me as he's leaving his office at the North British Insurance Company. At a pinch, I could even venture inside and ask to speak with him."

Christopher frowned. "That sounds rather dangerous, Jane."

"We'll take an unmarked carriage. Even a hansom cab. I'll wear widow's weeds and a heavy veil. Cosgrove won't be able to see my face properly."

Her husband tilted his head. "Very well," he said, but Jane could still see a shadow of apprehension clouding his blue eyes. Although when his gaze flicked to Jack O'Connor, Jane wondered if he had concerns about her venturing out with the private detective on her own. She could have offered to take a servant with her, but she didn't want anyone loyal to the duke to overhear what *she* was going to ask Mr. O'Connor to do.

"Of course, Your Grace," said O'Connor. "I'd be more than happy to escort Her Grace to Waterloo Place." The detective checked his notes, then looked up. "The only other thing I have to report is that I'm still tryin' to track down the whereabouts of Neville Phelps. Since his dishonorable discharge, he seems to have disappeared. His family hails from Tewkesbury in Gloucestershire, so I've approached one of my contacts in the local constabulary who says he'll make further discreet inquiries. And of course I will keep lookin.'"

Once the meeting had concluded, Jane repaired to her suite and with Elsie's help changed into a black taffeta gown, black bonnet, and heavy black veil. Before she descended the main stairs to meet Mr. O'Connor, Christopher appeared on the landing. Without a word, he caught her in his arms, threw back her veil, and kissed her. Hard.

It was a possessive kiss, full of barely restrained hunger.

A branding. There was no doubt Mr. O'Connor and the footman on duty would have seen everything if they'd glanced up the staircase to the floor above. Could her husband be jealous of the fact she was about to go out alone with the young and attractive private detective?

Never in her life had she inspired such passion in anyone before. It was a novel sensation. Being wanted so fiercely. Rightly or wrongly, Jane thought she rather liked it.

"Take care, Jane," Christopher murmured when he released her from his embrace.

"I will," she promised, her voice hushed and breathless. "I want to catch this perpetrator so very badly too. But I wouldn't worry too much. I'm sure Simon Cosgrove will barely notice me. If I do happen to be quizzed by him or anyone else, I'll use my mother's new surname. I'll be Mrs. Jane Pevensey."

"A very good idea." Christopher stroked her cheek. His eyes were filled with smoldering heat and his voice was low and soft as he added, "May I come to your bed tonight?"

"Of course." She smiled softly, seeking to reassure. "If you don't, I'll be sneaking into yours."

He gave her a swift kiss. "Hurry back." And then his expression grew serious. "I mean that. I'm not used to worrying about the safety of anyone else other than myself. It's only just occurred to me that you might become a target too."

"Me?"

"Yes, you, Jane." Christopher pressed a hand to her torso. Even through all the layers of her clothing—even her boned corset—Jane fancied she could feel his heat. "You're my wife and before long will be the mother of my heir. And that might place you in danger. I can't explain it. It's a feeling I have. That perhaps the person trying to hurt me might strike out at you too. Perhaps as an act of vengeance. Even just to spite me. I don't know what his motive is yet or how unhinged he might be." He shrugged a wide shoulder. "Call it a soldier's intuition. A gut instinct. Over the years I've learned to trust it. And I can't ignore it."

Jane shivered. She hadn't considered that by marrying Christopher, she'd inadvertently placed herself in the sights of a killer. It was an unnerving thought. "I promise I'll be careful," she whispered.

"I know you will." Christopher lowered her veil, and when Jane descended the stairs, she fancied her husband's eyes were upon her.

He was worried about her safety. That notion was even more fascinating to Jane than the idea he might be jealous. And, in a way, terrifying. Because it suggested her husband was beginning to care about *her*, not only what she could do for him.

And she had no idea what to do with that information. Not one whit.

Chapter Nineteen

THE OFFICES OF THE NORTH BRITISH INSURANCE COMPANY were located at 8 Waterloo Place. Jack O'Connor directed the hansom cab driver to stop in nearby Pall Mall, and then after he leapt out, he handed Jane down.

It was late afternoon, and the thoroughfare was aswarm with traffic. Both carriages and pedestrians jostled for space in the rapidly dwindling light.

"I hope we're not too late to catch a glimpse of Mr. Cosgrove," said Jane. On the way to Waterloo Place, Mr. O'Connor had described the man as being six feet tall and lean with brown eyes, medium-brown hair, and neatly trimmed muttonchops.

"He's due to finish at five o'clock, and his footman claims he's quite a punctual sort of man," said Mr. O'Connor as they crossed the road. "With any luck, we'll spot him as he walks outside. Although…" The detective frowned. "It's so busy, you might not get a good look."

"Perhaps I could wait in the entry hall of the insurance company," said Jane. "It would be quieter in there."

"True," agreed Mr. O'Connor. "I might linger back in the shadows though. It's better for the investigation if Cosgrove doesn't notice I'm watching him."

Jane inclined her head. "Of course. Perhaps you could give me a signal when you see him. Cough or whistle or drop your journal or a pencil."

"I'm a fine whistler." O'Connor winked. "I'll give you a rendition of 'The Rose of Tralee.'"

You're also a fine flirt, thought Jane. But she thought Mr. O'Connor was harmless enough. He escorted her into the lobby of the North British Insurance Company and Jane hovered by a marble column, not far from the bottom of a divided staircase of polished oak. The doorman seemed disinterested in both her and Mr. O'Connor. No doubt he was waiting for the end of the working day and keen to go home. The detective had retreated to one end of the chamber and appeared to be engrossed in studying the portraits of poker-faced gentlemen who were probably on the company's board.

There was a walnut longcase clock by the stairs, and when it was precisely five minutes to five, another woman entered the lobby in a flurry of blue silk. She was pretty with a heart-shaped face and clusters of pale-blond curls framing her rosy cheeks.

Jane recognized her immediately. It was Daisy Cosgrove.

The doorman greeted her by name. "Your husband shouldn't be too long. Always on time, he is."

"Yes. Yes, he is," said Daisy with a sweeter-than-spun-sugar smile. As she turned away from the doorman—a portly, older gentleman—she rolled her eyes, but then her gaze grew keener as it settled on Mr. O'Connor's back. It was clear she was admiring the snug fit of the Irishman's coat and the width of his shoulders. Not that Jane could blame her. His shoulders were rather impressive. Not quite as impressive as Christopher's, of course, but noteworthy nonetheless.

Perhaps Daisy sensed that she was being watched as her interest transferred to Jane. Her bright-blue gaze wandered over Jane's widow's weeds before lingering on her veiled face, as though she was trying to discern Jane's features. Even though Jane trusted Daisy wouldn't be able to see much through the heavy lace, she bent her head and pretended to dig about for something in her reticule. By the time she'd retrieved a lawn kerchief, Daisy Cosgrove had refocused her attention upon the staircase. Beneath her bell-like skirts, Jane fancied the woman tapped her toe.

A pair of starchy-looking gentlemen descended the stairs, and Mr. O'Connor turned his head but didn't whistle. Another elderly fellow appeared on the landing at the stroke of five, and a few seconds later, a tall brown-haired man wearing a fierce frown along with a top hat followed.

Mr. O'Connor began to softly whistle a pretty tune as Daisy's countenance broke into a smile. "Simon," she called as her husband made his way toward her. Despite the fact his handsome face was marred with a scowl, she continued, "I finished my shopping early, so I thought I'd surprise you by stopping by. We can share a hansom cab home."

Simon Cosgrove snorted as his wife took his arm. "Run out of credit on your account at the milliner's and the modiste's again, did you?"

Daisy affected a small tinkling laugh. "Now, now. You know I want to look my best tomorrow night when we go to the theater. It's not *every* day that one gets invited to share a private box…"

Her voice trailed away as the pair exited the building and were absorbed by the gloaming and the throng of pedestrians. Jack O'Connor sauntered over to Jane. "It seems like there might be trouble in paradise still," he observed quietly.

"I agree," replied Jane. "Simon Cosgrove is a rather forbidding character, isn't he?"

"Aye. I'll be sure to make further discreet inquiries about the Cosgroves' finances too," said Mr. O'Connor. "And whose theater box they're sharing. Would you like to return home now, Your Grace?"

"Yes, thank you. I would."

Once they were safely installed in another hansom cab, Jane mustered the courage to broach the topic she'd been wanting to raise with the Irishman all afternoon. Even though nerves twisted her belly into knots, she inhaled a steadying breath and began. "Mr. O'Connor, I know my husband has employed you to investigate who's behind these terrible attacks on his person, but..." She swallowed as she lifted her veil. "It seems I have a problem of my own that I would like sorted out sooner rather than later. A problem that His Grace knows nothing about, and I would prefer to keep it that way. Before you say anything, I know I'm placing you in a difficult situation by asking you to keep quiet and maintain my confidence. And of course I will pay you for your trouble..."

In the dim interior of the hansom cab, Mr. O'Connor's eyes gleamed. "You can trust me, Your Grace," he said quietly. "I won't say a word to your husband."

"Thank you." Jane felt her cheeks grow hot, but she trusted the shadows would hide her embarrassment as she shared the details of her problem. Well, *most* of the details. She didn't disclose what her pamphlet series would be about. Only that her journal contained private information she didn't want to be disclosed to the public.

The detective's expression was thoughtful. "And you have no idea who this person might be? Who might bear you a grudge?"

"None at all," said Jane.

"The handwritten blackmail letters you've been sent, though, they would contain some sort of clues. The language used sounds quite vitriolic for one thing, but what else is of note? Is the handwriting neat or messy? Masculine or feminine? What sort of paper is it written on? Does the person seem educated or not?"

Jane frowned at the passing traffic outside the cab's window as she pictured the handwriting in her mind. "I cannot tell the sex of the writer, but the script is neat. Whoever it is has good literacy skills and, I would venture, a degree of intelligence. There are shades of dark humor and wordplay within the text. And the paper and envelopes are of decent quality. There is no postmark, so I assume the notes have been posted through the letter box at Delaney's by the blackmailer."

Mr. O'Connor's mouth tilted with a wry smile. "So it could be anyone, really."

"Yes," agreed Jane. "Although…" She frowned. "When I left the last deposit at Mudie's, I thought I caught a glimpse of someone I knew. Not very well, though. But this woman—a governess named Miss Sharp—threatened to ruin the reputation of one of my good friends if she didn't comply with her demands. She wasn't trying to extort money, though. It was…more of a manipulation of the situation to suit her own ends. She didn't think my friend was a suitable fiancé for her employer."

"I see," said the detective. "Do you think that this woman might be behind this blackmail plot? It's been my experience that criminals often use a similar modus operandi when committing crimes."

"I'm not sure. Perhaps," said Jane. "I dismissed the idea initially because whoever stole my journal broke into my grandfather's bookstore. I simply can't imagine Miss Sharp doing such a thing."

"But you said that whoever it was didn't take much. Tell me, Your Grace, would this Miss Sharp know you had a secret to hide?"

Jane sighed. "I shouldn't think so, but from what I've heard, she was the sort of person who was quick to judge others for not being 'moral' enough. So perhaps she could have formed an unfavorable opinion of me simply based on my friendship with a woman she despised. I was never formally introduced to Miss Sharp though. In fact, I only caught a glimpse of her once when I was visiting the house where she worked. When her perfidy was exposed, she was dismissed by her employer and moved on to another governess position."

"So this Miss Sharp isn't wealthy. It's feasible she might need money if she's fallen on hard times for one reason or another. Or she could be seeking to take advantage of you. Especially now you're a duchess."

"I suppose," conceded Jane.

"Regardless of whether your blackmailer *is* this Miss Sharp or someone else, I think it's important that we lay a trap next time you need to make a payment." Mr. O'Connor leaned forward in his seat. "I know you are reluctant to confide in your husband, Your Grace, but is there anyone else you can confide in to enlist his or her help? Your friends that you've mentioned? If they know Miss Sharp, they might be willing to act as lookouts at Mudie's. The more pairs of eyes we have, the better."

Jane returned her gaze to the streets. The gas lamps glowed in the gathering gloom, bringing light to the dark, teeming streets. She needed some light. Some relief from the sense of impending doom dogging her heels. And from the guilt for not being totally honest with those she cared about.

For lying to her husband.

"I'll consider it," she said at length. And she would. She *had* to. Up until now, she'd been adamant that she'd solve this problem on her own. But her practical streak would have to concede that *maybe* she couldn't. After all, that's why she'd broached the subject with the private detective. "How much do I owe you for your services, Mr. O'Connor?" she added. "I'm afraid I don't know your rate."

"Nothing at all, Your Grace. Your husband pays me well, and staking out Mudie's on March 7 won't take up a great deal of my time."

Jane frowned. "Are you sure? I have the means to pay you."

"I'm sure you do, Your Grace. But as I said, I'm sure your issue will be resolved quickly."

Jane could but pray that his assessment was correct.

Chapter Twenty

WHEN JANE ARRIVED BACK AT ROXBY HOUSE, MRS. Harrigan the housekeeper approached her as she began to scale the stairs, heading for her suite.

"Forgive me for waylaying you, Your Grace, but I wanted to check with you about one of tonight's courses." The matron grimaced. "The turbot I'd promised for the fish course isn't quite up to snuff, so I wondered if you and His Grace would mind if Cook substituted it with plaice. The lemon, caper, and parsley butter sauce will complement it equally as well."

"That all sounds perfectly fine. I trust your judgment," said Jane as she removed her bonnet and veil.

"And eight o'clock still suits?"

"It does." Jane didn't see the need to alter Christopher's established routines. His comfort was important to her, especially at a difficult time like this. "Where is His Grace, by the way?" The house was awfully quiet. At this hour, Christopher could often be found in the drawing room, playing the pianoforte.

"He's in the arms room, Your Grace," replied the housekeeper. "With Featherstone."

"The arms room?"

"Yes, Your Grace. It's off the billiards room. But it's hard to spot. There's a jib door hidden in the wood paneling, and it's usually locked on account of all the weaponry kept inside. His Grace likes to train in there. Fencing and boxing and the like."

"I see," said Jane. No wonder her husband's physique was

so superb. But as a military man, she supposed he was used to being physically active.

"I'll show you where it is on my way back to the kitchen."

"Thank you." While she wouldn't have minded changing out of her widow's weeds, Jane wanted to see Christopher. To let him know that she was home and to share her account of her visit to Waterloo Place.

She also couldn't ignore the nagging sense that her husband *had* been worried about her spending time alone with Jack O'Connor. She wanted to reassure him that she had eyes only for him.

Daisy had jilted him for Simon Cosgrove, and Jane imagined that being rejected might still pain him. Miles Dempster's rejection had certainly cut her deeply. So much so that even after a decade, the wound had never quite healed. Jane knew that it was hard to trust again—indeed, to even think about loving again—following such a devastating blow. Just like her, Christopher was no doubt resistant to the idea of letting down his walls and risking his heart a second time.

After Mrs. Harrigan pointed out the jib door at the back of the billiards room and how to press the concealed latch to open it, Jane bid the housekeeper adieu. As she lingered by the door, she could hear a faint pounding tattoo. A steady rhythm of muffled thuds punctuated with the occasional grunt.

Good Lord… Someone was getting a drubbing and a half. *Was* her husband upset about the fact she'd gone out with Jack O'Connor on her own after all?

Jane drew a breath and opened the door without knocking.

Gas wall sconces illuminated a large airy chamber with a parquetry wood floor, not unlike a dance floor in a ballroom. Weaponry—swords and pistols and rifles of all descriptions— were mounted upon the wood-paneled walls or displayed in glass-fronted cabinets. A row of enormous mirrors that alternated with velvet-curtained windows lined another side of the room. The only furniture was a leather settee positioned by one of the mirrors. But Jane's attention wasn't claimed by any of these things.

No, her gaze was riveted to the sight of Christopher, clad in nothing but buckskin breeches, rhythmically throwing bare-knuckle punches at an enormous leather bag—a "punching" bag she supposed—that was suspended from the ceiling. Featherstone stood behind, holding the bag steady. The valet needed to, given the force and speed with which his master was delivering each blow. It was a veritable barrage. If it wasn't for the cloth wrapped around Christopher's knuckles, she imagined they would be bloodied and bruised.

Jane cleared her throat. "Your Grace..." she began, then forgot what she was going to say next. Because how could one concentrate on finding words and formulating sentences when faced with the spectacle of a shirtless man with the physique of a Viking warrior going through his paces? Christopher's sleek muscles, glistening with perspiration, bulged and flexed and even rippled with his movements. His athletic display was violent and elegant and frightening and beautiful all at once.

As she stood there gaping like a hen-wit, Christopher stopped beating the punching bag and swiped a hand through his sweat-damp hair, raking it away from his eyes. His gaze connected with hers. "Jane," he said, his broad chest rising and falling with the increased pace of his breathing. "You're back. I'm glad."

"Yes..." Perhaps he wasn't annoyed then. Her gaze darted to Featherstone, and Christopher's did too.

"That'll be all for now," he said to his valet. "I'll be up shortly to get ready for dinner."

Featherstone handed his master a towel, which Christopher wiped over his face then draped around his shoulders. "I'll arrange yer bath, Yer Grace," said the valet, and then he quit the room.

Once the jib door shut behind him, Christopher turned his attention back to Jane. His gaze was assessing. Perhaps even hard. "Did you have success?"

Jane swallowed. Oh, she couldn't read if her husband was miffed with her or the situation. Whatever the case was, it was clear that Christopher was strung as tightly as a bowstring that was about to snap. Or a lion about to pounce. He was all rigidly coiled muscle and wariness and calculation.

Her skin prickled with awareness as she moved closer to the center of the room where he stood. "Yes," she said. "I saw Simon Cosgrove. And Daisy as well." And then she told Christopher about the Cosgroves' less-than-amicable interaction. "Mr. O'Connor mentioned that he would look into their finances a bit more."

"Fair enough." Christopher began to unwind the strip of fabric from one of his hands. "Although I doubt my death would have any effect on the Cosgroves' fortunes."

"I've thought about that. Being in financial difficulty might be another cause of tension and dissatisfaction within the marriage," Jane ventured. "If Daisy is spending more than they can afford and her husband feels she is ungrateful, if she's comparing him to you, perhaps Simon Cosgrove feels emasculated. And that might make him angry. More likely to lash out at you."

"You make good points." Christopher crossed the room and tossed the length of fabric onto the leather settee where his discarded clothing was draped. Then he set about unwrapping his other hand. His movements were unhurried. Purposeful.

When he was done, he looked up, and Jane swore his eyes

were fairly smoldering with heat. "It will be interesting to see what sort of information we can glean tomorrow night. Jealousy can make a man do all sorts of unexpected things. Feel unexpected things…"

Jane fancied the air surrounding them began to crackle with a strange energy. There was a hushed expectancy. An excruciating yet exquisite tension that made Jane's pulse race. "Yes… I'd say that's true for a woman too. Daisy Cosgrove is exceedingly pretty and I…" She released a tight breath. "I would own to feeling a trifle envious of her attractiveness."

Christopher's brows plunged into a frown, and he set his hands on his lean hips. "You're not worried that I still hold some affection for her, are you? Because I don't. The woman might be pretty, but she's also vapid and inconstant and vindictive. I have no idea what I saw in her."

Jane nodded. She would take her husband at his word. She had no reason *not* to trust him about this. Just as he had no reason not to trust her when she was with Jack O'Connor. And he needed to hear that, along with the fact she no longer cared for Miles Dempster.

"Christopher, I want you to know that I no longer have any affection for my former fiancé either," she said, solemnity weighting her words. "You can trust me to remain loyal to you. Fidelity is important to me. I'm your wife now. I would never betray you."

Christopher held her gaze. "I believe you." He tossed the towel that had been draped about his shoulders onto the floor, then prowled toward her. "I know I said I'd wait to come to your bed tonight, Jane," he continued, his voice a low, deep purr that she felt all the way to her toes, "but I have need of you now. What do you say to that?"

Jane swallowed, and when her own voice emerged, it was

husky with desire. "I will do whatever you want me to do, Your Grace." She meant it. She was happy to play along. She might not trust her husband with her heart, but she trusted him to bring her sexual pleasure.

Christopher halted a few feet away from her and crossed his arms over his chest. His eyes glinted with carnal intent as he said, "I don't like seeing you in black widow's weeds, Jane. Take off your gown."

"Very well," she whispered. She raised her hands to her gown's collar, and then she slowly slid the jet buttons securing the bodice undone. Christopher followed her every movement, and when the dress at last lay in a pool of black taffeta at her feet, his mouth twitched with a smile.

"I don't like those petticoats either," he said. "They hide your deliciously long legs."

Jane slid a fingertip along the low neckline of her corset. Her breathing had quickened, and her breasts strained against the garment's confining cage. Her taut nipples ached to be free. She decided she liked this wicked game. Not only was it thrilling and arousing, but she also felt powerful. Even though Christopher was telling her what to do, she suspected he was very much caught in *her* thrall. Especially when she licked her lips and then pressed her teeth into her bottom lip. The man's gaze was riveted to her mouth. "Would you like me to remove my corset too?" she murmured.

"At once," Christopher said sternly. Although considering the way his mouth kept hitching at the corner, Jane knew his apparent display of displeasure was nothing but an act.

"Of course." She loosened the tapes holding her crinoline cage and petticoats in place, and once they were also on the floor, she released the hooks and eyes securing her corset. The garment sagged open, and when Christopher caught sight of her nipples and the way they impudently poked against the thin lawn of her shift, he lost his battle with suppressing his smile. It was wide and wolfish and made Jane's stomach flutter with excitement.

"Your chemise will have to go too," he commanded. "And your drawers."

Jane grasped the hem of her shift and removed it in one movement. And then she loosened the ribbon securing her drawers and pushed them down her legs. Apart from her stockings and kid half-boots, she was now completely and unashamedly naked. Judging by the slickness between her thighs, she was also undeniably aroused.

And so was Christopher. His impressive erection tented the front of his breeches.

Jane swallowed. "What of my stockings?" she whispered, reaching for one of the ribbon garters. "Shall I take them off too?"

"No, those can stay on. Along with your shoes."

The lust simmering in her blood made Jane bold, and she jutted a hip. "What now, Your Grace?"

Heat flared in her husband's blue eyes as his gaze slowly wandered over her. It lingered on her breasts and the dark triangle at the apex of her thighs before returning to her face. "Go over to the settee."

Jane stepped out of her puddled clothing and crossed to the leather chair where Christopher's own discarded clothes were draped. One of the mirrors captured her reflection and her breath hitched at the sight of herself. So brazen and not like the Jane of old at all. The Jane who drifted around the edges of ballrooms and in the shadows of bookcases. The woman who men glanced at, then hastily looked away. The Jane who was barely ever regarded, let alone desired. That Jane was gone.

This Jane, the one she could see looking back at herself, the one Christopher was staring at so hungrily, was confident and beautiful. Her cheeks were flushed and her green eyes gleamed. Her peaked nipples were a deep berry-red. When she reached the settee, she turned to glance back over her shoulder at Christopher, who was padding after her with predatory intent.

"Shall I sit?" she asked but her husband shook his head.

"No. I have other ideas, my dark-haired temptress." He leaned down and snagged something from the arm of the chair. His black neckcloth. "Hold out your hands," he said in a tone that brooked no argument. When Jane complied, he deftly looped the black silk about her wrists, tethering them together. Then he hauled her bare body against his.

There was no mistaking his rampant arousal now. It prodded into Jane's sex and lower belly as Christopher lashed an arm about her waist and seized her mouth in a fierce kiss. "I want you helpless," he breathed against her lips when he at last came up for air. "Writhing in ecstasy and completely at my mercy. I'm going to take you, and take you some more until you are shuddering and boneless and incoherent with pleasure. Do you understand, Jane?"

"Yes," she whispered. Christopher's eyes were bright, yet his pupils were so dilated Jane thought she might drown in them. In truth, his scent—clean sweat and cologne and leather—threatened to overwhelm her as well. "I'm yours, Christopher. Yours to command. Yours to have. In any way that you want."

"Do you mean that?" he growled. "Truly?"

She nodded, breathless. "Yes."

Almost immediately, Christopher spun her around, and Jane found herself bent over the stuffed arm of the chair. Her bound hands landed on the seat, and she had to brace her elbows to stop herself from falling too far forward.

"Spread your legs, Jane. Open for me."

She did. When she turned her head to the side, she could see over the low back of the settee to the mirror...and she was mesmerized by the entire erotic tableau. Her naked torso, bare derriere, and stocking-clad legs. Christopher standing behind her, unbuttoning the fall of his breeches and then freeing his engorged cock. He took it in hand and then pressed himself against her buttock cheeks. He was hot and hard and the *feel* of him made Jane want him inside her even more.

Gripping her hip with one hand, Christopher slipped his other hand between her thighs, then groaned when he touched her drenched sex. "Sweet Jesus, Jane. I love how wet you are. So slick. So ready." As he spoke, he stroked her slit, making Jane moan. Her eyes closed, and she curled her fingers into a velvet cushion. Rocked her hips, seeking more contact.

If Christopher would only focus his attention on her clit—

"Look at me," he ordered, and Jane immediately obeyed. Locking eyes with Christopher in the mirror, she watched him suck his glistening fingers quite deliberately, like a man sampling something exquisite. It was shocking and lewd and wicked and the most decadently wonderful thing Jane had ever seen.

"I'd make you come with my mouth," he murmured, his deep voice vibrating with raw need as he fisted his cock again, "but I'm too impatient to have you. A week without you has been too long. An eternity."

"I want you too," she whispered. "Inside me."

A low, purely animal sound like a growl emanated from Christopher's throat as he tilted his hips and pushed his cock between her slippery folds. "A word of warning, I'm not going to be gentle. I'm going to fuck you hard and fast."

"Good," Jane returned, arching her back, urging him to take her. The sensation of his hot, rigid length sliding toward her entrance but not pushing inside was pure torture. "I want that too. I want you hard and fast, and I want your wicked, filthy words. I want all of it. Don't spare me. Give me everything."

He bent forward and clasped her jaw. Turned her face toward his so he could claim her mouth with a brief, ravaging kiss. "Then you shall have it, Jane, and more."

And then he straightened, grasped her hips roughly, and thrust deeply as though staking his claim...and in that moment, Jane knew that this coupling was going to be magnificent.

———

Oh God.

The sensation of Jane's greedy sex, so hot and wet and tight, almost had Christopher spending at once.

If he were being perfectly honest with himself, he would own that taking Jane in this desperate, almost ruthless way wasn't only about his need to come after a week of abstinence. No, he wanted to claim her. Possess her. He knew it was irratio- nal, but he'd hated seeing her walk out the door of Roxby House in the company of Jack O'Connor.

He trusted Jane, but some base male instinct inside him made him wary of the charming Irishman. And while he was reassured by Jane's profession of fidelity, it wasn't enough.

He needed more than that. He needed his wife to know that he wanted only her and that she was his and his alone. That the past was dead and buried and that no one else mattered. Not Daisy or any of the other women he'd been with over the years.

He also hated the fact that she'd been wearing dour black widow's weeds. It was a stark reminder of what was at stake.

What he might lose if he was killed...

All these wild dark thoughts careened around Christopher's head as he fought for control. The urge to let go was overwhelm- ing, but he gritted his teeth, seized the gorgeously plump globes of Jane's arse, and then set up a steady, pounding rhythm. His strokes were hard, forceful, unrelenting, but Jane matched him thrust for thrust. Kept up with his reckless pace. She panted and moaned with abandon as she pushed back. Her movements increased the friction. Sent his lust spiraling.

Oh, but she was wonderful. His desire for his wife knew no bounds. And he was determined to make her see that. To know it right down to her bones.

Sweat dripped from Christopher's brow as he looked down and watched his steel-hard cock plunging in and out of Jane's luscious wet heat. The sight was almost his undoing. But he wanted, needed, *more*. He wasn't ready for this frantic joining to end.

"You are mine and I am yours," he rasped between hectic thrusts. He gripped the back of her head, scattering hairpins so that her lustrous dark hair tumbled about her shoulders. "Do you agree?"

"Yes," she whimpered. "God, yes."

"We are one. Do not ever forget that," he continued, thrusting harder and faster. His blood was roaring, his head spinning. His heart crashed against his ribs and his balls throbbed. He needed to climax. And so did Jane.

Bending forward, he reached between her legs and thumbed the pearl of her clitoris. "Let go, Jane," he grunted, his voice harsh. Stripped raw. "Come with me. Fall with me over the edge."

Jane gasped, then cried out. A keening sound spilled from her throat and her whole body arched as her sheath clenched around him. Her intimate muscles spasmed with such force, Christopher's control shattered. The power of his release was cataclysmic. Thought-robbing pleasure shot through him like lightning, stealing his breath, and all he could do was groan and gasp and jerk and swear as a hot pulsating torrent of his seed poured into Jane.

He collapsed forward, his sweat-slick body covering his wife's. One of his arms had snaked around her, binding them together. He could feel her trembling, sighing beneath him. Whispering his name. And in that moment, he never wished to let this woman go.

Christopher's breathing stilled.

What the hell was he thinking? The afterglow of lovemaking was making him go soft in the head.

It's just the rampant lust talking, he told himself. And to his shame, his sudden attack of possessiveness had been triggered by an unhealthy dose of jealousy.

Christopher forced himself to open his eyes and release Jane from his embrace. Pushing himself up, he caught sight of his reflection in the mirror behind the settee. And he froze as the man staring back at him was instantly familiar. He knew those blue eyes, that nose, that mouth, that jaw.

They were his. Not a complete stranger's.

Christ. He closed his eyes. He still hadn't withdrawn from Jane's body, and he really should let her get up. They should repair upstairs and share the bath waiting for him in his rooms.

He was almost too afraid to open his eyes lest the man in the mirror became a stranger again. But he did. Christopher glared at his reflection, a challenge, perhaps even an accusation in his gaze, but he still knew himself. All at once relief and hope surged to join the bone-deep satisfaction humming through his veins.

Somehow, by some miracle, the sixth Duke of Roxby was slightly less afflicted than he had been before.

Chapter Twenty-one

"THERE'S NO NEED TO BE NERVOUS, JANE," SAID CHRISTOPHER as his town coach inched its way down Bow Street toward the Royal Italian Opera House in Covent Garden. Throngs of well-dressed theatergoers were pouring through the doors below the grand colonnaded front entrance. It looked like the last performance of *Il trovatore* before Lent would be packed to the gunwales.

"You can tell?" she asked, turning away from the window to regard her husband. Tonight, he was the epitome of "handsome as sin" in his elegant black evening attire.

"The way you're gripping me and the handle on the door, I'm certain your knuckles are white beneath your gloves." Christopher's smile was wry, but nevertheless he gave her hand a reassuring squeeze. "I know I said it before we left Roxby House, but you look beautiful. People will stare at the Duchess of Roxby, but not for the reason you think."

"Oh, I'm not nervous about everyone looking at me and my scar," said Jane. "I'm used to that. I'm worried about you, Christopher. About what will happen when you encounter Simon Cosgrove. Not only that, but there are so many other people here. What if someone else means you harm? Someone we don't know about?"

Christopher shrugged a wide shoulder. "I can only hope that person wouldn't be foolish enough to murder a duke in cold blood in such a crowded public place. I know there was an attempt to end me on Piccadilly, but once we're inside the theater, there are considerably fewer escape routes. At least, that's what I'm counting on."

"I still marvel at the fact you held all those parties at Roxby House," said Jane. "Your killer could have gained entrance and done you a mischief at any time. Well, if they managed to guess the password. Weren't you worried about that?"

In the dimly lit interior of the carriage, Christopher's blue eyes gleamed. "There never was a correct password. It was simply a device my footmen used to try and limit the number of guests gaining entrance on any one night. Despite appearances, I didn't want Roxby House to get too overrun. Everyone who turned up was given three guesses, and then whoever was on duty would decide if the guest could come inside based on their manner and appearance. A title or a claim to some sort of artistic fame always helped but wasn't essential. But to answer your question, I suppose I was wary rather than worried. Part of me hoped to draw the perpetrator out on my home soil. On my terms. Call it a soldier's instinct, perhaps. I always had several weapons secreted on my person. I know how to defend myself."

"I don't doubt that for a minute," said Jane, recalling the sight of Christopher boxing and all the weapons in the arms room. She was certain he would know how to use each one expertly.

"After I'd made an appearance in the ballroom and drawing room, and the carousing seemed to be in full swing," continued Christopher, "I'd disappear into my library and wait. Most of the time, the only people who stumbled into the room were looking for a place to have a tryst. I'd make my presence known and then they'd leave. Featherstone, who would shadow me for most of the night, would also watch everyone's comings and goings from a secret alcove in the corridor outside."

"You were laying a trap."

"I suppose you could say that." Christopher's smile was devilish. "It seems I caught you instead."

Jane smiled back. "Yes. You did. Red-handed."

Christopher's hand drifted to her seafoam-green silk skirts and somehow managed to squeeze her thigh through all the layers of fabric and her crinoline cage. "I'll never forget the sight of you lifting your gown and brazenly tying that book to your leg."

Jane arched an eyebrow. "I thought it was my face that was unforgettable."

"That too," said Christopher. His gaze warmed. "I wish you knew how beautiful you are, Jane. When everyone sees you sitting beside me in my private box tonight, resplendent in that gorgeous gown and that emerald parure from the Roxby estate collection, they'll be so in awe, they'll hardly want to watch the stage."

Jane's cheeks grew warm as she gave a nervous laugh. "Now I know you're jesting."

"But I'm not," said Christopher. In fact, his expression had grown deadly serious. "I wish you could see what I see when I look at you. You take my breath away."

"Thank you," Jane whispered. "You take my breath away too."

And then she glanced away out the window because the moment was too much to take in. Too much to bear. Because for the first time ever, she actually believed Christopher. And that was dangerous.

No, surely it's just desire talking, not love, Jane told herself as her reflection stared back at her. Christopher wanted her. That was all there was to such a pronouncement.

The Royal Italian Opera House was one of the most opulent theaters Jane had ever laid eyes on. If truth be told, as

Christopher escorted her up the grand marble staircase and then along crimson-carpeted corridors flanked with marble columns and sculptures, she was quite overawed.

Of course, there'd been the odd occasion when she accompanied her mother, Kitty, and Henry Pevensey to a pantomime or melodrama showing at another Covent Garden theater, but those establishments couldn't compare to this. Jane had certainly never been to the opera before, nor occupied a private box.

Christopher had given her a brief description of *Il trovatore's* premise on the way to Covent Garden, and if not for their own situation, Jane might have been amused to hear that Verdi's tragic opera was about two men vying for the love of a woman named Leonora. A story about murder, jealousy, curses, and revenge seemed a little too close for comfort at the moment.

Nevertheless, Christopher's mood was outwardly buoyant despite the fact he was about to engineer a confrontation with his former fiancée's husband. Jane marveled at his sangfroid. Even though Christopher's main aim was simply to get a rise out of Cosgrove in the hope the man might say something to incriminate himself, not to start a fight, Jane wasn't certain that things *wouldn't* turn violent. She supposed she would have to trust her husband's skills when it came to physical combat. He'd survived years of service in the military and had recently disarmed an attacker with a knife in a dark alley, after all.

According to Jack O'Connor, the Cosgroves would be sharing the box of Viscount Yarmouth, who was on the board of the North British Insurance Company. The viscount's box was farther back from the stage than Christopher's but apparently on the same level. Christopher had already informed Jane that he planned to "bump into" Simon Cosgrove in the theater's private saloon during the intermission. Many of the guests who owned private boxes often repaired there for a tipple or two before the production resumed.

Once Jane was seated beside Christopher, she gazed out upon the crowded theater. Everywhere she looked was a feast for the eyes: the deep-red velvet curtains shielding the stage and bracketing their box; the dazzling gas chandelier suspended above the stalls; the gilt wall sconces and the ornate gold plasterwork decorating the vaulted ceiling and the balconies.

She dared not look at the sea of faces below or across from where she and Christopher sat in case she saw people focusing their attention on her. Despite her husband's words of praise and support—despite the fact she was used to being stared at by complete strangers every single day—she hadn't the patience for it tonight.

She felt unsettled. Expectant. A peculiar mixture of trepidation and excitement buzzed through her like a bolt of lightning. Or perhaps she'd been overwhelmed by some strange fever. One that made her cheeks hot and her stomach flutter and her attention dart about the auditorium whenever there was a shout or a burst of laughter from the stalls below or an unexpected flurry of notes from the orchestra pit.

She supposed it wasn't helping that Christopher had tugged off one of her satin gloves and was lightly brushing his bare thumb in the most distracting way up and down the inside of her wrist, provoking delicious shivers. Ever since their incendiary bout of lovemaking in the arms room yesterday evening, Jane's body had become more sensitive. All her senses were heightened as though her nerve endings, everywhere, had come alive. When she'd awoken this morning, the slide of Christopher's bedsheets against her bare limbs had been beyond pleasurable. The whisper of her silken undergarments against her skin raised gooseflesh. If she caught a whiff of Christopher's cologne or shaving soap, she had to stop herself from burying her nose in his neck so she could inhale more of him.

Christopher must have noticed her agitation, as he leaned closer and murmured, "Are you sure you're all right, my darling wife? I swear you're as skittish as a cat on hot bricks."

She affected a laugh. "Is it that obvious?"

"Yes…" His gaze was hot and heavy, his voice dark and low as he added, "I can think of something I could do for you that would relax you. When the performance starts, we could draw one of the curtains and no one would know what I'm doing beneath your skirts. I swear I could hide an entire battalion underneath a crinoline cage."

Jane felt herself blushing even as the fluttering in her belly settled lower, gathering between her thighs. "You're insatiable, Your Grace. And incorrigible."

"Yes," he said with a wicked grin as he reached for her thigh. "I am."

She rapped his knuckles playfully with her fan. "You'll make me miss the performance."

"I can guarantee that I'll bring you more pleasure though. I always find *Il trovatore* to be quite overwrought. It's not to my taste. Whereas you, my dear duchess, are."

Her laugh was genuine this time. "Your arrogance and wickedness know no bounds."

He cocked a brow, challenge in his gaze. "But I'm right a good deal of the time, am I not?"

She sighed. "You are… The problem is I'm still worried about what the night ahead will bring."

Christopher frowned. "I promise you that nothing untoward will happen," he said. "If anything, we might find out if Cosgrove is the one responsible for these attacks. Or not."

Jane nodded. Before she could say anything else, the gaslights dimmed and the orchestra started to play a rousing overture. The opera had begun.

Jane tried very hard to concentrate on the first act, but the libretto was in Italian and she found her attention wandering yet again. During the second act, she had to stifle a yawn. Opera was clearly not for her. Christopher, ever attuned to her moods, leaned closer during a particularly melodramatic aria and murmured in her ear, "Why don't you go to the ladies' retiring room, remove your drawers, and we'll see what happens when you return?"

Jane bit her lip. Her cheeks were flaming, and she was grateful for the dim lighting. "Very well," she whispered back, then made a discreet exit. Or so she hoped.

It was but a short distance to the retiring room, and within a few minutes she'd removed her silk drawers and had left them in a dark corner behind a leafy potted palm. They wouldn't fit into her reticule, so she had little choice. She'd begun to check her appearance in one of the mirrors—one of her curls was in danger of coming loose from the elaborate arrangement Elsie had created for her and needed to be repinned—when she caught sight of Daisy Cosgrove right behind her.

Blast.

The young woman's reflected gaze met Jane's.

"Oh, so *you're* the Duchess of Roxby," said Daisy, a condescending smile transforming her pretty features into something quite unattractive.

Jane forgot about her errant curl and turned to face the smirking young woman. "And you are?" she asked, pretending she had no idea.

"Mrs. Daisy Cosgrove." Daisy tossed her perfectly styled blond curls. "Come now, I'm sure you've heard of me, Your

Grace. I'm your husband's former fiancée." She laughed. "Well, back then when I jilted him I was Daisy Byrd, so perhaps you know me by that name."

Jane arched a brow. "And how do you know who I am, pray tell?" Of course, Jane could hazard a guess, but she wanted Daisy to admit it.

"Well, I think it's rather obvious." The woman spoke to Jane as if she were dull-witted. "Everyone who's anyone in polite society has been talking about you and that hideous scar on your face. Honestly"—Daisy lowered her voice and leaned closer, as though she were about to share a confidence, not another insult—"I must say I don't know what the duke sees in you."

Jane somehow affected a look of nonchalance even though she was fuming. "Evidently something worthwhile because *I'm* the woman he married. Not you, *Mrs.* Cosgrove."

Daisy and several other women in the room gave a collective gasp, which Jane found most satisfying, and then she flounced from the room.

Oh, what a horrible, dreadful, spiteful cow!

Jane was still bristling with anger when she returned to Christopher's side. Even though the box's heavy velvet curtains were now partly drawn and her husband's face was in deep shadow, there was enough ambient light for Jane to discern that his brow had furrowed into a deep frown.

"What's wrong?" he murmured as she settled upon her seat.

"I crossed paths with Daisy," she whispered. "She knew who I was because of my scar and the gossip circulating about Town. It was not a very pleasant encounter."

"I'm sorry." Christopher reached for her hand and squeezed it. The contact of his strong, bare fingers surrounding hers was both reassuring and arousing. "We can leave now if you like."

"No, we should stay," she returned firmly. "You need to speak with Simon."

Christopher's answering smile was grim. "Yes, I do." His gaze returned to the stage where the villainous Count di Luna was singing of his love for Leonora, a woman in love with another man. A muscle was working in his jaw.

Oh, blast again. Was Christopher going to renege on his wicked offer to distract her? Although after her encounter with Daisy, Jane owned that she also wanted reassurance that Christopher wanted only her.

She sighed. She shouldn't be selfish, and she couldn't really blame him for changing his mind—

All of a sudden, Christopher's lips brushed her ear. His breath was warm as he whispered, "Spread your lovely legs, Jane. I'm going to make you forget about every damn thing except for me and how I make you feel."

Before she knew what he was about, he'd slipped to his knees on the carpeted floor of the box, and then he was determinedly burrowing beneath her skirts.

Good Lord. His wide shoulders pushed Jane's thighs apart, and as her hips tipped forward, she had to grip the arms of her chair lest she fall. A moment later, Christopher's fingers were gently prizing open her slippery folds even more and his hot mouth was on her, his wicked tongue licking along her slit before finding her clitoris with unerring accuracy. His tongue tip fluttered over the sensitive nub of flesh, and it wasn't long before Jane was biting her lip to stifle whimpers and moans.

Thank God the action on the stage was noisy. Thank heavens she was in deep shadow, because for the life of her she couldn't focus on anything else but the wild passion sizzling through her veins. Of the blazing firestorm of sensation threatening to engulf her from head to toe. If anyone *could* actually see her, she didn't much care. In fact, the idea that someone *might* see her enflamed Jane's desire even more. If they guessed what was going on beneath her voluminous skirts, she hoped they were envious. The Duchess of Roxby's husband was rumored to be a wicked libertine anyway, so it wasn't like this sort of debauched behavior was entirely unexpected. And she could hardly deny her husband. She *had* promised to obey him…

Oh, how shockingly wanton she'd become. And how unremorseful. To own one's joy in sexual pleasure was liberating and she wouldn't be ashamed about that.

At least that's what Jane told herself as she opened herself even wider and her body began to quake with tremors of anticipation. Perhaps sensing she was on the edge of ecstasy but that she needed an extra nudge to let go, Christopher's lips fastened on Jane's clitoris, and he suckled her so exquisitely she couldn't help but succumb to pleasure's brightly beckoning flames. Her whole body arched, and her ardor-soaked cry coalesced with the soaring notes of an aria.

As the pulsating waves of pleasure abated, Jane slumped in her chair and her head fell to the side. She idly wondered if she'd be able to walk out of the theater or if Christopher would have to carry her.

She cracked an eyelid and spied Christopher. He was back in his seat beside her, his tawny hair thoroughly disheveled, the smuggest smile she'd ever seen spreading across his face as he regarded her.

She straightened a little, drawing her shaky legs together. "At the risk of inflating your already overblown self-confidence, you were right," she murmured into the velvet shadows. "I forgot everything but you."

Christopher caught her hand and raised it to his lips. "Now you know how I feel," he murmured. "All I see is you, Jane. All I think about is you. You consume me. I've never experienced anything like it. And I think you should know that." His voice might be soft and low and masked by the swelling music and vocal acrobatics of the performers, but Jane felt his words. Their import. They sank into her. Resonated through her.

Christopher was consumed by thoughts of her.

What did that really mean? Was this merely lust, or was he starting to feel affection for her? *Real* affection?

Was he falling in love?

Jane hardly knew what to do with such a fantastical notion. It was...it was too much, too fast, too soon.

Too tempting.

Her husband's unexpected confession pierced her heart with a shard of such acute longing that it stole her breath. The urge to let loose the tight bonds securing her own emotions was strong. Tenderness—perhaps even an emotion akin to love— was stirring in her breast, threatening to bud and grow and unfurl into something glorious.

Jane squeezed her eyes shut, fighting for control. She wanted to let go, to *feel* all of it. But something was stopping her. Weighing her down.

It wasn't only the fact she feared heartbreak again. It was her guilt. Guilt that she wasn't being open and honest with Christopher. That she was keeping part of herself closed off from him. Separate.

All of a sudden, the weight of her secret felt like something she couldn't bear to carry any longer. "Christopher..." she began, but her voice was lost in the cacophony of the opera.

And then her husband surprised her yet again. He slid a gentle hand behind her neck, drawing her closer. His breath warmed her ear as he whispered, "I have a secret to share with you. Not here though. In the carriage on the way home," and all Jane could do was nod.

Fear gripped her tongue. Held it in check. Now would have been the perfect opportunity to tell Christopher that she had a secret to share with him too. But hers wasn't wonderful. It was shameful and would expose how underhanded and dishonest she was. The warm light in Christopher's eyes would surely dim.

And she didn't want that.

You'll deal with your blackmailer soon, she told herself. *All that awfulness will end.*

But then what, Jane? Then what?

She still wanted to publish her controversial pamphlet. If Christopher found out about her project, he might stop her from doing what she wanted. What she *needed* to do to feel whole and useful again. Her past suffering at the hands of the wrong man wouldn't be for naught. It had to mean something. She would use her hurt and pain to make a difference in the world for other women. Come what may.

Not yet, Jane, her mind whispered. *Don't fall for your husband just yet.*

When you know him better, when you're certain he'll understand you, perhaps then you can let him in.

Perhaps then and only then she'd be able to let herself love again.

Chapter Twenty-two

THE OPERA HOUSE'S SALOON WAS A HIVE OF ACTIVITY WHEN Christopher escorted Jane into the room on his arm. Her cheeks were still flushed and her eyes aglow, and he liked to think it was because of the pleasure he'd brought her.

She was breathtakingly beautiful, and she was also a damned distraction. One thing he couldn't afford to be right now was inattentive. Not when he needed to be on his guard. Not only because Simon Cosgrove was somewhere in the crowd, but because anyone could approach him and he wouldn't have a damned clue who that person was.

He was in danger of looking and sounding like he'd lost his mind. Thank God he had Jane to support him.

Christopher snagged a glass of champagne for each of them and maneuvered them into a position close to the main door. It always paid to have an exit route worked out. Just as it also paid to have a weapon on hand. Even though he'd foregone bringing a pistol—the close cut of his evening jacket wouldn't accommodate the extra bulk at his waist—he had a knife strapped to his ankle. And then, marble sculptures and champagne glasses and his fists could be used as weapons too.

Hopefully he wouldn't be trading blows with Simon Cosgrove, but his military training and service would not allow him to be anything less than vigilant of his surroundings.

"I'll point out Simon as soon as I catch a glimpse of him," said Jane. "He's tall—not quite as tall as you, though—with brown hair and brown eyes. Fairly lean with neatly trimmed muttonchops."

"Thank you," said Christopher. "No doubt Daisy will be on his arm."

A line appeared between Jane's elegant dark brows. Leaning close to his ear, she murmured, "I'm afraid one of my stockings is in danger of slipping and I need to check my garter. Can you bear it if I desert you to dash to the ladies' retiring room? I'll only be gone for a minute or two."

"Of course." Even though Christopher's gut tightened, he offered her a reassuring smile. "I'm a battle-hardened soldier. I'm sure I can survive for that long."

Jane squeezed his arm and handed him her champagne. "I'll be as quick as I can."

As Christopher waited by the door, he slid a scowl into place. If he'd been on edge before, he was even more so now. Appearing inconspicuous was almost impossible when one was six foot four and a notorious duke. He prayed that his forbidding expression would make anyone think twice about approaching him for a chat.

"Roxby, old chap. It's been an absolute age," boomed a voice near Christopher's right shoulder at the same moment a hearty clap landed on his back. "How have you been?"

Damn bloody damn. One of Christopher's worst nightmares *was* coming to life. Turning his head, he found himself regarding a complete stranger. An immaculately dressed, middle-aged gentleman with silver sprinkled though his dark hair smiled broadly at him, and Christopher had no idea who he was.

To mask his confusion, Christopher plastered a smile on his own face, hoping to hell he could brazen this encounter out without sounding like he'd lost his marbles. "Capital, just capital," he lied. "And you?" *Whoever you are...*

The man gave a guffaw. "I'm in fine fettle. Never better, in fact. But tell me more about you, Roxby. I haven't seen you around the usual haunts lately. What have you been up to?" The fellow laughed again. "Now, that's a ridiculous question, isn't it? Rumor has it that you're now leg-shackled. That's no doubt hamstrung you a bit." He gave Christopher a wink. "No more wild soirees, hey what?"

"Quite," said Christopher tightly and sipped his champagne as he racked his brain. What did this stranger mean by "the usual haunts"? Did he mean the House of Lords, or a particular gentlemen's club? This man *might* be a fellow peer. He also might have attended one of Christopher's parties. The touch of gray in the chap's hair suggested he might be at least a decade older than Christopher, but that wasn't enough to go on. This stranger could be *anybody*.

The man gave him a nudge, suggesting they were on familiar terms. "So where's this new wife of yours? I caught a glimpse of her before I came over. I'd love an introduction."

Bloody hell. Christopher sipped his champagne again, trying to hide his rising panic. The stranger's expectant look shifted into frown territory as the awkward pause lengthened into the realm of "hideously uncomfortable." How could he introduce this man to Jane when he had no idea what his goddamn name was? He should move away before he made a complete fool of himself. Make some excuse to leave, to find Jane, but then she might come back anyway and—

At that moment, Jane, God bless her, appeared at Christopher's side and without hesitation, leapt into the strained silence. "How do you do, sir? I'm Jane, the Duchess of Roxby," she said, all her natural poise coming to the fore. "And you are?"

"Your Grace." The fellow beamed and then bowed over her

proffered hand. "Dunhill's the name. I was just saying to your husband how much I'd like to meet his lovely bride, and now here you are."

Baron Dunhill. Of course. Relief surged through Christopher as Jane smiled disarmingly. "You have a way with words, my lord. Pray tell, how do you know my husband?"

"Dunhill served with me in the Crimea," said Christopher smoothly. He was on sure ground now. "But since then, we've crossed paths on the odd occasion at White's and Brooks's."

"Don't forget Tattersall's," added the baron. "I was most miffed when you outbid me on that black Thoroughbred last Season." Then he winked. "Now that you have this prize filly in your stable, Roxby, I expect I'll see even less of you. And I can't say that I blame you." Turning to Jane, he smiled. "I hope you don't mind the old cavalry officer talk, Your Grace."

"Not at all," returned Jane with a gracious inclination of her head. Although Christopher did notice a slight stiffening of her smile. Which was entirely understandable. Men like Dunhill could say the most asinine things at times.

He was about to inquire after the man's own wife when Dunhill leaned closer. "I think I should warn you, Roxby. Your former fiancée and her husband are both here. I spied them on the other side of the room where I left my wife in the company of the Yarmouths. In any event, you might want to give that end of the saloon a wide berth. Best to avoid any awkward encounters, hey what?"

Christopher gave a tight smile. "No doubt." Awkward was what he wanted when it came to Simon Cosgrove. Uncomfortable was even better. The more riled Cosgrove was, the more likely he would be to say something telling in the heat of the moment.

Thankfully, Dunhill caught sight of someone else he wanted to chat to and drifted away.

"I suppose we're going to venture down to the other end of the saloon?" said Jane quietly.

"Yes." Christopher downed his champagne in a few swallows, then handed the glass to a nearby footman. "There's no time like the present."

Within a minute, Jane had located the Cosgroves amongst the throng of other well-heeled theatergoers. "Daisy is wearing a gown of butter-yellow silk and Simon is to her very left," she murmured.

Christopher narrowed his gaze. "I see him." He drew a steadying breath. "All right. Let's get this over with, shall we?"

As he approached the Cosgroves, the blond woman Jane had identified as Daisy turned and smiled. "Christopher... I mean, Your Grace. Fancy meeting you here." She nudged the dark-haired man beside her. "Look, Simon. It's the Duke of Roxby."

Cosgrove's face contorted with a sneer as his gaze settled on Christopher. "What the hell are you doing here?" he all but growled. "Come to sniff around my wife's skirts again, have you?"

A middle-aged woman in their party— perhaps it was Lady Yarmouth—gasped at Cosgrove's crudity, while the gray-haired man beside her uttered a rather loud "ahem" before adding, "Now see here, Cosgrove. That's not the sort of talk one expects in mixed company."

Cosgrove tilted into a small bow. "My apologies to your lady and to you, my lord. But Roxby is an absolute bounder. Everyone knows it. A leopard can't change his spots."

The blonde in butter-yellow—Daisy—affected a tinkling laugh. "Now, now, Simon," she said. "That unpleasant business is all behind us. Look"—she gestured with her chin toward Jane— "His Grace is even married now. He's turned over a new leaf."

Cosgrove's dark gaze flickered over Jane. "Bully for you,

Roxby," he said. "That doesn't mean you still don't wish to chase after my wife."

Christopher cocked a brow. "If you'd let me get a word in, Cosgrove, you'd be surprised to learn that I came over here to apologize for what happened last year. Now that I am most happily wed, I have a better understanding of why you reacted the way that you did."

Cosgrove snorted. "I don't believe a thing that comes out of your mouth."

Christopher drew a bracing breath as he prepared to land a well-placed verbal blow. "Look, it's never easy to hear that your wife might still be in love with another man. But really, Cosgrove, if you're going to keep a mistress, you can't be too heartbroken—"

With that, Cosgrove let out an almighty roar and lunged at Christopher. They wrestled for a moment, then dropped to the carpeted floor. Cosgrove managed to plant a punch on Christopher's jaw before Christopher rolled, landing on top, pinning his attacker down. His elbow connected with the man's face, and he was about to deliver his own blow in retaliation—Cosgrove was an absolute ass, and Christopher's jaw *bloody* hurt—when a deluge of freezing water and shards of ice rained down on them.

"My God, stop it, you two." Jane's voice snapped over them like a whiplash. In her hand, she held a silver champagne bucket. "That's quite enough. You're grown, supposedly civilized men. Not brawling schoolboys or barbarians."

Christopher climbed off Cosgrove and wiped a hand across his face. His cheek was smarting too, and when he looked down at his fingers, they were streaked with blood.

Bastard. But then again, Christopher *had* provoked the man with malice aforethought.

Cosgrove—easily identifiable by the wet hair plastered

across his brow, heaving chest, and a split lip—had clambered to his feet and was now glowering at Christopher from across the room. Daisy—at least Christopher thought it was Daisy, given her fair hair and yellow gown—was clutching her husband's arm and wailing like the end of days was coming.

And Jane... Jane was magnificent. Her green eyes were flashing with fire and her cheekbones were marked with high color. "We should leave," she said.

Christopher nodded. "Agreed." He sketched a mocking bow the Cosgroves' way, then took Jane's arm and quit the saloon.

But as soon as they reached the bottom of the opera house's grand marble staircase, he pulled Jane close and kissed her fiercely.

"Thank you," he murmured roughly. "You stopped me from pounding Cosgrove into mincemeat."

"Well, that wasn't my motivation for breaking up the fight entirely," said Jane. "I was worried that he might have a knife secreted on his person. Like you do. I just wanted it all to end before someone—before you—got hurt."

Christopher couldn't stop his mouth from kicking into a smile. "You were worried about me?"

"Of course. How could I not be?" said Jane softly. Even though her cheeks had pinkened as though she were embarrassed about making such an admission, she reached up and brushed her fingertips across his bruised jaw. "I worry about you all the time."

Christopher threaded his fingers through hers, and they began walking toward the foyer and the exit leading onto Bow Street. It was a novel sensation to have someone show concern for his well-being. Christopher wasn't sure if he'd ever get used to the idea. But he decided he rather liked it.

Once they were safely installed in his carriage, and Jane

was nestled against his cambric shirtfront—Christopher had removed his wet evening jacket as soon as he'd entered the coach—he blew out a sigh. "I really don't know if Simon Cosgrove is behind all these attacks."

Jane straightened, and the soft golden glow of the carriage's lamp revealed her frown. "You can't be serious. He launched himself at you. His eyes were fairly blazing with fury."

"But he merely tackled me and threw punches. And he owned his anger. He wasn't trying to hide from it. All the other attacks have been executed stealthily. From a distance. In the dark. In the fog. In a crowd. And they've always come out of nowhere. While there's no doubt that Simon Cosgrove is a jealous sort of husband, my gut tells me he's not the one trying to kill me. Aside from all that, there was a room full of witnesses tonight. If Cosgrove really did have murder on his mind, I don't think he'd want to draw attention to himself."

Jane leaned back again.

"You make good points," she said. "And I suppose if he really did want to do away with you, he *could* call you out."

"Exactly," said Christopher. He placed a kiss on her temple. "I never did thank you for helping me to avoid looking like an imbecile in front of Lord Dunhill."

"There's no need to thank me," said Jane. "That's what I'm here for. Actually..." She turned in his arms, then murmured huskily, "That's not all I'm here for." Her fingers danced across his chest before sliding a button of his satin waistcoat undone. And then another. "I rather think that I should be thanking you for what you did for me in your box... Turnabout is fair play after all..."

Christopher chuckled even as his cock immediately started to harden. "Don't you want to hear my secret first?"

Jane's fingers froze and Christopher crooked a finger under

her chin, tilting her head up so she couldn't escape his gaze. "It's not a frightening secret. In fact, it's rather wonderful."

She swallowed. "Of course I want to hear it," she said. But even so, there was a look of hesitation in her eyes. A catch in her voice that gave Christopher pause. But then the moment passed, and her mouth curved in a smile. "Tell me."

Christopher directed her attention to the window where their reflections stared back at them. "Yesterday, when we made love in the arms room, I caught a glimpse of myself in the mirror and I recognized my face. I didn't want to tell you straightaway unless my memory failed again. But more than a day later, it hasn't. When I look at you and at me"—he nodded at the window again—"I see us together. Not you in the arms of a stranger. I can't describe how wonderfully amazing that feels."

"Oh my God. That *is* wonderful." Jane caught his face between her hands and kissed him softly. "I'm so happy for you," she murmured as she drew back.

Christopher swallowed, suddenly overwhelmed with a surge of strong emotion. He'd been determined not to let down his guard and develop any feelings beyond lust or a fond regard for his wife. But perhaps he had begun to care for Jane, just a little, despite his best efforts not to… He was jealous as hell whenever Jack O'Connor paid her any sort of attention. He'd been worried about Jane's safety for days. He was touched by her obvious care for his well-being and all the little things she did to make his life easier. He couldn't deny their close physical connection. He'd never known anything like it before.

It was a sobering notion, how much change Jane had wrought in his life—in him—in such a short space of time, but tonight he wouldn't turn away from whatever "this" was. Or what it could be in time if he was given half a chance. If his life wasn't cut short.

Tonight, he would revel in it.

"I want to celebrate you," he said. "Us. Right here, right now." He brushed a stray lock of her glossy brown hair behind her ear. "There's something about you, Jane, that has brought me to life again. For the first time in a very long time, I have hope." And then he kissed his beautiful wife with all the passion he could muster. His hand swept up her back to settle at her nape. Tipping her head back, he plundered her mouth thoroughly, deliberately, his tongue stroking deep. His cock was throbbing, demanding attention, but he ignored it until Jane's fingers drifted to the tented front of his trousers. Thwarted lust made him hiss with frustration.

"Let me pleasure you. Let me use my mouth on you," whispered Jane huskily as she began to slide his trouser buttons undone, freeing his engorged length.

He caught her hand. "No. I'd love you to, but no. Not this time. I want to be inside you. I need to feel how hot and wet and tight you are. Ride me, Jane. And then I can watch you come."

―――――

"Very well," Jane whispered.

She could hardly fathom what Christopher had disclosed. It was, indeed, wonderful. Perhaps even miraculous. Something to rejoice.

And yes, she wanted to celebrate with Christopher "right here, right now," just as he'd declared. His deep voice, graveled with lust, had made her blood heat and her toes curl.

She wanted nothing more than to banish all their troubles into the shadows of the night. They could be dealt with tomorrow.

Christopher's blue eyes were alight with deep desire, a passionate fire that mirrored her own as she deftly dispensed with her crinoline petticoat. While she shimmied out of the wire cage and left it in a heap on the carriage floor, he drew the carriage's curtains.

Even though Jane had found it arousing beyond measure to be surreptitiously pleasured in a theater box, she was pleased that these special moments would be for them and them alone to share. The luxurious town coach trundling through the noisy, foggy London streets had become their own private world. A safe place where nothing and no one else existed but them. A haven for exploring their mutual passion.

Christopher was leaning back against the velvet upholstered bench, watching her through heavy-lidded eyes. In the muted glow of the carriage's lamp, he was a beautiful creature of light and shadow. The strong lines and planes of his harshly handsome countenance seemed even more sharply defined. A bruise was blooming along his jaw and there was an angry-looking cut upon his cheekbone. He looked appealingly dangerous and exactly like the barbarian she'd accused him of being a short time ago.

And then there was his magnificent cock. He was running his fisted hand up and down its engorged, rigid length as he waited for her to climb onto his lap.

Jane licked her lips. Gathering up her skirts, she then straddled Christopher. Her hands settled on his wide shoulders and her wet quim grazed his shaft, pulling an agonized groan from his throat.

"Jane," he breathed. "I must have you."

"Then take me," she whispered, deliberately teasing him by undulating her hips and sliding her slippery folds all over him.

"God, yes." He grasped her waist, holding her steady while his other hand dragged the head of his cock toward her entrance. "Fuck me. Use me. I'll give you everything I have and more."

His crude words enflamed Jane's own desire to blazing proportions. She reached beneath her skirts, fitted herself more securely over Christopher's cock, then plunged downward. She moaned and gripped his shoulders. His hot, pulsating length filled her so completely, so perfectly, it took her breath away.

And then Christopher ruthlessly yanked down her bodice and corset, exposing her breasts. He suckled one puckered peak then the other before spearing one of his hands into her hair, pulling her down for a ravenous, uncompromising kiss. At the same time he rocked his hips, encouraging Jane to move. And she did. Slowly at first, gliding up then sinking down upon him with studied purpose. Setting a deliberately torturous pace, prolonging the exquisite friction of each intimate stroke of her body. Her sole intention was to drive Christopher wild. To build his need until he was cursing and groaning and begging her to go faster.

It wasn't long before Christopher was gripping her waist and determinedly pumping his hips, pistoning his cock in and out of her. Jane matched his frantic, punishing pace. She rode Christopher, just like he'd asked her to do. Both of them were hurtling headlong toward ecstasy. She could feel the coiling tension inside her, pulling tighter and tighter. Christopher was sweating and grunting, and she was panting and gasping. But the most thrilling thing of all was the way Christopher's burning gaze was locked with hers.

She was mesmerized. Entranced. So totally consumed by this intense, unbridled ride that they were sharing that all she could do was hold on until passion claimed her.

In fact, it didn't take long at all. Her orgasm when it hit was brilliant. It burst over her, engulfing her, and Jane cried out as wave after wave of unadulterated bliss washed through her. Her sheath rippled and clenched, squeezing Christopher's cock, and then he came too.

Her name fell from his lips followed by a desperate groan as his body jerked beneath hers, his hot seed flooding her welcoming womb. And she watched his face. The way his brow furrowed and his eyes squeezed shut as though the sensations claiming him were almost too much. How his whole body tensed, his fingers digging into her hips. The way the cords of his neck stood out.

Oh, how she reveled in the satisfaction she was able to give this wonderful man too.

Jane buried her face in Christopher's neck. Inhaled his intoxicating scent as his arms slid around her, cradling her. She was delirious with satisfaction. Floating in a dreamlike state on a cloud as her lips grazed Christopher's jaw.

If only this were *a dream*, her mind whispered, breaking through the hum of contentment radiating through her body.

Then she wouldn't have to wake up and face tomorrow. She wouldn't be afraid to take Christopher into her confidence.

She wouldn't be so terrified of falling in love.

In her heart of hearts, she knew that was her greatest fear of all. That she would love this man and then she would lose him. Not at the hands of some killer, but because of her own rampant stubbornness, pridefulness, and foolishness.

In the coming days, somehow, some way she'd have to muster the courage to lay bare all her secrets, no matter the consequences. She couldn't keep lying to her husband.

She had to be honest with him. It was the right thing to do.

Chapter Twenty-three

THE LONGCASE CLOCK IN THE CORNER OF DARTMOOR House's elegant drawing room tick, tick, ticked into the shocked silence that followed Jane's announcement that she was being blackmailed.

It had taken several days for her to work up her courage to confess all to her Byronic Book Club friends. To face the attendant feelings of embarrassment and shame. And guilt, not only for keeping something so momentous from them but also for dragging them into such an awful mess after all this time. For weeks now, Jane had been shouldering this burden on her own—and perhaps, to some degree, pride and a degree of stubbornness had made her hold her tongue. She'd only lately realized that she also hated appearing weak. For years she'd maintained a stiff upper lip and soldiered on, no matter how much she'd been put upon by her mother and the rest of her family. Because that was what was expected of her. Jane was always there to be relied upon. Depended upon. Jane would fix things. Be the stopgap when something went wrong.

But Jack O'Connor had been right. She *did* need help. She *couldn't* fix this on her own. And she trusted Artemis and Lucy more than anyone in the whole world.

Lucy's eyes were as wide as saucers as she put down her cup of tea with a clatter, then declared, "You can't be serious. Who would do such a horrendous thing to you, Jane? And why?"

"You poor thing," murmured Artemis, compassion softening her brown gaze. "What can we do to help?"

Jane put down her own fine bone-china cup amid the piles of Gothic novels and tea things on the mahogany table between them all. Not only was she touched beyond measure, but she was also relieved that she had at last decided to confide in her friends. It was only four days until the one-hundred-pound payment was due, and this Byronic Book Club meeting had seemed like the perfect opportunity to lay all her cards on the table.

"I'm afraid I'm entirely serious, dear Lucy," Jane said with a sigh. "Though I have no idea who is behind it. And if you would be willing to help me"—she shifted her gaze to Artemis and offered a smile—"I would be most grateful. But..." She inhaled a steadying breath before continuing. "I'm sure you would like to know what you're dealing with before committing yourselves to the cause, so to speak."

"We're here to listen to whatever you wish to tell us," said Lucy with an emphatic nod of her head.

"And no matter what you say, we'll help anyway," added Artemis. "Because that's what friends are for. We've been through thick and thin together over the years. Lucy and I will not abandon you now."

Jane pleated her fingers together in her lap and willed away the grateful tears that were threatening to gather. "Thank you both," she said. "You're going to tell me that I'm a dunderhead and that I should have come to you sooner, but you know how proud and determined I am to make my own way in this world. It's my nature not to be a bother and to just get on with things, no matter how unpleasant or difficult."

"We know," said Artemis kindly. "And I understand because I'm much the same."

"And *I* would never call you a dunderhead," added Lucy. "Artemis, on the other hand..."

Artemis's mouth twitched with a smile. "Well, yes, I might call you a dunderhead, Jane, but I will say it in a loving, entirely supportive way. Now confess all before I expire from curiosity."

Jane nodded, then drew a deep breath. "Very well," she said, then proceeded to describe the robbery at her grandfather's shop, how her journal containing the various drafts of her proposed pamphlet series *A Practical Woman's Guide to Self-Determination and Lasting Fulfillment* had been taken, and the horrible threats and letters of demand that had followed. Of the payments she'd left at Mudie's Lending Library.

"So *that's* why you were there," said Lucy. "That's why you were acting so oddly when I bumped into you."

"Yes." Jane winced. "I was trying to catch the blackmailer in the act."

Artemis frowned. "And you told me later on that day—when we met up at Madame Blanchard's boutique—that you both glimpsed a woman you thought might be Miss Sharp at Mudie's. I must say, my suspicions are more than a little aroused."

"Did you find out if Miss Sharp *is* back in London?" asked Lucy.

Artemis shook her head. "Alas, no. Dominic made some discreet inquiries through his man of business up north, and while it seems that Miss Sharp *did* leave her post in Liverpool, where she went next is a mystery. Her employer certainly wasn't forthcoming on the matter. In fact, Dominic's man of business said the fellow was quite terse. I know I sound ungracious and unduly suspicious, but it does make one wonder what the woman might have done this time around. It doesn't sound like the parting was on good terms."

"You have every right to be ungracious and suspicious," said

Jane. "Miss Sharp did threaten you to get what she wanted. It does make me wonder about her too." Jane shared a bit more about the nature of the blackmailer's letters. The language used, the tone of the messages, and the neatness of the handwriting. "So a woman *might* have penned them," she concluded. "Jack O'Connor said—"

Lucy's brows shot up. "Jack O'Connor? Who's that?"

Jane inwardly cursed her slip of the tongue. "He's a private detective my husband employs on occasion for, ah, certain things," she admitted. "I recently asked for his opinion about the letters and the best way to go about catching the blackmailer."

Artemis's far-too-perceptive gaze settled on Jane. "Hmmm. You haven't yet told us what your husband thinks about all of this. I'm sure he'd have an opinion."

"He…" Jane swallowed. "He doesn't know."

Lucy frowned. "Jane…" she said gently. "Why wouldn't you tell him?"

"Because," said Jane, "I don't know Christopher well enough yet. I don't know how he'll react to my disclosure. I'm worried he'll think less of me. I'm worried he'll try to stop me from publishing my controversial pamphlets. Duchesses do *not* write, publish, and disseminate information about sexual congress and methods of contraception to the general public."

"No, they do not," said Artemis. "Not usually. But then, I would contend that duchesses are not supposed to pen and publish licentious Gothic romance novels either. However, it would seem that *some* husbands don't mind if their wives do."

"I think reasonable, decent men like your Dominic are not all that easy to find," said Jane. She smiled at Lucy. "Your husband, Will, fits the 'reasonable and decent' category too."

"That may be quite true," acknowledged Artemis. "And in my case, it *did* take me a very long time to find someone as wonderful as Dominic. But let me go back to something else you mentioned, Jane. You said that you're worried that Christopher will think less of you..." Artemis's eyes were kind as she added, "My darling friend, are you falling in love with your husband?"

Jane blushed. "Perhaps. Maybe. I'm not sure... It's only been a few weeks since we first met and...for various reasons, things have been a little tumultuous."

"I suspect there's more to the story of how you first met and how your duke came to propose to you than you're letting on," said Artemis gently.

"Yes, there is. But some of it..." Jane sighed. "A great deal of the reason I'm being so vague is that it's related to other people's secrets. Secrets I'm not at liberty to tell."

Lucy reached out across the table and gave Jane's hand a brief squeeze. "I understand more than you could ever know. As I said earlier, please do not feel obligated to share more than you are comfortable with."

Jane nodded as she nervously fiddled with the handle of her teacup. "At the risk of incurring your displeasure, my friends, I suppose I should confess that part of the reason I married Christopher was that I needed money. Not just because I was being blackmailed but because my grandfather was in danger of losing his bookstore. And...and I really couldn't face the idea of asking you to bail me out. It's not your place to do so and...and when I met Christopher, he offered me a unique proposition. An opportunity to change the course of my life that I couldn't resist."

"You want a baby too," said Artemis, her hand moving to rest on the front of her skirts. "I hope you don't mind that I told Lucy."

"No, I don't mind," said Jane, her cheeks warming. She cast Lucy an apologetic smile. "I should have told you myself."

"That's quite all right." Lucy's answering smile was kind. "And I happen to think it's wonderful that you are getting what you want at long last. I too remember when that complete bounder Miles abandoned you. How much he hurt you. How it took months and months for you to even smile again. What he did was unforgivable."

"Yes…" Jane sighed heavily. "It was. Of course, he's the reason I dismissed the idea of getting married and having a baby for so long. But Christopher's proposal made me reconsider everything about my life. And now that we're getting closer, I don't want to ruin it all. If we can catch my blackmailer in the act, Christopher need never know about this whole horrible chapter of my life."

"But what about your desire to publish these pamphlets?" asked Lucy. "Will you go ahead with it behind his back?"

"I wouldn't advise it," said Artemis. "I kept my career as a Gothic romance novelist hidden from Dominic while we were engaged, and the guilt nearly destroyed me. And then when he found out, I discovered that my fears that he would think less of me were totally unfounded. Perhaps Christopher will surprise you too."

"I *want* to trust him with my secret," admitted Jane. "And I'll think on all you've said, Artemis. But first things first."

"We need to catch the culprit," said Lucy. "If we think it might be Rosalind Sharp, I'd suggest we don disguises. We don't want to alert her to our presence. She might go to ground."

"Yes," agreed Jane. She cast her mind back to her recent visit to Waterloo Place. "Widow's weeds and veiled bonnets might work at a pinch. And wouldn't invite too much comment."

"That sounds perfect," said Artemis as she replenished their cups of tea. "And very Gothic. A trio of mysterious women in black. I like the idea so much I might even use it in one of my books." She smiled. "Well, my friends, it looks like our next Byronic Book Club meeting will be at Mudie's Lending Library."

Chapter Twenty-four

THE NEXT FEW DAYS LEADING UP TO MARCH 7 DRAGGED BY for Jane. She tried to keep herself busy to stop dwelling on whether her blackmailer would be caught or not and the consequences of both eventualities. She also tried not to think about the ever-present guilt that quietly gnawed away at her. That kept her awake at night as she lay in Christopher's arms after they made love. She wanted to be open and honest with her husband as her friends had suggested. Her logical side insisted that she *should* tell him everything. But stultifying fear held her back. It wasn't rational, and in her heart she knew it was wrong and cowardly. But Jane couldn't seem to make herself share that part of her, even with a man who'd done nothing but help her. Who made her feel like she was wanted and maybe even cared for. That she *mattered*.

At least not yet.

Miles Dempster had destroyed so many things that long-ago summer. Perhaps the worst injury of all had been the irreparable damage he'd done to her ability to trust a man ever again.

The day after the Byronic Book Club meeting, Jane paid a visit to the Pevensey house to see how her mother was faring. Jane had taken away one of her chief joys in life—gambling at the card table—and she was worried that her mother might be down in the doldrums. But to Jane's surprise and relief, Leonora Pevensey was in fine spirits, taking tea in the small courtyard garden of the Pelham Crescent townhouse with Kitty, enjoying the bright spring day. They'd chatted and laughed, and her mother and Kitty had shared their plans for Kitty's coming Season, and Jane was satisfied that her mother was at last finding renewed purpose in life.

The following day, Jane visited Delaney's Bookshop to see her grandfather. He too was well, and the store was so busy that he didn't have time to take tea with her at Fortnum & Mason's. But he promised that he would the following week when a new employee was due to start.

Jane had then returned home to Roxby House to find Christopher meeting with Jack O'Connor in the library. The private detective was providing an update on the dishonorably discharged officer, Neville Phelps. The constabulary in Tewkesbury had reported that Phelps's father was a man of the cloth—an Anglican minister—and he and his wife had moved on to the village of Reigate in Surrey about a year ago. Apart from that, they hadn't provided anything else useful by way of information other than Neville Phelps didn't have any sort of criminal record. Christopher determined that perhaps he would travel to Surrey to call on Phelps's parents himself. The journey was but an hour or so by train, and Jane, of course, offered to accompany him.

"We'll go on Monday," said Christopher.

"This coming Monday? The seventh?"

Christopher cocked a brow. "Yes. Is there a problem?"

Oh dear, that was the day the blackmail payment was due. Even though guilt pinched, Jane attempted to affect an air of nonchalance as she said, "I promised my friends Lucy and Artemis that I would help them with some pressing charity work. A...a new project we're working on to provide aid to women... Women in need, if you take my meaning."

Oh, she was not very good at dissembling, but she pressed

on with her half-cocked story regardless. "We're meeting at Lucy's house in the morning. Perhaps we could go to Surrey tomorrow, even though it's Sunday? Or later in the afternoon on Monday? Or even on Tuesday at a pinch?"

Christopher frowned. "You know you can invite your friends here to Roxby House at any time, Jane. It's your home now too. As for visiting Surrey tomorrow..." He drummed his fingers on the blotter. "Phelps's father is a vicar, so he's likely to be quite busy, given it's the Sabbath. I feel he might be more amenable to a visit from complete strangers during the week when he's likely to have less on his agenda. Let's go Tuesday. I have some other business I should attend to on Monday anyway."

"I'm sure you're right about Phelps's father." Jane forced a smile and tried to ignore the feeling that Jack O'Connor was watching her closely. "And Tuesday also suits me."

The meeting came to an end and Jack O'Connor took his leave. Jane excused herself as well and caught up with the Irishman in the entry hall as he was donning his beaver hat.

"A moment, Mr. O'Connor," she called. Glancing back the way she'd come, Jane couldn't see any sign of Christopher, so she drew closer to the private detective.

"I take it you wish to speak with me about Monday, Your Grace?" he said in a low voice. "I trust that you still plan to go ahead with your plan to catch your, ahem..." He cast his gaze toward the door where the footman was waiting. "Well, you know who I mean."

"Yes. I do...wish to speak with you. About that matter." Jane rushed on in a hushed voice, "My two friends and I will be outside Mudie's at half past nine. The New Oxford Street entrance. We'll all be disguised in black mourning attire including veiled bonnets. You are still willing to help keep watch with us? We all think it might be the woman I glimpsed last time. Miss Sharp."

Mr. O'Connor tilted his head. "I am, Your Grace. Rest assured I'll be there at half past nine. On the dot."

"Thank you," said Jane. "I shall see you then."

The Irishman bowed, then nodded at the footman who opened the front door. Before Jane even turned around, she had the oddest feeling that she was being watched. But when she did turn back, she could see no one in the hall or on the grand stairs leading to the upper floors or in the shadows of the grand gallery that took one to the drawing room and of course the library.

Jane's guilty conscience was clearly playing tricks on her. Hopefully, come this time tomorrow this blackmailing business would be over with once and for all.

Monday the seventh of March dawned at last, and it was freezing cold and miserable. Indeed, the rain was coming down in buckets as Jane huddled beneath a heavy black cloak and enormous black umbrella and hastened down Eaton Square toward Lucy's residence, Kyleburn House.

The Countess of Kyle's carriage was already waiting outside, and when Jane climbed in, she found Lucy and Artemis armed with blankets and warmed bricks and flasks of hot sweet tea, along with a basket of freshly baked cinnamon buns. Even though they were all somberly attired in widow's weeds, it almost felt like they were embarking on a seaside holiday rather than heading out to catch a criminal red-handed.

It was only when they were drawing close to New Oxford Street that Artemis said, "I take it this Jack O'Connor will be there to step in if this blackmailer is some horrid burly man, not someone like Miss Sharp."

Jane swallowed her mouthful of tea before responding.

"Yes. He seems quite a capable fellow. He was once with Scotland Yard."

"Oh?" said Lucy. "You should have said. Will might know him."

"It's my understanding that he was a bobby," said Jane. "In any event, he's the cousin of Christopher's valet. I'm certain he's both reliable and trustworthy. Christopher wouldn't have hired him to—" Jane broke off. She really *had* to be more careful lest she betray her husband's confidence. "Well, he wouldn't have hired him if he wasn't any of those things," she concluded.

Both Lucy and Artemis gave her a speaking look, but nevertheless they didn't say anything else.

Apart from the occasional pedestrian scuttling by beneath an umbrella, the street in front of Mudie's Lending Library was almost empty of foot traffic when the Countess of Kyle's carriage drew to a stop. Jane couldn't see Jack O'Connor. Perhaps he was waiting inside, which would be the sensible thing to do.

Jane suggested that they should all do that as well. "There's no point in catching colds," she said as one of Lucy's footmen, armed with a massive umbrella, appeared by the carriage window.

"I agree," said Lucy with a dramatic shiver. "It's certainly weather for ducks."

"Hmmm, I'm a trifle worried that it might be harder for us to remain inconspicuous if there aren't many customers inside Mudie's today," added Artemis as she gathered up her bombazine skirts, preparing to alight. "I know we all have disguises, but we'll still have to take care."

"Yes, we don't want to stick out like a trio of sore thumbs." Lucy gestured at the footman to open the door. "We should probably disperse as quickly as possible. If Miss Sharp *is* behind this horrible plot, Jane, at least she doesn't know your Mr. O'Connor."

Your Mr. O'Connor...

Of course, he wasn't *her* Mr. O'Connor at all. But Lucy's choice of words gave Jane pause.

After she'd farewelled the Irishman two days ago, she'd wondered if she had detected a slight change in Christopher's demeanor. Nothing was overtly wrong. He was still as wonderfully attentive in the bedroom, and their conversational exchanges during dinner had remained lively and entertaining. But every now and again she thought she'd caught Christopher studying her. She'd feel the weight of his stare, but when she looked up his attention was upon something else. Like that moment in the entry hall when she'd felt as though someone had been watching her, she put it down to her guilty conscience.

Very soon, all going well, she'd have nothing to feel guilty about anymore.

As soon as Jane entered Mudie's with her veiled friends, Jack O'Connor stepped forward to greet them. He bowed with due deference as Jane made the introductions and then they all retreated to a quiet, shadowy corner behind a set of bookshelves to discuss their plan of attack.

"After I've ascertained the precise location of the Dickens book Her Grace is to leave the one hundred pounds in —*Oliver Twist* if I recall correctly—I suggest we all take up various lookout positions about the library," said O'Connor. "The upper balcony and the marble column adjacent to the bookcase where *Oliver Twist* is shelved would be good spots. Meanwhile, I'll wait with one of you near the library's lending desk. On the side near the exit. I take it you all know what this Miss Sharp looks like?"

"Yes," said Jane. "She's quite petite with brown hair and hazel eyes. If it *is* her, we'll recognize her immediately. Artemis especially."

"Very well then," said Mr. O'Connor. "After you've placed the money in the book, Your Grace, perhaps you could join me at the desk. No doubt the blackmailer will be watching at that point, so I think it's best if you look like you're leaving as instructed." He turned to Artemis and Lucy. "Whoever takes the position on the upper balcony, I'd like you to wave when you see anyone at all picking up the copy of *Oliver Twist*. I'll then step forward and intercept whoever it is, and hopefully it will be the blackmailer I'm confronting."

"I'll go to the balcony," said Artemis. "If it *is* Miss Sharp, it's best if I make myself scarce. My bonnet covers most of my red hair and my face is veiled, but if she did somehow manage to recognize me, it would undoubtedly ruin things."

"I'll hide near the column," said Lucy.

"Excellent," said Mr. O'Connor. "After you're all in position, I'll find that book, pretend to make a quick perusal of it so you can see what it looks like from a distance, then I'll put it back in the same spot. Ladies, I'm sure this campaign will be a success."

The lending library's copy of *Oliver Twist* was easy enough to identify when Jack O'Connor slid it from the shelf and made a show of riffling through its pages. Even from across the room, Jane could see it had a distinctive vermilion-hued leather cover. If her memory served her correctly, it appeared to be right beside *The Pickwick Papers*.

As Jane lingered by the lending library desk, waiting impatiently for ten o'clock to arrive, she tried not to fidget or stare too much at anyone who walked through the doors or browsed for titles near the Dickens section.

"We'll catch this person, Your Grace," said Mr. O'Connor, who'd returned to her side. "Do not worry."

"Is it that obvious that I'm nervous?" asked Jane.

"Aye," said the Irishman with a grin.

"I must thank you again for your help," said Jane. "I know it's a bit awkward, going behind my husband's back."

"It's nothing at all. I'm happy to be of assistance."

Mr. O'Connor's blue eyes held Jane's for a moment too long, and she found herself blushing behind her veil. Maybe Christopher did have good reason to be wary of the far-too-charming Irishman and his motives. "I am going to tell His Grace about all this," added Jane after a slightly uncomfortable pause. "I just want this part to be over with. It was my problem before we married and I feel it's my responsibility to solve it."

"I understand," said Mr. O'Connor. His gaze slid to the front door, then returned to Jane. "A short woman shrouded in a hooded cloak of dark-gray wool just walked in, Your Grace. I can't see her hair, but perhaps you could glance her way to see if it's Miss Sharp. She's approaching the far end of the lending desk right about now."

Jane dipped her head, and while she pretended to peruse a book, she looked up to spy on the woman in question. "It might be Miss Sharp," she murmured. Her skin had begun to prickle with awareness and her stomach was a bundle of tightly cinched knots. Beneath all that, anger nipped. If Miss Sharp was behind this horrible campaign... Jane pressed her lips together to prevent herself from saying something she ought not to.

O'Connor's attention returned to the shrouded woman who was now apparently studying the spines of books on a shelf not too far from the Dickens section. "I'll keep an eye on her." He pulled a pocket watch from his waistcoat and checked the time. "I'd suggest you get ready to put that one-hundred-pound payment in place, Your Grace," he added softly. "It's two minutes to ten."

Jane inhaled a fortifying breath as she pulled the envelope containing the money from a pocket in her own cloak. She'd had no problem withdrawing the sum from her bank account where her pin money was now deposited. "Wish me luck," she whispered, then started toward the shelves.

She tried not to look directly at the woman who might be Miss Sharp. Instead, she focused on locating *Oliver Twist*. And that was when she bumped into a Mudie's employee who was rushing past with a pile of books in his arms. The books went flying, and so did Jane's envelope. It skittered beneath the bookcase. *Damn it.*

The employee apologized profusely as they both dropped to the floor to retrieve their things. Fortunately, Jane's envelope hadn't disappeared completely beneath the enormous bookcase. She grasped a protruding corner, and with a quick tug, it was free. By the time the Mudie's worker had reclaimed his books and had moved on, Jane imagined it must be a minute or two after ten o'clock. But there was nothing she could do about it. With any luck, the blackmailer wouldn't be put off by the minor kerfuffle. One hundred pounds was a substantial sum and would be hard to pass up.

Again, Jane looked for *Oliver Twist*, located it, then slid it from the shelf. It might have been her imagination, but she sensed that she was being watched. The hairs on the back of her neck were standing to attention as she placed the payment inside *Oliver Twist*, then put the book back in its place.

Then, resisting the urge to look around, she turned and retreated to the far side of the lending library desk. As she rounded the corner, Jack O'Connor strode past her. Glancing up to the balcony, she could see Artemis waving a gloved hand, and Jane's heart leapt with hope.

This plan *might* actually work.

In the next instant, Jane heard a commotion coming from the other side of the library.

"Unhand me, you...you brute," cried a woman. "And give me back my book! This instant!"

Jane spun around to discover Mr. O'Connor was holding *Oliver Twist* aloft while the petite woman in the gray cloak was scrabbling to get it back. Except she couldn't reach it because O'Connor had his other hand on the woman's shoulder, keeping her at bay. In the struggle her hood fell back, and Jane saw that it *was* Miss Rosalind Sharp.

Jane rushed back over to the bookcase and threw back her veil. "Miss Sharp," she snapped, fury sharpening her tone. "Stop squawking like a banshee and drawing attention to yourself. It's most unseemly. The game is up. You've been caught red-handed."

The governess, who was as crimson as a beet, rounded on Jane. "You...you have no right to accuse me of behaving indecorously, Your Grace," she hissed. And then her face crumpled, and she burst into a storm of violent tears. Her gloved hands covered her face, and her slight body shook with the force of her racking sobs, so much so that she subsided to the floor in a heap of damp wool and muddied skirts.

Good Lord. Jane *almost* felt sorry for the woman. And then her gaze fell to the front of Miss Sharp's gown and heartfelt sympathy *did* well up inside her.

The governess was pregnant. *Very* pregnant.

About-to-have-a-baby-any-day-now pregnant.

Jane knelt on the floor. Miss Sharp was still crying, and in between gasping breaths and sobs, Jane detected the odd word or phrase. Things like "my poor baby," and being "abandoned," along with "God save me."

"Miss Sharp," she said, her voice low, "I think I know why you need money so desperately. And whether you want me to or not, I *am* going to help you."

The governess swiped at her runny nose and glared back at Jane. "You think you know me, but you don't. I'm not like you *or* your friends with your love of depraved Gothic romance books and your ridiculous Byronic Book Club and your…your loose morals. I'm not a wicked person. I'm not. I have standards and I'm—"

"In trouble," finished Artemis. She had joined the small group along with Lucy. Both of them had lifted their veils too.

"Yes. Yes, I am," whispered Miss Sharp. Her bottom lip trembled, and fresh tears brimmed in her hazel eyes. "And I don't know what to do."

Compassion softened the Duchess of Dartmoor's gaze as she sank to the floor beside the distraught woman. "As Jane said, we'll help you, Miss Sharp, whether you want us to or not. We might be wicked in your eyes, but we also understand. More than you could ever know."

Chapter Twenty-five

AFTER JANE BID MR. O'CONNOR FAREWELL, LUCY suggested that they all repair to Kyleburn House to regroup. To Jane's surprise, Miss Sharp readily agreed.

The governess was subdued during the journey back to Eaton Square, staring out the rain-streaked panes of the carriage window at the sodden, traffic-congested streets, dabbing at her eyes with Jane's lawn handkerchief every now and again. As Jane regarded her from the opposite bench seat, she tried to sort through her tangled thoughts and emotions. While part of Jane was still angry at the governess for the hell she'd been put through, Jane also couldn't help but wonder what sort of ill fortune had befallen the young woman since she'd been dismissed from the Duke of Dartmoor's employ. She supposed they would soon find out.

Once they were all safely installed in Kyleburn House's drawing room and Miss Sharp had been made comfortable before the fire and had been plied with hot tea, the young woman seemed both calm and amenable enough to discuss her situation. Especially after Jane reassured her that no matter what she disclosed, she wouldn't be in any trouble with the law.

"Are you able to talk about your pregnancy, Miss Sharp? I...or I *should* say we"—Jane gestured at Artemis and Lucy who sat on a nearby settee—"recently heard via the Duke of Dartmoor that you'd left your position in Liverpool. And that your employer wasn't very forthcoming about the details."

Miss Sharp put down her cup of tea, the cup rattling against the saucer. "I can well imagine," she said with a watery sniff. "Arthur Grimsby is his name. He's a wealthy textile merchant with a rather large family. Six children to be exact, and I was governess to the three youngest ones. Needless to say, Mr. Grimsby was most upset to discover that I was with child, and when he did I was summarily dismissed. Four months ago. After I could no longer hide my..." She pressed her hands protectively against the swell of her belly. "Well, when I could no longer hide *this*."

"And who is the father of your baby? If you don't mind me asking," Lucy said, her expression soft.

Miss Sharp's bottom lip wobbled. "No, I don't mind," she said thickly. "The father is the man that I love. With my whole heart. His name is Ned and he's Arthur Grimsby's oldest son. But his father sent him away shortly after he and I..." The governess blushed. "Shortly after Ned and I consummated our love." She shot Artemis a mulish look. "And yes, I know what you're thinking, Your Grace. That I'm a hypocrite for condemning you for the very same transgression when you were engaged to the Duke of Dartmoor. But...but Ned and I truly love each other. At least, I believed he was being sincere when we...when we gave in to our baser urges. But then he left, and even though I've tried to find out where he is so that I may write to him to tell him about my situation, I've had no luck at all. He hasn't written to me either."

A sigh shivered out of Miss Sharp. "I don't want to believe that Ned lied to me about his feelings in order to get what he wanted"—her eyes glistened with fresh tears—"but of course I've had to face the very real possibility that I'm the biggest fool in Christendom. A small part of me still hopes that Ned hasn't forsaken me. But given his lack of communication—he hasn't written to me in eight months—it seems that I have indeed been duped."

"I'm so sorry," said Jane softly. "I, too, was once abandoned by a man who I thought loved me sincerely. Since you lost your position, I take it you've had to resort to drastic measures in order to support yourself and the baby you're about to have? Is that why you broke into Delaney's Bookshop and stole my journal?"

Miss Sharp dabbed at her eyes with the limp kerchief. "Yes. I–I did." She swallowed. "Because the Duke of Dartmoor made me sign a contract stating that I would do no harm to Miss Jones, I mean Her Grace"—Miss Sharp nodded Artemis's way—"or I'd face prosecution, I couldn't do anything that might affect her. I knew that you and Her Grace were good friends and I'd heard via servant gossip at Dartmoor House that your grandfather owned Delaney's...so I decided to break in. I know stealing is sinful, but I have no family to speak of and it was midwinter and freezing cold and I'd already gone through all of my savings. And no one would hire a disgraced governess who's pregnant. The fact was I desperately needed money for rent and food and heating."

Miss Sharp's breath hitched. "I couldn't bear the idea of going to a workhouse, or dying on the streets, or...or..." She dropped her gaze to her lap where she was twisting the handkerchief in her fingers. "I might have given myself to a man once, but I didn't want to become a prostitute. I'd rather die."

"I understand," said Jane, smiling gently. Her mind returned to Saint Valentine's Day and what she'd been prepared to do to save her grandfather's bookshop and her mother's reputation. And her own. "Sometimes desperate times do call for desperate measures."

Miss Sharp nodded. "Yes. Yes, they do. When I didn't find

more than a handful of coins in your grandfather's bookshop that night, I began looking for other things I might be able to pawn. And then I found your scandalous journal, Your Grace, with all your plans about your wicked pamphlet series, and of course it reminded me of the scandalous books Artemis—I mean Lydia Lovelace—writes. I surmised that you might not want your secret to be shared with the world either, and that you might be willing to pay me to keep it a secret. Especially when I heard you'd become the Duchess of Roxby and must have access to a sizable fortune."

"I see," said Jane. "Tell me, Miss Sharp, did it ever occur to you that perhaps you could have approached Artemis or me or even Lady Kyle for help? The reason I want to share advice about sexual congress and how to prevent conception is so that women *won't* get into trouble. It's not wicked to possess such knowledge. I believe it's every woman's right to learn about these things. I believe the greater sin is keeping women in the dark."

"Yes, it's really just a question of educating women about their own biology," added Lucy. "How can any of us make informed decisions about what we do with our bodies if we don't know how they work?"

Miss Sharp hiked up her chin. "I already know all this and it didn't help me. Some women, like me, are simply fools who put their faith in the wrong man. There's no way to prevent *that*. I should have abstained. I should have waited until Ned and I were wed. But I was weak and succumbed to temptation."

"And Ned could have taken precautions *not* to get you with child," said Artemis gently. "If a man truly cares for you, he *will* be careful. Because he wants what's best for you. He shouldn't only be thinking of himself and his needs in the moment."

"Humph." The governess sniffed. "I cannot fault your logic, Your Grace."

"I know you disapprove of us and the way we think about

the world," said Jane. "But I don't think that makes us wicked. It makes us open-minded and compassionate. And I for one am willing to do what I can to make sure you aren't forced to steal or do anything else of a questionable nature in order to have everything that you and that your child will need."

Miss Sharp nodded. A tear slid down her cheek. "Thank you," she whispered. "I never expected such kindness from those I've wronged."

"Tell us, Miss Sharp," said Artemis. "What do *you* want? How can we help to make your situation better?"

"I suppose, in my heart of hearts, I would like to find out where Ned is. I'd like him to know that I'm pregnant with his child. I want to know what he thinks about that."

Artemis nodded. "I'm sure between us we can manage to find the whereabouts of Ned Grimsby."

"My husband has properties up north. In Cumberland and the south of Scotland," said Lucy. "I'm certain we could offer you a place to stay to have your baby safely. And when you are ready, we could offer you employment. Actually, I believe there's a vacancy for a housekeeper at our country house near Bowness by Lake Windermere. We have ample staff on hand who would be able to assist you with looking after your little one."

"You...you would do that for me, Lady Kyle?" Miss Sharp's hazel eyes glimmered with a light that might be hope. "Someone you hardly know who's treated your friends so abominably?"

"I would." Lucy smiled. "And even though it would be playing a little fast and loose with the truth, I'm wondering if we should introduce you to everyone as *Mrs.* Sharp. Just for the sake of propriety."

"It's customary for housekeepers to be addressed that way," added Artemis. "So it's not a terrible fib in the grand scheme of things. At least I don't think so."

"I think it would be a sensible thing to do," said Miss Sharp. "And Cumberland isn't so very far from Liverpool by train. If Ned can be found..." The governess huffed out a breath. "I'm getting ahead of myself. I need to have this baby first. I'm not exactly certain when I'm due, but maybe toward the end of this month... And then I suppose I shall see what the future holds." Her gaze shifted between Lucy and Artemis, and then settled on Jane. Her eyes were definitely looking brighter. "Thank you. All of you. I know I've been quick to pass judgment and I've said and done terrible things. It's only now that I'm beginning to realize that I was so very wrong about all of you. I hope that one day you can forgive me. And Your Grace..." She was looking at Jane again. "I shall return your journal to you. It's with my things in the room I rent in Marylebone."

"Thank you," said Jane. It was almost too soon to let relief into her heart.

Perhaps when she had her journal back in her hands.

Perhaps later, after she'd confessed all to Christopher.

As to whether he would forgive her for her subterfuge, whether or not he would stop her from achieving her goal, Jane had no idea.

The only thing she could be certain about was that the time to be honest with her husband had well and truly arrived.

Chapter Twenty-six

When Jane arrived back at Roxby House, a dismal dusk was beginning to fall. A steady chill rain had set in, and Jane wanted nothing more than to retire to her room with her hard-won journal and curl up in bed and sleep for a week. Anything to avoid the conversation which must be had.

Upon reaching the hall outside the ducal suite, she bumped into Featherstone, who informed her that His Grace had just finished a vigorous bout of boxing and was "soaking his tired muscles in the tub," as was his custom.

As the valet discreetly hastened away, Jane quietly entered Christopher's sitting room and approached the bedroom. Through the half-open door, she could see that the enormous copper bath her husband favored had been set up in front of a roaring fire.

As Jane lingered on the threshold, her heart in her mouth, her stomach knotted with tension, she couldn't help but take a moment to admire Christopher's impressive physique as tendrils of steam curled up around him.

His eyes were closed and his head was tipped back, resting against the edge of the tub. The firelight gilded his long, tautly muscled limbs and burnished his damp, slicked-back locks to a deep caramel brown. Water droplets glistened on the mounds of his broad chest.

Oh, but he was magnificent. Jane longed to shed her own damp, cumbersome clothes and join him in the warm water.

But she couldn't. Her guilt wouldn't let her. Her fingers curled around the edges of her scandalous journal, and she imagined the scarlet leather was burning her flesh.

She cleared her throat. "Christopher," she murmured, not wishing to startle him, and he immediately opened his eyes and turned to look at her from beneath drowsy lids. His sharply cut lips curved in a soft smile.

"I'm sorry to disturb you," she continued. Oh, she did not want to break his contented mood, but she must. "I–I need to speak with you."

Something about her hesitant manner made him frown and he straightened. Ran his fingers through his damp hair. "You look like you've had a very long, challenging day, my love," he said, then held out a large hand in invitation. His voice, low and soft, swept over her like a warm velvet caress. "Come and join me. I'll make you forget about all your troubles."

My love? Oh no, don't call me that. Guilt sliced through Jane's heart, cutting her to the bone. She recalled the words he'd said to her just over a week ago: *You are mine and I am yours. We are one.* And then in the carriage on the way home from the theater the very next day: *There's something about you, Jane, that has brought me to life again. For the first time in a very long time, I have hope.*

Was she about to ruin it all?

"I'd love to," she said, drawing closer to the gleaming tub, clutching her journal against her chest. "I absolutely would, and I'm sure you *could* make me forget about everything. But this matter can't wait. I–I don't know how to begin, really. You've done so much for me already, Christopher. I can't begin to describe the relief I felt when you saved my grandfather's bookshop but—"

"Blast, did Featherstone say something to you?"

Christopher's frown returned, deeper this time. "I heard his voice in the hall a few moments ago. He better not have spoiled my surprise."

"Surprise?" repeated Jane. "I have no idea what you're talking about. Featherstone didn't say anything at all about a surprise."

"Oh, good." Christopher's stern expression lifted and his smile returned. In fact it was almost sheepish as he added, "I suppose the cat's out of the bag now though. If you go over to the bed, you'll find a document on the bedside table. I want you to take a look."

A document?

Jane crossed the room, put down her journal, then picked up the parchment. She pulled the red ribbon securing it undone, then unfurled it. When she took in what was written on the paper, she gasped.

It was a business transaction—a bill of sale—indicating that her mother, Mrs. Leonora Pevensey, had sold her share of Delaney's Antiquarian Bookshop in Sackville Street, Piccadilly, to the Duke of Roxby for the grand sum of fifteen hundred pounds.

"Christopher," she whispered, meeting his warm gaze, "is this true? Do you now own half of my grandfather's bookshop?"

"Yes, it's true." His answering grin dazzled her. "But I won't own it for much longer. Because I'm going to gift it to your grandfather. My man of business here in London is drawing up the papers as we speak."

"But...but why? Why would you do this?" Jane whispered as the full import of her husband's words hit her. "You've already done so much. Too much. You've spent two and a half thousand pounds on this shop. I'm certain that's more than it's worth."

"My dear Jane, seeing your reaction, I'd pay much more than that. But to answer your question as to why I've done this...it's because I know how much you love that shop. And how much your grandfather loves it too. I don't want him, or you, to have to worry about the store's safety ever again. Besides, you know how much I love books. During my 'wild soirees', as you like to describe them, I spent countless hours in that library downstairs, perusing my great-uncle's collection. I like to think that I can count on your grandfather to value and restore any of the titles that might need some care and attention. I trust him. Just like I trust you."

Oh God. Christopher's words threatened to cleave Jane's heart in two. She didn't deserve such care and consideration. She certainly didn't deserve Christopher's trust. Tears pricked at her eyes as she carefully rolled up the parchment and secured it with the ribbon.

Tears of joy and relief and sorrow.

"I hope those are happy tears, Jane," murmured Christopher. A frown furrowed his brow.

"I…" She swallowed. "I'm happy and grateful beyond measure. You'll never know how much your generosity means to me…" She trailed off and wiped away a tear that had slipped onto her cheek. Oh, this was going to be so hard. Harder than she'd ever imagined. "It's just that…while my grandfather is a worthy recipient of such a gift, I'm afraid I am not."

Christopher's eyes narrowed. Concern clouded his blue gaze. "Whatever do you mean by that?"

Jane inhaled a steadying breath. Braced her heart for the pain which she knew was headed her way and Christopher's as she said, "I've been keeping secrets from you. Lying to you from the very beginning. I'm not the woman that you think I am. And I cannot bear to hide the truth from you any longer."

A sliver of apprehension penetrated Christopher's chest. This was *not* how he'd anticipated this conversation would unfold. He attempted a smile and a quip to alleviate the razor-sharp tension. Anything to dispel the despair and self-recrimination in Jane's gaze.

"What, are you going to confess you're my would-be murderer, Jane?" he asked. "Or that you're a bigamist?"

She shook her head. "No. It's not quite that bad."

He forced himself to ask his next question, even though his heart crashed against his ribs and foreboding curled through his gut. "Is there...is there someone else? Another man you've been seeing?" he asked softly. *Someone like the far-too-charming Jack O'Connor?*

Again she shook her head.

Thank God.

"No. It's not anything like that," she whispered.

Her face was so stricken that Christopher wanted to draw her into his arms and kiss away her tears. But something else held him back. Wariness. Fear.

Suspicion.

Christopher climbed from the bath and snagged a towel from a nearby table. He roughly toweled himself dry, then threw on a pair of trousers and a dark-blue satin banyan that Featherstone had draped over a chair.

"Let's move into the sitting room," he said, unable to soften the grim edge to his voice. Jane winced at the harshness of his tone, and while part of him regretted it, he couldn't seem to control how he sounded. Not when deep unease coursed through his veins.

Jane claimed her usual seat by the fire, a short distance from Christopher's leather wingback chair. She was as taut as a piano wire and seemed to be looking everywhere but at him.

"What's going on, Jane?" he asked, trying to temper his tone. And then his gaze fell on the red leather book she clutched tightly, so tightly her knuckles were white. "You need to speak plainly. I'm afraid I have no idea what you're talking about."

Jane nodded. Drew a breath. "When I tried to steal *The Canterbury Tales* from you, I didn't need money just to save my grandfather's bookshop," she began. "I also needed money because I was being blackmailed."

"Blackmailed?" If Jane had grown a mermaid's tail or sprouted fairy wings, Christopher would have been less surprised. "How...? What sort of scandalous secret could you possibly be hiding?"

She lifted the red book she still clutched in her hands. "This journal was stolen from my grandfather's bookshop in January. It contains my notes for a pamphlet series I hope to anonymously publish one day entitled *A Practical Woman's Guide to Self-Determination and Lasting Fulfillment*. While it sounds innocuous, the pamphlets are about topics that most of society would classify as taboo. Subjects such as sexual congress and how to prevent pregnancy and venereal infections. Subjects many women know next to nothing about, but they *should* know about...before it's too late."

"Ah, I see," said Christopher. While he was impressed by Jane's open-mindedness and the humanitarian nature of her venture, he still needed to voice his concerns. "I'm sure I'm stating the obvious, but such a project *would* be deemed scandalous, despite your worthy intentions. The public outcry that would result should word get out that you are the author of these pamphlets would be enormous. Polite society would be pitiless in its treatment of you. Your good name would be ruined. Even though you are a duchess, you would be shunned."

"I know," whispered Jane. "I know all this. To be fair, I

conceived the idea for my pamphlet series before I'd even met you. And of course I never dreamed that anyone would steal my journal and blackmail me."

"But someone did," said Christopher grimly. "Putting aside my deep reservations about your proposed project—I feel that is a discussion we should have at another time—I see you have the journal back. So the immediate threat to your reputation is over?"

Jane nodded. "Yes. It is."

"And how did you get it back? I trust the blackmailer has been caught?"

"Yes, she has. Earlier today, in fact." And then Christopher listened in shock as Jane disclosed that the perpetrator, a Miss Rosalind Sharp, had once been the governess of the Duke of Dartmoor's daughter but had been dismissed for similar unconscionable behavior. That this Miss Sharp had since fallen pregnant and had been blackmailing Jane to save herself from destitution. That she'd been caught this morning at Mudie's Lending Library, the place where Jane was instructed to deliver a one-hundred-pound payment.

"She broke into my grandfather's shop because, I'm afraid to say, she did not think much of me or my friends Artemis and Lucy," said Jane. "Or our Byronic Book Club. When she discovered my journal, she had no compunction about using it to extort money from me. But she's exactly the sort of woman I want to help. If her lover had taken precautions, she wouldn't have ended up in the terrible situation she found herself in. Part of me is sympathetic to her plight. So much so that I do not wish to take the matter further. Aside from the fact it would be awkward to go to the police about it— the fewer people who know about my journal, the better— someone like Miss Sharp needs help, not censure. Lucy has offered her employment as a housekeeper at one of her husband's properties up north."

"I must say, I'm flabbergasted," admitted Christopher. "Not only by who the blackmailer turned out to be, but by your ability to forgive such a malicious crime. You have a kind heart, Jane. Perhaps too kind." Narrowing his gaze, he added, "I'm curious though…how did you manage to catch this Miss Sharp? You mentioned your friend Lady Kyle knows about all this. I take it the Duchess of Dartmoor has been involved too?"

Jane worried at her lower lip. "Yes… I enlisted their help recently when I realized it would be difficult to catch the blackmailer on my own. And while I should have told you about all this even before we wed, I simply couldn't, Christopher. You already have so much to deal with. I didn't think it was fair that I would be foisting yet another problem onto you. A problem that was not of your making."

"I see," said Christopher carefully. "But you went to your friends… And were they with you this morning at Mudie's when this Miss Sharp was apprehended?"

"Yes. Lucy and Artemis acted as lookouts while Mr.—" Jane broke off and blushed. Looked away.

"Mr. who?" asked Christopher, suspicion uncoiling like a viper in his belly.

"Mr. O'Connor," Jane whispered.

"Jack O'Connor. The private detective *I* employ."

Jane at last met his gaze. "Yes… It's not his fault for keeping all this from you. I was the one who asked for his advice on the matter. And his help this morning. We needed all the sets of eyes we could find in Mudie's Lending Library to keep watch."

Christopher surged to his feet. "No doubt the fact I can't recognize anyone at all apart from you and my own reflection factored into your decision to exclude me from your scheme," he grated out. He was unable to hide the bitterness in his voice. Impotent frustration squeezed his lungs, tightened his throat. Made him clench his fists. He suddenly wanted to strike a wall or a door or upend a table. Smash something. Anything.

Jack O'Connor's bloody face would do. The sly bastard.

Not that it would help to lay the Irishman flat on his back.

Christopher strode over to the oak cabinet where he kept a small supply of spirits and sloshed brandy into a tumbler. He needed to calm down. The plain, hard, ugly truth was that Jane had gone to another man for help. This affliction, this blindness for faces made Christopher worse than useless.

Indeed, he'd never felt so hopeless.

"Christopher…" The sound of Jane's voice, so soft and so hesitant, tore at Christopher's gut. His display of temper had no doubt frightened her, and he instantly regretted it.

He turned, glass in hand, and immediately noticed her green eyes were shining with tears. Oh God, he'd made her cry.

But she'd hurt him too. Even now, he could feel the prick of tears at the back of his own eyes. He hadn't cried in years.

Fuck. What the hell was wrong with him?

"Christopher, I'm so, so sorry." Jane got to her feet, took a few tentative steps toward him, then stopped. "I can see how upset I've made you. I…I never set out to hurt you or make you feel excluded, but I fear that I have. I truly wanted to shield you from *my* mess. It was *my* responsibility to extricate myself—"

"Yet you had no trouble using my money and my private detective," he bit out before he could stop himself, and Jane winced. Her face began to crumple, but then she bit her lip as though that would stem her tears.

Christ. He was such an insensitive brute. He was like a wounded lion, roaring and lashing out without thought.

He threw back his brandy, then poured himself another. Then drank that too for good measure.

When he turned back, it was to discover Jane had retreated to the fireside. The flames picked out strands of deep mahogany and even gold in her thick lustrous locks. Part of him wanted nothing more than to draw her into his arms, offer her comfort for the ordeal she'd been through. No doubt she'd been fretting and anxious for weeks.

But his pride wouldn't let him.

She'd gone to another man for help. She'd gone behind his back. And he'd only ever been open and honest with her. About everything.

He couldn't get past it.

He wondered if he ever would.

Jane lifted her head and looked at him across a gulf that seemed wider and deeper than the Atlantic Ocean. "I understand that you feel as though I've betrayed you by not confiding in you," she said softly, her voice thick with emotion. "My only defense, which you may think is weak but nonetheless it is the only one I have, is that I find it very difficult to trust. To share everything with someone else. Like you, my heart was broken. Like you, I've avoided any sort of intimacy—both physical and emotional—with anyone for a very long time. And I think now is the time to tell you why. Of course, I know it can't excuse what I've done, but perhaps it will help you to understand."

"Very well," said Christopher. He reclaimed his chair. "I'll listen, Jane. I think if this marriage is to work, we both need to understand each other."

Jane nodded. "I'm glad you agree." She subsided into her chair again and a resigned sigh shivered out of her. "You know some but not all of my history with Miles Dempster. I think it's important that I share the parts I've left out. The parts no one else knows about except for my mother..."

She pressed her fingers to her lips, then placed her hands on her skirts, rubbing her palms up and down the silk fabric. She seemed agitated. Restless. It was as though she didn't know how to begin. That her emotions were roiling around inside her so much, she couldn't order her thoughts.

Despite his own bruised feelings, Christopher's heart cramped with compassion. "If it's too difficult to speak about, you don't need to," he said gently.

"No. No, I want to," said Jane, her expression graver than Christopher had ever seen it. "I *need* to. I suppose a large degree of my apprehension is related to the fact that my conscience plagues me. Actually, it has done so ever since you first proposed and then I accepted. We both agreed that we would share a bed, that I would bear you an heir. And while I do want that, with my whole heart I want that, what I didn't disclose is that when I was nineteen..." She paused. Swallowed. Her hands shifted to the arms of the chair and she curled her fingers into the damask. "When I was nineteen, after Miles proposed and we made love, after the accident..." Her voice cracked and she inhaled a quick breath. "After the accident," she continued, her voice now steady, "after Miles called off the engagement, I discovered I was with child. And then I lost it."

Oh God. Christopher's chest tightened with so much pain on her behalf, he almost couldn't breathe. He put down his glass of brandy with a clatter on the table. "Jane, I'm so sorry. I had no idea."

She shrugged. Her mouth twisted with a small broken smile that wasn't really a smile at all. "How could you know? As I said, no one knows except my mother. Not even darling Artemis and Lucy. I lost the baby quite early on. In fact, I was pregnant but a handful of weeks. Weeks in which I was simultaneously filled with secret joy and terror. I wanted a baby, but I didn't want to be an unwed mother."

"That's completely understandable," said Christopher. "Did you tell Miles?"

Jane shook her head. "No. After he jilted me, he left to begin his next semester at Oxford. He was studying law, like my brother. I miscarried before I got the chance to tell him. He never knew. In hindsight, I doubt it would have made much difference. He was so horrified by what had happened to me—to my face—that he couldn't even bear to be in the same room with me. He couldn't stand the guilt."

Christopher's jaw had tightened so much it cracked. "What a weak bastard, Jane. What a puling excuse for a man. If I ever cross paths with him, that sniveling swine will rue the day he was born."

At last, Jane's mouth did twitch with a genuine smile. "I think I should like to see that. In any event, my physician assured me that I would still be able to have children in the future—that it was probably the ordeal I had been through, both physical and emotional that had contributed to the loss of my baby. But I suppose I've always wondered if maybe there is something lacking within me as a woman. It was wrong of me not to share that with you, Christopher, considering the bargain we made. But we'd only just met… We barely knew other…and as you know, I was desperate. And deep down in my heart, I wanted the chance to have another baby. I *still* want that. That isn't a lie."

"Jane… I…" Christopher shook his head. "I told you at the start that my main reason for making that bargain with you was to ensure you and I would be sharing a bed. And while I will need an heir one day…" His words trailed away. He flexed his hands on his thighs. "I want you, Jane, there's no denying it.

But the fact that you went behind my back, that you've kept so much from me, shut me out... I too find it hard to trust. After Daisy left me for Simon Cosgrove, I've always feared that might happen again."

Jane's gaze was unwavering as it met his. "I want to reassure you that I haven't betrayed you the way Daisy did. I may have gone to ask Jack O'Connor for help, but that's all. I haven't been unfaithful. I would never do that."

"But that's just it, Jane. You might not have been unfaithful to me in a physical sense, but to me, what you've done is almost worse than that. I can't help but feel a sense of emotional betrayal. From the very beginning, I shared everything with you. My affliction. The fact someone is trying to kill me... I've never been so vulnerable with anyone before. And now to hear you couldn't confide in me or ask for my help... Yes, it's been hard for me to trust anyone after Daisy. She hurt me. Deeply. And the way I feel right now, in this moment, it's as though you've cut me to the quick too."

It was true. He felt beaten and bruised and raw. Like his insides were splitting apart. Like the stitches holding his heart together were coming undone.

"Christopher." Jane's whisper was leaden with remorse. "I never expected you to feel this way. We've only been wed a few weeks. All this time, I've been telling myself that we could never have more than the marriage of convenience we agreed to. I thought you would do the same."

Christopher shook his head. "Even though I never promised you love, I was beginning to care for you, Jane. I thought that in time I might even develop feelings beyond mere affection and lust. I suppose I was a fool to hope that you would see that or feel it too."

Anger flared in Jane's gaze. "That's not fair. You cannot

blame me for having doubts. For being wary. For protecting my heart. I cannot read your mind. I cannot know what's in *your* heart if you do not share it."

"And you cannot even be honest," he returned heatedly, hating how cruel he sounded. How she winced as though he'd wounded her too. Even though it was true he'd never voiced such sentiments before, deep down he'd started to wonder if Jane *had* begun to care, just like he had.

He strove to temper his tone. "I appreciate that you've been open with me tonight, how brave you've been to share so many difficult, tragic things from your past. While I understand your reluctance to confide in me to some extent, I cannot simply set aside how *I* feel. Which is misled and deceived." He rose and dragged a hand down his face. A dull throb had begun at the base of his skull, and he knew it wouldn't be long until his whole head was pounding. "I'm sorry, but I need some time to myself, Jane. I fear I have a megrim coming on. We will not share a bed tonight."

And then he quit the room, closing his bedroom door on the woman he'd begun to believe he could fall in love with. Whether this marriage had all been a huge mistake—the worst of his life—only time would tell.

Chapter Twenty-seven

WHEN JANE AWOKE THE NEXT MORNING, ALONE IN HER OWN bed, the rain had at last abated but her low spirits had not.

After Christopher had retreated to his bedroom, closing the door on her, she'd gone to her own room, shed her clothes, climbed into her bed, and then had sobbed herself to sleep. Never in her life had she felt quite so wretched. In the dark hours of the night, she'd woken and wept again. Silent tears had slid from beneath her lids into her pillow until it was damp. The rift between her and her husband seemed irreparable.

And she had no one to blame but herself.

While she took breakfast in her room—a cup of tea and half a piece of toast was all she had the appetite for— Elsie relayed a message from Featherstone. His Grace wished to depart for Waterloo Bridge Station by nine o'clock so they could catch the ten o'clock train to Reigate.

Jane almost cried with relief. At least Christopher wasn't going to shun her completely. He still needed her in some capacity, and she would count that as a blessing.

Perhaps there was hope for them after all.

Elsie helped Jane to dress in one of her new creations from the modiste, a smart traveling gown of burgundy wool trimmed with black velvet and jet buttons. But when Jane took in her reflection in the looking glass, she realized that the gown's hue only made her eyes look redder and puffier. She'd have changed into something else, but it was ten minutes to nine and she hadn't the time to spare.

With a sigh, she donned a black bonnet and selected a matching beaded reticule and then exited her room…and barreled straight into Christopher.

He caught her about the shoulders to hold her steady. "My apologies, Jane," he said softly. "I wasn't looking where I was going."

"Neither was I," she returned. Her gaze searched his face, trying to ascertain his mood. There were shadows of fatigue beneath his blue eyes and lines of strain bracketed his mouth, so perhaps he hadn't slept well either. Or perhaps he was in pain. "Has your headache abated?"

He released her and as he headed for the stairs, she fell into step with him. "It's faded but not completely gone." He patted his breast pocket. "I have a little laudanum on me in case it gets worse."

"Are you sure we should go at all—" she began but Christopher cut her off.

"Yes, I'm sure," he said with uncharacteristic brusqueness. "I'm keen to at least eliminate another suspect from my list besides Harry Wexford. Even Cosgrove is still a maybe in my mind." He halted at the head of the stairs and raked a hand through his already disheveled hair. "God, I'm sorry, Jane. I'm just so damn frustrated with the lack of progress. For months I've felt as though I'm looking over my shoulder, starting at shadows, waiting for the next attack, and it's wearing me down. I can't even go for a bloody ride in Hyde Park in case I'm shot at again. Every time I step outside this house, I wonder if I'll ever return. It's…" He huffed out a heavy sigh. "It's just a lot."

Jane wanted to hug him, offer him comfort, but he might reject her, so she simply reached out and touched his arm. "I can't even begin to imagine how that feels," she said gently. "You know I'll do whatever I can to help."

"Thank you," he replied gruffly. "The carriage should be out front waiting for us." Then he proceeded down the stairs. Without her.

The carriage ride to Waterloo Bridge Station and the subsequent train trip to Reigate was filled with awkward, heavy silence. For most of the journey, Christopher's attention was either fixed on the passing scenery outside his window, or he would close his eyes and tip his head back against the seat.

Jane hoped his megrim wasn't getting worse.

She lamented the fact she hadn't brought any sort of diversion with her. Although she doubted she'd be able to concentrate on a book right now. So she stared out her window too and tried not to fret about the complete hash she'd made of her relationship with Christopher.

Time heals all wounds, she reminded herself. *Christopher will see that I'm trustworthy. That he hasn't a reason to doubt me.*

Jane's thoughts strayed to other parts of their fraught discussion yesterday. Fragments drifted through her mind and an ember of hope flickered in her heart. Although Christopher had stated that he had reservations about her pamphlet scheme, he'd also said that they would discuss it in the future. If he was willing to do that, it meant he hadn't dismissed her idea outright. Perhaps when the person behind these attacks on Christopher was caught, she could revisit the matter.

Jane certainly wouldn't bring the subject up today.

They reached Reigate shortly after eleven o'clock and Christopher sought directions to St. Mary's from the station master. The church was apparently in Chart Lane, a little over half a mile away.

The day was cool and overcast, but it didn't feel like there was rain in the air as she and Christopher set out.

"Have you thought of how you're going to broach the topic of Neville with his parents?" asked Jane as they traipsed along a quiet road, heading for the center of the village.

"I don't see much point in dissembling," said Christopher. He looked a bit brighter now that they were out in the fresh air. A light wind ruffled his hair, pushing it back from his high forehead, and his eyes seemed clearer. "I'll simply ask Reverend Phelps where he is. That I've a desire to see how his son is faring after all this time."

"I'm sure you're right," said Jane. "I'm afraid I forgot to take another look at that sketch you have of Neville, the one taken from the newspaper. I don't imagine he'll be here in Reigate, but it would have been useful to refresh my memory all the same."

Christopher reached into his pocket. "I have it here."

Jane took the newspaper cutting and felt a pinch of hurt when she noticed how carefully Christopher had passed it to her. He'd avoided any sort of physical contact. Any accidental brushing of fingers. How on earth were they to beget a child if he couldn't even bear something as innocuous as that?

Telling herself his aversion to touching her would pass, Jane studied the engraving as they continued on their way. Lieutenant Neville Phelps had been a handsome young man with short, cropped hair and neatly trimmed side-whiskers. His jaw was strong and his features regular. The way he stared so confidently out from the sketch, Jane could well imagine he'd been a rakish sort of chap. Tupping the commanding officer's wife was certainly daring, if not altogether audacious. It was undoubtedly imprudent.

Whether or not Reverend Phelps and his wife would share anything about their son remained to be seen.

Within fifteen minutes, Jane and Christopher arrived at the church. A tall, crenellated tower of pale-gray stone dominated the grassy knoll upon which it sat, casting a long, dark shadow over the mossy flagged footpath and ancient gravestones in the churchyard.

The arched wooden door appeared firmly shut, but when Christopher tried the handle, it yielded. He ushered Jane into the hushed, shadowy interior, and she paused in the vestibule, studying the nave with its empty pews, the vaulted ceiling, and the elegant stained-glass window above the alter at the far end.

Christopher drew alongside her. "I'm not a deeply religious man," he murmured, "but I hope to God we can find some answers today."

She turned her head and was heartened when Christopher met her gaze unflinchingly. "I pray that we do too. You deserve to be happy. More than anything, I want that for you..." She inhaled a steadying breath to add "and for us," but before the words emerged, the creak of a door and the scuff of a footstep on flagstones drew Christopher's attention away.

"Can I help you?" A gray-haired gentleman appeared in the chancel. He was attired in black with a white minister's stock at his throat. As he advanced toward them with unhurried steps, his gaze was politely curious.

"Yes," returned Christopher. "If you have a moment to spare for a brief chat, Reverend Phelps, I'd be most grateful."

A warm smile broke over the minister's distinguished countenance. "I've always got time for a chat," he said. "But you have me at a disadvantage, sir. You know my name but I do not know yours, or that of your charming companion."

Christopher's smile grew a little tighter. "Forgive me, Reverend. My name is Christopher Marsden, and my charming companion, as you so aptly described her, is my wife, Jane."

At the mention of their names, Reverend Phelps's own smile instantly dimmed. "Marsden, you say."

"Yes. I once served in the same light dragoon regiment as your son, Lieutenant Phelps. I was formerly Major Marsden."

"Ah...that's why I know the name," said the minister, his expression smoothing into professional neutrality again. "You say 'formerly'?"

"Yes. I resigned my commission when I inherited my great-uncle's title. I'm now the Duke of Roxby."

"Oh...oh, I see. My goodness gracious, Your Grace. I had no idea." The flummoxed minister bowed to Christopher. "Your Grace," he added, bowing even lower to Jane. "Please forgive my rudeness."

Jane offered Reverend Phelps a reassuring smile. They really needed this man to open up to them, and honey caught more flies than vinegar. "That's quite all right. How were you to know?"

"Yes," said Christopher, adding a charming smile of his own. "No harm done."

Their ploy worked because the minister beamed back at them. "So, Your Grace, what brings you to Reigate? What can I do for you? Would you care to join me in the vicarage for tea? My wife is currently out and about, but I'm sure our housekeeper could manage to produce a tea cake. She makes a delightful one with cinnamon—"

"That won't be necessary," said Christopher. "I don't want to put you to any trouble. But to answer your initial question, I will be quite frank. I'm actually here to find out how Neville is after all this time. I must confess it has been weighing heavily on my mind that I played a significant role in his discharge from the regiment. It was a difficult business all around."

The minster's cheeks took on a ruddy hue. "Yes. Yes, it was," he said gravely. "And I want you to know, Your Grace, that neither my wife nor I bear you any ill will for the part you played in our son's dismissal. What Neville did was shameful. Unchristian. It was just and right that he was called to account for—" He broke off and his flush deepened to a rather startling shade of crimson. "For what he did. I thought my wife and I had brought him up to be better than that."

"If it's any consolation, he served the regiment well in the Crimea," said Christopher.

"Right. Yes..." Reverend Phelps's narrow shoulders rose and fell on a sigh. "Be that as it may, I'm much relieved that that period of his life is behind him now. But to answer *your* question, Your Grace, I'm proud to say that Neville is doing very well for himself. He's a changed man." The vicar beamed. "He's now happily wed to the daughter of a local landowner and manages his father-in-law's farm and estate. In fact, Alice—that's his lovely wife—is about to give birth to their second child any day now. My wife, Margaret, is visiting them as we speak. If you'd like to stop by, Brookfield Farm is only a few miles away on the outskirts of the neighboring village, Redhill."

"I don't want to create any discord or dredge up bad memories," said Christopher.

"Oh no, I'm sure Neville would welcome the chance to see you again, Your Grace. He doesn't blame you at all for what happened. He's taken his punishment on the chin and has well and truly moved on."

Jane smiled. "It's wonderful to hear that Neville is so content."

"It's wonderful what the love of a good woman can do

to change a man," returned the vicar warmly. He winked at Christopher. "I'm sure I don't need to tell you that, Your Grace."

Christopher's tight smile slid back into place. "Quite," he said. "Tell me, Reverend, is there a train between here and Redhill?"

The vicar nodded. "Yes, there is. But it would be uncharitable of me not to take you to Brookfield myself. The curate and the sexton have everything well in hand here. It will take but ten minutes to ready the dogcart and then it's a fifteen-minute journey, if that."

"That is very generous of you," said Jane, even as dismay began to swirl in her belly. Tightened her chest. *A dogcart.* She had avoided riding in a dogcart for years. Nearly a whole decade in fact. She could ride in an enclosed hansom cab and any other sort of carriage. Catch an omnibus and a train.

But a dogcart?

They followed Reverend Phelps outside into the churchyard, and after he disappeared to ready the cart, Christopher grasped her elbow. "Jane, are you all right? You've gone awfully pale."

"I..." She mustered a smile. Christopher needed to meet with Neville, and he was relying on her to help him associate names with faces. She wouldn't let him down. Not again. "I'm fine. Just a little tired, I expect."

Christopher relinquished his hold on her. "Very well," he said, although he didn't look at all convinced.

When Reverend Phelps pulled up outside his church in the dogcart a short time later, Jane felt no better at all. Indeed, her stomach churned with so much panic, she thought she might cast up her accounts as Christopher helped her into the back of the small two-wheeled vehicle.

She clutched the railing with one hand and the bench seat with the other and tried to calm her breathing. *You'll be all right. You'll be all right,* she told herself over and over again as Christopher leapt in beside her and the dogcart started off at a sedate pace down the narrow lane. *Reverend Phelps isn't Miles Dempster. He won't drive too fast. He hasn't been drinking champagne. You're safe.*

But try as she might, Jane couldn't seem to slow down her galloping heart or the increased rate of her breathing. Her lungs refused to draw in enough air. When the dogcart reached the open road, and the pony pulling it picked up its pace, Jane wondered if she might faint and topple out to meet her end. She screwed her eyes shut and tried to imagine she was safe inside Christopher's carriage. That the window was open and that's why she could feel the wind tugging at her bonnet and hair and whipping around her skirts. That she wasn't perched precariously on an open bench seat with nothing to stop her falling.

They hit a bump in the country road, and she emitted a whimper.

"Jane…" She felt Christopher's arm slide around her, drawing her close. "Christ, you're shaking like a leaf."

"I'm…I'm…I'm afraid I'm not good with dogcarts," she whispered through clenched teeth. "After the accident…"

"Devil take you, woman, you should have said something!"

"Didn't…didn't want to create a fuss," she managed. If she wasn't so terrified, she was certain she'd enjoy the feeling of being held against her husband's wide chest. The press of his muscular thigh against her own leg. But all she could do was hold on. "I'm sure we'll be there soon."

"I've got you," Christopher murmured near her ear. "I won't let you go." Then he called out, "I say, Reverend, would you mind slowing down a bit? My wife's feeling a tad poorly."

"Oh, of course," returned the vicar. "So sorry. Clover hasn't been out for a while and she's a trifle enthusiastic."

Almost at once, the dogcart began to slow, and Jane began to believe that she might survive after all. When they at last turned into a narrow poplar-lined lane, heading toward a rambling whitewashed house upon a low rise, she was nothing but relieved.

As soon as the cart halted by the house's front door, Christopher vaulted from the seat and lifted Jane down. "You goose," he said softly. His arms were about her, his hands resting lightly on her waist. "If I'd known how difficult this would be for you, I would have quite happily taken the train or walked the whole way."

She nodded and sucked in a shaky breath. "I'm an enormous goose if we're being honest. But we're here now. That's all that matters."

"Yes…" Christopher's gaze slid past the dogcart to the farmhouse. "Hopefully Reverend Phelps's assessment of his son's opinion of me is accurate. I'm not in the mood for a bout of fisticuffs today."

"I can't see why the reverend would lie," said Jane.

"No, neither can I," Christopher began, and then his whole body went rigid. "Jane, is that Neville at the door?"

Her stomach fluttering with unease, Jane turned and eyed the tall, dark-haired man lingering on the threshold. A small child with a mop of brown curls—a little boy who couldn't have been older than three—was clinging to the fellow's trouser leg with one chubby fist. "Yes, it is," she murmured. With them obscured by the back of the dogcart, Neville hadn't noticed her and Christopher yet. She wondered how he would respond when he did.

The young man called a greeting to his father, who was in the process of tethering the pony's reins to an iron ring set in a nearby garden wall. And then Neville Phelps's gaze drifted to the cart and his eyebrows shot up into the vicinity of his hair-line. "Major Marsden? Is that you?"

Christopher offered Jane his arm and then they both stepped forward. "Yes, it is, Phelps," he returned, then lifted his chin. "And this is my wife, Jane, the Duchess of Roxby."

Jane inclined her head and smiled, hoping she didn't look as wary and tense as she felt. Neville Phelps didn't look like he was spoiling for a fight or worse, but one never knew...

"Duchess?" Neville's startled gaze flitted to Jane, then back to Christopher. "Does that mean that you're—"

"The Duke of Roxby?" interjected Reverend Phelps with a wide grin. "Why, yes, it does, my dear boy. It does. Just think, a duke and a duchess have come calling at Brookfield Farm."

Neville inclined his head. "I see," he said carefully. "I must say I never thought I'd see you again, Major Marsden... I mean Your Grace. So I hope you'll forgive me for asking you quite bluntly why are you here?"

"Papa"—the child tugged on his father's trousers— "Who dat?"

"Who *is* that?" gently prompted Neville as he swung the child into his arms. "It's a man your papa used to work with a long time ago. And the fine lady he's married to. They're a duke and duchess and we are to call them 'Your Grace.'"

"Your Gwace," repeated the child. His nose scrunched up as he fiddled with his father's shirt collar. "Wike Aunty Gwace?"

Jane's heart swelled with a bittersweet ache, not only for the babe she'd lost but for what might never be if she and Christopher couldn't find a way to repair their fractured relationship. One of her hands involuntarily fluttered to her waist. If she were lucky enough to have a little boy, would Christopher pick him up and hold him just like Neville Phelps was doing? Would he speak to him with such warmth and patience? It was almost too much for her to bear thinking about.

Reverend Phelps approached the door, and the child threw out his arms. A bright smile split his rosy cheeks. "Gwandpapa, Gwandmama's here too."

The vicar laughed and took his grandson from Neville. "I know, I know, Charlie. Fancy that. We can all have lunch together."

"Cook's making wabbit stew. I don't wike wabbit stew," said Charlie as Reverend Phelps took him inside.

"I don't care for it much either, my boy. But it will fill our bellies all the same."

When they'd disappeared into the house, Neville crossed his arms over his chest. "You still haven't answered my question, Your Grace. Why are you here?"

Christopher inclined his head. "I've come to see how life is treating you, Phelps."

"I'm sorry. I don't believe you," said the former lieutenant. "There's some other reason, but you won't say."

"Yes, it's true. There is," returned Christopher after a moment's hesitation. "But I'm not sure if it would be prudent of me to share it with you."

"I see…" The man rubbed his jaw, his gaze assessing. "Look, Your Grace, if you've come here to gloat at my fall from honor, or even if you're seeking a personal apology for trying to strike you when I was drunk, I'm afraid you are out of luck on both counts. I've paid for my foolishness, in spades, and I've moved on. That arrogant, hot-headed young officer is gone. In fact, now that I'm a farmer, I'm as happy as a pig in mud. I have a beautiful wife and a wonderful son, and it won't be long before I'm a father again. You may not believe it, but leaving the cavalry was the best thing I ever did."

Christopher smiled. "I don't know if *you'll* believe *me*, Phelps, but I'm very happy to hear it." He took a few steps forward and offered the man his hand. "I wish you and your young family nothing but the best in life."

Neville tilted his head in acknowledgment and then shook Christopher's hand. "Thank you, Your Grace. I appreciate your kind words." His gaze traveled to Jane. "You and your wife are welcome to share our humble lunch of rabbit stew if you'd like to stay. There's plenty."

Christopher glanced at Jane. "What say you, my wife?"

"I think I should like that very much," she returned warmly. And she meant it.

"Very good," said Phelps, and for the first time he smiled at Christopher. "Welcome to Brookfield Farm, Your Grace. Won't you and your wife come inside?"

Chapter Twenty-eight

IF JANE HAD THOUGHT THE RETURN TRIP TO LONDON would be less awkward and strained than their earlier trip to Reigate, she was sorely mistaken.

While they'd shared lunch with Neville Phelps and his family, Christopher had appeared to be in far better spirits. He hadn't been so withdrawn, chatting freely and even laughing at the charming antics of little Charlie Phelps, which had touched Jane immeasurably. It was a tantalizing glimpse of what the future might hold if Christopher could find it in his heart to forgive her.

Jane had also been heartened and relieved when Christopher had suggested they walk the short distance to the nearby village of Redhill rather than return to Reigate in Reverend Phelps's dogcart. She'd even begun to believe that her husband no longer eschewed physical contact with her—he'd offered her his arm as they'd walked along meandering country lanes and had readily handed her onto the train. But as soon as the train had pulled out of the station, the atmosphere inside their first-class carriage had changed. Sitting on the opposite seat to her, Christopher had once more lapsed into a brooding silence.

Even though she feared she might make things worse, Jane gathered her courage to discuss Neville Phelps and where their investigation should go to next. It was a topic that couldn't be avoided. It's why they'd embarked on this journey to Surrey in the first place.

"Neville was so amiable during lunch, I do think he's genuinely happy with his lot in life," she said. "I don't think he's behind these attacks. But I'd be interested to hear your thoughts."

Christopher agreed with her. "I don't think it's Neville either. I kept looking for signs that he was insincere, or that he might harbor a grudge below the surface of all that bonhomie, but I couldn't detect that anything was amiss."

A peculiar mix of relief and dismay suddenly welled in Jane's chest along with a rush of icy foreboding. "So if Harry Wexford and Neville Phelps are now crossed off your list, and you don't think Simon Cosgrove is responsible, who could be behind these attempts on your life?"

Christopher's brows gathered into a deep frown. Shadows darkened his blue gaze and perhaps there was even a note of despair in his voice as he said, "I don't know... I truly don't know. I've been racking my brain since we left Brookfield Farm, but I honestly haven't a clue."

Jane's heart clenched. She wanted to join her husband on the opposite side of the carriage and draw him into her arms, to soothe him, but she wasn't sure how such a gesture would be received. She couldn't bear it if Christopher pushed her away. So she stayed in her own seat and looked out the window.

Yet again, her mind drifted to Neville Phelps's young family and her own deep desire to have a baby with Christopher...and then her pulse began to hurtle as another thought occurred to her. Something potentially significant that could make all the difference to their stalled investigation.

"Christopher..." She was unable to hide the note of excitement in her voice as she continued, "This might seem like a far-fetched idea, but what about Daphne, your cousin-in-law? I know each time you've been attacked it was a man, but what if...what if Daphne hired someone to kill you? You told me that her son, Oliver, is currently the next heir to the dukedom. If something happened to you before *you* fathered a son, wouldn't he inherit the title?"

Christopher's gaze narrowed in thought. "Yes, he would. But I never... It never occurred to me..." He sat forward and his voice contained renewed vigor as he said, "I never considered Daphne, but it's not beyond the realm of possibility. She does have a strong motive. She's certainly never approved of me. Given my notoriety, I suspect she thinks I'm a reprobate of the highest order. You're bloody brilliant, Jane."

Upon hearing Christopher's praise, Jane couldn't suppress a smile and a small rush of attendant pleasure. Her mind returned to her visit to the Whisteria Club. "I didn't mention this before because I wasn't sure it was important, but..." She told Christopher about what she'd observed that afternoon as she was leaving. How she thought she'd seen Daphne Marsden. "At the time I didn't think anything of it. But what if she needs money? When I met her at Roxby House, she asked you for a check. She said it was to buy new clothes for Oliver, but what if she lied? What if she has a gambling problem like my mother? Or she's using the money for something else nefarious?"

Christopher's expression was grim. "Like hiring a killer..." He rubbed a hand down his face. "Round-the-clock surveillance of my cousin-in-law's comings and goings would be useful at this juncture. I'd be interested to find out if she *is* actually a member of this Whisteria Club and if she's running low on funds. Or if she has won a substantial sum, what is she using the money for?"

"So how will you go about monitoring Daphne's movements?" Jane ventured, her voice breathless with nerves. "Will you...will you ask Mr. O'Connor to watch her?"

Christopher's expression became shuttered, and his voice

was frost-laden as he said, "At this point, I'm reluctant to share my particular circumstances with another private detective, so yes, I will continue to use the scoundrel's services. Although if O'Connor didn't have an association with Featherstone, I'd be quite literally booting him out the door."

His words stung, but Jane wouldn't shy away from continuing a discussion that needed to be had. "This anger you feel toward Mr. O'Connor… I do understand it, but remember, I'm the one who's responsible for creating all this discord in the first place. I asked Mr. O'Connor to keep my secret from you. It wasn't his secret to share. At the very least, he's demonstrated he won't breach client confidentiality no matter what."

Christopher made a low sound in his throat which might have been a harrumph but sounded more like a low growl. "Client confidentiality, my arse," he muttered. But after a moment, he blew out a sigh. "Look, Jane, I'm sorry for snapping at you. I just need some time to come to terms with what's happened. I need some space for my wounded male ego to heal. That being said, I do want to thank you for coming to Reigate and then to Brookfield with me today."

She tried to smile but suspected that the movement of her lips was little more than a quiver. "There's no need to thank me. I want you to know that I'll continue to help in whatever way that I can. And not only out of a sense of obligation. I *want* to help you."

Christopher's expression softened. "I appreciate everything you've done for me. Especially today. It can't have been easy getting into that dogcart. You were very brave."

She nodded, then bit her lip as unbidden tears welled. "Thank you," she whispered.

"Oh, Jane, don't cry." Christopher's brow creased with a frown and his own voice sounded thick with emotion as he added, "I don't like seeing you so unhappy."

She brushed away a tear. "I could say the same thing about you, Christopher. I know we're both still feeling our way forward. Tiptoeing carefully around each other. And at the risk of reopening scarcely healed wounds, I've noticed how you can barely tolerate touching me. I don't wish to push you into anything you don't want to do, but if we are to make a baby..." Despite everything they'd done together, Jane felt her face grow hot. "How are we to manage that if we don't..." She swallowed. "If we don't have sexual congress?"

A muscle flickered in Christopher's lean jaw and heat flashed in his blue eyes. "Make no mistake, I want you, Jane. Perhaps too much. In fact, even after your disclosure yesterday I want you. I wish to God that I didn't. Then I wouldn't be constantly fighting with myself. My body wants you—there's no escaping my desire—but my pride is bruised."

"Is it only your pride?" she whispered.

That muscle in his jaw twitched again. "I think you know it's more than that. And I don't know how to get past this hurt. At least not yet."

Jane's breath hitched. To hear Christopher confirm that it wasn't only his pride that had been wounded—to see the pain in his eyes—it made her wonder if she'd underestimated the depth of his feelings. She'd sensed that he'd begun to care for her, but had he actually started to fall in love? *Well, until you ruined it all, Jane...with your duplicity...*

But she wasn't brave enough to give voice to any of that, so she simply said, "I understand, and I'm sorry if I sounded mercenary and selfish for bringing up the matter of begetting a child so soon. But it's within my nature to fix things. To make them better. I hate what I've done to us."

They lapsed into silence again, both of them staring out of the window and the landscape rushing by in a blur of gray and green. Although Jane suspected that her view was hazy because of the tears which kept brimming in her eyes.

As the train pulled into Waterloo Bridge Station, Christopher surprised her. As he got to his feet, he offered her his arm. "I'll come to your room tonight. If you want me to."

"Do *you* want to?" she asked, her eyes searching his. "Only come if you want to."

He gave a brusque nod. "I do." And then below his breath, "God help me, I do."

Jane began to respond, but then they were caught up in the rush of disembarking. But perhaps her words were no longer needed.

Perhaps making love, letting their bodies talk for them, was the only way forward. In her heart, she prayed it would be true.

———————

The firelight in his sitting room made the brandy in his glass glow as Christopher studied the golden-brown spirit though the cut crystal. Then he sighed and put the drink down. He wanted the fiery liquid to take the edge off his raw emotions, to take away his pain, yet at the same time he didn't want it.

It was the same when it came to Jane. He wanted her with a fiery passion, yet he also didn't want her, didn't want to feel this way at all. So bruised and so fucking vulnerable. Like a wounded animal with a gaping, sucking wound in his chest. After Daisy, Christopher had sworn to himself that he would never feel anything for a woman again.

Yet he did. Damn it all to hell, he did.

He couldn't explain what he felt for Jane. Or how he fell for her so quickly.

It defied logic. Like the moon and the stars, his feelings for her—the ones he dared not put a name to—just *were*. And he rather suspected those cursed feelings, just like the moon and stars, were as equally enduring. They wouldn't fade away, no matter what he did.

He was also angry with himself for behaving like a surly child. Jane wasn't like Daisy. She *hadn't* been unfaithful. He *believed* that she didn't want Jack O'Connor.

But the problem was Jane *had* gone to O'Connor for help. This wasn't simply about a base emotion like jealousy. It was more complicated than that. The cold, hard truth was that Christopher felt emasculated. Less of a man.

Yes, he was less than he used to be, and maybe he would always be this way. A man who couldn't come to his wife's aid when she was in trouble. A man who couldn't discriminate between faces. A man who couldn't move freely about polite society in case his affliction was exposed and he was deemed mad. A duke who couldn't freely mix with his peers unless they were inebriated and they thought he was too.

Christ, he was lucky that Jane desired him at all.

He knew she was in her suite next door, waiting for him. The mantel clock indicated it was close to nine, and he really should get on with fulfilling his conjugal duties.

Conjugal duties...

It shouldn't be a duty. Jane deserved more than that.

She deserved a husband who could truly make love to her. A man who could fulfill her every need.

He still didn't know if he could be that man.

His heart thudding, his loins hardening in anticipation, Christopher opened the connecting door that led to Jane's bedroom. He found her, just as he'd expected, in her tester bed, reclining against a pile of plump snowy pillows. Upon seeing him, she greeted him with an uncertain smile and put the book she'd been reading aside.

She wasn't naked, but she wasn't far from it. Christopher's hungry gaze swept over her. She'd donned a thin-as-gossamer amber nightgown that clung to her slender body: her long legs, the undulating curves of her hips and waist, and the luscious mounds of her pert breasts. His attention lingered on her nipples, and he had to suppress a groan as those taut little nubs seemed to harden even more beneath his gaze, poking impudently against the silk as though beckoning him closer, urging him to tease and taste and fondle.

And then there was the allure of Jane's unbound hair. How the rich brown locks tumbling in glorious abandon around her shoulders transfixed him, tempting him to sift the silken strands through his fingers. Or he could wrap a thick glossy skein of it around his fist and then tip Jane's head back and ruthlessly claim her delectable mouth. Plunder that sweet recess with deep strokes of his tongue until her head was spinning and they were both breathless.

He swallowed, licked his lips, and Jane's gaze fell to his mouth and then to the front of his robe where his cock stood at full attention. Her breathing quickened.

He approached the side of the bed, and he sensed her gaze searching his face. "Christopher, are you certain you want to do this?" There was a note of hesitation in her voice. A brittle edge.

His mouth curved in an ironic smile. "I think it's rather obvious that I do."

"No, that's not what I mean," she said. "I feel like you're not really looking at me."

"Oh, I'm looking at you."

"No. No, you're not," she said sadly. "You…you can't even look me in the eye."

It was true. He couldn't. He dragged his gaze to hers. Saw the shadows in Jane's lovely green eyes. The hurt.

"I can't do this, Christopher," she whispered. "Not if you're going to treat me like I'm not really here. That you're…that in your head you're making love to someone else just to get through it. The idea is too lowering."

"That's not…" Christopher inhaled a shuddering breath. "That's not how it would be. I don't want anyone else."

"But still, it won't be same, will it? It won't be like before. When you trusted me."

Confusion swirled through Christopher, dampening his ardor. "What do you want from me, Jane?"

She lifted her chin, and her gaze was both unflinching and infinitely sad. "I want… I think I want what *you* want. A certain something that both of us are too afraid to admit. And until we *are* brave enough to be honest with each other, I don't think we're ready for this." She gestured at the room. The bed. At him. "I think it would be a mistake."

"I think you're right," he murmured huskily. Then because he couldn't help himself, he gently cradled Jane's jaw, then dropped a kiss on her temple. "Good night, Jane," he whispered. And then he quit the room.

Because everything she'd stated was true, and for now there really was nothing else left to say.

Christopher—his company, his witty conversation, his smiles meant only for her? His unforgettable lovemaking? Why else did she cry herself to sleep every night, aching for his touch?

And Jane rather thought that Christopher might love her too. But the problem was she didn't *really* know, and she was too terrified to ask.

She couldn't work up the courage to make a confession about how she felt, or to ask him to do the same, in case she was wrong about him. So it seemed they were at an impasse, both of them skirting around the issue at the center of everything. The words she'd said to Christopher when he'd last come to her room ran through her mind: *I think I want what you want. A certain something that both of us are too afraid to admit.*

That was the crux of the matter. That was the heart of the problem. Unless and until one of them was brave enough to say what needed to be said, they'd both remain stranded on opposite shores with an ocean of uncertainty and hurt between them.

When the papers that conferred the entire ownership of Delaney's Antiquarian Bookshop to her grandfather arrived at Roxby House ten days after her estrangement with Christopher had begun, it was Shelby who delivered them to her in the drawing room. She took them with a murmured thanks, and then, after she learned from Featherstone that his master was ensconced in his study with his man of business and didn't wish to be disturbed—apparently Jane hadn't been required to confirm the man's identity—she dressed in one of her loveliest day ensembles to at least affect an appearance of cheerfulness, then quit the house. At least she could make her grandfather happy.

And indeed, he was. As soon as her grandfather registered the import of the business papers he had in his hands, a bright smile broke across his lined countenance, and he gathered Jane into a

Chapter Twenty-nine

ANOTHER HORRID, INTERMINABLE WEEK DRAGGED BY IN which Jane and Christopher continued to walk on egg-shells around each other. Instead of working in the library, he decamped to another room, a small private study upstairs not far from the ducal suite. He explained that he'd moved out in order to give her unfettered access to the books she loved so much. She could continue to catalog and rearrange to her heart's content, freeing herself from his brooding presence. But in truth, Jane knew he'd abandoned the library because it was a way for him to avoid *her*.

She breakfasted alone in her bedroom, and he took his dinner on a tray in his study. If they passed each other in the hall or on the stairs, falsely polite smiles and awkward, altogether impersonal pleasantries were exchanged.

Jane had never felt so lonely or completely at a loss of what to do in her whole life. This couldn't go on, but she didn't know how to make things right. How to breach the gulf between her and Christopher. A gulf which seemed to be widening by the day.

She loved this extraordinary man with her entire heart... She knew it now. She'd tried so very hard not to fall in love with him, but it had happened anyway. Yes, she could no longer deny or hide from the powerful emotions swirling around inside her. Why else would this distance between her and her husband hurt so much if she wasn't in love? Why else did she long for hug. "I can barely believe it," he said when he drew back. "I know your mother has never been particularly interested in Delaney's, so it wouldn't have been hard to convince her to sell her half, but for your duke to then gift the share to me... Yes, I can scarcely fathom it." A small frown creased his brow. "Do you know what prompted his actions, Jane? Did you ask him to do this for me?"

"No, I didn't," she said. "But he does know how much the store means to me and to you. He's a generous man."

"He's more than that. He's a good man, Jane. I'm so delighted for you, my girl. You seem like a match made in heaven."

Oh, but that was a lie. Jane forced herself to smile even though her heart ached. "Yes, we are," she agreed. "We couldn't be happier." Because what else could she say?

The following day, Jane met with Artemis and Lucy at Fortnum & Mason's tearoom for a Byronic Book Club meeting. The invitation had been delivered by one of Kyleburn House's footmen, and Jane and her friends shared Lucy's carriage to Piccadilly. Jane had relayed a message to Christopher via Shelby about her whereabouts before she'd left rather than do it herself. She wondered how long Christopher's cold-shoulder treatment of her could go on. It wouldn't be too long before she marched into his study and did something drastic like throw a cup of tea in his face, or strip off all her clothes and lie across the papers on his desk, just to provoke *some* sort of reaction from him. Oh, how she missed him. Quite desperately.

But she couldn't say any of this to her friends as they sat at an elegant table in the middle of the tearoom, sharing tea and cakes and sandwiches. If she did, she risked bursting into tears, and the last thing she wanted to do was make a public spectacle of herself.

In her mind's eye she could already see the headline in the *London Tatler*: TROUBLE IN PARADISE? THE WIFE OF THE MOST SCANDALOUS DUKE IN LONDON IN TEARS IN A PICCADILLY TEAROOM. WHAT HAS THE SCOUNDREL DONE NOW?

The irony was he wasn't a scoundrel and he'd done nothing at all. She was the one who'd made the mess, but this time she couldn't fix it.

To Jane's relief, neither Artemis nor Lucy questioned her about whether she'd told Christopher about Miss Sharp's blackmailing scheme. Instead, Artemis proudly announced that they'd come up with an idea to enact Jane's plan to print and distribute her pamphlet series. A plan that would involve "minimal risk" to Jane's reputation. Or theirs.

"Because of course we are going to help you make your vision a reality, Jane," said Lucy as she helped herself to a delicate petit four covered in snowy royal icing and topped with a crystallized violet.

"Yes, once you shared your scheme with us, we knew we had to help," added Artemis. "We don't know what you've shared with your husband, but if he has any concerns, perhaps our plan—if you agree to it—will ameliorate them."

Jane swallowed past a sudden lump clogging her throat. Despite her resolve not to cry in Fortnum & Mason's, it seemed she was unable to hold her emotions in check for very long at all. "I don't know what to say other than thank you," she managed after she took a sip of scalding hot tea. "I certainly didn't expect you to become champions of my cause, considering it's such a risky venture."

Artemis waved a dismissive hand. "'Risky venture' should be my middle name," she declared. "Since when have I ever shied away from anything controversial in nature?"

"And you know how unconventional I am," added Lucy.

"None of us are the epitome of 'perfectly proper' or 'genteel,' are we?"

"But now that we have funds and influence, we can make a difference," said Artemis. "We just have to go about it the right way."

"Or rather, we'll utilize whatever means we can within the current system," said Lucy.

Jane was intrigued. "So, tell me, what have you come up with?" she asked. "I'm all ears."

"Well," began Artemis as she poured milk into her tea, "being the patroness of the Dartmoor Ladies' College has afforded me innumerable opportunities to associate with some of the finest, most forward-thinking female minds of the day. Apart from our minds, of course," she added as she dropped two sugar lumps in her cup.

"Of course," said Jane. "I take it you've met other like-minded women who would be willing to further my cause?"

"I have," said Artemis. "One of these women is a Miss Elizabeth Garrett who recently became a member of the Society for Promoting the Employment of Women. Not only does she possess similar views to ours about women's education and employment, but she has also lately decided that she would like to pursue a career in medicine. She wishes to become a doctor."

"A doctor?" repeated Jane. "A *female* doctor? How marvelous would that be!"

"Marvelous beyond words," said Lucy. "It's not unheard of, of course. There are female doctors in America. Women like Dr. Elizabeth Blackwell."

"Sadly, Britain is not as progressive," Artemis said, sighing. "But I digress. What I'm trying to say is Miss Garrett believes there's a place for literature like yours in medical dispensaries. We were discussing how wonderful it would be if there were special clinics just for women, in which open-minded doctors and nurses could share pamphlets like yours. Especially in poorer areas."

"Yes, when I was looking for my brother last year in the St. Giles Rookery, I was struck by how terrible the conditions were," said Lucy. "I can't even begin to imagine how a woman manages to take care of a young family, let alone herself, when she has barely any money to speak of. I've often wondered if she had a choice to control how many children she had, would she exercise that control? If she was provided with access to information and a ready supply of things like sponges and French letters—disseminated freely via funds raised by a charity that we could start—perhaps her life might be a little easier."

"You want us to form a charity that raises money for distributing my pamphlets and paraphernalia for birth control?" said Jane. "But won't that risk our reputations too?"

"Not if we recruit the right sort of medical staff in the medical dispensaries we will manage as benefactresses," said Artemis. "Yes, we will need to be careful and strategic about it all, but anyone who holds similar views to us would not condemn us. The use of sponges and condoms is not illegal. The issue is many women don't know about them or can't afford them. And there's nothing wrong with medical practitioners delivering appropriate advice about sexual congress and how to prevent the spread of venereal disease to their patients. The scope of your project won't be as wide or as big as you'd anticipated, Jane. And it will take some time to establish our charity and a medical dispensary and to find the right sort of staff for it. And then there's the question of raising funds to keep it all up and running on an ongoing basis. But it won't result in public censure."

"Your ideas are wonderful, and you've given me a lot to think about," said Jane, her heart swelling with gratitude. "And you're right, what you're suggesting is a much safer proposition.

I do still wonder if anyone would be willing to publish my pamphlet series to begin with, given the nature of the information."

"I have sounded someone out already," said Lucy with a smile. "There's a progressive group called the Ladies of Langham Place who publish the *English Woman's Journal* every month via Victoria Press. Emily Faithfull, who is a member of the Langham group and the founder of the publishing firm, would be happy to print your pamphlets as long as it is done so discreetly and anonymously."

"My goodness, it's you two who are marvelous," said Jane. Tears misted her vision. "I never could have conceived of such a wonderful scheme. Like you say, this venture of mine—or should I now say *our* venture?—might not be as far-reaching as I'd initially anticipated, but it will undoubtedly have longevity."

"And who knows," said Artemis with a sly smile, "perhaps rogue copies of *A Practical Woman's Guide to Self-Determination and Lasting Fulfillment* might end up on the occasional street corner every so often in St. Giles and Whitechapel and *even* pockets of Belgravia. I think we have the wherewithal to accomplish that without exposing any of our identities."

Considering Artemis had been able to conceal the fact she was the Gothic romance author Lydia Lovelace for years, Jane had every faith in her friend's ability to achieve such a feat again. If Artemis could do it, then she, Jane Roxby, could do it too.

If only she could share the plan with Christopher. She wouldn't keep secrets from him. Never again. But for now her project could wait.

Over the coming days, repairing her marriage and catching her husband's would-be killer would be Jane's priorities. Because the thought of living without Christopher, the man she loved, was almost too much to bear.

Chapter Thirty

WHEN JANE RETURNED TO ROXBY HOUSE LATER THAT AFTER-
noon, Jack O'Connor was leaving. The way he politely doffed
his hat and gave her a tight smile before he swiftly disappeared
out the door made Jane wonder what his exchange with
Christopher had been like. She wished she could have been a
fly on the wall to witness it. Then she would know how her husband was feeling.

Christopher had claimed his pride was bruised and that he
needed time for his "wounded male ego" to heal, so she could
well imagine that sending the private detective away with a flea
in his ear might help to some extent. At least Mr. O'Connor
didn't appear to be sporting any obvious injuries. Although
Jane suspected her husband would have preferred giving the
man a sound thrashing with his fists rather than delivering a
mere verbal setdown.

The fact that there was any sort of friction at all between the
two men was her fault, Jane disconsolately reminded herself as
she slowly climbed the stairs to her room. Guilt seemed to be
her constant companion these days, following her around like a
shadow. And she didn't know how to make it go away.

Indeed, Jane's mood was as gloomy as the weather for the
rest of the afternoon and the evening. A heavy rain set in, and
she found that she couldn't concentrate on anything she tried
to put her mind or hand to. The new book she'd picked up from
Delaney's held little appeal. She was not in the mood for sewing

or writing in her journal. So she sat in a chair in her sitting room, listlessly watching the rain lash the windowpanes, wishing that she didn't keep listening for Christopher.

She wanted to go to him, to ask how he was, to tell him about her day, to find out what was happening with Mr. O'Connor and the investigation, but she also feared what might happen if she did. That somehow she might make the situation worse. So in the end she'd picked at her simple dinner of a boiled egg and tea and toast, donned the plainest cotton nightgown she owned—there was no point in wearing any of the flimsy night attire that Madame Bouchard had created for her—and then curled up in bed, telling Elsie she didn't want to be disturbed because she feared she might be coming down with a cold.

By the time the mantel clock in her bedroom struck the hour of eleven, Jane's bed was a mess of tangled sheets and thumped pillows. Even the sweet oblivion of sleep eluded her. It probably didn't help that a ferocious storm had blown in. The flashes of lightning and constant rumbles of thunder that shook the windows were disconcerting and kept jolting Jane awake whenever she began to drift off.

Giving up on sleep, she slid from her bed, thrust her feet into slippers, wrapped a cashmere shawl about her shoulders, and then quit her room, heading for the library.

Save for the storm raging about Roxby House, all was silent as the grave. Some thoughtful servant had left several gas lamps burning so she wasn't stumbling through a dark house as she made her way downstairs. Hopefully she would find another book that would engage her.

When she pushed through the oak doors into the library, she discovered the fire had almost burned down to ashes. The lamp on Christopher's desk was still alight, but he was nowhere to be seen. Even the dark corner where he'd lurked the first evening they'd met was empty. Relief and acute disappointment welled in her heart. She wanted to bump into him, yet she didn't.

What a contrary creature she was.

With a sigh, she crossed to the fire and lit a small branch of candles. Then, candelabra in hand, she began to peruse the bookcase on the far side of the room where she'd shelved the novels and volumes of poetry. She already knew what was there, and there wasn't a great deal that appealed.

Sir Walter Scott. Byron. Keats. Dickens.

Ha! Dickens. If she never saw another title by Dickens ever again, she'd be happy indeed.

Jane's shawl slipped, and she put the branch of candles down on a table. Roxby House really had a dearth of books by female authors. Nothing by Austen or any of the Brontës. She'd have to rectify the situation.

Tipping her head back, she spied several titles by Thackeray on a shelf she couldn't quite reach. She'd read *Vanity Fair*, but not *Barry Lyndon*, or *Pendennis* which her grandfather had once recommended because it was quite amusing.

Amusing would be welcome right now.

She pushed the library ladder over to the bookcase, kicked off her slippers, shrugged off her shawl, then scaled a few rungs. If she stood on tiptoe, she would be able to reach *Pendennis*...

She reached up and then she felt a large, warm hand settle on her hip.

"Careful, my duchess." Christopher's voice was as low and smooth as a sip of fine French brandy. "I wouldn't want you to slip and fall."

Jane froze. Closed her eyes as a wave of deep longing threatened to turn her knees into sun-warmed butter. "I–I won't," she stammered breathlessly, even though she wondered if she just might.

"Are you sure you want to read right now?" Christopher's other hand slid beneath the hem of her nightgown and his fingers brushed up her calf then down again, raising gooseflesh. "I can think of something else you could do that would be more diverting."

Before Jane could respond, both of his hands moved to her waist and then he was lifting her down from the ladder.

Christopher spun her around and then she was pressed between his long, lean body and the bookcase. Thunder rolled, deep and low, and Jane felt it all the way to her bones. It was as though the tempest had invaded the library and the very air around her and Christopher crackled with energy and excruciating expectation.

Her hands came up to rest against his chest. Through the thin cambric of his shirt, she could feel the steady thud of his heart. The heat of his skin. The hardness of unyielding muscle.

"Christopher," she murmured, searching her husband's far-too-handsome face. It was taut with hunger. And his blue eyes... They were burning so brightly, so intently, it was as though he was staring straight into her very soul. She couldn't look away. "Are...are you sure you want to do this?"

"The one thing I *am* sure about, my beautiful, maddening wife, is how much I've missed you. How much I need you." He pushed his hips against her so she would be in no doubt about what he wanted. Pressed a hand to the base of her throat where her pulse fluttered wildly, as though he was scared she might disappear. "I've tried to distract myself with work, but all I can think about is you," he continued, his voice hoarse with desperation. "Thoughts of you consume me, morning and night. I can't concentrate. I can't eat. I can't sleep. I should be trying to track down my attacker, but I can't even focus on that. If you can bear hearing the truth, I'm in agony, Jane." He grazed his lips along her jaw, then he groaned. "I can't stand this distance between us. I toss and turn all night, aching for you. When I dream, it's about you. When I wake and you're not there, I feel hollow and empty. Like all the light has gone out of my life. That I have nothing to look forward to."

"I'm right here," she whispered, her heart rejoicing yet aching at the same time. "I'll always be here. And I'm yours." She touched his cheek. "Only yours."

"You're sure?" His mouth hovered over hers, his breath caressing, teasing. "Am I enough for you, Jane?" Again, another push of his hips. Another searing graze of his mouth across her cheek.

"Yes. I've never been more certain of anything in my life."

"Thank God." Christopher's mouth claimed hers in a hard, possessive, unrelenting kiss. The hand at her throat slid to her breast, covering it possessively, and Jane moaned her pleasure at the firm contact.

"You like that?" he rasped against her mouth, squeezing her tender flesh, making her nipple tighten to a hard aching point.

"Yes."

"Tell me what you want, Jane. I've fantasized about what I want to do with you when I've taken myself in hand. When I've stroked my hard, aching cock." He ground his rampant erection against Jane's belly, pulling another moan from her throat. "But I want you to say it." He thumbed her nipple through the cotton of her nightgown. "You know I'm generous." He nuzzled her ear, his breath hot, his voice raw with lust. "If you want it, you can have it. I'll do anything you ask."

"I want your mouth on me," she whispered as liquid desire pooled between her feminine folds. "On my sex. Everywhere."

He growled his approval, drew back, and then before she knew what he was about, his hands had seized the neckline of her nightgown and then he was ripping the thin cotton, rending the garment in two. The halves fell open, exposing her body. The way his ravenous gaze raked over her bare breasts and her belly before finally landing on the thatch of dark curls at the apex of her thighs made Jane quiver with anticipation. She'd never felt so desired. So adored.

He fell to his knees. "Lift your leg," he commanded, and Jane complied immediately. She hooked her foot onto a rung of the ladder, opening herself to Christopher's avid gaze.

He licked his lips. Slid a long, wicked finger along her slick furrow, spreading the welling moisture up to her throbbing clitoris. "So pretty, so wet," he crooned. "And all for me." In the next instant, he parted her folds and set his mouth on her, and all Jane could do was whimper in delight. Clutch at his head as he tightened the seal and increased the exquisite suction until she almost couldn't bear it. And then he released her and began working her with his tongue, lapping and flicking and taunting her to the point of madness.

Oh God. It was too good. It was too much.

Jane moaned and her fingers tightened in Christopher's hair. She gripped his scalp and called his name, but that only seemed to spur him on. He plunged one finger then another into her tight, wet heat, expertly stroking her, building the excruciating tension inside her, setting her ablaze.

He was relentless in the way he pleasured her. There would be no respite. Jane knew he wouldn't stop until she was mindless and begging and could no longer stand. And she wanted that too. His hunger. His ruthless need to command and possess her. She was his in every way.

His lips delicately suckling at her clitoris once more was Jane's final undoing. Her orgasm crashed over her, her legs buckling beneath her, but Christopher held her about the hips, supporting her body as it was racked with spasms of breath-stealing bliss.

When she could hold her own weight, Christopher stood, and his hands swept up to her arms. With a swift tug he dispensed with the remnants of her nightgown, and then he lashed her body against his. "I'm going to lift you. Hold onto my shoulders and wrap your legs about me."

Hoisting her into his arms, Christopher claimed her mouth, then carried her over to his desk. Deposited her bare behind upon the leather blotter, scattering papers and books and the inkwell.

"I'm going to take you hard and fast. I won't be gentle," he said gruffly as he tore off his shirt and threw it on the floor. His burning gaze locked with hers. "Are you ready for that, Jane?"

"Yes," she breathed. "I want that too."

"Good." He swore as he fumbled with the opening of his trousers. The moment he was free, he didn't hesitate. He gripped Jane's hips, and with one sure thrust he filled her with his hot, pulsing length, stealing her breath all over again. She gripped his shoulders as he began to pump in and out of her with perfect precision. Each incursion was merciless, each deep stroke was so exquisite that it wasn't long before Jane could feel another climax gathering inside her. Approaching inexorably like an oncoming storm. Burning, blazing, consuming. Uniting them. Fusing their very souls.

Perhaps Christopher felt the power of their joining too, because he speared his fingers in her hair and his smoldering blue gaze trapped hers. "Come for me, Jane," he grunted between panted breaths. "I want to watch you come around my ramming cock. I want to watch your face as I fill you with my seed."

The urgency in his voice, the potency of his words, the

searing heat of his possession, everything coalesced and ignited and Jane was lost to thought-robbing pleasure yet again. Her sheath clenched around Christopher's cock, and almost at once he came too. He gasped and cried out her name. Clutched her head and shuddered and jerked his hips.

Satisfaction and sheer joy rushed through Jane as she collapsed against Christopher's sweat-slick chest, as she buried her face in his neck and kissed the place where his pulse beat strong and true. Their bout of lovemaking had been sublime. Profound. It had transcended every other experience she'd ever had.

It was, quite simply, unforgettable.

At least for her it had been.

If only she could be brave enough to own how she felt in words. To confess those feelings to Christopher. Despite his heartfelt confession earlier—that he'd missed her, that without her his life felt hollow and empty—something inside her still held her back.

It was doubt. It was fear. Because what if Christopher *didn't* actually love her? That it was merely animal lust and jealousy and the fact another man had usurped his position as "protector" that had been behind his recent malaise? That had prompted this passionate reclaiming in the middle of the night? She didn't want things to be awkward between them. Nothing could be worse than professing your love for someone but then your lover couldn't say it back.

When she raised her head, Christopher cradled her face between his hands and kissed her deeply with lingering tenderness, and Jane was all at sea again. This didn't feel like animal lust alone. It felt like *more*. But when Christopher broke the kiss and whispered, "I'm going to take you upstairs now. To my bed. And I'm going to have you again. Long and slow this time,"

Jane couldn't help but take note of his choice of words. That he would "have" her. He hadn't described it as "making love."

So she simply smiled and said, "That sounds perfect to me." Because she would take whatever she could get from this man. No, if she were being honest with herself, she would revel in it.

If the words "I love you" *had* been hovering on the tip of her tongue, the moment to say them slipped away when Christopher withdrew from her body. He was all business as he did up his trousers then bent to retrieve his shirt and slid it over her head.

"To preserve your modesty as I carry you upstairs," he said as he began to fasten the buttons for her. "I don't think we'll bump into any of the servants, but one never knows."

"Yes," she said, because dealing with practicalities and keeping the tone light and breezy was far easier than being honest. "Very sensible. Although *not* ripping a perfectly good nightgown to shreds might have been the wiser course of action. I have no idea what my maid will say. Or what any of the servants will think when they see the mess we've made in here."

Christopher chuckled. "It's not anything they haven't seen before around Roxby House." He finished sliding the last button in place and then swept her up into his arms as though she weighed nothing at all. "And I wouldn't fret about your nightgown being destroyed," he said, heading for the library door. "It was truly hideous and you know it. In fact, I forbid you to wear anything so monstrous again. You'll wear flimsy silk and lacy confections or nothing at all."

"What about your shirt?" she asked as the door shut behind them and Christopher carried her down the shadowy gallery toward the main stairs. "I quite like it. It smells like you and whatever cologne it is that you wear."

He laughed at that. "Now that's the first time I've ever heard anyone say that."

"You *do* smell delicious," she asserted.

He cocked a brow. "Have you had a recent knock to the head? Or have you been drinking?"

"No. I'm just drunk with..." Her voice trailed away, and she bit her lip. *Damn.*

Christopher paused at the foot of the staircase. "Drunk with what, Jane?"

She felt herself blushing beneath the weight of his stare. It would be easy to evade answering his question truthfully. The words *happiness* or *lust* would fit equally as well.

Although heavy rain still lashed the windows and Eaton Square outside, the hall itself was cloaked in velvet-soft silence. Jane's heart beat loudly in her ears.

"Desire," she murmured. "I'm drunk with desire. I've missed you too, Christopher. More than you could know. I can't wait to share your bed again." And then she cradled his jaw and kissed him in case she did say more.

She'd have to let her body speak for her whenever they made love. Because she knew, deep down, for her that's exactly what it was.

―――――――――

In the quiet hours of the night, after they'd found satisfaction again, Jane shared her day with Christopher, along with her friends' suggestions about how to disseminate her *Practical Woman's Guide* pamphlet series without earning public censure. At least she could be honest with him about that.

Christopher listened intently to all she said, asked insightful questions, and in the end agreed that it might just work. "It's a scheme I can get behind," he said. "And whatever funds you need to start up a charitable foundation and a medical dispensary for women, I'll be more than happy to provide them."

Jane raised her head from where it had been resting against Christopher's chest and met his heavy-lidded gaze. "You will?"

"I will."

She kissed him. "You make me so very happy," she said softly. "I should never have doubted you, and I'm so sorry for the pain I've caused you. If I could take it all back—"

"Shhh." He pressed a finger to her lips. "All is forgiven."

Jane turned her head and kissed his palm. "Now, to be perfectly content, I just need to know that you are safe."

"Yes." Christopher's expression grew grim. Talk turned to what they would do next to hurry up the progress of the investigation.

"I need to confirm whether my initial suspicions about Cosgrove were, in fact, unfounded. Even though my gut tells me he's not involved, I should try to rule him out definitively."

"Do you have any ideas how you might accomplish that?" asked Jane.

"It might be risky, but I think I should engineer another conversation with the man. He's a member of White's, so it would be easy enough to cross paths with him there. It will be neutral territory if nothing else. Committing murder in the middle of a gentlemen's club isn't the done thing, so I should be safe enough. At least in a physical sense." Christopher sighed. "Providing I don't make a spectacle of myself when I can't place anyone's face."

"Yes. That might be a problem. And of course I can't go with you to point Cosgrove out. How will you recognize him to begin with? And how will you know if he's even there?"

"O'Connor has provided me with a list of Cosgrove's usual habits. If I wait outside White's in the carriage with you, you might catch a glimpse of him going inside. If you can tell me what he's wearing, it might be enough for me to go on so I don't accost the wrong person."

"I'll do anything you ask," said Jane. She slid her fingers through Christopher's chest hair, then traced her fingers along the line of one of his ribs. "I do have to ask, though, what of your cousin-in-law Daphne? Do you have any more information on her activities or her financial situation?"

"Not much. It seems she lives a fairly sedate existence with a regular routine. Whether or not she's a member of the Whisteria Club remains a mystery. Even if she is a member, it might mean nothing at all. Unfortunately, O'Connor didn't unearth anything particularly useful about her..." Christopher paused, then said quietly, "I dismissed him this afternoon."

Oh... Guilt pinched inside Jane's chest. Poor O'Connor. That he'd lost his job *was* her fault. But she didn't want to talk about the man, not when she and Christopher had begun to mend their own relationship. Instead, she simply said, "I understand," before redirecting the conversation back to the subject of Daphne. "There must be some way to draw her out. To glean some sort of useful information about her recent dealings and her true feelings about you. Perhaps if I invited her to tea or even better dropped by her house and engaged her in conversation, she might make some sort of verbal blunder. In fact, we could both do that. You could distract her while I search some of her things. She must have papers and bills or even a diary."

Although Jane wasn't looking at Christopher, she could hear the frown in his voice. "We'd need to be careful. If she is plotting to do away with me, I wouldn't want to provoke her into doing anything rash on the spur of the moment. I don't want to put you in her sights either."

"Doing nothing isn't getting us anywhere though."

"True." Christopher dropped a kiss on her brow. "All right.

We'll visit my cousin-in-law. I'm truly sick and tired of this cloak-and-dagger existence."

"We'll work this out. I know we will," Jane said and snuggled against her husband's chest. A wave of drowsiness washed over her and her eyelids drooped. She couldn't seem to keep them open.

"I pray that you are right," Christopher murmured against her temple. He whispered something else which might have been "my love," but as Jane was tugged toward the arms of sleep, she surmised that was probably wishful thinking.

Chapter Thirty-one

CHRISTOPHER'S UNMARKED CARRIAGE DREW TO A HALT ON St James's Street not far from the corner of Jermyn Street as a chill, gray dusk was beginning to fall. The front door of White's was close by, and Christopher trusted that when Simon Cosgrove left Waterloo Place at the end of his working day, he'd likely walk along this section of the street to reach the club.

It had been three days since he and Jane had reconciled. Three days of heavenly conjugal bliss, both in and out of the bedroom. They'd talked and laughed and spent every waking minute together. Christopher had become obsessed with finding out everything he could about Jane. As they'd cataloged books together, he'd quizzed her about her childhood in Heathwick Green, her family life, and how she'd become friends with Artemis and Lucy. How they'd come to form their Byronic Book Club. He wanted to learn about topics both large and small—from why she'd once wanted to forge a career in journalism to what was her favorite book (*Jane Eyre*) and her favorite meal (roast chicken and roast potatoes with lashings of gravy). He'd promised to teach her to ride a horse because she'd never ridden anything larger than a pony.

Jane had found out about his parents—how his beloved mother, Catherine, had died from pneumonia when he was thirteen and his father, who'd been a military man too, had passed away just after Christopher had finished his schooling at Eton. How his guardian, his great-uncle, the former Duke

of Roxby, had been opposed to the idea of Christopher joining the cavalry but Christopher had insisted it was what he'd
wanted. That his mother was the one who'd taught him to play
the pianoforte and that he owed his musical ear to her.

And of course they'd made love both in and out of the bedroom. In the library again and on the stairs late one night. Even
on his pianoforte after dinner.

Christopher's cock twitched at the memory of it despite
the fact he was also on edge about the coming interview with
Simon Cosgrove…if he showed up.

His gaze crossed to Jane. She sat on the opposite bench seat
in the carriage, a slender figure in russet velvet, peering intently
out the window, watching out for Cosgrove. If identifying the
man wasn't the goal of this foray, Christopher would be hauling
her across his lap so he could kiss her to his heart's content. He
might even have his wicked way with her right here in this carriage, just like they'd done the night they'd attended the opera.

Christopher checked his pocket watch. It was a quarter past
five and there wasn't much light left. Luckily, there was a gas
lamp on the corner of St James's Street and Jermyn Street that
would illuminate anyone who walked beneath it.

He trusted O'Connor's intelligence was reliable. Apparently,
it was Cosgrove's habit to visit White's between five and five
thirty on a Wednesday. He would take dinner at the club,
and then he'd visit his mistress in rented rooms he paid for in
Cheyne Row in Chelsea.

"That's him," Jane said, pointing to a man who'd passed
beneath the gas lamp. "In the charcoal-gray suit. I think he's also
wearing a pin-striped waistcoat with silver buttons."

Christopher narrowed his gaze as he watched the fellow—a
complete stranger with dark hair and muttonchops—stride
past the carriage then mount the short flight of stairs to the

TALL, DUKE, AND SCANDALOUS

front door of the club. "Yes, his waistcoat is striped. Let's hope no one else in White's is wearing something similar."

"Yes," agreed Jane. In the dim light of the carriage, he could see that a furrow had formed between her delicately drawn brows. "Please be careful, Christopher."

He put on his top hat and then leaned across the space between them to kiss her. "Always," he said. "All going well, I should be back within half an hour."

At this hour, White's was still fairly quiet. As Christopher scanned the main club floor, he was dismayed to discover that almost everyone was wearing a dark jacket and trousers. Many of the gentlemen had dark hair of varying shades of black and brown as well.

Although at least several men had beards, which ruled them out. Christopher knew that Cosgrove was clean-shaven. Another chap was portly, and another wore glasses. He couldn't see anyone who was sporting a striped waistcoat.

Frustration and uneasiness tightened Christopher's gut as he walked through the club, looking right and left, trying not to invite attention. At times like this, he found traversing a room full of strangers to be more nerve-racking then entering a battlefield. If truth be told, his pulse raced like a cavalry horse bolting pell-mell into the fray.

Here, all he was armed with was a set of deficient wits. If someone he knew began talking to him, and he couldn't work out who the fellow was... If he seemed like he was unhinged, rumors might begin to spread that the Duke of Roxby wasn't in his right mind. And he could ill afford that sort of gossip. If Daphne Marsden heard it, it wouldn't be long before she might mount a full-frontal assault. She might question his sanity and his right to hold the dukedom at all. He'd lose control of everything he held dear. And he couldn't have that.

Steady on, he told himself as he scanned another room, looking for a glimpse of a pin-striped waistcoat on a dark-haired gentlemen. *If anyone approaches you, just affect aloofness as though you're bored with the conversation. Respond in a noncommittal way. Talk in generalities. Better to be thought of as an arrogant prick than a man who's gone mad.*

There. A tall, broad-shouldered man with dark-brown hair. Beneath his well-cut jacket of dark wool, he wore a striped silk waistcoat in shades of gray and silver. He was brandishing a glass of spirits while flicking through a newspaper. It *might* be Cosgrove.

Swallowing his fear, Christopher pulled back his shoulders and approached the stranger. "Cosgrove?" he asked in the drollest, most world-weary voice he could muster.

The man looked up from the newspaper and his marked brows dipped into a frown. "I'm verra sorry, but I'm afraid you've got the wrong man," he said. "I dinna ken Cosgrove well, but I think I spied him over by the fire. Through there." He gestured with his glass toward the next room. His frown grew deeper, and his dark-blue eyes narrowed. "I feel like I should know you. That I've met you before… Are you no' the Duke of Roxby?"

Christopher swallowed. This man recognized him, but their connection sounded vague, so he might survive this encounter. "I am," he said with a slight tilt of his head. "But Roxby will do. And you are?"

"William Lockhart, the Earl of Kyle," said the Scotsman. "I believe we're practically neighbors. Not only that, but our wives know each other. I also have a wee suspicion that we've crossed paths before. My wife, Lucy, mentioned you were once a military man."

"Ah," said Christopher. "As a matter of fact, I was. But back

then I was Major Marsden. We should swap stories sometime."
Hopefully when my wife is around…

"I would verra much like that," said Lord Kyle. "Actually, Lucy keeps talking about having you and your wife over for dinner. The Duke of Dartmoor and his wife, Artemis, as well." The earl raised a brow. "Do you know Dartmoor? He's a member here too."

"Other than hearing him speak in the House of Lords, I'm afraid I don't," said Christopher.

"We should rectify that this evening," said Lord Kyle. "Dartmoor will be joining me shortly."

God, no. The longer he lingered in White's, the more chance there was that Christopher really would put his foot in his mouth in spectacular fashion. He might be able to manage a conversation with Lord Kyle and the Duke of Dartmoor if he could stay focused on those two men alone, but if others joined the conversation he was sure to get confused and make a monumental fool of himself. Besides, Jane was waiting for him outside and he didn't want to worry her.

Christopher affected a smile. "Thank you for the invitation, Kyle, but I do actually need to speak with Cosgrove. It's about a…a rather pressing matter. I hope you understand."

"Aye, of course. Dinna worry." Kyle's mouth tilted into a lopsided grin, and he waved his glass in the air. "I'm sure that dinner invitation willna be far away if my wife has anything to do with it. Would next week suit? I'll let her know if it does."

Christopher's smile was genuine this time. He decided he liked the earl. He certainly seemed affable enough. "Yes, next week will be fine," he said. "My wife has been talking about arranging a dinner party too, so she will be most happy to hear that I'm at last going to meet all of her friends and their respective spouses. I look forward to it."

He farewelled Lord Kyle and headed into the adjacent room to find Cosgrove.

Straightaway, Christopher spied a dark-haired gentleman by the fire who was also wearing a pinstripe waistcoat beneath his charcoal gray jacket. He had a decanter of red wine by his elbow, and he was perusing a copy of the *Times*. In fact, he looked like he'd settled in for the night.

As Christopher approached, the man looked up and then scowled at him over the top of the paper. "What the hell are you doing here, Roxby? Throwing insults at me at the opera wasn't enough?"

It certainly sounded like Cosgrove. Despite the hostility of the man's demeanor, Christopher selected a nearby seat. Perhaps sensing the tension between them, the bespectacled gentleman who was reclining in a wingback chair opposite Cosgrove got up and moved away with his copy of the *Illustrated London News*.

"No, that's not my intention, Cosgrove," said Christopher. "Actually, I came here to apologize to you for the way I behaved that night. For bringing up the fact you have a mistress in front of so many people, and for implying your wife might still hold a torch for me. It was exceedingly rude and uncalled for."

Cosgrove snorted. "Damn right it was uncalled for." He set aside the *Times*, then reached for his wineglass. "On the other hand, what you said wasn't wrong. On both counts. My wife does still moon over you. That's why I have taken up with a mistress. If I had a guinea for every time Daisy mentioned how wonderful the Duke of bloody Roxby is, and how much she regrets jilting you, I'd be a far richer man. As rich as you."

Christopher humphed in surprise. "I certainly didn't expect such honesty, Cosgrove. But I do appreciate it."

Cosgrove's mouth twisted with a wry smile. "There's no

point in denying it. Not now." He took a large swig of wine. "You see, I'm going to divorce my cow of a wife. In fact, tomorrow morning I have an appointment with a lawyer to start the ball rolling. I'm utterly sick of her carping on about you. I want to marry someone who actually wants to spend her life with me."

If someone had attempted to knock Christopher over with a feather in that moment, they would have succeeded. "I'm sorry to hear that," he said after he'd picked his jaw up from the floor. "I mean it. Considering Daisy broke things off with me, I'd assumed she'd found a love match with you."

Another snort from Cosgrove. "Love match? Does such a thing exist? After Daisy, I'd settle for a woman who just actually likes me."

A woman who just actually likes me…

As Christopher took his leave and returned to his carriage, he knew without a shadow of a doubt that he was wed to a woman who definitely desired *and* liked him. The last few days had been a testament to that.

But did she *love* him?

After they'd reconciled, when Christopher had carried Jane up to his bedchamber, there'd been a moment when she'd owned to feeling drunk with desire. But at the time, Christopher had wondered if she might have been about to say something else. That her choice of the word *desire* hadn't been entirely accurate. But he hadn't pressed her because he wasn't sure if he was ready to hear that she *might* actually have fallen in love with him. Because that would mean he might have to examine his own feelings for Jane, and he hadn't been ready for that. Everything he'd told her that night—about being in agony when she wasn't with him, about missing her—all of it had been true.

But he'd attributed those feelings to thwarted lust along with a purely masculine need to assuage his bruised pride. To reassert that Jane was indeed his in every way that mattered after all that business with that far-too-cocky-for-his-own-good Jack O'Connor.

Christopher climbed back into the carriage and filled in Jane on how he'd accidentally crossed paths with the Earl of Kyle and that a dinner invitation was on the cards for the following week. And then he'd recounted his interview with Cosgrove. "Given the man is divorcing Daisy, I'm certain he's not the culprit. Which leaves Daphne Marsden..."

"Yes," agreed Jane. "I think we might need to seriously consider her as a suspect."

"When we get home, I'd suggest we refine our plan to tackle her tomorrow. I want this over with, Jane. There's no point in delaying."

As they headed back to Eaton Square, sitting side by side in the carriage, Jane's hand in Christopher's, they both lapsed into companiable silence. It was almost as though they were reassuring each other that they'd get through this. That it wouldn't be long before Christopher's life was no longer in danger.

Each of them had only agreed to a marriage of convenience. When Jane had produced the heir Christopher needed, he'd always anticipated that they'd lead separate lives.

And perhaps that was all for the best. No matter how much he enjoyed Jane's company, no matter how much he *liked* her, it might be better to break things off sooner rather than later. As soon as Jane was pregnant, as soon as they'd caught the person or persons attempting to end his life—and now he'd all but eliminated everyone except Daphne from his suspect list, that should be very soon—perhaps he'd suggest that she move into her own residence in London or farther afield.

Except...except he'd come to rely on her in other ways. He still needed her to help him hide his facial blindness.

And really, perhaps that was the real reason he was reluctant to let Jane go. She was his anchor. The one constant in his life. His need for her wasn't rooted in tenderness. Aside from wanting her in his bed, he simply needed her in a practical sense, and he was beginning to misinterpret that as love.

He was a former military officer, battle-hardened, practical, and unsentimental. A man who eschewed the very notion of love, especially after being let down by Daisy.

If he were honest with himself though, what he'd felt for his former fiancée paled into insignificance when he compared it to what he felt for his wife. And Jane was nothing like Daisy. She was intelligent and kind and giving and loyal...

Devil take him, he so wanted to believe she was loyal.

His fingers tightened around Jane's, and she turned her head to him and smiled.

And Christopher's chest was immediately flooded with the sweetest ache. God help him, whatever this was—this bond developing between him and Jane—he wanted more of it, not less. He could reason with himself all day, even tell himself lies, but the truth was he *might* be falling in love.

As a former cavalry officer, he'd grown used to facing danger, even death. Strange how the prospect of losing his heart to his wife suddenly seemed more terrifying.

Chapter Thirty-two

DAPHNE MARSDEN AND HER SON, OLIVER, LIVED IN A MODEST town house in Russell Square. As Christopher's town coach made its way through the snarls of London traffic, he explained to Jane that the rent was drawn from Oliver's trust fund.

"Are you Oliver's sole guardian?" she asked. She was so nervous about the coming interview with Christopher's cousin-in-law that her belly was churning uncomfortably. Talking seemed like the best way to distract herself from dwelling on all the things that might go wrong this afternoon. Daphne might not be at home. Jane might be caught going through Daphne's personal papers by a servant or even Daphne herself. Jane recalled how cold and prickly the woman had been when they'd first met all those weeks ago. She couldn't imagine Daphne being any more welcoming today, considering their visit was impromptu.

"No, I'm not," said Christopher in response to her question. "There's another gentleman, a solicitor, who ensures that everything is aboveboard when it comes to payments. Aside from her widow's jointure, Daphne also receives a monthly allowance from Oliver's trust fund to cover household and other sundry expenses. But if she needs extra money for whatever reason, she must come to me or speak with the solicitor. If what she's asking for seems reasonable—like her recent request for money to cover a new wardrobe for Oliver—I usually just write her a personal check. I don't see much point in draining the boy's trust fund for something as mundane as new shirts and shoes."

"It would be useful to find out if she does need more money than she's able to access," said Jane. "That's the main reason my mother started gambling at the Whisteria Club. But given the play is not for those with shallow pockets, it wouldn't take long to end up in trouble. If Daphne *is* in deep financial straits, she might want access to the Roxby family fortune." She sighed. "At the risk of dredging up a difficult subject with my mother—I'm sure she's still annoyed with me for canceling her membership at the club—I really should ask her if *she* knows Daphne at all. I probably should have done so sooner."

"O'Connor failed to find out if she's a member of the club, so please do not feel as though you haven't done enough already," said Christopher, squeezing her hand. "And you don't have to go through with our plan this afternoon, you know. I could employ another private detective."

"Unless the detective breaks into Daphne's house, I don't see how he or she could find out anything more than Mr. O'Connor did," said Jane.

"You're right. But I hate seeing you so nervous." Christopher's blue eyes suddenly glinted with mischief. "You're so pale, I'm tempted to whisper filthy suggestions in your ear just to bring the color back into your cheeks."

Jane laughed at that. "I'd settle for an enthusiastic kiss," she returned. "If you say anything too wicked, I'll be too distracted and will probably make a hash of this reconnaissance mission."

"Done," said Christopher, and he kissed Jane so deeply, it didn't take long for her fear to be washed away in a tide of longing. When they came up for air, it was to discover that the coach was turning into Russell Square.

"Do I look all right?" asked Jane, straightening her bonnet, which had been knocked slightly askew during their kiss.

"You look perfect," said Christopher. "And you're definitely not pale anymore. I hope those nerves have faded." He lifted her gloved hand to his lips and kissed it. "We can do this. I just hope Daphne is at home. I want this over with."

Jane couldn't have agreed more.

As luck would have it, Daphne Marsden *was* at home. She was also most put out that the Duke and Duchess of Roxby had stopped by.

"Your Graces, do come in, but honestly you should have sent word," she said after she'd curtsied to both of them in the narrow hall. "I haven't anything remotely decent to serve you for afternoon tea. I think there are some ginger biscuits. Or Cook could make a batch of scones, although we haven't any cream to go with them. Only butter and jam."

Jane smiled. "Tea and biscuits would be perfectly fine. We don't want to put you to any trouble."

Daphne Marsden's brows arrowed into a troubled frown. "Please pardon my bluntness, but why exactly *are* you here?"

Christopher removed his top hat and handed it to a hovering housemaid who was staring at him in wide-eyed awe. "We were in the area, and I thought it's been quite some time since I saw you and Oliver. And of course Jane has yet to meet him."

"Oh, he's not here," said Daphne. "He's gone on an excursion to the British Museum with his tutor. I don't expect they'll be back for another hour. Perhaps two."

"That's no matter," replied Christopher. "We can still chat."

"Yes, I've been looking forward to furthering our acquaintance for some weeks now," said Jane. "We're family now."

"Oh. Yes. Quite," said Daphne stiffly. To Jane, she looked as though she'd rather swallow a prickly conker than acknowledge the connection. Nevertheless, she ushered Jane and Christopher into a neatly furnished parlor and bade them take seats by the fire.

Christopher selected an overstuffed armchair by the hearth and Jane sat upon a shepherdess chair upholstered in faded blue silk, which she suspected might be Daphne's preferred seat. Daphne perched on the edge of a hardbacked chair, looking as though she wanted to bolt from the room at the first opportunity.

In fact, the woman seemed so ill at ease that her knuckles stood out starkly as she clasped her hands together in her lap. Jane initiated a bland conversation about the weather and then the parlor's charming view of the park in the middle of Russell Square. Both topics went nowhere. After the tea service arrived, Jane attempted to quiz Daphne about her background and interests, but again, it was like wringing water from a stone. The scantest of details emerged, whatever the subject.

Jane learned Daphne was the only child of a vicar and had grown up in Hertfordshire, but nothing more about her family. When Jane shared her own particular tastes in literature and fashion and music, Daphne offered little in return. On the subject of card games like whist, Christopher's cousin remained distinctly tight-lipped, especially when Jane mentioned her own mother had once been a member of the Whisteria Club. Daphne maintained she'd never heard of it.

Throughout it all, Christopher nodded and smiled, only offering the odd comment here or there. For the most part, Daphne ignored him too. It was almost as though he wasn't in the room. The entire encounter was nothing but awkward and uncomfortable, and Jane was almost looking forward to escaping from the parlor to undertake her search.

Indeed, when Daphne offered to replenish her cup of tea,

Jane decided it was time to make her move. "My apologies, Daphne. As lovely as the tea is, I'm afraid something isn't sitting well with me. In fact, I might need to excuse myself for a few minutes. Is there a retiring room I could use?"

"Oh…" Daphne frowned, and her cheeks grew quite red. It was clear that she was of the opinion that proper ladies should never mention anything as vulgar as retiring rooms in mixed company. But her next comment made it clear why she looked so embarrassed. "I'm certain the milk is fresh."

"No. It's not that." Jane managed a reassuring smile. "It's possibly the smoked kippers I had for breakfast." Now, that was a lie. Jane couldn't abide kippers and she never touched them, but it seemed like a plausible excuse.

Considering Daphne's nose wrinkled in apparent revulsion, she did too. "If you go upstairs, there's a washroom with a necessary at the end of the hall," she said. "Otherwise, there's a water closet near the kitchen downstairs."

Jane inclined her head as she put down her napkin. "I'll go upstairs," she said, affecting a weak smile. She caught Christopher's eye. "Hopefully I won't be too long."

Christopher nodded. "Take as long as you need, my dear. I will chat with Daphne about Oliver's studies."

Jane found the small washroom easily enough. She opened and shut the door with a loud click for show, then turned back to the narrow hall. It was so quiet she could hear Christopher's deep voice floating up the stairs. There were three other doors, all closed. Jane assumed one of them was Daphne's bedroom and that perhaps she had some sort of private study somewhere. If it was downstairs, it would almost be impossible to search it in secret.

Jane tried each of the doors in turn. One led into a bedroom that she assumed was Oliver's, given the blue quilt upon the bed and the masculine pair of shoes set by a wardrobe. The next door led into Daphne's room, and the third door by the head of the stairs opened onto a small sitting-room-cum-study.

Perfect. Ignoring the mad fluttering of her pulse, Jane slipped inside and quietly closed the door behind her. There was a rosewood escritoire and a bookcase with shelves above and drawers and cupboards below. She'd search here first, and if she didn't find anything, she'd then look through the dressing table, wardrobe, and bedside table in Daphne's bedroom.

Jane sat down at the escritoire and was relieved to discover that nothing was locked. There was a neat stack of bills that were related to mundane purchases, a large ledger that Daphne used to keep track of the household budget including the servants' wages, and a small pocket-sized diary which contained calendar entries and notes about appointments.

Aha! Jane eagerly flipped through the diary's pages, looking for anything of import. Christopher had been shot at in Hyde Park on the fifteenth of February, and lo and behold, on that exact day Daphne had marked the page with a cross in red ink and the word *Jervis.* Of course, the cross might mean anything, and it was impossible to tell if *Jervis* was a name or a place or if it meant nothing at all. But the same word *Jervis*, along with another red cross, appeared on the seventeenth of February, the day someone tried to push Christopher into the path of an oncoming hansom cab on Piccadilly.

Unfortunately, the diary started on January 1, so Jane couldn't check if the dates that coincided with the knife attack in December and the original attempt on Christopher's life seven—or was it now eight?—months ago were marked in a similar fashion.

But there were a number of entries for appointments at the "W Club," including one for the following week, the same day she and Christopher had been invited to dinner at Kyleburn House. So much for Daphne's assertion she'd never heard of the Whisteria Club.

Whether Daphne's penchant for high-stakes card play on a regular basis had anything to do with Christopher remained to be seen, although it was interesting that she'd lied about it.

While Jane was tempted to search for the preceding year's diary, her instincts told her she'd lingered here long enough. Even if Daphne didn't come looking for her, a housemaid might enter the study at any moment.

She slipped the diary into the pocket of her woolen gown— she'd come prepared and wasn't going to strap the book to her leg—then closed the lid of the escritoire.

And then she opened it again. *Jervis.*

It *was* a name; she was certain of it. She'd seen it some-where else during her search. In the ledger listing the names of Daphne's staff perhaps? Or was it in the pile of bills?

She quickly riffled through the bills again and came up empty-handed, but when she went back through the ledger where the staff wages were recorded, she found more than half a dozen entries for an Archie Jervis. Several in July and December of the preceding year, and several more in February. Whoever Archie Jervis was, he'd been paid two hundred pounds on each occasion over two installments. One hundred pounds before each date that coincided with an attack on Christopher, and then another hundred pounds the day after.

Good Lord. That *had* to mean something. Had Daphne in fact hired this Jervis fellow to kill Christopher?

The ledger was far too large to hide on her person and Jane was most definitely taking too long. On an impulse, she tore each of the pages of interest from the heavy leather-bound tome, folded them, then thrust them into her pocket too. That was the best she could do.

She slipped out of Daphne's study and was relieved to see the hallway and stairs were still devoid of occupants. When she entered the parlor, it was to discover that Oliver Marsden had returned home. He was a tall thirteen-year-old youth with brown hair and light-blue eyes exactly like Christopher's. He bowed and smiled shyly at Jane when Christopher made the introductions.

"We were just talking about Eton," explained Christopher.

"Yes, I'm most excited to start after Easter," said Oliver, his eyes alight with enthusiasm. "I'm really keen to join the cricket team."

"Well, we'll see about that," said Daphne stiffly. "You don't want to overtax yourself, Oliver. And those cricket balls are awfully hard. I think shuttlecock or croquet would be safer options for a boy your age."

Oliver rolled his eyes, and Jane noticed a flicker of annoyance in Christopher's gaze. Her husband cocked a brow. "I'm sure he'll be safe enough playing cricket, dear cousin. It didn't do me any harm."

"Yes. Well," returned Daphne with a sniff. It was obvious she didn't agree. She turned her attention back to Jane. "Are you feeling better, Your Grace?" Her manner was cool, her gaze appraising as Jane took her seat. "You were gone for so long, I was beginning to wonder if I should check on you."

"I'm much better. Thank you," replied Jane smoothly, even though her pulse rate kicked up a notch. *Damn.* Daphne was sure to notice her diary was missing. Jane had rather hoped the woman might simply think she'd misplaced it, but if she also noticed that several pages had been torn from her meticulously kept ledger...

Jane inwardly shivered. Of course, it was doubtful Daphne

Marsden would actually accuse the Duchess of Roxby of stealing. But as Jane and Christopher had discussed the night before, Daphne might also be provoked into taking some sort of reckless action if she feared they'd unearthed her secret.

Although the evidence Jane had gathered was vague at best, at least it was better than nothing. If only they could find out who this Archie Jervis might be.

Jane wondered if it was about time that they consulted Lucy's husband, Lord Kyle, to help. Christopher had been reluctant to involve anyone else in the investigation, but Lord Kyle had once worked for Scotland Yard and Jane was certain he could be trusted.

As far as Jane was concerned, next week's dinner party at Kyleburn House couldn't arrive soon enough.

Chapter Thirty-three

"Well, I must say, your duke's cook is very good," said Leonora Pevensey as she selected a tiny gooseberry tartlet and a delicate cucumber sandwich for her plate. "Be careful you don't get too plump, Jane."

Plump? Jane nearly choked on her tea. For years her mother had harped on about the fact Jane was far too thin in her eyes. Trust her mother to always find fault.

Jane, her mother, and Kitty were currently ensconced in Roxby House's elegant drawing room, enjoying a sumptuous afternoon tea. At least Kitty and her mother were. Ever since Jane and Christopher had visited Daphne last week, Jane had found that she did feel a little off now and again.

Talk turned to some of the gowns Kitty had ordered from Madame Blanchard for the coming Season. "I know it's rather wicked to say so, but I do find Lent rather a bore," said Kitty. "I cannot wait for it to be over so I can start attending balls and soirees again."

"Considering the new connections I've made through the Widows and Orphans of Crimea Society, we should have quite a few invitations flowing through the door after Easter, my dear Kitty," returned Leonora proudly. "Oh, and of course Jane is a duchess. That will help."

"Yes, I expect so," said Jane dryly. Secretly, she was pleased her mother was engaging in worthwhile charity work instead of wasting time and money at the Whisteria Club. Which reminded her...

Putting down her tea, Jane cleared her throat. "Mother, I've actually been meaning to ask you about someone you might have crossed paths with at one of your clubs or societies. A woman who's the war widow of Christopher's cousin. Her name is Daphne Marsden. She's quite a petite woman and bears a strong resemblance to Queen Victoria herself. I hear she might be fond of playing cards. Whist in particular."

Her mother's cheeks instantly turned bright red. "Daphne Marsden, you say? I'm...I'm not sure." She emitted a nervous laugh. "I've met so many new people of late, and I have a terrible memory for faces."

Jane knew in that moment her mother must be lying. She had an excellent memory for both names and faces. "Oh, Christopher has a photograph of her and her late husband right here." Jane rose and retrieved the framed picture from the oak sideboard where it was kept. "Do you know her at all? I'd very much appreciate it if you could think on it."

Her mother took the picture and studied the daguerre-otype within the silver frame. "Yes, she does look a little like our queen... I might have seen her about. Where, though, I couldn't say."

She handed the picture back to Jane with a tight smile, and Jane knew that her mother *had* recognized Daphne.

"I don't like to spread gossip at all, but Christopher has been concerned that his cousin has become far too fond of whist and that she's lost a fair bit of money at some female-only gaming hell called the Whisteria Club," said Jane as she placed the pho-tograph on a side table.

"A female-only gaming hell?" exclaimed Kitty. "I never knew such a thing existed."

"It certainly does," said Jane. "Christopher and I are both terribly worried about Daphne and her card-playing habit, but we trust she'll come to her senses and soon see that there are other pursuits in life that are far more worthwhile. Like joining charitable organizations such as your Widows and Orphans of Crimea Society, Mama." On an impulse, Jane reached out and grasped her mother's hand and gave it a gentle squeeze. "I'm proud of you, you know," she said softly. "You of all people should know how hard it is being a widow. How challenging it is when one is pressed for money. I think you'll do a wonderful job helping others."

"Yes…yes, I do know how difficult it can be," said her mother. Her cheeks had pinkened and tears brimmed in her eyes. "And thank you, Jane. I've never said it before, but I'm proud of you too. I'm not the easiest person to get along with and sometimes I've been my own worst enemy. You've put up with a lot."

"I'm just glad to see you so settled and happy now," said Jane. "When the Season proper begins, Christopher and I will be sure to host a ball here at Roxby House, and you and Henry and Kitty will all be invited."

With promises to catch up sooner rather than later, Jane's mother and Kitty took their leave. Christopher made an appearance in the hall to bid them farewell too. As soon as the door closed behind them, Jane told Christopher about the fact her mother had recognized Daphne.

"Because Kitty was present, we had to talk around the topic of the Whisteria Club. So I'm not sure if Daphne has been involved in high-stakes play all that often. But still, at least we now know your cousin-in-law is definitely a member."

"Yes," agreed Christopher. "She's so conservative in all other respects—a holier-than-thou stickler for the rules—that she doesn't strike me as the sort of woman who would be interested in gambling of any kind. It makes me wonder why."

"She certainly didn't want to admit she was a member when I quizzed her about it last week," said Jane. "Actually, I keep expecting her to turn up on the doorstep of Roxby House to accuse me of theft."

Christopher frowned. "Perhaps it's equally as telling that she hasn't. To me it suggests she has something to hide."

"So, what do we do next?"

Her husband sighed and scratched his jaw. "As much as I don't want to involve anyone else, I think it *is* time to recruit others to the cause. I trust your judgment, Jane. I'll speak with Lord Kyle tonight. And the Duke of Dartmoor too. Hopefully, I'll convince them that I'm not as mad as a hatter during dinner."

"Of course you're not," said Jane. "They'll see straightaway how intelligent and capable you are. From what I've heard, they are very understanding men. Just like you."

"Stop that now. You're making me blush," Christopher said, his voice gruff. "And I don't blush easily."

Jane laughed. "No, you don't." She loved how easy the banter was between them again. The camaraderie. They headed toward the main staircase, but a knock on the front door had them turning back.

Christopher frowned. "Were you expecting anyone else this afternoon?"

"No," Jane returned. "Were you?"

"No…" Even though Christopher gave her a reassuring smile, Jane sensed that he was on alert, as though preparing for something unexpected to happen. "It's probably a courier. My solicitor mentioned he might send over some documents for me to sign."

"You're worried that Daphne might be planning another attack, aren't you?" murmured Jane.

Christopher grimaced. "Is it that obvious?"

"Yes." Jane squeezed his arm. "What are we going to do tonight? Do you propose we send for your carriage when it's but a five-minute walk to Kyleburn House?"

"Don't tempt me," growled Christopher. "I'd do anything to ensure your safety."

The knock came again, more frantic this time, and Christopher gestured for the burly footman on duty, Beattie, to answer the door. When it swung open, it was to reveal none other than Daisy Cosgrove.

Jane's surprise must have shown on her face as Christopher asked, "Who is it?"

"Daisy," she murmured just as the capricious, odious woman called past Beattie's wide shoulder.

"Your Grace? Christopher? Might I have a word?"

Christopher's mouth flattened into a grim line. "I really don't have the time or inclination for this," he muttered beneath his breath. Nevertheless, he waved Daisy into the hall. "What is it, Mrs. Cosgrove?" he asked coldly. Jane had never seen his eyes turn such a shade of arctic blue.

"Goodness, aren't we all stiff and formal this afternoon!" Daisy replied with a little laugh. Jane didn't fail to notice how her gaze drifted knowingly to the front of Christopher's trousers when she'd uttered the word *stiff*.

"My time and patience are both limited, Daisy," Christopher said, crossing his arms over his chest. "Please state your business. I have other matters I need to attend to."

Daisy sniffed and tossed her blond curls. "Are we going to have this conversation in the hall? In front of"—she looked Jane up and down as though she were a stray cat who'd slunk in the door after her—"others."

"You mean my wife, the Duchess of Roxby?" said Christopher, cocking a brow. "Why, yes, we are."

"Very well then." Daisy lifted her pointed little chin and her eyes glinted. "I've come because I wanted to let you know that Simon is divorcing me. He told me this morning. In fact, he even handed me papers from his solicitor."

"I'm sorry to hear that," said Christopher gravely. "My sincerest condolences to you."

Daisy waved a gloved hand. "Oh, I'm not sad or even mad about it. Of course, it will be a trifle embarrassing in the short term, but just knowing there's a chance for us to rekindle—"

Christopher's eyes narrowed. "*Chance* for us? What *are* you talking about?"

"Oh, don't pretend you don't know *exactly* what I mean, Christopher." Ignoring Jane's presence altogether, Daisy sauntered closer, her pale-pink skirts swaying. "I've always thought that after that night we shared together last year that you and I might—"

"Night you shared together?" repeated Jane. Foreboding was brewing inside her as her gaze met her husband's. A memory stirred, and the words Christopher had said to her a few weeks ago slid through her mind: *Here, don't you go thinking that I'm a good man or any sort of hero, Jane. There are things that I've done in my past that are not honorable.*

"Was this the night Daisy came here during your end-of-Season ball and propositioned you?" whispered Jane. Her throat was so dry she could barely speak. "You told me that nothing of import happened."

Christopher waved away the goggle-eyed footman before he responded. "Yes, it was. But Daisy is misrepresenting the whole affair."

Daisy raised a brow and smirked at Jane. "Oh, no, I'm not," she said. "Your husband kissed me, and then we—"

"Enough, Daisy," growled Christopher. "I'm happily married

to Jane now, and you'll show her the respect she deserves by not uttering another single word about that night. There is no chance for us. There is no you and I. Whatever love I once had for you is gone. Dead and buried."

Daisy's eyes hardened. "But I thought... After last year..." She crossed her arms and scowled. "When we made love that night, you led me to believe—"

"My God, Daisy." Christopher shoved a hand though his hair, turning its artfully tousled waves into wild spikes. "We did *not* make love. Your lies must stop. The lengths you will go to to get your own way both astound and appall me. In fact, I'm beginning to think you're quite delusional. Please leave now before I have you thrown out."

Daisy's mouth dropped open. "Well, I never," she managed after a frost-laden pause. She drew herself up and cast a disdainful glare Jane's way. "If you think he'll be happy with you, Your Grace, *you're* the one who's delusional."

"Out." Christopher's voice rumbled like oncoming thunder as he pointed at the door. "Get out now."

Daisy sniffed, then turned on her heel. "You'll be begging me to come back to you. I know you will, Christopher," she called over her shoulder. A red-faced Beattie appeared from the shadows of the cloakroom and opened the door for her. "A love like ours—"

The door slammed, cutting off her words, and if Jane wasn't so perturbed she might have laughed. "I think we need to talk, Christopher," she murmured, wrapping her arms about herself. She suddenly felt far too cold. And perhaps a little ill.

"Yes, we do." A muscle worked in Christopher's jaw. "Let's repair to the library."

As soon as the door closed behind Christopher, he stalked across the room and poured two sizable nips of brandy into crystal tumblers. "I'm so sorry, Jane." His words were leaden with remorse as he passed her one of the drinks. "That scene should never have happened. I knew Daisy could be cold-hearted, but her vitriol and false accusations were beyond the pale."

"Are her accusations false, though?" challenged Jane. She crossed to the fire to ward off the chill that seemed to have set-tled in the pit of her stomach.

She wanted to believe Christopher, but had he commit-ted adultery with a married woman? Was that what he meant when he'd told her that he'd done something dishonorable? She felt bruised inside. As though her heart had suddenly been trampled on. "You told me once that 'nothing of import' had occurred that night Daisy turned up here uninvited. I know it was months ago, before we'd even met, but did you and Daisy…?" Her voice faltered, but she made herself press on. "*Did* you and Daisy make love? Please tell me the truth."

Christopher rubbed his jaw and Jane's heart sank. She had the distinct feeling he was weighing up what he was going to tell her. Choosing his words. "We kissed," he said. "And we began to…" His throat worked in a swallow and his expression, while earnest, was also ravaged with regret. "I will tell you everything if you want me to, but I don't think a precise description of what we did or didn't do that night will help matters. Suffice it to say we didn't go very far. I had an attack of conscience and I stopped before…"

He blew out a heavy sigh, but his gaze was steady as it met hers. "We did *not* have sexual congress, Jane. May God strike me dead if I'm lying. I was wrong to even kiss Daisy. And to be perfectly honest, I did so for entirely dishonorable rea-sons. It was out of spite. I was angry at her for breaking my heart, and part of me wanted to show her what she'd missed out on. What she could have had if she hadn't thrown it all away. And yes, I was jealous of Simon Cosgrove for stealing her away from me, so kissing Daisy, perhaps even bedding her, would have been a way for me to get back at him. It was petty and vindictive and grubby, and I'm so damn ashamed that the whole incident ever happened."

He put down his glass and crossed to the fireplace where Jane hovered on the hearthrug. "I told you I wasn't a good man. I should have told you about what happened that night a lot sooner. I was a coward not to confess all. The simple truth is I was worried that you'd think less of me. That I couldn't be the sort of man whom you could—" He broke off and looked away. Looked back. "I just pray that you can forgive me for withholding the truth for so long."

That I couldn't be the sort of man whom you could love? Was that what Christopher had been about to say?

Jane's heart began to crash against her ribs. "I believe everything you've told me, and I don't think less of you. Although I'm shocked and a little hurt about what I've learned, I do understand. No one is perfect, and God knows I've made mistakes too. Mistakes that have hurt you. So of course I forgive you." She placed her untouched brandy on the mantelpiece. "It seems we've both been worried about the same thing. To be perfectly frank, that's one of the reasons why I didn't tell you about my blackmailer. I didn't want you to think less of me either. That *I* couldn't be the sort of woman whom you could…whom you could live with."

Oh, she couldn't say it. She was a coward too.

"*Live* with, Jane?" Christopher's mouth curved into a bittersweet smile. "I was a cavalry officer, yet it seems that confessing how I feel about you is one of the hardest things I've ever had to do. I keep wondering why, and it's only just now that I've realized it's because I'm nervous about *your* reaction to what I

have to say. But I'm going to say it. Oh God, I *need* to say it…"
Christopher inhaled deeply and drew Jane into the circle of his
arms. "Two weeks ago, after we made love in this very room,
you told me that you were drunk with desire."

"Yes, I did," whispered Jane.

"But," continued Christopher, tilting up her chin with a
crooked finger so she couldn't escape his gaze, "since that night,
I've often wondered if you were about to say that you were
drunk with something else, some other emotion, but changed
your mind."

Jane's cheeks grew hot, but she couldn't look away. She was not
used to being so honest. To sharing how she felt. Not even with
herself. But it was time. "I might have," she murmured huskily.

"Would it help if I told you that I, too, know that feeling of
being drunk with deep emotion?" added Christopher in a low,
tender voice. "That whenever I'm with you like this, I feel as
though I'm intoxicated. As though I've downed an entire bottle
of potent brandy and my head is spinning with the wonder
of it all. And when you're not here, it feels like all the air has
gone out of the room. That all the lights have been snuffed out.
That somehow my day is not complete unless you are in it."
Christopher caressed her cheek with gentle fingers, then murmured, "Is it like that for you too?"

"Yes, it's exactly like that," she whispered.

"Well, it seems that somehow we've both fallen in love…
Jane…" Christopher's eyes stared so deeply into hers, Jane felt
as though he touched her very soul. "I love you."

Oh, dear heaven. Could it be true? "Are you sure?" she whispered as tears welled in her eyes.

"I possess not a single doubt. My heart, my body, my soul,
everything that I am belongs to you."

Jane swallowed past a lump of emotion jamming her

throat. "Oh, Christopher, I love you too. With my whole heart, I love you."

"My love. My heart." Christopher captured her face between his hands and kissed her deeply. Reverently. With such tender passion Jane wasn't sure if she ever wanted this breath-stealing, glorious moment to end.

Somehow, some way, despite all the trial and tribulations they'd been through and were yet to face, they'd forged an unbreakable bond. An everlasting love. Jane could feel it in Christopher's kiss. In his touch as his hands swept over her body.

It resonated in her heart. She could hear it singing in her blood.

Every single part of her, every little piece, *knew* it.

When they drew apart, Christopher's eyes were aflame with desire. "Do you think we have time to make love before we go to dinner at Kyleburn House, my darling wife?"

Jane smiled. "Of course we do. You can have me right here in the library if you like..."

Her husband laughed. "It's like you read my mind," he said as he swung her into his arms and carried her over to the desk. And then words were no longer needed as they showed each other everything that was in their hearts.

Chapter Thirty-four

THE DINNER AT KYLEBURN HOUSE WAS OF SUCH EXCEL-
lent quality and the company so convivial that Christopher
wondered why on earth he'd been so reluctant to meet with
Jane's friends for so long. He should have listened to his
clever wife sooner.

For one thing, Christopher had no trouble at all keeping
track of who was who at the dinner table, which was a huge
relief in and of itself. William, Lord Kyle, was easily identifiable
by his Scots accent, and Dominic, the Duke of Dartmoor, had
a smattering of silver in his jet-black hair. Lucy, Lady Kyle, was
blond, while Artemis, the Duchess of Dartmoor, had flaming-
red hair. It really was impossible to mix any of them up, even
if Christopher couldn't recall their faces from one moment to
the next.

By the time the dessert dishes had been cleared from the
table, Christopher felt relaxed enough to stay in the dining room
drinking spirits and port with the men while Jane repaired to
the drawing room for a postprandial cup of tea with her Byronic
Book Club friends.

This afternoon's visit from Daisy Cosgrove had in many
ways been a godsend, Christopher thought to himself as Lord
Kyle poured him a whisky. It had been the catalyst that had
forced him to open his heart and be completely honest with
Jane. He was blessed indeed that she hadn't judged him for his
past transgression. She understood him. Knew him inside and

out like no one else in the entire world. And she accepted him for who he was despite his faults and imperfections.

It was also a huge relief to finally confess how he felt about her. That he loved Jane beyond reason, and she felt exactly the same way about him. In many respects, the pressure to effectively deal with the threat hanging over his head, and perhaps Jane's, was more urgent than ever.

Before they'd arrived here at Kyleburn House, Jane had insisted that her friends Artemis and Lucy and their respective spouses would be nothing but understanding if Christopher shared his closely guarded secrets. He just had to choose the right moment to bring up such complicated and fraught subjects.

They discussed politics for a while before Kyle struck up a conversation with Christopher about his military service in the Crimea. And then Christopher asked the Scots earl about his time at Scotland Yard after he resigned his officer's commission.

"I've learned from my wife that you conducted clandestine investigations, Kyle."

"Aye," said the Scotsman and his mouth twisted with a wry smirk. "Unfortunately, I canna really divulge anything about any of the cases I worked on. If I did, I might have to kill you. It wouldna be personal though."

Christopher swirled his whisky about in his glass, watching the amber-hued whirlpool. Now was the perfect opportunity for him to disclose everything he needed to—the fact that someone *was* actually trying to kill him, and that the first attempt on his life had resulted in facial blindness. But despite Jane's earlier reassurances, the words seemed to stick in his throat.

"You've gone rather quiet there, Roxby," said Dartmoor in his distinctive cultured baritone.

"Aye," agreed Kyle as he put down his own whisky glass. "I

can assure you that I was joking." His gaze narrowed a little as he added, "There isna anything wrong, is there?"

Christopher gave a small snort. "Actually, there is." And then he inhaled a long breath and shared everything. He didn't withhold a single detail, and as he told his story, he was heartened by both Kyle's and Dartmoor's reassuring responses and insightful questions.

By the time Christopher had finished, he knew beyond a doubt that these men would support him. They didn't think he was mad or incompetent. In fact, they were concerned about his safety and Jane's.

"I havena heard of anyone by the name of Archie Jervis in connection with any particular crime," said Kyle. "But that doesna mean he isn't a killer for hire. First thing tomorrow, I'll check with one of my main contacts at the Yard. A Detective John Lawrence." He cocked a brow. "I could also ask Detective Lawrence to pay a visit to your cousin-in-law to ask her a few questions. If nothing else, I'm sure he'd be interested to hear about this Whisteria Club. A dowager viscountess might own the establishment, but it still sounds like an illegal gaming hell to me."

"I just wish I knew what the man or men who've been attacking me actually look like," said Christopher after Kyle had replenished their whisky. "I have nothing to go on except the name Jervis, which might be a red herring. Although my gut also tells me that there'll be another attack soon. Jane and I have undoubtedly provoked Daphne by taking her diary and several pages from her ledger. I'm worried she'll retaliate."

"A military man should always trust his gut," said Kyle. "I did wonder why you arrived by carriage tonight with a small army of footmen in tow. I thought the cavalry had descended on Kyleburn House."

"I'm not taking any chances," said Christopher. "Especially when it comes to my wife."

"I for one do think it's rather interesting that your cousin-in-law hasn't turned up at Roxby House to ask you or your wife if you had anything to do with her diary's disappearance," said Dartmoor. "I think that could be quite significant."

"Aye, I agree," said Kyle. "I'm beginning to think that perhaps we need to have your cousin watched. If she's hired this Archie Jervis to kill you, I imagine she'll have to meet with him sometime to make a payment. I know of several excellent men who I could recommend for the job."

Christopher inclined his head. "I'll definitely take you up on that offer."

"Gentlemen, it sounds like we have a firm plan of action," said Kyle. "And rest assured, Roxby, while I'm in Town, you willna be left to flounder at White's or at any other social event you attend."

"I'll do the same for you whenever you make an appearance in the House of Lords," said Dartmoor. "No one will dare question your soundness of mind."

"Thank you," said Christopher. It suddenly felt like something the size of a boulder had become lodged in his throat, and he had to swallow hard to clear it. "I'm very grateful for your support."

Lord Kyle reached for the whisky decanter and topped up all their glasses again. "Let's drink to newfound friendship and your good health, Roxby. And then we'll join our good wives."

"Yes, God knows what they're plotting," said Dartmoor with a grin. "I know Artemis is brewing up something with your wife in particular, Roxby. Something to do with pamphlets and medical dispensaries for women. I swear she has fingers in more pies than I do these days. Which is saying something. But I wouldn't have it any other way."

"You ken what they say: busy wife, happy life," said Kyle. "At least that's true for my Lucy. I thank God every day for the simple fact I'm by her side and that I can support her in her endeavors, whatever they might be."

"I feel the exact same way about Jane," said Christopher. He raised his glass. "Do you mind if I amend the toast, gentlemen? Here's to newfound friendship, good health, *and* to our wives who bring so much joy to our lives."

"Hear, hear," chorused Dartmoor and Kyle as they all touched glasses. As Christopher took a sip of his whisky, he also sent up a silent prayer to heaven that his days with Jane would not be numbered.

─────────

When Christopher joined her in the drawing room, Jane could immediately tell that his discussion with Lord Kyle and the Duke of Dartmoor had gone well. He'd never seemed so relaxed in the company of others, and she was so relieved.

With Christopher's agreement, Jane had already disclosed to Artemis and Lucy that her husband suffered from a rare condition that made him unable to recall most people's faces. Of course, they were sympathy personified. They were also horrified to hear that someone was threatening Christopher's life. Moreover, both Artemis and Lucy had offered their country homes as a place for Jane to seek refuge if it all became too much for her to bear.

Jane, while grateful, had politely declined. Now wasn't the time to quit London. Not when she and Christopher were closing in on the perpetrator. With the help of Lord Kyle and Scotland Yard, Jane was confident the person or persons responsible for these insidious attacks would be caught and brought to justice.

Jane also learned from Lucy and Artemis that "Mrs." Rosalind Sharp had been reunited with Ned Grimsby, and if they weren't wed already, they would be very soon. Dominic had managed to find out that Ned's father had sent his son to Paris to establish a Continental base for their expanding business, and he'd then lied to Ned about the governess's whereabouts. Ned had been told that Miss Sharp had run off with one of the footmen, and because he'd been so heartbroken, he'd buried himself in work. As soon as he'd heard the truth from Dominic, he'd sought out Miss Sharp at Lucy and Will's estate in Cumberland.

While Miss Sharp had created havoc in Artemis's life and Jane's, Jane was nevertheless pleased to hear the misguided governess would get a happy rather than a tragic end to her love story.

The merry party had continued on until almost midnight. When Jane and Christopher at last decided it was time to quit Kyleburn House, the weather had turned inclement. A sheeting rain swept over Eaton Square, and Jane was thankful Christopher had decided to use his carriage to transport them the short distance to Lucy and Will's residence.

Beattie, the footman, held an umbrella for Jane as she lifted her midnight-blue silk skirts and carefully negotiated the slick stairs and pavement as she crossed to the carriage. Christopher, cloaked in a greatcoat, handed her inside before leaping up to join her.

"I do feel sorry for the staff," said Jane as the carriage moved off.

Christopher shrugged. "I'm sure the footmen took turns to enjoy a brew or two in Kyleburn House's kitchen while they waited for us," he said. "It's the driver who's had the worst of it, watching the horses all night, poor sod. I'll be sure to slip him an extra guinea for his pains."

"At least we don't have far to go." Jane had noticed Franklin, the coach driver, huddled on his seat with his hat pulled down over his eyes and the collar of his oilskin turned up to ward off the freezing needles of rain as she'd approached the carriage. "But I agree that he deserves a tip for his trouble on a night like this. It feels like the Arctic has decided to send an icy blast our way."

Within a minute or two, they were drawing up outside Roxby House. A gust of wind rocked the carriage and Christopher swore. "Umbrellas aren't going to cut the mustard in this weather," he said as he shrugged off his black wool greatcoat. "Here, put this on, my love. I don't want you to catch cold."

Jane laughed. "You're such a mother hen, but I love it," she said, kissing his lean cheek. His night beard was already beginning to grow, and she relished the feel of the rasp of it against her lips.

"Good Lord, I'll have to make sure that I perform well when I take you to bed, Jane. Call me vain, but I'd much rather you thought of me as something far more manly, like a rampant stallion or a rutting buck or even a randy cock. But a chicken?"

"I look forward to your complete demonstration very shortly." Anticipation bubbled inside Jane as she added huskily, "I'm sure I'll be soaking wet by the time I reach your bedchamber. Perhaps we can make love before the fire."

Christopher gave a low growl of approval and nipped at her ear. "A capital idea," he began, but then the carriage door swung open, and Beattie was waiting to hand her down.

Jane pulled Christopher's coat around her tightly as she hastened toward the front door of Roxby House, which

Shelby held wide open. Beyond the butler, she could see the grand entrance hall illuminated by the enormous gas chandelier and she was immediately transported back to Saint Valentine's Day and how she'd taken a chance and had rushed up these same stairs.

She had no regrets at all. Not a single one—

There was an earsplitting crack in the night. For the briefest of moments, as Jane was knocked sideways, she wondered if thunder had clapped right over her head. But then the searing pain in her right arm put paid to that idea. With a cry, she fell to her knees on the pavement.

If she hadn't been struck by lightning, she must have been shot.

Shot. Oh God.

"Jane!" Christopher's voice was a faint echo in her ears. She felt his hands gripping her shoulders, and then his beloved face was hovering in front of hers. Somewhere behind her she heard a horse whinny and the clatter of hooves. Shouting. And then dark spots began to dance in front of her eyes as though someone had pulled a black lacy veil over her face.

"It's my arm," she whispered, not knowing if Christopher heard her. "It's on fire."

"I've got you, my love." In the next instant, her husband was sweeping her up into his arms. And then Jane's world turned black.

━━━━━━━

Christ. He couldn't believe it. His Jane had been shot.

Shot.

As Christopher lifted his injured wife into his arms, a white-faced man rushed down the stairs toward him. His name tag identified him as Shelby. "Your Grace... Shall I take her...?"

"No…" There was a commotion behind them—shouts and grunts and scuffling—and Christopher glanced over his shoulder. Even though it was dark and raining, there was enough light from a nearby gaslight for him to discern that everything was under control. His footmen had wrestled the shooter—the carriage driver, by the looks of things—to the ground. But Christopher's priority right now was Jane. The love of his life.

If anything happened to her… If she didn't survive this…

God damn it, the bullet had been meant for him…

Christopher gritted his teeth as guilt twisted his guts and a white-hot fury coursed through his veins. As much as he wanted to pull the dog who'd hurt his wife to pieces, he'd have to deal with the shooter later.

Chapter Thirty-five

EVEN THOUGH CHRISTOPHER ALREADY KNEW IT, THE attending physician, Dr. Hamilton, declared that the gunshot wound to Jane's right upper arm was a graze. A deep one, but nothing life-threatening…unless infection set in.

"It will need to be cleaned with chloride of lime and stitched, Your Grace." The doctor addressed Jane directly. "And that will hurt, a lot, unless I administer chloroform. You simply inhale it and it will make you go to sleep for a little while. In fact, you'll feel nothing at all while I attend to your wound. And afterward when you wake, you can take laudanum to take the edge off the pain."

"I don't want anything like that," said Jane. Even though she was sitting before a roaring fire in her bedchamber, her face was ashen and she couldn't seem to stop shivering. Her dark-blue evening gown was wet and muddy, and the right sleeve had been cut away to reveal the nasty gash across the top of her arm. In fact, the sight of his wife in so much pain and in such a forlorn state made Christopher want to grind the person responsible for this vile atrocity into dust.

Christopher squatted down beside Jane and took one of her slender hands between his, hoping he could suffuse her with warmth. "My love, perhaps you should do as the doctor suggests. I've been grazed by bullets before and getting stitches is terribly painful. I don't want you to have to suffer needlessly." He brought her palm to his cheek, then kissed it. "My heart is already shredded by the thought that bullet was meant for me, not you. Please assuage my guilt just a little."

Jane's beautiful green eyes were clouded with pain, but she met Christopher's gaze steadily as she said softly, "It's not your fault, my darling man. Please don't feel guilty."

"But I do. I cannot help it."

"Christopher, you did everything you could to keep us safe. If it weren't for you and your valiant footmen, you wouldn't have caught this Jervis character."

Christopher's jaw tightened. "It wasn't me who stopped the swine from getting away though. I should have known something was wrong. I should have noticed it wasn't Franklin up there in the driver's seat. Good God, the man could be dead too. This should never have happened."

When Jane had been shot and Christopher had rushed to her aid, it was the alert young footman, Beattie, who'd first noticed that the carriage driver was the shooter. Or, to be more precise, Archie Jervis who'd taken the place of Franklin, the real driver.

In fact, Beattie, despite the danger, had stopped Jervis driving off after the worthless cur had fired at Jane. The footman had held onto the horses while another pair of footmen had seized Jervis and had tackled him to the ground. The hired killer was now tied up and being guarded in Roxby House's stables until the police arrived. The only thing he would admit to was his name.

So far... For now...

Jane reached out with her uninjured arm and touched Christopher's cheek. "It doesn't matter that it wasn't you who apprehended Jervis. You employed good men. Brave men. And you were brave too. Indeed, how many men would come to the aid of someone else with no thought for their own safety? Jervis could have fired another shot. But no, you rushed straight into the line of fire to protect me."

"How could I not? I would do anything for you. I love you. And I hate seeing you in so much pain."

"I'll be all right," she returned. "'Tis but a graze. And as to whether the doctor should administer the chloroform or not..." Jane paused and drew a small breath. "There's a very good reason that I *don't* want him to use it. Nor do I want to take laudanum..." She smiled softly. "You see, I'm late..."

"Late?" Christopher frowned in confusion.

"Yes, by a week." She shook her head in apparent exasperation when it was clear he still didn't take her meaning. "You dunderhead. I'm beginning to wonder if I might be with child."

"Pregnant? You think you might be pregnant?" whispered Christopher. He could scarcely believe it.

"I'm not entirely certain, but aside from being late, I've been feeling ill on and off for the past five days. So it is a possibility..."

"Oh my God, Jane. That's wonderful news." Joy along with a wave of fierce protectiveness surged in Christopher's chest. He wanted to gather his wife into his arms and kiss her soundly, but he was also aware of her injured arm. Instead, he settled for placing a gentle kiss upon her forehead. "I'm so happy, my heart can hardly contain it."

But beneath all that, he was also angry. Livid that some dog had quite possibly taken the life of Franklin, his coachman, and had then taken a shot at Jane. But he didn't want to spoil this tender moment between him and his wife.

The doctor cleared his throat. "I hope you can forgive me for overhearing some of what you disclosed, Your Grace," he said to Jane. "But perhaps it would interest you to know that it will be quite safe for me to administer chloroform even if you are pregnant. It's routinely used in childbirth. Even our good queen used it to ease her labor pains during the birth of Prince Leopold and then Princess Beatrice."

"It's up to you, my love," said Christopher. "I support whatever decision you make."

She gave a little sigh. "Very well, I'll let Dr. Hamilton use the chloroform. But I'll wait to see if I need to take any laudanum. If I can manage the pain without it, I'd prefer not to use it."

"Believe me, it will be better this way," said Christopher gently. "Seeing you suffer so hurts me too."

Jane's maid, Elsie, emerged from the sitting room with hot water and clean linen, and after she'd assisted Jane to remove her cumbersome crinoline cage, Christopher helped Jane to the bed.

He stayed by Jane's side while she drifted into a deep sleep, and when the wound had been stitched and she was resting comfortably, he donned another greatcoat, quit Roxby House, and then made his way through the rain to the mews.

He had business to attend to in the stables.

———

Close to dawn, Jane awoke to find herself alone in her bed.

Even though she was groggy from the chloroform and her arm throbbed and burned, she pushed herself up against the pillows. Someone, probably Elsie, had managed to get her out of her soiled evening gown and into a plain cotton nightgown, the sort Christopher hated.

Well, he'd just have to put up with the visually offensive garment for the time being. Jane smiled to herself as her drowsy gaze searched the room for her husband. Ah, there he was, fast asleep in the chair beside her bed, head tipped back, breathing deeply and evenly. The light of the bedside lamp gilded his sharply cut profile and picked out strands of guinea gold and burnt caramel in his tousled tawny hair.

Darling man. He probably hadn't wanted to bump her

injured arm in his sleep. He was still dressed in his black evening trousers, leather shoes, and white cambric shirt, although it wasn't as pristine as the night before. Jane winced when she spied a dark-red stain near one rolled-up cuff that must be her blood. But then the knuckles of Christopher's right hand were also bruised and grazed...

Had he been fighting? And if so, with whom?

She frowned. She remembered nothing at all after Dr. Hamilton had given her the chloroform. Which she supposed was a blessing. She slid a hand beneath the covers of her bed and laid it upon her belly.

Could it really be true that she was pregnant? A toe-curling thrill of sweet anticipation unfurled inside Jane and she smiled. Despite the fear and pain of last night, she was so happy to be able to share her suspicion with Christopher. To see the joyful light in his eyes when he realized what she was telling him.

She'd only begun to suspect she was expecting last night. So much had gone on of late that she hadn't kept track of her courses. But as she'd taken tea with Artemis and Lucy in Kyleburn House's drawing room, she'd felt a little "off" and had declined the glass of sherry that Lucy had offered her. Artemis had also declined taking sherry, and as Jane had studied her friend's slightly full figure, the realization that her period hadn't arrived when it should have had struck her. She'd always been as regular as clockwork, so the fact that her courses were almost a week late *must* mean something.

She prayed it was indeed the case.

It was still raining outside. Jane could hear the drops pattering steadily against the windows. The clock on the mantelpiece indicated it was almost half past six. She really needed to use the necessary in her dressing room, but she didn't want to ring for Elsie because then she'd disturb Christopher. Even though it was painful to do so, she carefully slid from the bed.

When she returned to the bedroom a short time later, Christopher stirred. He yawned and scrubbed a hand down his face, and when he saw her hovering by the end of the bed, he frowned.

"What the devil, Jane?" he growled. "What are you doing up and about?"

She laughed. "I was shot in the arm, not the leg," she said as she approached him. "I can still walk."

"Humph. Even so..." Despite his early morning display of grumpy indignation, he stood and greeted her with a soft kiss. "Good morning, my darling wife. How is your arm? How do you feel? Can I get you anything?"

"Perhaps you could ring for a cup of tea and some toast. But first of all, I want to hear about poor Franklin and what you've learned from Jervis." She picked up Christopher's hand and lightly kissed his abraded knuckles. "I don't think you were sparring in the arms room in the wee hours, were you?"

Christopher grimaced. "No, your assumption is correct."

"I take it that Jervis might be sporting a bruise or two on his person?"

"Yes, but not as many as I'd like, to be honest. Alas, the former military officer in me won't let me take justice into my own hands, even though another part of me would very much like to."

"And everyone believes you're such a scoundrel when you're nothing but noble." Jane kissed her husband's hand again. "So where is Jervis now?"

"In police custody," said Christopher. "No doubt in a matter of hours he'll be charged with multiple counts of attempted murder and assault. Aside from sporting a sizable bump on his head, you'll be pleased to hear that Franklin is all right though, thank God."

Christopher quickly filled her in on how Jervis had managed to take the place of the coach driver. Apparently, the hired killer had been hiding in the mews behind Kyleburn House, and when Franklin had ducked down the alley to relieve himself just before midnight, Jervis had knocked him out with a blow to the back of the head. He'd purloined the coachman's oilskin and hat, and in the darkness and the rain the other footmen hadn't noticed that it was Jervis, not Franklin, who'd climbed back into the driver's seat of the carriage.

Well, not until it was too late.

"Why don't you hop back into bed, my love? Then after I have a quick word with Featherstone next door about arranging a breakfast tray, I'll come back and tell you everything else that I know. Detective John Lawrence from Scotland Yard has been assigned to the case, and if he hasn't already paid a visit to Russell Square to speak with Daphne, no doubt he will be doing so very soon. I'm confident we'll be hearing of her arrest in the next few hours."

Jane nodded. "Poor Oliver. It will be a shock for the boy to hear what his mother has been up to. I take it that Jervis admitted that it was Daphne who hired him to kill you, then?"

"Yes, he did," Christopher said grimly, but then the gravity lacing his tone softened as he added, "I'm afraid he was hired to do away with you too. After we paid a visit to Daphne's house last week, it seems she was worried you might be pregnant. You'd mentioned you weren't feeling well, remember?"

Oh, good heavens. What a foolish slip of the tongue that had been. Jane's stomach pitched and Christopher immediately noticed. "Jane, you've gone awfully pale. I really do think you should stay in bed."

She couldn't disagree. She dutifully complied with

Christopher's request, and after he'd tucked her in, she closed her eyes.

"I'll be back soon," he murmured, and then she heard the door click shut behind him.

Jane sighed and snuggled into her pillow. Not only was she weary to the bone, but she also felt oh so terrible. She'd unwittingly put herself in Daphne's sights too.

But perhaps that always would have been the case. As soon as she'd wed Christopher, she'd become a threat to the woman's plans.

The woman was diabolical. Pure evil.

A Lady Macbeth come to life who'd resort to murder to seize the dukedom for her own son.

Thank God the Scotland Yard detective would soon be questioning Daphne, perhaps even arresting her, and then this whole nightmare would be over.

The door to Jane's bedchamber snicked open again. Goodness, Christopher had been quick. Or was it Elsie who'd popped in to draw the curtains back and stoke the fire?

Jane opened her eyes and then gasped. Horror froze her blood.

Daphne Marsden was standing in the middle of her room, holding a gun trained straight at Jane.

Even though ice-cold fear constricted her throat, somehow Jane made her voice work. "H-how did you get in here?" she whispered as she pushed herself into a sitting position. She was so petrified that she barely even noticed the pain in her arm as the stitches pulled.

The woman sneered and pushed a bedraggled lock of hair away from her face. Her pale-blue eyes were filled with contempt as she hissed, "Shut up, you baseborn bitch. And don't you dare think about screaming for help."

"I–I won't," said Jane. "I promise I won't."

Oh God, if Christopher came in, would Daphne shoot him too? Jane's gaze fell to the pistol Daphne held with both her hands. It looked like a dueling pistol. Her grip was tight, but her aim was unsteady. Did Daphne even know how to use the thing?

Jane wasn't going to take any chances. Perhaps if she kept Daphne talking, Christopher might hear them through the door and not stumble into his cousin-in-law's sights too.

If anything happened to him… If anything happened to their child…

Jane stopped herself from placing her hand upon her belly. She didn't want to provoke Daphne. The woman was clearly unstable, if not altogether mad.

She swallowed to moisten her dry mouth. "What do you want?" she managed at last through stiff, frozen lips. "Surely you don't mean to hurt me. Just think of poor Oliver. If you put the gun down, I'm sure we can work—"

"Shut up, I said." Daphne's gaze darted to the bedroom door leading to the hall, then back to Jane. Perhaps she'd heard a noise outside? "I'm trying to think. There are so many damn servants in this house—"

"Yes, there are," interrupted Jane. "In fact, I'm amazed you even managed to reach my room without getting caught. That must have taken some skill."

Daphne smirked. "I sneaked in last night after you got shot and all hell broke loose. I've been hiding in the library, in amongst the bookcases, waiting for my chance to finish what Jervis couldn't. The fool."

"It doesn't sound like he's worth the price you paid for his services. Is that why you joined the Whisteria Club, by the way? Because you didn't have enough money and needed to acquire it by gambling at a gaming hell?"

"The Whisteria Club is *not* a gaming hell," Daphne snapped. "It's a card-playing establishment for ladies of quality." She moved several steps closer to the bed and aimed the pistol at Jane's head. "Now, be quiet before—" She broke off as a wide yawn split her face.

Daphne was clearly exhausted. There were shadows of fatigue beneath her eyes and lines of strain bracketing her mouth. The idea that the woman had been lurking downstairs in the library for hours and hours made Jane's stomach roil. But it also didn't make sense. The house was waking up for the day. The woman could have invaded Jane's room when she and Christopher were both fast asleep and no one was about. Jane's gaze wandered over the woman again. Her hair was a mess, and her black gown was crumpled. "You fell asleep downstairs, didn't you? It seems to me that you're not that much better than Jervis."

"So what if I did fall asleep?" Daphne replied. "It hardly signifies."

"Well, I think it does," said Jane. "I mean, how on earth do you think you're going to get away with this at this hour of the morning? If you shoot me now, everyone will hear the pistol go off and come running. And it's a dueling pistol, isn't it? Have you even loaded it correctly? Because you clearly don't know how to cock it. Besides that, it's only got one bullet in it, so if Christopher or anyone else enters this room, who are you going to shoot first? Really, Daphne, you haven't thought this through, have you?"

"Shut up! Shut up! Shut up," the woman screamed. In the next instant, the door connecting Jane's suite to Christopher's swung open and there was her husband, standing on the threshold, his own pistol trained on Daphne.

His eyes were icy cold as he said quite calmly, "My dear cousin, I'd suggest you put that gun down immediately, or you'll find that I've put a bullet right between your eyes before you can even blink. And I can assure you I won't miss."

Daphne whirled around and with a furious cry lobbed her pistol at Christopher. As he dodged the weapon, she bolted for the bedroom door that led to the hall.

"I'm all right. Go after her," urged Jane as her husband's concerned gaze swept over her. "I'm worried that she'll—"

A scream rent the air, followed by shouts.

Oh God. What had happened now?

Jane scrambled from the bed and followed Christopher out the door and along the hallway. And then she gasped as her gaze traveled down the main staircase to the entry hall below.

Sprawled at the bottom of the stairs was Daphne's body. Even in the gray morning light, it was clear the woman was dead. Her neck was twisted at an odd angle and a dark puddle of blood was beginning to pool on the marble tiles around her head. Whether she'd tripped and fallen to her death or had thrown herself down the stairs deliberately, Jane had no idea.

In any event, Daphne would no longer be a threat to her and Christopher. And perhaps that's all that really mattered.

Christopher gathered Jane close, and she buried her face in his shoulder.

"Jane, my love…" Christopher's lips were at her temple. "I'm so sorry you had to go through that. I'm so sorry for all of it. If anything had happened to you…"

Jane lifted her head. There were tears in Christopher's eyes, and her own heart clenched. Indeed, it felt oddly light yet heavy at the same time. While it was brimming with relief and hope for the future, it was also weighted with sadness for all the terrible things that had occurred. For the difficult times that were to come. Oliver Marsden had just lost his mother, and she and Christopher would have to break the tragic news to him.

Still, Jane's heart was filled with love. For this man who looked at her with such adoration. For the blessing of the child who may already be growing inside her belly.

"I'm here. I'm whole," she murmured thickly, caressing her husband's jaw. "And none of this is your fault. None of it, so do not blame yourself. You are not responsible for the actions of a madwoman."

Christopher swallowed, then nodded. "I have something else to tell you, Jane. Something important."

"Yes?"

"Before I even burst into your room, I knew Daphne was in there threatening you. I could hear your voices. But as soon as I opened the door and took aim at her, I swear to God I recognized her face. She wasn't a stranger to me."

"Oh, dear heaven," whispered Jane.

"It is a blessed relief to think this cursed affliction might be resolving," he murmured. "But even if I never recognize anyone else's face ever again, I don't care. Because, my beautiful Jane, it's your face alone that I value above all others. You are the one person who matters to me." His mouth curved in a small smile as one of his hands, large and warm, pressed against her belly. "Well, and this little person too."

Featherstone appeared in the hall behind Christopher and cleared his throat. "My apologies for interrupting, Yer Grace. Shall I deal with...?" He gestured with his head toward the hall.

"Yes, thank you, Featherstone," said Christopher. "And send word to Detective Lawrence at Scotland Yard about what's happened as well."

The valet bowed. "Of course. At once."

Christopher swept Jane off her feet and started carrying her toward their suites.

"I'm beginning to get used to this," she said softly.

"What? Being in my arms? I should hope so," Christopher said as he nudged the door to his bedchamber open with his foot, then back-heeled it closed behind them. He laid her very gently on the bed, then carefully slid in alongside her. Caressed her cheek. "In case you didn't already know, my love, I never intend to let you go. I belong to you, and you belong to me."

Jane twined her uninjured arm around Christopher's neck and her gaze locked with his. "We were made for each other," she whispered huskily. And then Christopher lowered his head, and they sealed their undeniable love with a kiss.

Epilogue

Roxby Hall, Hertfordshire. Four years later...

THE MIDSUMMER SKY WAS HEAVENLY BLUE AND COMPLETELY cloudless as Jane, Artemis, and Lucy shared afternoon tea in the dappled shade of an enormous chestnut tree on the grounds of Roxby Hall.

It was the third day of the week-long house party that Jane and Christopher had decided to throw for their closest friends. Indeed, at this precise moment, Jane could hear whoops and squeals of laughter as Oliver Marsden, home for the holidays before his final semester at Eton, played with her daughter, little Catherine, and Lucien, Artemis and Dominic's three-year-old son.

Since Daphne's death—a coroner had decreed it had been a terrible accident—Oliver had come to live with Jane and Christopher, and Jane believed the boy was settled and content. Even though Archie Jervis had testified at his trial that Daphne had hired him to kill the Duke and Duchess of Roxby, he couldn't prove his claim. Both Jane and Christopher agreed that for Oliver's sake, it was best that the evidence they had unearthed should stay buried. A well-known petty criminal, Jervis's accusation against Daphne was dismissed and any scandal soon died down after the man met his end upon the scaffold at Newgate Prison.

Jane thanked God every day that that terrible chapter in her life and Christopher's was well and truly closed. And that since that time, so many new and beautiful chapters had begun.

Jane sighed contentedly as her gaze settled on the perambulator beside her where her infant son, James Joseph, slept peacefully. His nurse had the afternoon off, and Jane was happy for the private interlude with her family and friends. Gone were the days when burly footmen seemed to be on guard around her and Christopher every single minute.

Bees droned in the nearby lavender and rosebushes while a light breeze ruffled the chestnut boughs above their heads and the tranquil waters of the ornamental lake a handful of yards away. Jane trusted Christopher, Dominic, and Will would be back soon. On a whim, they'd gone out riding around Roxby Hall's vast estate.

Life had never seemed so perfect, and Jane had never been so content. If she could capture these blissful moments and seal them in a bottle, she would.

Lucy, now the Duchess of Ayr, reached for more cake. "Jane, your cook here is positively evil. One slice of her Victoria sponge is never enough. Before this week is through, I swear I won't be able to fit into my clothes anymore." She patted her round belly beneath her silk wrapper for emphasis.

"Oh, fie," admonished Artemis playfully. "Even though you're seven months pregnant, Lucy, one can hardly tell. Goodness, when I was at that stage, I swear I was as big as Moby Dick."

"You were not," said Jane with a smile.

"Well, perhaps not," conceded Artemis, "but it certainly felt that way. Especially when my ankles puffed up. It's the only time in my life that I've been truly grateful for the god-awful skirts we are compelled to wear. They hide a multitude of sins."

Jane felt her cheeks grow warm as her mind was cast back to that night at the Royal Italian Opera when Christopher had aptly demonstrated that fact.

Of course, Artemis immediately noticed the change of color in Jane's countenance. "Why on earth are you blushing, Jane?"

Then her smile turned sly. "It was my remark about our skirts, wasn't it? Confess now. What were you thinking?"

"Yes, confess," said Lucy around a mouthful of cake. "You cannot keep secrets from us."

Jane drew a deep breath. "Very well," she said, and then she gave her friends a brief description of what had happened that night in Christopher's private theater box.

"How positively scandalous," declared Artemis, her brown eyes glinting with mischief. "It's almost as scandalous as the time Dominic and I made love on a train. We were engaged and it was in Dominic's private carriage of course, but still."

"Or that time Will and I made love in the conservatory at Dartmoor House," said Lucy with a laugh, "*before* we were engaged."

"You didn't!" cried Artemis with mock horror. "And here I was thinking we were all such paragons of propriety. What on earth would everyone say if they knew what the Duchess of Dartmoor, the Duchess of Roxby, and the Duchess of Ayr were really like?"

"Pooh to propriety," said Lucy. "I'd rather be happy and satisfied. And I'm also proud of all our achievements, no matter how controversial."

Jane smiled in agreement. Her own controversial project had been realized not long after Catherine had been born. Her anonymously published pamphlet on birth control was now readily available through the St. Giles Dispensary for Women and Children, and there were plans for two more clinics on the cards—one in Whitechapel and another in Southwark. And Jane couldn't have done it without Lucy or Artemis. Or Christopher, and she said as much.

"Let us toast each other's accomplishments with tea like 'proper' gentlewomen,'" she said, picking up the silver teapot to replenish their cups. "And give thanks for our husbands."

Artemis concurred. "I'd once declared at one of our Byronic

Book Club meetings that it is a truth *never* universally acknowledged that a single woman—whether she is in possession of a good fortune or not—doesn't necessarily want or even need a husband. And how wrong I was. While I might not *need* a husband, I will readily acknowledge that I do want mine. He might not be quite as wicked as some of the brooding Byronic book heroes we used to swoon over when we were younger, but he's certainly *my* hero."

Jane raised her brimming teacup. "Here's to us and here's to the wonderful men in our lives."

"Hear, hear," chorused Artemis and Lucy, and they all drank.

"Ah, speak of the devil," said Artemis. She nodded toward the path by the lake, and sure enough all their husbands were making their way toward them along with Oliver, Catherine, and Lucien. Lucien was riding on his father's broad shoulders, and Will and Christopher were swinging Catherine up in the air with every few steps that they took.

Her delighted squeals and bright peals of laughter warmed Jane's heart.

When the small party reached the chestnut tree, Catherine immediately clambered onto Jane's lap, and Jane passed her one of her favorite petit fours and several summer strawberries on a plate. Lucien climbed onto Artemis's lap and asked for cake too.

"Why are you always looking at books, Mama?" asked Lucien as Artemis reached past a pile of their latest Gothic novel finds to select a petit four for her son.

"It's because I love a good story," said Artemis.

"I love cake," said Catherine as she ignored the strawberries and nibbled at the icing on her petit four.

Christopher laughed. "I do too," he said.

"Oh, I thought you preferred muffins," murmured Jane, looking up at him.

He grinned before he bent low and whispered in her ear, "Only if it's yours."

At that moment, little James stirred in his perambulator and Christopher picked him up. The sight of her austerely beautiful husband cradling his son and making silly faces at him brought sweet tears of joy to Jane's eyes.

Not just because it was so endearing, but because Christopher knew his own son's face. And Catherine's as well. In the days following Daphne Marsden's death, Christopher's facial blindness continued to resolve. He began to consistently recognize Featherstone, then Shelby, and the housekeeper, Mrs. Harrigan. Then Beattie and all the other footmen, and of course Artemis and Dominic and Lucy and Will.

It was truly a miracle, Jane thought. A blessing.

And she was blessed too.

It seemed her life had only truly begun that long-ago night when she'd dared to sneak into the Duke of Roxby's library to steal a book. Who knew that she'd meet a man who was more precious than a priceless tome and even better than any Byronic hero she'd read about in a Gothic romance novel. A man who'd managed to break down all her defenses and had, in the end, stolen her fiercely guarded heart.

Yes, who needed fairy tales and princes or even a brooding antihero when one could have something like this? A real happily-ever-after with a good man. The best of men.

Christopher smiled at her over their son's downy head, and Jane rested her chin on the top of Catherine's silky golden hair and smiled back.

This was the perfect ending to the perfect day, and in her heart of hearts, Jane knew that she'd never want anything more than what she had right here.

Read on for a sneak peek into the
first Byronic Book Club book

AMY ROSE
BENNETT

Up All
Night with
a
Good
Duke

THE BYRONIC BOOK CLUB

Chapter One

APPARENTLY, THERE ARE SOME THINGS A YOUNG WOMAN shouldn't say, especially if that woman is genteelly impoverished and must behave decorously at all times in order to maintain her teaching position at an exclusive young ladies' finishing school in Bath.

So when Mrs. Parsons, the exacting headmistress of the Avon Academy for Young Ladies of Quality, summoned Miss Artemis Jones to her private study and then accused her of corrupting her charges' minds by exposing them to an entirely frivolous, some might even say *dangerous* novel, Artemis really shouldn't have muttered "Beelzebub's ballocks" beneath her breath.

"I beg your pardon." Behind her wire-rimmed spectacles, Mrs. Parsons's pale eyes narrowed with dislike and suspicion. "What did you say, Miss Jones?"

Artemis attempted a look of innocence while she inwardly cursed her ill-advised slip of the tongue. "I said, 'Of course, Mrs. Parsons.' I do see your point. *Sense and Sensibility* is entirely frivolous. It teaches young women nothing at all about the value of exercising good judgment or that possessing an overly romantic nature can lead one into trouble. Or that it would be wise for women to develop the skills, and therefore the means, to support themselves considering the protection of a male—whether husband, or father, or another form of guardian—cannot always be relied upon in this life. I could go on, but heaven forfend, I fear that I might inadvertently corrupt your mind too."

Mrs. Parsons bristled like a cat set out in the rain. "Sarcasm does not become you." Raising her bony hand, she then held her thumb and index finger an inch apart. "You are skating this close to dismissal. Do I make myself clear?"

Artemis tried to look contrite, which was no mean feat considering she didn't think much of the headmistress or the curriculum of her finishing school. But needs must when the devil drives, so Artemis bowed her head. "Perfectly. Although, it was only one student who read—"

Mrs. Parsons slapped the leather blotter on her desk. "And that is one student too many," she snapped. "You know as well as I that these young girls have impressionable minds. Aside from that, I shouldn't need to remind you that reading novels for pleasure is *not* part of our curriculum. Parents and guardians do not pay me good money to have their daughters' time wasted or, worse, have their heads filled with utter nonsense. These girls need to acquire solid accomplishments. Aside from displaying good manners, excellent deportment, and impeccable grooming at all times, they should be adept musically and artistically and be able to dance with grace, speak French moderately well, and be skilled at needlework and balancing domestic accounts. They should also have mastered the art of maintaining polite conversation and to have a thorough understanding of etiquette."

"And a thorough knowledge of geography, literature, and history." Artemis felt compelled to remind her employer about the subjects *she* taught the school's pupils. If she were ever fortunate enough to realize her own dream of starting an academic college for women, there wouldn't be a dancing master or an etiquette manual in sight.

Mrs. Parsons sniffed, her manner as prickly as the black woolen gown she wore. "Our girls only need to know the rudiments. Just enough to enable them to converse without making fools of themselves. It wouldn't do for our young women to graduate here with *more* knowledge than the men who will court them." She shuddered dramatically. "No gentleman wishes to wed a woman with a masculine level of intelligence. It's entirely unnatural."

Artemis pressed her lips together to quell a derisive huff. Oh, the things she could say to counter that. Instead, she uttered the sort of unpalatable tripe Mrs. Parsons wished to hear. "Yes, you're quite right. As if a woman's intellect could ever match that of a man's. After all, we are the weaker sex."

The headmistress nodded her approval. "Exactly, Miss Jones. A woman must know her place in the world. And that is what the Avon Academy excels at. Showing each young woman that her *rightful* place is at her husband's side, managing his domestic affairs, bearing his children, keeping him entertained, and being an indispensable helpmeet." One talon-like finger tapped the cover of Volume I of *Sense and Sensibility*. "She won't learn any of those things in ridiculous novels like these."

"No, of course not," agreed Artemis. "I don't know what I was thinking lending an impressionable student such a terrible, perhaps even subversive book. It won't happen again."

"No. It won't." Mrs. Parsons lifted her chin. "Because I've confiscated the whole set. And indeed all the other novels in your private quarters."

"I beg your pardon?" Artemis couldn't hide the outrage in her voice. It shook with the force of it and momentarily masked her fear that the headmistress could have unearthed something even more damning than her treasured collection of novels by Jane Austen. For instance, the latest Gothic romance manuscript her alter ego, Lydia Lovelace, was presently penning. "You...you went through my belongings?"

"I did." Mrs. Parsons rose to her feet and, eyes flashing, looked down her beak of a nose at Artemis. "You've proven yourself to be untrustworthy, Miss Jones. And you shan't have your dreadful novels back until you leave this establishment. Which might be sooner rather than later. One more black mark against your name, and you'll be dismissed, do you understand? And do stop gaping at me like a landed carp. The look does not become you."

Sometime during the course of the headmistress's admonitory speech, it seemed Artemis's jaw had indeed become unhinged. She shut her mouth with a snap and somehow swallowed her pride along with her burning anger. "Yes, Mrs. Parsons. I understand."

Dropping her gaze lest it further betray the depth of her ire, she then dipped into a respectful curtsy, something she rarely did. As much as she loathed the Avon Academy—indeed how she'd endured working here for three years quite amazed her—she couldn't afford to lose this position. Because if she did, she'd end up living with her fearsome aunt Roberta, Lady Wagstaff, who would parade her like a prize heifer for sale through London's ballrooms. Her aunt's unrelenting but ultimately fruitless quest was to marry both Artemis and her younger sister, Phoebe, off to "gentlemen of means." That eventuality didn't bear thinking about. Phoebe was dying to marry, but at nine-and-twenty, Artemis was firmly on the spinster's shelf and there she meant to stay.

Artemis was about to take her leave—it was only four o'clock in the afternoon, and she still had mountains of work to do before she could retire to her room to alternately fume and lick her wounds in private—when Mrs. Parsons pushed an envelope across the desk. "Some correspondence for you, Miss Jones. See that you read it in your own time."

"Yes, of course. Thank you." Artemis picked up the letter, and after she'd ascertained the sender was her dear friend, Lucy Bertram, she slid it into the pocket of her cambric pinafore. "I shan't look at it until after supper and prayers when the girls are all settled for the night," she added for good measure, even though that was a lie.

Indeed, as soon as Artemis gained the corridor, she ducked into a nearby music room that was currently vacant. Lucy, a baronet's daughter and her oldest friend from childhood—they'd both grown up in the hamlet of Heathwick Green near Hampstead Heath—was only a year younger than Artemis and equally happy with her lot in life as a spinster. She did write, but not all that often, so it was decidedly odd that she'd sent *another* letter on the heels of her last one, which had arrived but a fortnight ago.

A peculiar mixture of anticipation, curiosity, and concern buzzed about inside Artemis as she cracked the envelope's seal, unfolded the parchment, and started to read.

Dearest Artemis...

Lucy began in her beautifully flowing handwriting.

I hope this letter finds you well. I'm afraid I'm not particularly "in the pink" at the present moment, even though I stated that I was so in my last letter. And no doubt you're wondering why...
Actually, to be perfectly honest, I'm all at sixes and sevens. In fact, my hand is quite literally shaking as I write these words, so please do forgive my poor penmanship and what

might seem like my sudden, entirely out-of-character pen-
chant for hyperbole. I do not mean to cause alarm. But
you see, the news I'm about to impart is quite disconcert-
ing, if not altogether terrifying—to me at least.
My papa has decreed that I should have a Season and
absolutely must wed by summer's end. And I... Frankly, I
can think of nothing worse. At all. I'm not sure what ter-
rifies me the most: the thought of marriage to some man
who doesn't give a jot about me or my ambitions in life, or
the idea of actually having to venture into society to begin
with. And the idea of courting... I'd rather eat nothing
but chalk and charcoal for a year and a day than set foot
in one of London's ballrooms.

What? Artemis's jaw dropped open for the second time that afternoon, and she sank onto the piano stool behind her. Her knees suddenly felt as insubstantial as a freshly unmolded flummery.

Poor sweet Lucy. Just like Artemis, her dear friend had no love for London with its crowded, noisy streets and hectic pace. Or its members of high society. Gatherings any larger than a small, intimate dinner party or an afternoon tea with close acquaintances were anathema to her. Indeed, on countless occasions, Artemis had witnessed how Lucy's tongue would tie itself into hopeless knots when trying to summon a response to the simplest of questions from a stranger, and how she would blush redder than a platter of roasted beets when even a smattering of attention was directed her way.

Her heart clenching with sympathy for her friend's plight, Artemis quickly perused the remaining paragraphs of the letter.

I'm afraid there's no reasoning with Papa. He's absolutely
determined that this will happen, despite my genuine

trepidation and the fact that I'm surely too spinsterish and singular in my habits. Even though he will never admit it, I suspect he is terribly short of funds. No doubt his last expedition to Ceylon depleted the family coffers considerably. And then, my brother's tendency to live extravagantly has not helped. But of course, Monty is being as obstinate as an ox and will not even lift his little finger to win the hand of some biddable heiress. So apparently I am to be the sacrificial lamb who must save the family. Naturally, marrying me off to the highest bidder will certainly reduce Father's—or perhaps I should say our—financial difficulties. But I, for one, am not willing to pay the price. I cannot. I will not.

Artemis, you know better than anyone that I am not equipped for any of this. Unlike you, I've never even had one Season. You, my fearless, indomitable friend, are definitely cut from a different cloth.

Oh, hell's blasted bells. Artemis closed her eyes. Dread coiled through her belly. She knew what was coming even before she read her friend's next words. Lucy went on:

And so I had a slightly mad, but hopefully not altogether unappealing idea. If you were by my side, my dearest Artemis, helping me to navigate society's treacherous hunting grounds while fending off any potential suitors— I'm sure they will all be objectionable with not a Mr. Darcy or honorable version of Mr. Rochester amongst them—I'd perhaps stand a fighting chance of surviving unscathed this Season. I'd be forever grateful. Of course, I know I'm putting you in a horribly difficult position— asking you to give up your post at the Avon Academy to be my companion for a few months. But I need you most desperately, and I do so hope you will consider my request. Who knows, perhaps you could even court a sponsor for your own venture. Then you'd have your college and never have to work at a place like Mrs. Parsons's horrid finishing school ever again. And of course, we could reconvene our Byronic Book Club meetings with dear Jane at her grandfather's bookstore. Just think of the fun we could have, plotting and planning our futures while simultaneously swooning over our favorite book beaux. It would be like the old days. The three of us—unconventional and unrepentant—the heroines of our very own stories, forging our way through the world on our own terms. (Well, it's a lovely dream anyway.)

I await your reply with bated breath.

Ever your devoted friend,
Lucy

Artemis blew out a deep sigh as she rose to her feet and wandered over to a nearby window. For long moments, she stared out of the rain-streaked mullion panes and contemplated her future. The options that might be open to her if she were brave enough to chart a course that was different from the plodding pedestrian path she'd been following for years. While she loved being an author of lurid Gothic romance novels—her publisher advertised them as "literary" penny bloods—it was, for obvious reasons, a clandestine career and indeed must remain so if she were to achieve her ultimate goal. Unfortunately, her book sales, while steady, were such that it would still take her a few more years to save sufficient funds to start her ladies' college. The same could be said for the wages she earned as a teacher.

But if she could find a wealthy, forward-thinking patroness to support her project this Season while also coming to the aid of her closest friend...

If she did agree to Lucy's plan, she'd somehow have to manage both Aunt Roberta's and Phoebe's expectations. As soon as they learned Artemis would be in London for the Season, the cat really would be set amongst the pigeons. There'd be little respite from their nagging to "do her duty and find a husband." But she'd also have both Lucy and Jane to confide in when it all got too much to bear. Perhaps it *would* be like old times.

"Well," Artemis murmured at last as she pushed the letter back into her pocket, "nothing ventured, nothing gained." Her mind was made up. She couldn't abandon her darling friend to society's wolves. And she owed it to herself to at last pursue her own dream. Come what may.

Her heart tripping with anticipation, Artemis lifted her chin and marched straight back to the headmistress's office. After a cursory knock, she entered and announced with a wide smile and not one iota of regret, "Mrs. Parsons, I'd like my books back, please. I'm tendering my resignation, effective immediately."

Chapter Two

London

As Artemis stepped off the train onto Paddington Station's teeming Platform One, she squared her shoulders and pushed her way through the heaving fray of passengers and those there to greet or bid them farewell. Overhead, the enormous vaulted wrought-iron and glass roof revealed a leaden gray sky, while all around the platform swirled clouds of gritty steam that had been belched from the departing train on the adjacent track. The acrid odor of jostling bodies and burning coal filled the air.

Old Nick's nob. Artemis winced as a liveried footman accidentally elbowed her in the ribs. The hustle and bustle of city life was something she did not miss. At all. But it was too late to turn back now. She was actually here, in London, about to commence a brand-new chapter of her life. A *better* chapter. All going well…

Except things started to *not* go very well within a surprisingly short space of time. Within fifteen minutes, Artemis had ascertained that her two traveling trunks had gone missing and all she had in her possession besides her overstuffed carpetbag and coin purse was a great deal of simmering frustration.

After filing a "Missing Items" report at the Lost Property Office, she at last made her way toward the station's exit. Before she'd departed from Bath, she'd sent a telegram to Aunt Roberta and Phoebe where they resided at Wagstaff House in Cadogan Square, and one to Lucy, to let them all know she'd quit her post and would soon be arriving in London, but she hadn't mentioned precisely when.

While she wanted nothing more than to stay with Lucy, Artemis felt she owed it to her sister, Phoebe, to spend some time with her before the Season proper commenced in a fortnight. In any event, whether Artemis liked it or not, she was going to have to grin and bear it and stay with her difficult and overbearing aunt, at least for a little while.

Hefting her carpetbag from one gloved hand to the other, Artemis emerged onto Praed Street and scowled at the crowded pavement and traffic-congested road, then up at the sullen sky. It had begun to rain, and of course, she'd neglected to pack an umbrella. Thank goodness she had enough money to pay the cab fare to Cadogan Square. She'd rather not have to contend with a packed-to-the-gunwales omnibus.

Once she spied a gap in the sea of bodies and mushrooming umbrellas, she forged her way to the curb and for several frustrating minutes tried but failed to wave down a cab. The rain was growing heavier by the moment—the icy, needlelike drops pricked at her face and a sliver of her nape not protected by her bonnet and jacket's collar—and just when she thought she'd best look for an omnibus after all, a hackney splashed to a halt a few feet away. Artemis rushed toward the cab's door… and then crashed straight into an unyielding wall of masculine muscle that hadn't been there a moment ago.

What the devil?

As Artemis's shoulder connected with the wool-clad chest of the tall, solidly built stranger, she skidded and stumbled, and her full-to-bursting carpetbag flew out of her hand and onto the pavement. The battered clasp came undone, and several books fell out, skittering across the wet flagstones toward the gutter and the cab's wheels.

"Lucifer's love truncheon," Artemis muttered without thinking. And then her heart did an odd little tumble when she realized that the man had put out a hand to stop her from slipping. His fingers were curled about her elbow, and when she looked up, her gaze collided with his. Caught.

Lingered.

Lucifer's love truncheon indeed...

"I beg your pardon." The man's voice was a deep velvet stroke that Artemis felt all the way to her bones. From beneath the shadow of his top hat, storm-cloud gray eyes bore into hers and she was momentarily transfixed. Frozen.

It didn't seem to matter that her carpetbag was on the ground with her books, getting wetter by the moment.

Because this man. He was... Artemis's befogged brain struggled to function. To formulate a single thought. Retrieve a single word.

She had the oddest sensation of falling, plunging, as though this stranger's gaze was a turbulent ocean and she was being pulled into a maelstrom. Sucked below, sinking deeper and deeper. Or perhaps she'd been struck by lightning. Awareness shot through her body like a searing hot electrical charge, heating her blood and scalding her cheeks, despite the chill rain trickling down the back of her neck.

Artemis instinctively recognized this man was as formidable as a force of nature. And just as dangerous. Not only was he as handsome as sin—all austere good looks with his sharply cut jaw and jet-black hair save for a touch of silver at the temples—but he exuded an innate authority.

He was clearly an aristocrat. Wealthy, beautiful, and powerful beyond imagining.

Beneath the scent of damp wool and starched linen, even his cologne—clean and sharp like the sea—smelled powerful.

Somehow Artemis absorbed all of these impressions within

a few seconds. Between the space of one wildly pounding heartbeat and the next.

Then the stranger spoke again, rousing her from her stupor. "My sincerest apologies. It seems we were both intent on securing the same cab."

Artemis swallowed. Drew a shaky breath. A shiver dashed down her spine, and she wondered how she could feel hot yet so cold at the same time. As though she'd suddenly been afflicted by a strange fever. "Yes..." she managed at last. "May I offer my apologies as well. I was in a rush and not paying attention to my surroundings."

"No harm done at all. Not to me at least." The gentleman at last released her arm. "But your books... Let me make amends for my own carelessness."

In the next instant, he'd crouched down to retrieve her scattered belongings. His expertly tailored black trousers pulled tight over his muscular thighs, and Artemis had to remind herself not to stare at his legs or any other distinctly masculine parts in their immediate vicinity. *Artemis Jones, stop gawking like an utter ninny*, she silently admonished herself as she dropped to the ground beside him. *He's not the first indecently handsome man you've ever met. You'd do well to remember that the road to ruin is paved with lustful thoughts.*

Reaching for Mary Wollstonecraft's *A Vindication of the Rights of Woman*, she began, "You really don't have to—" but then her breath caught as the stranger grasped the book at the very same moment. Their fingers brushed, and Artemis felt a spark for a second time. An electrical crackle that mysteriously penetrated the kid leather of her glove, then radiated up her arm, making her flesh burn and tingle. Thunder rumbled overhead.

The man withdrew his hand, but she sensed his gaze upon

her, studying her face beneath the brim of her sodden bonnet. Had he felt that strange flicker of connection too?

"It's the least I can do," he said, handing over *Frankenstein; or, The Modern Prometheus* along with Artemis's own novel, *Lady Violetta and the Vengeful Vampyre*. One of his slashing black brows arched when he caught sight of the latter title. Or was it Mary Shelley's book that he looked upon with disdain? Or that of Mary Shelley's mother, Mary Wollstonecraft? The woman's reputation was much maligned in some circles.

His next observation made it clear. "I see you've a penchant for 'horrid' novels." His mouth twitched with a smile that bordered on sardonic. Even though his opinion shouldn't matter, his change in demeanor rankled Artemis more than she could say.

"The more horrid, the better," she rejoined, stuffing her books back into her bag and securing the clasp with jerky movements. Ignoring his proffered hand, she climbed to her feet, hoisting her carpetbag as she rose. "It might also shock you to know that I'm an outspoken bluestocking. And proud of it."

He stood too. "There's nothing wrong with being a bluestocking." His slightly amused manner seemed to belie his pronouncement though. Artemis bristled at the thought he might be laughing at her, but before she could mount any sort of defense, he reached for the hackney's door. "You take the cab. I insist." His good breeding required him to play the gentleman, despite the fact he clearly didn't think much of her taste in books.

Artemis's reply was stiff with grudging politeness. "Thank you."

She gave the driver her direction, then climbed into the dark confines of the carriage. It contained a musty odor, redolent of damp leather, tobacco smoke, horses, and stale sweat, and she wrinkled her nose. If it was the least bit socially acceptable—and the stranger hadn't mocked her reading choices—she would have invited him to share the hackney, just for the chance to smell his tempting cologne. She might be an unconventional bluestocking who would never be a perfect model of gentility, but she wasn't foolish. She had to maintain a veneer of respectability.

Once she'd deposited her bag on the seat, she reached for the door handle and was surprised to see the stranger still standing there. Raindrops glanced off his hat and impossibly wide shoulders, but he seemed oblivious to the downpour. Even though his perfectly chiseled mouth had compressed into a hard line, the light in his storm-cloud eyes was almost wistful rather than disdainful as he regarded her. "I wish you good day, Miss Bluestocking," he said in that deep, dark velveteen voice of his. And then the door shut, and he was gone.

As the hackney pulled away, Artemis couldn't resist the urge to look back and follow the forbiddingly handsome stranger's progress. But he'd already been swallowed by the crowd.

What a particularly odd and altogether disconcerting incident. In all of her twenty-nine years, Artemis had never been so singularly affected by a member of the opposite sex. Even the rake that had charmed and almost ruined her when she was a naive debutante a decade ago couldn't hold a candle to…well, whoever *that* enigmatic, mercurial man had been.

It was as though her imagination had conjured him up—the epitome of a darkly brooding, Byronic hero who'd stepped out of the pages of one of her own books. One thing was certain: A man like that—no matter how much he provoked her interest by a mere glance and a touch—was not of her world. Nor would he ever be. This had been a completely inconsequential, chance encounter, nothing more.

Author's Note

My dearest readers, just a quick note to let you know where I've played a little fast and loose with history in the telling of *Tall, Duke, and Scandalous*…

The village of Heathwick Green where my three Byronic Book Club heroines hail from is my own invention. I took my inspiration from the actual hamlet of Hatch's or Hatchett's Bottom near Hampstead Heath.

The tea rooms at Fortnum & Mason's weren't actually opened until 1926, so the tea salon appearing in this series is entirely fictional.

Lastly, I want to mention that Christopher's facial agnosia or prosopagnosia is a neurological disorder that my dear mother-in-law was also diagnosed with following a stroke eight years ago. For a period of time, she was unable to recognize familiar faces, even those of certain close family members. Her prosopagnosia has since resolved, but from my research, and from my time working as a speech pathologist, I'm very aware that for some, this condition—whether it's been acquired following a brain injury or is congenital—may be permanent. I hope I've portrayed Christopher's journey with sensitivity.

Acknowledgments

Thank you to the Sourcebooks Casablanca team for helping to make the whole Byronic Book Club series shine. Special thanks to my editor, Christa Désir, for your vision and insight.

As always, thanks must go to my wonderful agent, Jessica Alvarez.

And thanks to my husband and children for your boundless patience and understanding. And for keeping me fueled with coffee when required (which is often!).

About the Author

Amy Rose Bennett is an Australian author who has a passion for penning emotion-packed historical romances. Of course, her strong-willed heroines and rakish heroes always find their happily-ever-afters.

A former speech pathologist, Amy is happily married to her very own romantic hero and has two lovely, very accomplished adult daughters. When she's not creating stories, Amy loves to cook up a storm in the kitchen, lose herself in a good book or a witty rom-com, and, when she can afford it, travel to all the places she writes about.

Also by Amy Rose Bennett